I don't want to remember anymore.

I do not want to recall the day of my Selection, the Bloodbath of Shiratukh, the girls who dropped dead beside me while I sat unharmed. I do not want to recall the days that followed after, the fear that shadowed my every move.

I do not want to recall the day of Kavita's death, and how a void has carved my insides since then.

"It's up to you," he says. "I only act as far as you allow me to."

My throat tightens. He already knows my answer, yet he continues to dangle choices before me as if I truly have an alternative.

For a moment, I wonder what would have happened if Rashmatun actually existed. If Kavita's strange and cruel rituals had worked and the goddess magically came to me. Could I truly be rid of Ilam? Would I maintain my position without bloodshed? Or would I still concoct desperate schemes to ensure that Rashmatun stays with me?

I look at my hands. These are the hands of a murderer. Ilam is wrong. I haven't killed only once. I've killed ten times already.

What's one more count to the list?

My heart thrums against my chest, a loud, ferocious rhythm that may burst forth at any moment. I touch the yellow sapphire at my throat, its crude edges giving me comfort.

"I'll do it."

THE SCARLET THRONE

False Goddess Trilogy: Book One

AMY LEOW

orbit

orbitbooks.net

Copyright © 2024 by Amy Leow
Excerpt from *These Deathless Shores* copyright © 2024 by P. H. Low
Excerpt from *Fathomfolk* copyright © 2024 by Eliza Chan

Cover design by Lauren Panepinto
Cover illustration by Marcos Chin
Cover copyright © 2024 by Hachette Book Group, Inc.
Maps by Tim Paul
Author photograph by Alina Lee

Orbit
Hachette Book Group
1290 Avenue of the Americas
New York, NY 10104
orbitbooks.net

First Edition: September 2024
Simultaneously published in Great Britain by Orbit

Orbit is an imprint of Hachette Book Group.
The Orbit name and logo are registered trademarks of Little, Brown Book Group Limited.

The Hachette Speakers Bureau provides a wide range of authors for speaking events. To find out more, go to hachettespeakersbureau.com or email HachetteSpeakers@hbgusa.com.

Orbit books may be purchased in bulk for business, educational, or promotional use. For information, please contact your local bookseller or the Hachette Book Group Special Markets Department at special.markets@hbgusa.com.

Library of Congress Cataloging-in-Publication Data
Names: Leow, Amy, author.
Title: The Scarlet throne / Amy Leow.
Description: First edition. | New York : Orbit, 2024. | Series: False goddess trilogy: Book one
Identifiers: LCCN 2023057066 | ISBN 9780316562485 (trade paperback) | ISBN 9780316562706 (ebook)
Subjects: LCGFT: Fantasy fiction. | Novels.
Classification: LCC PR9530.9.L465 S23 2024 | DDC 899.28—dc23/ eng/20231214
LC record available at https://lccn.loc.gov/2023057066

ISBNs: 9780316562485 (trade paperback), 9780316562706 (ebook)

Printed in the United States of America

LSC-C

Printing 2, 2024

*To all the girls who were told that they were too angry and
too ambitious for their own good*

Author's Note

I first learned about the living goddess(es) of Nepal through a BBC mini documentary that popped up on my YouTube feed. It felt as though I was being drawn into a completely different world—one where deities were intimate with humans, where the line between human and god was blurred and transient. A question popped into my head the moment I finished watching the video: What if the living goddess wanted to continue being a goddess, and would do anything to do so? It must have been a great temptation, I imagined, to wield so much power and not be able to hold on to it. Those were the first seeds of *The Scarlet Throne*. The character of Binsa, the living goddess in my story, bloomed to life soon after.

The next question was to find a world where she belonged. I chose to depict a world inspired by Nepali culture because the tradition of the living goddess is one steeped in it, and to do something otherwise would not be doing Binsa's story justice. To me, traditions are not something that can be lifted from one culture to another—because they are rooted in a community's religion, beliefs, and worldview. Taking bits and pieces out of a centuries-old custom to fit into another culture did not sit right with me.

However, although my story draws from Nepali culture, it is not meant to be an all-encompassing representation of it. I am not a Nepali, nor am I from Nepal. I can only imagine the sights and smells there based on my readings and the encounters I've had with

South Asian culture in my own country. For example, while some of the names are actually Nepali (like Binsa), I constructed the fictional language in my book to be more reminiscent of Sanskrit, which had a huge influence on South and Southeast Asian languages. The food and dress are most certainly Nepali, but some nuances in the practices and worldviews of Nepalis may be missing.

I did my best to treat every single aspect of the book with delicacy and respect. I must also acknowledge that some parts of the book may not entirely resonate with South Asian experiences. Ultimately, this book was born from my imagination and my own interpretation of Nepal—and my desire to see more angry, vicious women on bookshelves. Thank you for picking up *The Scarlet Throne*, and I hope that no matter where you are from, you will be able to find familiarity or something new within its pages.

THE
SCARLET
THRONE

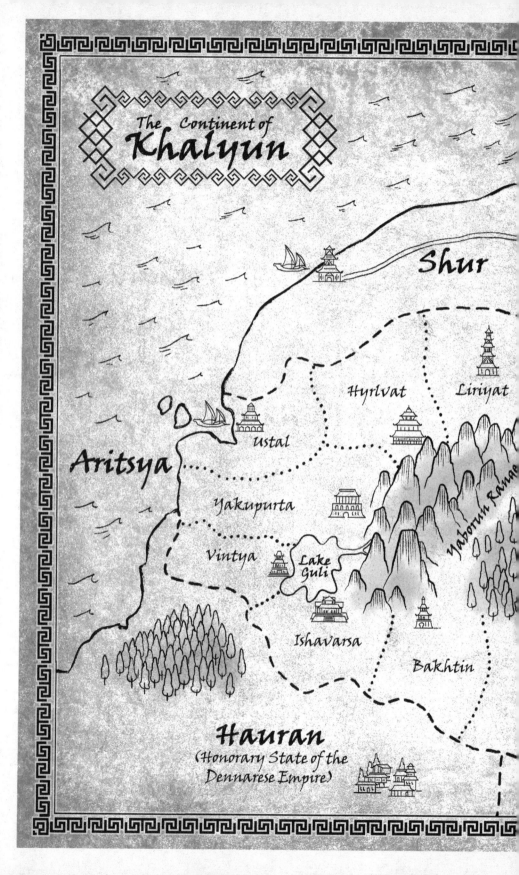

Sea of Taksul

Yanir

Farsal

Sulat

Dennar

Shimalu
Forest

Kheysa

Dennarese
Empire

Thiralu

Ashul

Ruins of Ritkar

Map by Tim Paul

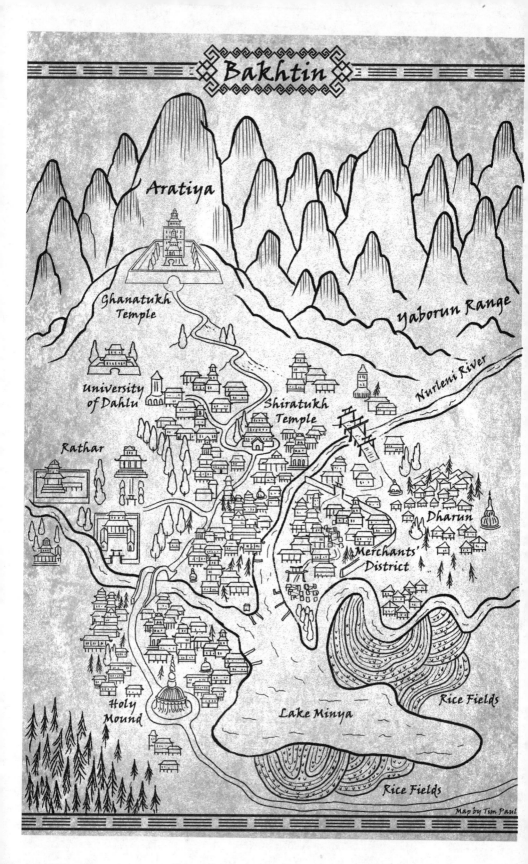

PART I

THE BLOODSTAINED GODDESS

Red and bright the skies will burn,
Our offerings mourn, and the ghosts return.
The skies darken with fear, trembling amidst the
     goddess's might,
The fallen stars shatter, and the seas rise.
At the end of it all, the Scarlet Throne bleeds,
The crown at her head rusts,
The ornaments turn to dust.

Hear our song of mourning, O Forgotten Goddess,
Hear our cries of despair!
Go back to whence you came from,
And leave us forevermore.
A sacrifice given, a sacrifice saved.
At the end of it all, a path of blood awaits.

The Prophecy of Geerkha, transcribed
by Ghushtar Abhijat Rijal, circa
Year 13 of the Age of Steel

1

The False Devotee

A woman had been crushed by a goat that fell from the sky.

Her husband, Uruvin Vashmaralim, humble spice merchant, now kneels before me, haggard bags underlining his eyes and tear stains slashing down his cheeks. He laments the loss of his wife and the suspicious circumstances hanging over her death. She was a pious woman, he claims, who always set the mangoes and wine before the family shrine and prayed to them three times a day. One day, however, a terrible illness befell her. She didn't place her offerings before the family shrine. She died the next week, not from illness, but from a goat falling on her while she was drawing water from the well.

Lies, a childlike voice hisses in my head.

The man bursts into sobs at the end of his tale. I observe him with my back straight and hands folded demurely on my lap. My lips are pressed into a thin line, but my brows are soft and relaxed. My brother has told me that this is my best regal pose, assuring everyone that the spirit of the goddess Rashmatun lives in me, with every muscle, every limb perfectly poised.

Even if Rashmatun never possessed me. Even if Rashmatun doesn't exist.

"My goddess!" the man wails. "Please, have mercy. I know not what my wife has done wrong, save for the one day she forgot to placate our ancestors' spirits. Her death has grieved me so. Rashmatun, what can I do to rectify the calamity that has fallen upon me?"

I stay silent, contemplating the situation. A goat dropped on an unsuspecting woman. It would have sounded ridiculous if not for Uruvin's solemnity as he delivered the tale. In fact, I am still in disbelief, even though I allow him to continue wailing.

Meanwhile, Ilam, the demon inside me, trails slow, taunting circles in my mind. His presence is as unnerving as a monster lying beneath still waters.

"Uruvin, how long has it been since your wife's demise?" I say, my reedy voice amplified with deeper, overlapping echoes. The acoustics of the concave niche carved into the wall behind my throne creates an incandescent quality to my tone. My brother did it himself, claiming that the sculpture of Anas, the ten-headed snake god, would protect the living goddess from any harm. What the temple dwellers do not know about is the hollow that lies beyond the niche, large enough for a grown man to squeeze into and eavesdrop on my daily audiences.

"Two weeks already, Your Grace," Uruvin replies. He wipes a tear away from the corner of his eye. "I miss her terribly."

Two weeks. Snivelling Sartas. They'd have cremated the body by now. "Pray tell," I resume smoothly, "was she a good woman?"

"Why, of course, Rashmatun! She was everything a man could ask for." He waves his arms in a vigorous manner, as if it can convince me of his sincerity. "A wonderful cook, a meticulous cleaner, a patient listener. Oh, my dear Dirka!"

He falls into another round of incoherent sobbing, forehead planted onto the fiery red carpet beneath him.

I narrow my eyes at Uruvin, studying him intently. The hems of his suruwal are suspiciously clean, neither a trace of ash nor dust on them. He probably never visited his wife's remains after the funeral. The Holy Mound is where we keep the ashes of our dead, open to the public and frequently flooded with visitors. If he were truly mourning her, he'd have spent plenty of time there.

Or perhaps he is so overwhelmed with grief that he cannot bear to step into the Mound.

Lies, lies, lies, Ilam chants with sadistic glee.

Where is the lie? I ask.

Open your eyes, girl. Open your eyes and see.

I draw in a breath, and Ilam gets to work. He worms his way to the front of my mind, shoving me aside and suffocating my thoughts. After nearly ten years of communing with a demon, you'd think I'd have become accustomed to the constant crawling up my spine.

But I endure it to have this power.

The demon burrows straight into Uruvin's mind; the man himself is unaware of the intrusion. A rush of resounding *truths* pours into me, and a brief flash of pain splits my skull before fading into a dull pulse. My senses sharpen, so sensitive that I can hear Uruvin's erratic heartbeat and catch the faint scent of perfume on his smooth, creaseless clothes. Ilam's magic amplifies the truths such details carry. Each of them pierces through my mind like a fire-tipped arrow streaking across a moonless night.

Throughout this, I maintain my tall, unflappable posture.

Then Ilam is done. He slowly retreats, and the world fades into its usual palette, the saturation of sounds and scents ebbing into the background. I inhale deeply. Using blood magic always leaves me with a discomfort that carves deep into my bones. After all these years, I still cannot tell if it's an inherent side effect of blood magic, or if it's my own revulsion towards the practice.

Meanwhile, Uruvin is still choking on melodramatic sobs.

I wait for him to swallow his tears. Now I see where the lie reveals itself. If not for Ilam, I would not have caught the subtle yet alluring fragrance of frangipani on him, commonly used as a perfume by Aritsyan women to usher good luck in love and life. I would not have seen the shrewd gleam in his eyes.

The part about the falling goat must be true—as absurd as it is—since Ilam did not say it was a lie. A mystery to be dealt with later. But Uruvin is no honest, grieving husband.

He hopes to earn some sort of compensation for his unprecedented losses. Just like many of the insufferable fools who walk in here. Some devotees are genuine, but plenty are out to take a bite out of the goddess Rashmatun's bursting coffers.

Fortunately, I'm not as gullible as these people would like me to be.

"You live by the banks of the Nurleni, Uruvin?" I ask after the man wrests his sobs under control.

"Yes, my goddess. I'm sure that the chief priest would have told you all you needed to know." He sniffs loudly. Perhaps he's wondering why the great Rashmatun is asking such menial questions.

"Is it Harun who will relieve you of your plight?" I say, allowing an edge of irritation to coat my tone. "No. It is I. So answer my questions without hesitation nor falsehood."

Uruvin's fingers drum against his thigh. "Yes, Your Grace. My humblest apologies, Rashmatun."

"Excellent." I tilt my head. "Is your business doing well, Uruvin?"

"Why, of course! The demand for spices is always there, no matter how poor the economy. And the river always brings good business." His fingers continue to *tap, tap, tap*.

Interesting. It hasn't been raining for the past few months; the waters of the river have receded so much that large boats can barely sail down without their bottoms scraping against rocks. Does the merchant think that I am ignorant to the workings of the world at large because I don't step foot outside temple grounds?

I stay silent for a while, tempering my anger.

"Do you think me a fool, my child?" I finally say, voice dangerously soft.

His eyes spark with alarm. "Your Grace?"

"I have given you a chance to speak the truth, and yet you have lied to me." I lean forward ever so slightly, careful to not let the weight of my headdress topple me forward. My shadow, cast by the braziers above my head and distorted by Anas's ten snake heads, stretches towards Uruvin. "You call yourself a follower of Rashmatun, yet you dare to let falsehoods fall from your tongue in my presence? Why must you use your wife, even in her death, to compensate for your failing business?"

Ilam cackles in delight. He loves it when I truly *become* a goddess, when none can defy me and all must bow to me.

Even I have to admit I enjoy the feeling.

The rhythm the merchant taps out grows even more erratic. "Your Grace. I assure you that I have been speaking nothing but the truth. My wife—"

"Is dead. That much is certain." I pitch my voice low; the echoes induce trembles in the man's limbs. "But for all her wifely qualities, you never did love her, did you?"

Uruvin's lips part dumbly. "I—I—Rashmatun, no," he stammers. "I loved her, with all my heart!"

"You are lying *again*." I slowly adjust my arm so that my elbow is propped atop the armrest encrusted with yellow sapphires, my temple resting against my fingers. "If you did love your wife so, why have you found yourself another lover already?"

His eyes widen in shock and guilt; his expression is stripped bare of pretence.

I cannot tell if the satisfaction welling in me is mine or Ilam's.

Uruvin sinks into a panicked bow. "Oh, Rashmatun!" he cries. "Your eyes see all. It was foolish of me to even think of deceiving you. Please, my goddess, I beg for your forgiveness! Please grant your servant mercy!"

I close my eyes, exasperated. Sweat trickles down my neck; the back of my jama is uncomfortably soaked. I am eager to peel off the four gold chains weighing down my neck, and my rump is sore from sitting the entire morning. I've given this man more than enough time to redeem himself.

"For your transgressions, you shall be prohibited from entering the temple for the next five years," I declare, opening my eyes languidly. "And you will pay a twenty percent increment of yearly taxes, since according to you, your business is bustling. My priests will ensure that the necessary paperwork is filled out."

His face takes on a sickly pallor. "My Rashmatun has been merciful," he murmurs.

"Get out," I say, quiet.

Uruvin ducks his head and rises to his feet. He scuttles backwards

until he is out of the worship hall. Ilam's amused laughter continues ringing somewhere at the back of my mind.

With a tired sigh, I sink into my throne. "Harun." A portly man
whose eyes resemble a bulging frog's steps into my direct line of
sight. I've grown somewhat accustomed to the chief priest's permanent expression of gross surprise. "Anyone else?"

"No, my goddess," Harun replies. He adjusts the orange sash
thrown over his left shoulder. "That was the last worshipper for
today."

"The maximum number of devotees is twelve." I pinch the
bridge of my nose. "That was the twentieth."

"The land is in a dire state now, Rashmatun. We did transport
a sizeable portion of our grain stores to the armies' supply centres before the drought hit us." He stares at me with his frog eyes.
"Your people are growing desperate. Many are flooding your temples, and more still wish to have an audience with you."

"I see."

Clever, clever goddess, Ilam laughs. *How your people love you so.*

I try not to bristle in reflex. No use getting furious at a demon
you cannot control.

Harun clutches the length of prayer beads around his neck; his
eyes slide towards the priests lining up behind him, their mouths
shut in an eerie, complete silence. "My goddess, perhaps if you
actually do something about the drought—"

"The Forebears bide their time, Harun," I say, waving a dismissive hand. "Is Hyrlvat thriving? Are the cornfields of Vintya lush
and abundant? The gods are staying our hands for reasons that will
be clear in a time to come."

Harun presses his lips into a thin line. I've been using that same
vague reason for the past two months now. Even as most of our
supplies are being given to the Aritsyan army, which has been bat-
tling the Dennarese Empire for decades, leaving precious little in
our silos. Even as our crops wither and the prospects of a hungry
winter grow exponentially with every passing day.

Do I have a choice? No. The only reason why the people of the
city of Bakhtin have not rioted against me is because the rest of the

country is suffering as well. Anyway, this is not the first time such a drought has occurred, and certainly not the first time Bakhtin's goddess abstained from bringing food to her people.

The chief priest still doesn't look convinced, though.

"Why do you not use your own magic to enchant the clouds, then?" I suggest scathingly. "If you're so worried about the drought?"

"My goddess, you know that our power has greatly weakened over the years. Besides, we can only cast enchantments—"

"When I'm around. Yes, I am well aware," I cut him off. *Excuses*, I think, but don't say out loud. The priests have no problem coaxing trees to bear fruit and casting needles to mend their elaborate garments when they think I'm out of sight. Minor spells, but ones that speak volumes about the temple's priorities. "Enough," I continue, vexation growing in me the longer this topic drags out. "I will only admit twelve devotees per day. At most. Am I clear?"

He dips his head in deference. "Yes, Your Grace."

"Good. And see to it that the necessary compensations and punishments are dispensed."

"Of course, Your Grace."

I dip my head. "Till tomorrow, Harun."

"Till tomorrow."

I stand up and step off the elevated dais. My bare foot touches the carpeted floor. Immediately my posture is not as straight, my head not held as high. I let my knees buckle, as if they were not accustomed to the weight of the ornaments I wear. Harun reaches forward to steady me, a fatherly smile on his face.

In a split second, I am no longer Rashmatun. I am Binsa, vessel of the goddess of wisdom, an ordinary girl whose life was touched by the extraordinary.

"What did she do today?" I ask Harun. My routine question after I've broken out of my "trance."

"Many things. Many great things." His routine answer.

"Will she bring rain soon?"

"She…" His grip on my shoulders tightens ever so slightly. He shakes his head and presses a hand against my back, guiding me out of the Paruvatar, the worship hall. "Come, child. You should rest."

I follow his lead without another word. We exit into a courtyard shadowed by long, straggling branches and lush emerald leaves. The rhododendron bushes planted all around the space are at full bloom, the vibrant red of the flowers resembling cloaks woven out of fresh blood. The sun overhead blazes bright, yet its full heat is lost on me with the mountain winds cocooning the temple, which lies high atop blustering cliffs. All enchantments by the hands of the priests; while the rest of the city withers, the sanctity of the temple must be maintained, which includes tending to its environment.

Harun claps his hands. Muscular palanquin bearers materialize before us. I step into the litter; the chief priest walks alongside.

The palanquin sways with a rhythmic lull as the bearers walk in perfect synchrony, marching through the various temples in Ghanatukh's complex at a languorous pace. They let me down before a two-tiered building, its red walls basking in the glow of the sun. I enter the Bakhal, the goddess's place of residence. A tall, imposing woman appears from behind one of the pillars, her generous girth clad in white. Jirtash claps her palms together and bows her head. Harun nods, leaving me to her care.

We wind our way through the sprawling maze of the pillars and shrines in the Bakhal's lowest floor, the scent of sandalwood drifting lazily through the air. We cut through another courtyard—a dry fountain in the middle, a luxury the priests didn't bother with— before arriving at my chambers. The furnishings hardly match the grandiosity of Rashmatun's power; while they are not falling into decay, they are as plain as a commoner's taste in fashion. The size of the room makes up for the lackluster decorations, though.

Any room is better than where I used to live, back when I was a child.

Jirtash tugs me towards a full-length mirror. I follow her like the obedient girl I'm supposed to be. She's the chief of the handmaidens and the oldest, having attended to four other vessels of Rashmatun before me. She carefully lifts the headdress away and places it on a finely embroidered cushion; the absence of its weight is liberating.

Meanwhile, Ilam has curled into a comfortable ball at the back of my mind. The demon rarely emerges during my day-to-day activities, only coming to life when something catches his interest or offends him, or when he wants to taunt me. Typical of a demon, only giving attention to matters that involve them, and remaining apathetic towards everything else.

More handmaidens scuttle towards me, peeling away the layers of my uniform with reverent efficiency. The four gold chains, each with a different design, representing the four cardinal directions. The bhota and jama, both fiery red and embroidered with golden flowers, catch the brilliant rays of sunlight streaming in through tall, narrow windows. My earrings and bangles are removed. Jirtash wipes my forehead with a cloth soaked in coconut oil, removing the seven-pronged star painted onto it. She whispers a quick prayer, a plea for forgiveness, as she temporarily breaks Rashmatun's connection to her chosen vessel. With the star gone, she moves on to the rest of my face—the thick lines of kohl around my eyes, my bloodred lips.

Soon I am left naked, save for a pendant of yellow sapphire hung from a crude length of woven threads. Its uneven surface rests comfortingly against my chest, where my ribs protrude beneath my skin. My arms and legs are as thin as sticks, and my breasts are pitifully small. Not that it matters, since no one dares to comment much about my appearance.

The handmaidens unwind the thick coils of hair piled atop my head. It falls almost to my knees, thick and luxuriant, a soft sheen running down its trails. The only physical trait I am proud of.

Jirtash takes my hand and leads me towards the bathtub. I sink into its waters, contentedly allowing the handmaidens to lift my arms and legs and scrub them clean. A layer of grime gathers and floats on the water.

When I'm done, Jirtash towels me down and outfits me in a red kurta—I must always wear a hint of red somewhere—and a loose-fitting suruwal. I sit before the vanity table, and she braids my hair as her helpers tidy up the place.

"Oh child, what a woman wouldn't give to have hair as gorgeous as yours." Jirtash sighs in admiration.

Ice seems to gather at the nape of my neck. The ghost of a rough hand yanks the ends of my hair and sets it aflame.

I play with a near-empty bottle of perfume on the table, pushing the memory away. Jirtash has combed my hair almost the past ten years. This is just another day, another routine. She has no ill intentions. She has nothing to do with my past, I remind myself.

A past that she can never learn about.

I hope she doesn't notice the tremor in my fingers as I run them over the perfume bottle. "Thank you," I murmur.

She doesn't say anything else. I know what is on her mind: If only the rest of me were as gorgeous as my hair. I am close to sixteen now. Other girls my age have developed bosoms and swelling hips already. Me? I might as well be a withering tree trunk.

It's unusual for a girl to not have menstruated already, she told me two weeks ago, and what is even more unusual is that I have not shown signs of puberty. She once suspected that I was malnourished, but quickly dismissed the notion when I pointed out that I ate three full meals a day.

I did not tell her that I always dispose of two of those meals.

She finishes braiding my hair and claps her hands over my shoulders. "All done," she says. "There now, don't you look pretty?"

I don't agree with the sentiment. My nose is too large for my pointed chin and thin lips, my cheeks are as hollow as empty bowls of alms, and my eyes are too large, too fierce. But she is trying to be kind, so I muster a smile. "Thank you."

She nods, then releases me from her grip. A platter of food has been served, placed on a table by the window. I polish off the meal thoroughly; it's my only one every day. When no one is watching, I retrieve a vial from under my table and pour a drop of its contents into the clay cup of water, turning it into a murky solution. I drain the cup, trying not to wince at the foul taste. This is forbidden medicine that poisons my ovaries—another one of my methods to delay my bleeding for as long as possible. A small price to remain a goddess for a little while longer.

But my medicine is running dangerously low.

I haven't heard from my supplier in weeks. I grit my teeth, suppressing the anxiety rising up my throat.

When I'm done, I head towards the exit. I sense a hint of grim disapproval from Jirtash. "Off to your lessons, now?" she asks, more out of courtesy than genuine interest. She does not think that I should be paying so much attention to books and education. I should be more concerned about growing into a woman and finding a good husband, like the many girls who came before me. The latter won't be too hard, considering that everyone wants to receive some form of blessing from a former living goddess. Assuming that I choose to marry.

However, that means that I have to give up my status as the vessel of Rashmatun. The thought hollows out my stomach, as if someone carved my skin open and emptied my insides.

Who am I, if I am Rashmatun no longer? A scrawny girl with no inherent title or wealth to her name. A nothing, someone whose face will fade from the memories of all who have seen her.

I shake the notion out of my mind. I am still a living goddess, I remind myself. "Of course, Jirtash!" I chirp innocently. "Lessons won't wait!"

I traipse out of the room.

2

Rumours

I climb the stairs leading to the second floor and enter the library, the ancient stone beneath my feet sanded smooth over time. The area stretches across the entire length of the Bakhal's second floor, gas lamps dimly illuminating the books and scrolls on their mahogany shelves, the musty scent of yellowing pages filling the air.

My brother is already waiting at one of the tables placed before the shelves, tinkering with one of his automatons. Ykta's eyes are bright and eager, and a silly grin splits his face as he winds up the little bird and releases the catch. The bird gives a few valiant flaps of its wings before plummeting onto the table with a crash. He frowns at his failed experiment.

"It's too heavy because it's made out of metal," I point out, closing the door behind me.

"I've hollowed out the wires. The structure is as close as it gets to the real thing."

"Have you considered using magic to fuel your funny little hobby?"

"And concede to using shortcuts? Never!" His cheeks puff in protest. "Besides, I'd have to grovel in front of yet another priest only for them to mutter some inane charms and wave their arms about like a fake shaman. No, thank you. I suck up to them on a daily basis already."

"Poor brother," I chuckle, ignoring Ilam's ruffled protest. The demon has a grudge against Ykta and his ardent disapproval of magic. "Sorry for loading you with the unpleasant work."

"You'd better appreciate me more. The goat you forced me to build cost me nearly three months of my sanity—even if it's just a head." He considers his automaton for another moment, then releases a defeated sigh. He turns his attention towards me, a mischievous glint in his eyes. "Speaking of which, I heard from the maidservants that there was a case with a falling goat today?"

I plunk myself onto a seat beside him, huffing. He wasn't hiding in the secret hollow behind my throne today, then, if he wants more details about the case. "I quickly settled that one. His grief over his wife's death was a lie. He was describing his 'dear Dirka' in too clinical a manner."

He quirks a curious brow. "What about the goat? Did it actually happen?"

"Of course not," I mutter, irritated. Ilam stays silent, refusing to clarify the truth.

"I could help you check if it actually happened," Ykta says, stretching his arms. He is the paragon of physical perfection that Jirtash would praise to the high heavens, with his lean, sturdy build and the dark, thick lashes framing his eyes. "The maidservants would be more than happy to share such outlandish gossip with me."

"No need. I'm a busy person, and I've no energy to waste with folktales of falling goats."

"For all you know, it might be a new pandemic plaguing Bakhtin. First the drought, now this. Rumours of the Prophecy of Geerkha are spreading among the common folk, you know? I heard from a few nosy uncles and aunties at the marketplace this morning: *Red and bright the skies will burn, our offerings mourn*—"

"Yes, yes. I know how it goes," I snap, waving a dismissive hand. I can't do much to control the tongues of my citizens. "Forget it. Let's begin the lesson."

Ykta shrugs. "What's your chosen reading for today?"

"*Theories and Principles of Aritsyan Magic for Beginners* by Vharla Privindu."

My brother stares at me. "Vharla *Privindu*? The blood shaman? Again? Are you trying to get yourself thrown out of Ghanatukh Temple before you abdicate the throne?"

"A few other scholars cited him in their works," I say. "I can't simply ignore him because of his reputation."

"A reputation that killed him and many other government officials." Ykta sighs. "How does the library here even have Privindu's book?"

"You could inform Harun about this, if you're that concerned."

"Fine, whatever. Don't blame me if someone catches you reading this." Ykta throws his hands up. Then his eyes widen and sparkle. "You know what, I have a better idea. Instead of keeping you cooped up in this stuffy place, why don't you come down to my workshop to take a look at the goat you commissioned? I can test it for you too."

I purse my lips. This isn't the first time he's tried to persuade me to escape enclosed grounds. Ykta has done enough skulking about the temple to be familiar with its inner arteries and hidden passageways, as evidenced by the subtle hand- and footholds he carved into the wall outside my room. I admit that I am tempted by his offer. He's described his goat head as a monstrous nightmare made out of brass and steel that can spit fire and roll its eyes backwards, and I am curious to see how it works.

However, he doesn't understand the full gravity of my position. A Rakhti is never allowed outside of temple grounds until she has retired, one of the many rules she must adhere to throughout her tenure. With my sanctity currently in question, considering my age and the issue of the drought, it is crucial, now more than ever, that I play the part of the perfect Rakhti.

After all, my position here was built on a falsehood: I do not hold a goddess, but I pretend to be one. I claim to be pure and virtuous, yet a demon lives within me.

Not even Ykta knows about Ilam, though he is aware I do not hold Rashmatun.

It's during moments like these that the gap between us shows. It's been almost ten years since we were first separated, and four since he returned to my side. So many things have happened during the six years in between. So many things happened during the years *before*, when our mother forced me to become Rakhti and abandoned Ykta to fend for himself. No one in the temple is even aware that we are siblings.

I take a deep breath, steadying my nerves. No. I cannot blame Ykta for thinking that I should be more light-hearted, more playful. I am younger than him by seven years. It is what anyone would expect. He had been fortunate to have been taken in by an eminent professor, who sent him to a university even though only the blood sons of kisharis are permitted to receive higher education. He had loved and been loved. He wouldn't be able to comprehend why I am so cautious.

"No, thank you," I reply at last, grabbing an ancient book from the stack on the table, its bindings barely keeping its pages together. "I'd much rather focus on the works of a controversial scholar."

My brother's face falls. He goes back to tinkering with his automatons in silence.

The mind is an ocean of limitless power—reality is limited only by your imagination. When does a falsehood become truth? Very simply, when you believe it to be true.

Only the opening of Privindu's book arrests my attention. The rest are dreary facts about how Aritsyan magic works—most of them already known to the general public. Like how shamans are descended from the Forebears themselves, which is why the kisharis' blood is regarded as sacred; and how the purity of a bloodline indicates the strength of a shaman. I've read this book plenty of times. I keep persisting, though, in hopes that I might find something new about blood magic when I read it with fresh eyes.

Today is not the day.

But of course. All books that explicitly contain information on blood magic have been banned from common circles and are kept under strict surveillance in university libraries. Privindu's book was my best hope; I had been overjoyed when I dug it out of a forgotten corner of the library the first time. Now it is another dead end.

"Your nose in yet another book, Little Mantis?" a voice abruptly rings out from behind. I whip my head around, startled, then relax at the sight of the lithe, sinewy silhouette emerging from the shadows of the racks. Keran must have taken one of the many hidden passageways he'd discovered. "Don't you have anything better to do than stuffing your head with formulas and dates and folktales?"

Ilam emits a low hiss.

The silhouette steps into the light, wearing a cocksure grin. Keran's pale skin contrasts against his dark clothing, and the scar slashing from his nose to his left ear adds a feral quality to his otherwise boyish face. Even without his unusual complexion, his eyes immediately single him out as a Dennarese—no one in Aritsya has eyes shaped like that, which curve into half moons when he grins wide enough. Half the time they are sharp as knives, and the other half they are unfocused, as though he were stuck in a dream.

Usually, it is easy to tell one's thoughts through their eyes; with his, I cannot gauge his mood, his mind. Every time I think he is unaware of something I do, he catches it and calls me out.

In short, I do not like him because I cannot control him. He is, however, a necessary part of my ongoing sham as a "goddess."

"You're three days late," I say.

"Mercy." He fishes out a small pouch from the satchel; the glass bottles inside clink as he sets it on the table. I nearly heave a sigh of relief. "Here you go. One month's worth."

I raise my brow. "I asked for two."

He bares a toothy smile; I detect the faintest undercurrent of unease from him. Surprising, considering that it's Keran, and Keran never gets uneasy. "Times are hard, Little Mantis. Your gods and goddesses are answering none of your prayers, and you haven't done anything to ease the situation."

I press my lips at the accusation. He's right, though. What can one girl do in the face of nature's wrath? Nothing. Not when I don't have a lick of the magic that the Rakhtas and their priests are supposed to have. Not when there are limits to the power one demon can provide.

"What news have you for me?" I ask, diverting the topic.

"Same old, same old," Keran says, going along with me. "The king is at his wit's end, constantly begging your fellow Rakhtas for some sign from the gods. Meanwhile, said Rakhtas are doing absolutely nothing to address the drought, and Rakhta Asahar's battles against the Dennarese Empire are still going terribly, for all his bluster. As for your city, rumours of falling goats are spreading, slowly but surely. Soon the entire country will know that your district is plagued by goats. Has anybody brought that case to you yet?"

Has there been more than one incident? Ykta casts me a side glance as my fingernails scrape against my palm. Keran is probably exaggerating the extent of the rumours; he just wants to see my nerves on edge. "None of your business," I say stiffly.

"Word spreads fast, you know. You should be more careful about your reputation."

I wait a while for him to speak more. He maintains his grin. "You really have nothing else to report?" I ask.

"Not really. News, I'm afraid, like the current state of your country, is rather stale."

Judging from the gleam in his dark eyes, there is something more that requires a lot more prodding—preferably with money.

"Ykta," I say. My brother takes out a heavy pouch from his suruwal and counts out payment for Keran. I reach over and pluck the pouch out of his hands, retrieving two more gurisi. I give the total sum to Keran, ignoring the dismay painted over my brother's features.

"A bonus," I say. "For all your troubles."

"Ah, I knew there was a reason you're one of my favourites." He tucks the gurisi away shamelessly. "I overheard an interesting conversation while I was sneaking my way here. It sounded like your chief priest and his sullen successor."

"Harun and Nudin," I supply the names. "What of them?"

"They are going to hold a Selection for the new Rakhti of

Bakhtin, regardless of whether Rashmatun grants them permission. 'It is high time,' they were saying, 'for a new vessel to be chosen. The current one has been in power for too long—Rashmatun is no longer blessing the city with the full spectrum of her abilities, a sure sign of the current vessel's decline in purity.'"

He pauses. I refuse to give him a reaction until he finishes talking, keeping my breaths long and even. Beside me, Ykta trembles with rage.

"Candidate nominations will open up in three days' time," he continues, quirking his brows. "They expect to have a new Rakhti by the next month."

I bob my head. My fingers idly play with the yellow sapphire around my neck. My stomach churns, even though I expected this to happen sooner or later.

"Oh, and your chief priest—Harun?—is currently exchanging correspondence with Rakhta Asahar."

Now *that* information gives me pause. My eyes sidle to meet Keran's. Bastard. Why didn't he mention that upfront? "What are those letters about?"

"Unfortunately, even my network isn't so extensive that I know everything that goes on in Aritsya. How on earth do you expect me to peek at letters written by Rakhtas and chief priests?"

I raise a brow at him. "Yet you managed to learn that Asahar often wastes his province's funds away in gambling dens? What a strange fellow you are, Keran."

"Scandalous information and confidential information are two different matters, Little Mantis." He wags a patronising finger at me; I still refuse to show my vexation. "It's up to you to decide what you wish to do with the information. My job is to supply it to you. Nothing more, nothing less."

I fold my arms and consider everything he's presented to me so far. The more immediate issue is the fact that Harun and Nudin are arranging for my removal sooner than I expected. Which means that I have to either give in to their plans or fight back.

"How ready is the goat automaton?" I ask Ykta.

My brother jumps at the abrupt question. "Eighty...ninety percent?

There's still some fine-tuning I need to do, but honestly it's functioning—"

"Can you move it by yourself?"

"Er—of course I could, in theory, but it depends on where I need to carry it to—"

"That will do." I turn back to Keran. "How willing are you to perform physical labour?"

The Dennarese's grin grows wider. "Depends on the price, as always."

"Another two gurisi."

Keran hums. "Quite a generous sum—for a regular labourer."

"Two gurisi and five hundred sharus, then."

"That sounds more like it," Keran says, stretching his hand towards Ykta. My brother gives me a hapless look before counting out the money. "What do I need to do?"

"Help Ykta move the goat automaton into Shiratukh Temple the night before the next Selection. He'll tell you how to do it."

Ykta glowers at Keran, who slaps Ykta on the back. "I'll be under your care. Make sure you treat me well, eh?"

My brother's scowl deepens.

Keran's peal of laughter is as light as the high, clear notes of cicadas. "I'll see you soon, and I'll see you next month." He directs the former phrase to Ykta, and the latter to me. He disappears beyond the racks, as soundlessly as he came in. The furious flap of wings startles me; I look towards the window to see the shadow of an eagle vanishing into the sky. This particular eagle always seems to accompany Keran wherever he goes, matching the Dennarese's stealth despite its size.

"I swear nearly a quarter of our yearly income goes to that pretentious, good-for-nothing swine," Ykta mutters.

"Come now, dear brother. He's a valuable asset—and valuable assets are not cheap to maintain." I replace the two glass vials into their pouch and shove them into my pocket.

"Little blood-leeching louse," he grumbles.

"Ykta," I groan. Honestly, I do not understand why my brother holds Keran in such low regard when he was the one who recruited the Dennarese in the first place. Apparently Keran had taken a liking to Ykta about three years ago, after witnessing how my brother exposed a swindler in the city, whose playing cards were marked by fingernail scratches. The Dennarese approached Ykta after that, and the two formed a strange bond—strong enough to convince Keran to help me, at least.

Still, I've never figured out why Ykta seems to despise Keran's presence, when I'm sure he's closer to the Dennarese than I am. He's even gone out of Ghanatukh Temple to meet Keran a few times for drinks and games. I could use blood magic to untangle the mystery, but—no. As much as I rely on Ilam to maintain my ruse as a goddess, it does not change the fact that I abhor blood magic.

All because of my mother.

Ykta releases a long exhale. "Fine. We need Keran. As much as I dislike him." He folds his arms across his chest. "And you! What were you thinking, dragging me into your Selection business? Are you actually trying to sabotage—"

"Dear brother"—I knit my fingers on my lap—"I am the current Rakhti. Of course I want to make sure the next vessel of Rashmatun is resilient and sharp of mind."

"But trying to scare the girls to death?"

"Are you here to help me or question me?"

"*Binsa*, I'm just concerned." Ykta runs his hands through his hair in frustration. "Haven't you thought about the consequences of re-electing yourself as Rakhti? You heard Keran just now. Asahar and Harun must be working together to remove you. Why would Harun pull off such a bold move otherwise? You know Asahar is not one to provoke. And your idea for the Selection...I hate to say this, but it sounds a lot like something Kavi—"

"Are you done lecturing me?" I interrupt him, just before he crosses the line. I pick my fingers. "As if I care about Asahar. None of the other Rakhtas liked me anyway ever since my Selection. But what do *you* know?"

His expression drops. Dismay lines the curve of his lips. My Rakhti Selection has always been a touchy subject for us—a haunting that perpetually scrapes at our backs, one that we desperately seek to banish.

"I'm sorry," he whispers. "I...I'm just worried about you."

I release a small breath. "I know."

He levels a stare at me. "Don't tell me you're planning to be Rakhti forever?"

"This is the only life I've ever known, Ykta," I reply, tone low. My eyelids shutter to a close; I cannot imagine a life beyond the temple walls, a life where I laugh and mingle carelessly with others, where I live out the rest of my days as a regular human being.

I left that life a long time ago, the constant worrying if I would get to eat the next day, the clothes that have been patched up so many times that scarcely a shred of their original fabric remains.

The temple walls guarantee comfort and power; a life outside does not.

That's what my mother told me. As much as I hated her, she was right.

"Whatever you say."

My fingers still. Whatever happens, I cannot have Ykta lose faith in me.

"Ykta, please. You're the only person I trust in this world." I place my hand over his and give it a reassuring squeeze. "If you won't help me, who will? You came back for me, even after... everything. Don't tell me you'll abandon me now?"

His countenance cracks. "Binsa..."

Then he doesn't say anything, simply places another hand atop mine. He clings on so tightly, afraid that if he let go I would disappear, like the fleeting light of a setting sun.

A grim determination settles over me. I have to protect Ykta, protect myself—and the only way I know how is by being Rakhti. If I don't hold my position as Rashmatun's chosen, I will be cast back into the streets with nothing but a handful of gurisi to my name, only enough to serve as my dowry. I'll be expected to fade into the background, to marry anyone who comes along—never mind that I have no more family on official records—and spend the rest of my life as a dutiful wife and mother. Ykta, the only blood family I have left, will have to leave me, and he will eventually forget all about my existence.

I recall today's audience with Uruvin, how he took advantage of his wife's death to plead for money. How her life was a mere tool, to be discarded and forgotten afterwards. Will that be my fate as well, if I return to a "normal" life?

No. I will continue to be Rashmatun's Rakhti.

And I will not let anybody dictate otherwise.

3

Promise of a Prophecy

I sit cross-legged in the middle of my room. Moonlight filters in through the windows, casting panels of silver onto the floor. A fog of calmness hangs heavy over the atmosphere, thick with the dreams of wishful maidens and innocent children. The occasional critter breaks through the silence, lending life to a drowsy night. The air is cool, quiet, free from the constant droning of innocuous gossip and scattered cacophony of the day.

I take a deep breath. The night is when I truly find my rest, the only time when I do not have to keep up an act and behave myself in front of people. Here, cocooned by the shadows, I feel safe—as though the darkness were providing me shelter from derisive eyes.

My dinner lies untouched on the table, a cold stew of spinach and cottage cheese accompanied by flatbread. Privindu's *Theories and Principles of Aritsyan Magic for Beginners* sits beside my bowl. Not many people go around looking for Privindu's works, considering his unsavoury reputation. No one will miss it.

The temple bell rings twelve times. I close my eyes and draw Ilam out of my mind.

It doesn't take much coaxing to get the demon out, much like reaching into a shelf and retrieving a well-worn tome. Ilam unfurls out of my body, stretching his length like a yawning cat. The process of physically separating ourselves sends a jolt of pain spiking straight into my temples. I grit my teeth and control my breathing, forcing myself to endure it.

The throbbing pain dissipates, and I open my eyes. The demon is prowling around the table, taking a black feline form, his preferred appearance. Ilam sticks his nose into my dinner without asking for permission. He doesn't actually have to eat human food; he simply enjoys the flavours.

A strange demon. Not that I am in a position to question anything he does.

When he is done polishing off the stew and flatbread, he turns around and faces me. His eyes glow an unnatural silver, perhaps even brighter than the moon itself. He licks his chops and yawns, baring his fangs. It's odd, seeing how he behaves like a normal cat. But the smoke that steams off his body is a clear indicator that he is not of this world.

He hops down from the table and slinks towards me. I push the sleeve of my kurta up and hold my hand out. Ilam sinks his teeth into my forearm.

Slow, sinking discomfort spreads throughout my body, like needles pricking beneath the surface of my skin.

Ilam is feeding on my blood—or, as he likes to call it, my soulstream.

This is how blood shamans keep their demons tethered to them. Demons crave flesh, and while they can consume animals, what makes human blood so delicious to them is the life force that flows inside. Ilam had once explained that by feeding on blood, demons feed on our souls—and it is the soul that keeps them sustained.

Apparently, the more powerful blood shamans can exert direct control over their companion by providing enough blood. I, on the other hand, have to contend with the fact that Ilam helps me at all. So long as I provide him soulstream at least once every month.

My limbs grow weaker with each passing second. Black spots dance before my eyes as Ilam unhinges his jaw from my arm. He sits on his haunches, his silvery eyes alight with the pleasure of a full meal.

"I noticed your book," he says, his voice surprisingly young for a demon far older than I am. "Still trying to do research on your own, I see. What do you intend to accomplish?"

"I need your help." My posture is ramrod straight, and I set my features into a neutral expression as best as I can—even as my guts knot and twist themselves.

"Don't you always," he replies in a condescending manner.

I maintain my stoic mask. "Ilam. Please."

"Tell me, what ambitions have you been hiding away in that pretty little brain of yours?" Ilam cocks his head. His muzzle curls into what almost resembles a smile. "What lies are you hiding behind? Have you discovered any of Privindu's secrets yet?"

"I have no secrets. I always share what I know with you, don't I?"

"Only if it's in your interest," Ilam purrs in amusement. He taught me early on how to hide my thoughts from him, after he deemed my inner voice too loud for his liking. When I'd turned his lesson against him by locking *him* up inside my mind, only allowing him passage when I want to so that he is not constantly prodding my thoughts, Ilam had been tickled. I suppose that's one other reason why he sticks around.

"I...need your help to summon rain." The words feel like rocks in my mouth.

Ilam stares at me, his silver gaze unnerving. I almost want to retract my statement.

He bursts into laughter; the sound resembles the crackle of burning wood. "After all these years," he says, still laughing, "and only now you want to tap further into blood magic? I thought consulting Privindu's books was enough for you!"

I curl my fingers into fists. "Yes, Ilam. I want to use more blood magic."

"Are you that desperate, little Binsa?"

"What's wrong with wanting to improve myself? My mind has been a bit stale lately."

"Or your tricks and schemes are starting to wear." His words scathe my nerves more than I'd like. "And you have nothing to turn to but the blood magic you so despise."

My eyebrows pinch together. "I don't despise blood magic. I'm just not very accustomed to it, is all."

"So you have no hard feelings against it because of Kavita?"

I press my lips into a thin line; heat flares in my veins. He knows how much I hate the mention of my mother's name. He knows how long it took for me to be able to go through my daily routines without having her ghost breathing down my neck—to be able to call my decisions and thoughts my own. Still, I keep my tone light as I say, "None whatsoever."

"Interesting." Ilam flicks his ears. "Are you prepared to pay the price?"

A sacrifice that will officially seal the new contract. As little as I know about blood shamans, I know that this is the very first step that enables one to successfully summon a demon or create a new pact. My current contract with Ilam is a special case—since it was my mother who passed him to me, I've never had to properly sacrifice anything to him before.

"Yes," I answer, my heart thrumming against my chest.

He blinks his unnerving eyes, as though he can see right through my mental walls, homing in on the fear that broils deep within me. "Fine. Give me three days to consider your request."

"All right," I say, despite my insides screaming for an immediate answer. Ilam is the one who holds power. I don't get to dictate what he can and cannot do.

When trading with demons, it's always best to understand one's position.

"Good." He pauses for a while. "I hope you truly know what this means."

"I do."

"I don't think so." Another pause, then he cackles. "But it matters not to me."

I incline my head, unsure of how to respond to that.

"Until next time, Binsa." His frame dissipates into smoke, which latches on to my skin and burns through me.

And he is there, curled up at the back of my mind.

I collapse onto the floor, all energy sapped from my body. Hosting a demon is demanding. The less skill you have, the more taxing it is on you. I'm lousy enough as it is, and coupled with my deliberate attempts to starve myself, it feels like I have just survived a hike to Aratiya, the summit of the Yaborun range behind the temple.

It takes a few minutes before I regain enough strength to sit upright. It takes another few before I can stand up and hobble towards my bed. I slump onto my blankets and stare at the ceiling, wondering if I'm going to be strong enough to take in more of Ilam's power.

No. There's no "if." I *must* be strong enough. No matter how I got here, I am the vessel of Rashmatun.

I *am* the goddess.

In but a few hours after I drift into a much-needed sleep, my hand-maidens ruthlessly haul me out of bed and plunge me into icy-cold water. A luxury, I suppose, considering that half the city is dying of thirst. But it's hard to appreciate one's privilege when you're bullied into taking a bath during the chilly hours of the wee morning. A distant bell chimes six times through the fog clouding my mind.

I am dressed in my off-duty kurta and suruwal. Jirtash walks me to the cleansing hall, a small building just to the west of the Bakhal, its frame held up by red and golden pillars. I kneel before a small channel that diverts some of the nearby waterfall into temple grounds. More water is doused over my head as Harun and several other priests form a semicircle around me, chanting their prayers and making signs with the bead necklaces wrapped around their hands. My limbs shiver violently; I keep my gaze pinned on the statue of Rashmatun standing beyond the channel, tall and imposing and glimmering with opalescent colours. For a deity that does not exist, her features are carved in exquisite detail, every hair on her arched brows perfectly trimmed, the line of her nose long and uncompromising.

Not for the first time in my life, I wonder if the priests know that Rashmatun is a lie. I wonder if the other nine Forebears—the greater gods of Aritsya—are fakes as well, and if my fellow Rakhtas are putting on an act. Like me.

But my wondering does not matter. I do not dare to speak the truth and risk losing my position.

When the priests are done with their morning prayers, I stand up and turn around to face them. Jirtash helps wipe my forehead dry. Harun steps forward with several small bowls of paint resting in one hand, dipping a brush into the white paint.

He swirls the sticky paint onto the centre of my forehead. At the same time, he begins to sing:

> *"Open, open,*
> *Open and see,*
> *Look at what our world offers to thee.*
> *Guide us, guide us,*
> *Guide us and tell,*
> *The hearts of men whom thou knoweth so well."*

He and the priests repeat the chant seven times, their voices coalescing into a low, sonorous mass. All the while Harun slowly but deftly wields the brush, layering yellow atop white. I do not need a mirror to see the seven-pronged star shining forth. The symbol of the goddess of wisdom, the ancient star that has travelled across the seven universes and has seen and heard all.

My countenance shifts. I stand straighter, shoulders back and neck tall. I stare at Harun, who falls onto his knees. Behind him, Jirtash and the rest of the priests do the same.

"Rise," I say after waiting an appropriate amount of time. "Now, can we get this body out of such dreadful threads?"

Ilam chortles, stirring to consciousness.

My day as Rashmatun begins.

"So you see, Your Grace," the elderly woman explains in a thin, placid tone, "it is fortunate that no one was harmed during the incident, since we were all outside the house. But now our home has been destroyed, and we have nowhere to go."

It is an unusual case that Harun has brought to me. Instead of one or two devotees, an entire family had been ushered in. There are five of them: an elderly woman, her son, and his three young children. They are dressed in the barest of threads, and the grandmother's gnarled hands bespeak years of hard labour. The father's face is wrinkled, his shoulders strong and lean and his skin a burnished bronze. Meanwhile, the mother is currently away at war, having joined the Aritsyan army in desperate hope that she would earn more to feed her family, despite the fact that Bakhtin is known for producing only crops and scholars, not warriors.

The family claims that their patch of land has completely dried out in the drought, and that they have been surviving on the meagre rations we distribute to needy citizens. As if that wasn't enough, a goat had dropped out of the sky and plunged through their roof.

Barely a day has passed, and another person has already come forward with yet another story of a falling goat.

Ilam's silence means that the family is telling nothing but the truth.

But even entertaining the idea of a falling goat sounds ridiculous. I wonder how all my devotees—Uruvin from yesterday, and the family from today—can talk about it with a straight face.

Then there's the matter of figuring out how one would drop these animals from the sky. Magic might help, but shamans in Aritsya are few and far between. Most of them are also too weak to do anything substantial, with the blood of the gods that run in them apparently watering down over the centuries. The remaining shamans who are strong enough to be of any use are all conscripted into the Holy Guard.

More importantly, why would anyone do this? How does harming innocent people help them in any way?

"My goddess, could it be...?" The elderly woman's voice cuts through my headache. "The Prophecy of Geerkha—is it coming to pass?"

> Red and bright the skies will burn,
> Our offerings mourn, and the ghosts return.
> The skies darken with fear, trembling amidst the goddess's might,

The fallen stars shatter, and the seas rise.
At the end of it all, the Scarlet Throne bleeds,
The crown at her head rusts,
The ornaments turn to dust.

The first verse of the Prophecy rings in my head, an ominous lullaby that sinks into my bones. I can even hear Kavita singing it, the incandescent quality of her voice eerie yet soothing...

A shudder runs through my limbs.

I recompose myself, quickly slipping back into the impenetrable armour of a goddess. I regard the old woman, whose eyes are filled with dread. Rage suddenly plumes inside me. Why do the words of a seer who died over five centuries ago hold more weight than my authority? Am I truly so unreliable that no one believes in my strength?

I temper my anger and hone it into a blade, its edge as thin as paper. My lips quirk into a benign smile. "My child, where have you heard rumours of the Prophecy?"

"Everyone is speaking of it, Your Grace. It may or may not be true, but the signs are there. We—we fear for our lives."

Perhaps Keran was right after all. Word spreads fast—fast enough to damage my reputation before I can stop it. Perhaps stories of the falling goats have already been circulated across the other districts, and soon the other Rakhtas will also doubt Binsa's ability to hold Rashmatun.

I recall Keran's news from yesterday—that Harun is planning to replace me. What an opportune moment to do so, as my position is being questioned by the subjects who have followed me faithfully for so many years.

My throat tightens.

I force myself to lean forward, my smile widening ever so slightly. "Do you not have faith in me, child?"

"I—I do," she gasps. "But you must understand that your child is anxious—that all of us are anxious."

Her son and his children gaze at me with baleful eyes. *Is Rashmatun still powerful?* they seem to say.

It is difficult to breathe all of a sudden. My eyes slide towards Harun. A small jolt spikes up my spine when I meet his frog eyes. He holds the stare, unflinching.

We know you are a sham, I imagine him saying. Then I see throngs of people surrounding him—men and women of all ages and ethnicities, dressed in tattered fabrics and goatskins for shoes. *And we will replace you, no matter what it takes.*

I stand up abruptly.

An audible breath escapes the old woman. The tension in the atmosphere spikes. Rashmatun *never* rises from her seat, save for when she is about to leave Binsa's body.

A memory flashes in my mind: Chandri, the previous Rakhti, rising from her throne. A murderer had been brought to trial before her. She lifts her arm, and when it falls, the murderer collapses to the ground, dead. The demure and gentle smile usually gracing Chandri's face has been replaced by a wrathful frown.

After the infamous trial of the Finger Butcher, stories of the goddess Rashmatun's righteous fury spread like wildfire, and crime rates dropped so drastically that Llaon, formerly Bakhtin's prison, became defunct.

That was the official story of Llaon's dismantlement. The unofficial story is that Bakhtin ran out of funds, and that Chandri had forced the prison's closure.

Chandri's frown fades from my mind, and the memory dissipates, even as I grasp at its threads and try to unspool more of it. It has always been like this. I want to remember Chandri. I want to know why her name is never mentioned in our temple halls. I want to know if Rashmatun actually—

I blink. What was I thinking about? I refocus my attention on the elderly woman, whose limbs tremble uncontrollably. She plants her forehead onto the ground, mumbling apologies and pleading for forgiveness. Her family does not move a muscle, too stricken to react.

I maintain my practiced smile and splay my arms.

All is still.

"Rain will come soon, my child. Spread the word amongst your neighbours," I declare, despite the violent pounding of my heart. "Rejoice, for the drought will end two weeks from now."

Ilam's laughter is more of a shriek, nearly splitting my head in two.

The woman lifts her head cautiously. Her gaze darts towards her arms, then at her family, as though surprised they are all still alive. "Truly, my goddess?" she asks. "You will bring rain in two weeks?"

"Indeed." I retake my seat on the Scarlet Throne. "And you will be compensated with a sum of ten gurisi for your losses."

"You are too gracious, my goddess." The woman bows once more.

With that, I send the family off. Harun shuffles forward, his eyes wide with disbelief. "Your Grace, surely my ears are not mistaken—you promise to bring rain in two weeks?"

"How many times must I repeat myself?" I retort sharply, although my stomach churns with the trepidation of boasting a miracle I cannot guarantee. Ilam's laughter does little to ease that worry. "Do you doubt my power?"

"My goddess, you do not have to succumb to your people's wishes!" Nudin jumps in. His usual gloomy expression is replaced with panic. "They are fools for doubting you!"

Harun and I stare at him, speechless. This is the first time Harun's son has ever spoken directly to Rashmatun of his own volition. He is usually so quiet that one would barely notice him in the room unless someone else pointed out his presence. "You are the fool for questioning me," I tell him, tucking my confusion aside for now.

He bows his head in deference.

"My apologies, Rashmatun! I do not know what this child has learned from me," Harun says. His hand twitches; I recognise it as the urge to slap his son. "Nudin, ask for Rashmatun's forgiveness, now!"

"I am sorry, my goddess," Nudin murmurs.

I study him. His heavy brows and obstinately square jaw are from his father, but he lacks Harun's potbelly and careful smile. His expression is a constant storm, as if nothing in life could ever please him. Even the older priests in the temple, renowned for their cantankerous dispositions, have at least cracked a grin at one of Ykta's jokes. Nudin is not irritable; he is, however, unnecessarily serious, adding at least ten years to his age of twenty-five.

He has never shown particular interest in the affairs of Rashmatun. What drove him to speak with such emotion?

But I have his traitorous father to deal with first. I wave my hand at Nudin. "Do not commit a slight like this ever again," I say. Then I turn my attention to Harun. "I heard that you wish to supplant Binsa before her time."

Colour drains from his face. "Rashmatun, I would never—"

"The old woman spoke of the Prophecy of Geerkha." I hold my chin high, sneering at Harun. "Tell me, does this rumour have anything to do with why you believe this current vessel to be tainted?"

Sweat beads between his thick, bushy brows. "The—the people believe that the drought is a signal of the skies burning red and bright. And surely you agree that the falling goats are in concordance with 'our offerings mourn,' since goats are traditionally used as ritual sacrifices."

He takes a pause to gulp. "All this is happening just as your current vessel is approaching her tenth year of tenure. Not one vessel has stayed this long on the Scarlet Throne before, Your Grace. Surely her purity has been compromised with age."

I take in all this with a cool mask of indifference. Inside, I am boiling with the impulse to cut his tongue. "Does her age have anything to do with her purity if I am still residing within her?"

"Of course not, my goddess. I—"

"How were you planning to elect a new Rakhti if I wasn't made aware of the nominations?"

Ilam purrs, amused.

Harun takes in a deep, shuddering breath. "I will immediately cancel Rakhti nominations—"

"No. You will do no such thing."

Summoning rain won't be enough to prove my worth as Rashmatun's vessel. To fully secure my position, I need to prove that I am the only Rakhti that my people will ever need—that no one else could possibly hope to replace me.

What better way to show that than by rejecting the next Rakhti?

"Go ahead with the Selection," I say.

Ilam's amusement continues to rattle my bones.

Harun doesn't bother to hide the relief in his expression. "Truly, Rashmatun?"

"Do not make me repeat myself."

"Yes, Your Grace." He dips his head in acquiescence. Nudin's face is shadowed with disappointment—or am I imagining things? "As you wish."

"Good. And do not forget to inform the other Rakhtas of the Trial of Divinity."

"But of course."

I straighten my back and briefly close my eyes. The Trial of Divinity. A three-day event where all the Rakhtas gather upon the crowning of a new Shira-Rakhta to assess and approve their soon-to-be colleague. It is up to the other Rakhtas to decide what the Trial will be, and it can range from taming wild beasts to solving puzzles. I remember that mine—fortunately—concerned simple interviews with the other Rakhtas. The Trial is more of a formality, though the final step is to bless the new Shira-Rakhti with magic.

Your chief priest is currently exchanging correspondence with Rakhta Asahar. Keran's words from yesterday ring in my ears.

Whatever Asahar's role in Harun's schemes, he will make a move during the Trial. Meetings between the ten Rakhtas are few and far between, as the vessels are not allowed to leave their areas of jurisdiction without conducting proper rituals. Apparently the lands only flourish because of our presence; once we're gone, there's no telling what harm might befall the people. A strange arrangement, really. If such powerful gods truly exist, their magic should be strong enough to protect their people, even if they leave their districts for an extended period of time. Maybe it's just a way to ensure that the Rakhtas do not interfere with one another's affairs.

But without a Shira-Rakhti, there will be no Trial.

With no Trial, there will be no Asahar to worry about.

I open my eyes and stare into the frog-like eyes of the chief priest. "Till tomorrow, Harun."

I haul myself to my feet and step off the dais. In a split second, I am small, harmless Binsa. I blink my eyes and look at Harun. "What did she do today?"

"A great many things," he replies, beaming at me. Snake. First he plots to replace me, then he treats me as though I were a friend. Binsa cannot speak against him, though. I have more power than him on paper, but he pulls a lot of the strings here. He's the chief priest, the mortal leader of Bakhtin's religious affairs—perhaps only the king and his family truly outrank him. Even then, the royal family is bound to religion in many inexplicable ways.

Binsa alone does not have the power to override him. Rashmatun's authority, though, is something else.

"Did she talk about choosing my successor? And about the rain?" I keep my tone as casual as possible.

"She communicated with you directly?" Harun asks in disbelief. I nod.

His composure is shaken ever so slightly. The precious little I've learned about playing Rashmatun over the years tells me that it's rare—or impossible, perhaps—for the goddess to converse with her vessel on a regular basis. I do not see why, though, and as a goddess, I *should* be free to bend my own rules.

Harun conjures a well-crafted smile. "Indeed. We are to organise the Selection in two days, my child," he replies at last. "And Rashmatun will bring rain in two weeks."

It's hard to maintain a polite expression. "I wish the new Rakhti all the best."

He laughs. "My child, why do you speak as though it is the end already? Come. You must be tired."

With that, he drops the topic. We converse of other things, of how the sun is wondrously bright and how the priests have procured a new collection of religious texts from Shur. He is trying to distract me from my impending dethronement, I can tell.

Never mind. If there's one thing I learned from my mother, it is patience.

4

The Selection

The headdress is uncomfortably heavy even though all I'm doing is sitting on a palanquin. I squint against the bright glare of my surroundings. The roar and clamour of the crowds is deafening; it's as though the cheers have solidified, jostling against me from all sides. Still, the path down to the city of Bakhtin is relatively clear, as no one dares stand in the way of their goddess.

The procession goes on for about an hour through brown, dusty streets and the dank stench of sweat smothering the air. The shift in temperature is startling. I hadn't realised how comfortable I was with the priests' wards around Ghanatukh Temple. It is a relief to arrive at the centre of the city. The Shiratukh Temple—the Lesser Temple—sits here, a smaller sister to my residence. Shiratukh is impressive, nonetheless, with gold-leafed carvings embossing its walls and its shimmering, sloped roofs.

Holy Guards—the elite force of Aritsya—keep vigil around the temple perimeters, all on high alert, their hands casually gripped around their sheathed kukris. New contraptions are slung over their backs. "Rifles," they are called, imported from the Western continent. I do not spot any shamans among their ranks; anyone who wields magic is much too precious to be deployed for regular guard duty.

Even unranked Holy Guards are more than equipped for the job, though. They are wary, determined to prevent another tragedy like the one ten years ago, on the day of my own Selection.

Their vigilance reminds me of that time. When the other candidates and I tipped the ceremonial wine down our throats, when the scent of charred flesh began to cloy the air—

No. I cannot remember. Not now. Not when my fate hangs on today's Selection.

I inhale deeply, loosening the tension building between my shoulders. *It'll be all right*, I tell myself. I have been managing the city *and* a demon for nearly the past ten years. I will be fine.

Will you, really? Ilam snorts. I pay him no heed.

The palanquin bearers set me down only when we are inside the temple proper; it'll never do for Rashmatun's feet to touch unholy ground, after all, and I get off with small, careful steps. The priests have just finished casting a soundproof barrier around the temple so that busybody onlookers are not able to eavesdrop on the Selection. Ten years ago, just one of them would have been enough to cast the spell. Now, it requires ten of them to accomplish the same effort.

Harun is already waiting inside. He gestures for me to follow him. We walk past sculptures of the ten Forebears of Aritsya and various lesser gods, some tall and imposing with their bared fangs, others small and meek with furred paws. The scent of smoke and incense wind into a thick coil in the air. The temple is dim, cool, as unfeeling and unmovable as the stone it is carved out of.

Harun and I walk along its length until we reach the first sanctum. Ten young girls kneel in single file, each of them no older than six, practically crammed against the walls.

Almost ten years ago, I was one of those girls—eager, hopeful, yet terrified. Terrified about what it meant to wield a goddess's power; and even more terrified about the consequences if I did not become one.

Now *I* am the goddess. I have the power to make or break each individual's life.

The girls press their palms together and bow their heads. "Your wisdom be upon us, Rashmatun," they chant in synchrony.

"The wisdom of the gods smiles upon you today," I complete the greeting. I wonder how I look to them. The image of Chandri abruptly surfaces in my mind—she was so tall, so regal, so composed. Above all, she was beautiful. Her eyes were as bright as stars in a cloudless night, and her lips as full and soft as flower petals.

When the voice that fell out of her mouth had the cold, distant tone of a goddess, I quavered in both fear and awe.

But as always, my memory of her—no matter how brilliant—fades into darkness. Frustration gnaws my nerves. Why? I should remember more, now that I'm in the place where I first met her. Why—

My thoughts return to the temple's sanctum, where the only source of light is the rays that stream in from the entrance. I scan the girls with a ruthless efficiency, like a hawk swooping down on prey. I imagine that the layers of rouge and powder are doing little to hide my gauntness, and I deign to give a reassuring smile. A few girls balk at my bearing; others manage to hold their nerve.

They would have already drunk the ceremonial wine before my arrival. None of them are showing any signs of weakness.

I release the tiniest breath.

"Chief Harun," I say. He ducks his head and treads out of the sanctum, leaving me alone with the candidates.

The selection process of the Rakhti of Bakhtin is a well-kept secret—only known to the Rakhtis themselves. Candidates who have failed the test are strictly forbidden from revealing the process, and any rumours that escape are quickly tamped down. The only constant is that the priests are to prepare a hundred goat heads and arrange them in the inner sanctum. The rest is up to Rashmatun.

Or in this case, the rest is up to *me*.

I would have had a reference point to conduct the Selection if the nine other girls alongside me hadn't died before the actual Trial. But I suppose it doesn't matter.

Time to shake these children up.

I point towards a random girl. She jumps in surprise. "You"—I pitch my voice low, taking advantage of the cavernous space—"tell me why you deserve to be Rakhti."

"I—I—"

"Speak, child. Do not waste my time."

"I—I passed the first test," she stutters. "I have the thirty-two virtues, my goddess. And—and I was born under a good star—"

"That goes the same for the nine other girls who are sitting alongside you. Try thinking of a better reason."

She opens her mouth, then closes it.

"You." I point at another girl. "Why do you deserve to be Rakhti?"

"I—" She stumbles for a moment, but recovers faster than the first girl: "It will bring honour and blessings to my family, Rashmatun." Clearly she is spewing what her parents have hammered into her head.

"Then what of the people you will govern? Will they not have a share in the blessings you will bring? How can a vessel of Rashmatun be selfish?"

Her gaze is wide, confused. Of course, I hadn't expected her to be able to reply to that.

I move on to the next child, then the next. Soon, most of them have faced my question, their answers growing more desperate and ostentatious. I work up a show of pacing down the narrow space agitatedly, contorting my features into a vicious scowl. The girls' postures shrink, their wide-eyed excitement reduced to slackened shoulders and solemn lips.

"You." I jerk my chin towards Girl Number Eight, who sits to the far right of the line. She sits quietly, composed, even as some of the other candidates burst into tears.

What a strange girl.

"Why do you deserve to be Rakhti?"

"Because I want to be Rakhti," she says evenly.

This time, I am the one who is stunned. I smooth over my shock with a trilling laugh. "Why do you *want* to be Rakhti, then?"

"No particular reason, my goddess."

A dismissive response. A rude response, in fact. Yet something about her tone keeps me from blowing up, and instead pulls me towards her.

I appraise the girl's features. She is as lovely as dew droplets on blades of grass, with her baby-smooth skin and her narrow, snub nose. Yet her beauty pales in comparison to the curiosity in her expression—just as I observe her, she observes me. It is merely budding, but I can already see the razor-like edge of her mind, her willingness to brave fire just to learn something new.

Maybe she doesn't realise it herself, but I sense the real motivation behind her answer. Indeed, she wants to be Rakhti—more than that, she wants to know what it *means* to be Rakhti.

Interesting, Ilam murmurs.

"Perhaps it will do you some good to think about why you want to be Rakhti, girl." I sweep away from her and move to the other end of the line. "We do not achieve something simply because we want to."

"Yes, Rashmatun," she says demurely.

I pose the same question to the last two girls and scorch their answers in rapid succession. All the while, the funny little girl stares at me. She's not like the others, who keep their eyes trained on me because they are trying to predict my unpredictability. She stares at me because she is genuinely drinking in my movements, noting the slightest shifts in my tone and posture, as though she wants to emulate them herself.

I do my best to ignore her as I rake my gaze over the entire line. "You will enter the inner sanctum one by one and stay there for five minutes," I say. "Count the seconds down yourself. If you leave earlier, you are to immediately exit Shiratukh Temple. If you come back screaming, crying, or having hysterics of any sort, you are disqualified as well. Am I understood?"

"Yes, Rashmatun," they chorus.

"You." I jerk my chin towards the strange girl. "You go first."

She inclines her head. "Yes, my goddess."

She climbs to her feet and turns towards the corridor, travelling deeper into the temple without any light to guide her way, her steps sure and steady. Either it's because she's truly brave, or it's because she does not know of any horrors that lurk in the dark.

I recall how Ykta had appeared at my window before the sun

had risen this morning, hair dishevelled and face smothered in dirt. "The automaton's in Shiratukh," he'd blurted, panting. "I'll be there later to operate it."

A living, moving, fire-breathing goat among all the dead ones.

The first time I'd seen an animal carcass, I had been too frightened to move. The smell of rot overpowering. The tang of blood and crawling of maggots terrifying. Kavita had forced me to touch it—a rooster or a duck, I cannot remember—and hold it close. Sink my fingers into its cold, slimy flesh. I sobbed and begged Kavita to let me go, but she held me by the neck and told me to overcome my fear of death—to embrace it.

I was such a child back then. But children are easily frightened.

This strange little girl will be no different.

I smother the smirk playing on my lips. *Have fun*, I think.

We wait in silence, the girls and I. The seconds tick by, agonizingly slow. A frown begins to crease my forehead. Has it been two minutes or three? Has she reached the inner sanctum yet? Why do I not hear anything? I know that the inner sanctum lies far down the temple, but its space is narrow and dense—not a whisper escapes these walls. I should be hearing screams by now.

Or has Ykta failed his task?

Then I hear the padding of bare feet against stone. My stomach clenches in dread.

The girl reemerges into the outer sanctum, whole and unscathed. Every fold in her sari is perfectly in place. She retakes her seat and directs a smile at me, lashes shielding her gaze. I stare at her; my breathing stops for a long, excruciating heartbeat.

She has ruined everything. She was supposed to shriek, to burst into horrified sobs. She was not supposed to pass the Selection.

None of them are meant to pass the Selection.

Clever, clever goddess! Ilam laughs.

I square my shoulders and re-collect myself, in spite of how the demon's taunts are chipping away at my composure. I must see the

Selection to the very end and give all candidates a chance before making my final decision. I wrangle the strain in my voice to a steady monotone as I call the next candidate.

The second girl struts down the hallway, emboldened by the previous candidate's composure. She comes back screaming in less than a minute.

The rest of them experience the test similarly: They go in, see things no child should ever see, and run back out with their throats hoarse from shrieking and tears streaming down their cheeks. I signal their failure with a cutting glare; they hobble out of the temple, broken and defeated.

When it's done, only the strange girl and I are left in the sanctum. I peer down the length of my nose, inspecting her as though she were an overgrown clump of fungus.

My head spins. How am I supposed to get rid of her?

"You will be the next Rakhti," I say, biting every word out. "Come, let us go out and rejoice."

She continues to hold her head in a bow. Surprisingly, she does not reply. Not even a "thank you." Perhaps she has indeed entered a trance, instilled with the strength of Rashmatun.

No. Impossible. Rashmatun never came to me. Why would she come to this girl?

Maybe she's as good at pretending as you are, Ilam suggests.

I wheel around and head out of the temple, cold sweat slicking across my palms. The soft footfalls of the girl echo mine. When the first rays of light hit my face, the crowd rises into another round of raucous cheers. The clanging of bells and the pounding of drums reverberate through the air, the cacophony burrowing into my marrow.

I hold up a hand. A veil of silence falls.

"Who will come forward to claim this daughter?" I ask.

There is a moment of abated quiet before someone responds, the crowd automatically parting for her. It's a tall, spindly woman whose beauty—although greyed with age—is striking, further enhanced by the cobalt blue sari she wears. A Dennarese servant shadows her, the younger woman's narrow, full nose and pasty skin reminding me of Keran's.

"My goddess." The woman presses her palms together in greeting; the numerous bangles running along her forearms clink a joyous tune. "I am her mother, Adarsh Yankaran, wife of Ranjit Yankaran. Unfortunately, my husband has taken ill and cannot join us on this momentous occasion."

"Wisdom be upon you, Adarsh, and may your husband recover soon," I reply, holding myself as tall as possible. "Have you any wish to accompany your daughter in Ghanatukh Temple after she is crowned Rakhti?"

A Rakhti can have one family member at a time join them within the temple walls, if only to help their transition into a life of total seclusion. This is exactly how Kavita first wormed her way into the temple, extending her claws around me and controlling me so finely that not even the priests nor the handmaidens had a voice in what I did or said. She strove to be the only person in my life after Chandri's retirement.

"I do not have such a wish, my goddess." She offers a placid smile. "My husband and I only desire to spend the rest of our lives together in peace."

I lift my brows. Surely this woman can't mean to abandon her daughter for at least the next five years.

"However, we will have another family member accompany our precious Medha." So that's the strange girl's name. My gaze briefly flits towards her; the girl stares at her mother, the smile on her face gone. "My goddess, please do take Nali, Medha's half sister. She may be half-Dennarese, but I assure you that she has full and utter devotion to the Forebears. If it pleases you, she will gladly serve as your handmaiden."

Audible gasps escape everyone's mouths.

On my left, Harun's and Nudin's expressions harden. The latter's glare of utter contempt directed at the former takes me aback, and I recall his outburst from a few days ago. The chief priest and his son were supposed to filter through the families—ensure that only the best girls from the best bloodlines were nominated as candidates. Apparently they did not filter well enough.

We have been at war with the Dennarese Empire for decades, and now one of them is a relative of a future Rakhti.

By all means, Aritsya itself is a diverse potpourri of immigrants and outsiders; centuries at the heart of a trading route invited various cultures and tribes to settle down here. But our war with Dennar still rages on our borders, and its refugees, though mostly innocent folk who seek to start life anew, will never be able to obtain the status and opportunities presented to an Aritsyan. Temple attendants, especially, are selected through stringent processes that only accept the "purest" of Aritsyan descendants.

Until now.

Ilam emits a soft snicker.

The young woman who I thought was Adarsh's servant shuffles forward, her head bowed low and palms pressed together. I resist clenching my fists. I cannot deny her now. It would mean that Rashmatun made a wrong choice, and Rashmatun *never* makes a wrong choice.

"Lift your head, Nali Yankaran," I declare. "You shall join Ghanatukh Temple in service to me today."

"My goddess is merciful," the Dennarese woman murmurs.

"As for you, Medha Yankaran"—I turn towards the girl, her burnished skin and sharply cut profile making her look like an apsara come alive—"from this day forth you are mine." Harun hurries forward with a tray of paints in his hands. I sketch the Star of Rashmatun on her forehead, as I have on my own. "You are a servant to me and me only. You will keep your body pure and your soul purer. You will be the brightest of girls, the fairest of ladies. You will be granted the wisdom of a thousand stars that have witnessed all the secrets of the universe, and you will be granted the foresight of the winds that have seen and heard everything. For soon you will no longer be Medha Yankaran. You will be Rashmatun."

I finish drawing the final prong just as I conclude my speech. The silence over the crowd breaks; another wave of roars fills my ears, although it is somewhat subdued compared to earlier. I turn to face my subjects, offering them an elated smile. The palanquin arrives to transport me back to Ghanatukh Temple. This time, I do not ride alone. Little Medha squeezes in beside me, smiling and waving to the people who will bow to her one day.

The heat is stifling, yet my insides burn with cold, helpless rage whenever I see the little girl.

It takes about an hour and a half before we arrive. The halls of Ghanatukh echo with emptiness, as visitors are not allowed into the temple today and only a few priests are left to maintain the place. The majority of them—including Harun—are tasked with wrapping up the ceremony back at Shiratukh Temple. Medha gets down from the palanquin first. She has not spoken a single word throughout the ride. Which is a blessing in disguise; if she had said anything in the litter, I might have strangled her there and then. Now my anger has *mostly* subsided.

"Once my foot touches the ground, the girl named Binsa will speak with you instead," I say to her. "Understand?"

She nods mutely.

I tamp down the urge to call out her lack of tact, for not answering in words when I talk to her. "Excellent. From now on, you do everything she says. She is your guardian above all, including your sister. She will raise you into a vessel worthy of my presence."

With that last dramatic flourish, I hop onto the ground and stagger a little. When I lift my head into focus, I look at Medha as if it's my first time meeting her. "Oh, hello. You must be the Shira-Rakhti."

She bobs her head.

I grin to conceal the frustration building in me once more. "Shy now, aren't we? Come on. It's all right. No need to be afraid. Your family will join us soon."

She just stares at me.

I swallow an impatient sigh. "You must be tired. I've no idea what you went through during the Selection." More accurately, I've no idea how this girl managed to sit in the presence of a walking headless goat without screaming her head off. Ykta must be throwing a fit right now, considering all his efforts over the past three days; it couldn't have been easy to sneak a hulking mass of bronze into Shiratukh, even with the secret passageways that link the temples and with Keran's help. "Why don't we get you freshened up and settled down first? Rakhti training can wait."

She gives another nod.

It's worse than talking to a wall. I cannot tell what's going on in little Medha's head, and it aggravates me.

What I wouldn't give to have the authority to slap her.

I turn towards one of the older priests. "Have Jirtash prepare a bath and food for her."

His brows pinch in disapproval of being relegated to servant duties. But my wishes—even though I am Binsa now—cannot be denied. I am still Rakhti. I still have Rashmatun in me. He transfers the task to a younger priest, who totters off in search of Jirtash.

By the time the girl and I enter the Bakhal, it is in a flurry of excitement; the young priest has delivered the message already, it seems. The women skirt around me and Medha, never coming so close that they have to greet us. It's as though we are showpieces, meant to be gawked at and never to be touched.

We enter my chambers. Jirtash is inside, waiting by the door. "Binsa, I've arranged for the girl to take the room beside yours."

"Thank you. Now, I'd like to be alone with her."

Jirtash cocks her head in curiosity but doesn't question my request. "The bath has been heated up. Are you fine taking off your clothes yourself?"

"I'll manage," I reply.

"I shall leave you two, then. You need only to call out if you require me."

"Will do," I say, keeping my voice cheery.

The old woman exits my room with a doubtful look. Once she's out, I guide Medha into the washroom. It's a little farther away from the door, so it's harder for eavesdropping ears to listen in. "What is your name, girl?" I ask.

Medha looks at me, lips still sealed.

I crouch so that I stare straight into her eyes. "I can't do anything for you if I don't even know your name." *Calm*, I tell myself. *Calm.* "Don't be afraid. I'm here to help."

The girl's mouth is tighter than an uncooked clam's.

"Would you like to take a bath, or do you want to eat first? Maybe you're hungry?"

She shakes her head.

"Gods damn it, girl!" I explode. "What the hell do I have to do to get you to talk?"

She doesn't emit so much as a frightened gasp.

"That's it." I shove my fingers into Medha's mouth. Ykta will probably admonish me for treating a child this way, but I don't care. My mother had hurt me often enough—and I survived. The girl yelps and clamps her teeth down. I clench my jaw and endure the pain. It takes considerable effort to get her mouth open, my hands seeping red.

How can one little girl be so vicious? Then again, who am I to talk? Wait. It's not just my blood. There's too much of it. There's no way my hands are bleeding this much...

Then I take a proper look at Medha—at the grimace in her expression, at the slow, dark blood dribbling out of her mouth. I simultaneously want to throw her *and* throw myself out the window. So that was how she kept herself from screaming.

The little brat literally bit her own tongue.

5

The Contract

A gasp of horror escapes me. "What were you—" I realise I am shouting, and immediately tone it down: "What were you thinking?"

An unbridled cackle escapes Ilam. His sudden burst of energy makes my vision dim for a moment.

"Ah tauf—" She attempts to answer, but a wince jolts throughout her tiny frame.

I haul her towards the window, inspecting her wound with better lighting. It's red and dark and swollen, and it looks downright nasty. She has left it unattended for nearly two hours now. How did she manage to sit through the entire procession?

More importantly, why would she do something like this?

You're not above doing such desperate things, Ilam reminds me.

"Listen to me." I grab Medha by the shoulders and shoot her an intent glare. "Stay put here. I'm going to fetch my tutor. If anyone will know how to take care of you, it's him. No matter what, do *not* go out. Rashmatun help us all if someone finds out that you passed the Selection by deceiving us."

The little brat gives a single, determined nod. The light in her eyes dims, as if she finally understands the gravity of her actions.

With a huff, I exit the room. Unsurprisingly, Jirtash is hovering right outside. "Is everything all right, Binsa?" she asks.

"Perfectly fine." I force my lips into a winsome smile. "I just need to grab something from the library."

"Shall I attend to Medha, then?"

"No!"

Jirtash's lips part in bewilderment. I rarely display such outbursts of emotions, and I mentally chide myself for allowing panic to get the better of me.

"No," I repeat, rectifying my tone. "She's still in shock and doesn't want to see anyone for now."

Jirtash clucks her tongue sympathetically. "Ah. Just like Lutna— that girl refused to come out of her room for two weeks and would only accept her mother as an attendant!"

Tales like these are not uncommon. The transition from mortal to immortal is a sudden one, and even the most perfect of girls would have difficulty acclimatising to such a life. I had no such problem, considering that Kavita would sooner kill me than allow me to mope around.

"Anyway, she seems to be fine with me," I continue. "Bring her meals and her clothing to my room. I'll take them to her."

Fortunately for me and Medha, a Rakhti is the primary person in charge of training her successor. Thus, I am given sole authority in managing her well-being for my remaining time as Rakhti. Meaning that no one, not even Medha's sister, will be able to interfere with her training.

Meaning that no one will question my decision to keep Medha in her room for the time being.

"If you say so, child," Jirtash replies.

I finally make for the library, where Ykta *should* be waiting. I try to slow my pace so that I don't look too flustered. My heart slams rapidly against my chest; cold sweat skims my palms. My brain is addled with worry. I force myself to take a few deep breaths, restoring some of the clarity I usually have.

Meanwhile, Ilam continues to be nothing but highly amused by all this. I wonder if he knew all along. Perhaps.

It'll be all right, I tell myself. It's not like Medha completely bit her tongue off. It'll recover, as all wounds do. Perhaps she'll have a scar, but it's a small price to pay for her folly. Do tongue wounds even leave scars?

It feels like an eternity before I reach the library. A sigh of relief escapes me when I see my brother's sooty face.

"Sorry about just now," he says sheepishly. "The automaton malfunctioned at the exact moment you sent that first girl in. I managed to get it up and running at the last minute, though."

"You—what?" My eyes widen. Was that why Medha had been able to hold out for so long?

"I'm sorry, all right? I wouldn't have been so stressed if I hadn't been so rushed. You knew that the goat automaton was a proto-type. Do you know how difficult it is to get lifeless objects to move by themselves, especially one as large as that?"

"You—" I wave my arms exasperatedly. "That's not the point. I need your medical expertise now—"

"Which is as advanced as a fish's cognitive capabilities."

"Quiet, dammit!" I snarl. I'm in no mood to exchange quips with my brother. "Listen to me. That stupid girl bit her own tongue to get through the Selection. If she cannot speak anymore because of that, I'm dead. If the priests find out that she has a defect on her body, I'm dead. You know why? Because Rashmatun chose some-one blemished in character and body while she was occupying me. And that means I, Binsa, am blemished as well."

I step closer towards him. I may be more than a head shorter, but I've always been the more menacing sibling, the one in control. Ykta holds his ground, yet fright spreads across his features. "Do you know what that means, Saran?" I hiss.

His expression crumples, as if I had just backhanded him. Guilt twinges in me. He doesn't like his old name—it is the name Kavita and our father gave him. A name that binds him to a past of empty stomachs and bare feet, of unprovoked beatings and ear-shattering shrieks. It reminds him of the life before our mother abandoned him. I wish I could forget that life too. That's why I use that name sparingly.

But at the same time, I don't want him to forget—that would

mean forsaking our connection, as if we were never brother and sister in the first place.

I need to convince him to stay by my side.

"How bad is the wound?" he asks, regaining his composure.

I pause for a moment, recalling my brief examination of Medha's injury. "Lacerations, mostly. They'll heal with time."

"Which we don't have." He fills in the gaps himself.

"Correct. Not that we can do much about it."

He gives a curt nod. "I'll go find supplies. What about the maidservants?"

"I've taken care of that."

"Always efficient." Ykta pauses a few seconds before continuing: "You sure you don't want the help of a physician? I have a few friends from Dahlu who have clinics."

His trusted contacts in the city. But just because he trusts them doesn't mean I trust them. "No. The less people who know, the better."

He purses his lips. "You'd better pray that the one introductory course I took is enough."

"It *has* to be enough."

"I'll come by the window," Ykta says. "Keep it open for me."

Since Ykta is known only as my tutor, and since no one actually knows that we're siblings, he cannot be seen entering my room. "Got it. Good luck."

"You too."

Despite the panic wracking my nerves, we realise that Medha's tongue wound is not as bad as I initially thought. However, it still requires a few stitches, and it is up to Ykta to perform the sutures while I help hold the girl still. To Medha's credit, she does not release a single scream throughout the entire procedure, only emitting occasional gurgles of pain. The medicine I usually take to poison my womb helps ease the pain during the surgery. Medha's lids blink heavily after she consumes nearly half the bottle, to my stifled horror. The medicine costs enough to feed ten families for an entire month.

Then we are all done, sweating, panting heavily, and bones weary with exhaustion. But Medha's wound will heal, and no one will question the sanctity of Rashmatun's vessel.

After Ykta leaves through the window, I drag—more than carry—a sleepy Medha to the other room adjoined to the washroom, and manage to settle her onto the bed in spite of my aching arms. She croaks, and her lips move, but her limbs stiffen in agony. I massage my temples with my fingertips.

She's going to be a handful.

The full moon hangs bright like a silver plate, glowing against the darkness of the night sky and silhouetting the outlines of my room. Anxiety lines my belly. I inhale deeply, trying to dispel the tension between my shoulders.

It's been three days. Ilam will give his answer today.

I clear my mind, opening a mental passage for Ilam to make his way out. His energy burns throughout my limbs. When he emerges, his first course of action is to consume my dinner. Then he sates the remainder of his hunger by taking a bite out of me.

As per usual. A hungry demon is a nasty demon to deal with.

When he is done, he gives his full attention to me. "Was your pretty little promise to the old woman a strategy to force me into your contract?"

"You know I'd never force you into something," I reply in monotone.

Ilam explodes into hysterics, the piercing noise driving nails into my skull. "What will you do if I refuse to give you my magic?"

I swallow a lump in my throat and raise my fingers to my yellow sapphire. I do not recall how this came into my possession—perhaps it was a gift from Kavita before she went mad—but calmness always washes over me when I touch it, as if it were a memento of brighter, happier days.

"I'll find another way," I say.

He cackles even louder.

I do not know how I maintain my unflappable mask. His blatant mockery is like a slap across the cheek.

"Fortunately for you, I believe that an extended partnership will benefit the two of us greatly," Ilam says once his laughter is under control. "All you need to do is sacrifice something."

"Done."

"You're not going to ask about what I want?" he asks with a note of surprise. "Negotiate a little, maybe?"

"No need."

Ilam bares his fangs in a contemptuous impression of a smile. "Good girl. I knew there was a reason I liked you."

Meaning that he likes an acquiescent, obedient vessel.

"In exchange for the power to summon rain," he resumes, "you will give me your capacity to bear children."

The possibilities race through my head with that single statement. I don't have to constantly starve myself and take medicine to delay my bleeding. I will always be considered a girl by Aritsyan standards. I will never be able to marry, to have children and live out my days as a normal woman.

I can be Rakhti for a long time to come.

Excitement flutters in my chest. Then my brows furrow in confusion. Why would he offer a proposition so advantageous to me? Ilam is a demon. He is never concerned about my welfare. Besides, just *that* for such powerful blood magic? He must be joking.

"It benefits you, doesn't it? Why do you look so worried?" Ilam says.

I press my lips into a thin line.

"I have my reasons for asking, little Binsa," Ilam says, as if in reply to my unspoken questions. "You needn't pry into the matter. Besides, you already agreed to it." Ilam's voice is a quiet growl, one that immediately makes my skin crawl and my stomach lurch. His muzzle is curled into a terrifying blend of a snarl and a smile. I bow my head.

"I understand," I murmur.

"Good." Ilam's eyes pierce through the darkness shrouding my room. "And it is done."

There is no lightning cleaving the sky, no sudden clap of magic that seals the transaction. But something shifts, nonetheless, as though the composition of my body is transforming—as though the very sense of *me* is changing. I cannot place the precise feeling, and I cannot tell where it starts and where it ends.

Cold dread permeates my bones; I take deep breaths. The contract has been sealed. I cannot go back on my word now.

Until now I have avoided blood magic. There are unimaginable costs that one must pay to be a competent blood shaman—stories whispered among children at night, about those who have lost their eyes, their limbs. Some who even sacrificed family members in exchange for power.

My mother was a testament to those horror stories.

Now, though, the circumstances are different. Binsa alone cannot manage the drought. Binsa alone cannot create miracles. Ilam is not strong enough in his current capacity. It is not enough to see through tricks and discern lies from truths.

I have no choice, I tell myself, even as my guts churn at the thought of using the same magic that Kavita had used to keep me in line—the magic she used to singe the ends of my hair off or break my bones and mend them back together whenever my actions displeased her.

I have no choice.

"You need to strengthen your body as well." Perhaps I am delusional, but Ilam seems to have grown in size. I blink twice, observing him intently. No—he *has* grown bigger. The shadows that coil out of his body have also thickened, and his voice is pitched deeper. "Your shrivelling frame serves as a poor medium for my magic."

"Will do." I incline my head. "Thank you, Ilam."

His ears twitch. "You can thank me later," he comments loftily, "when you become so powerful that you can challenge the gods."

He dissolves into smog, melding into my body.

An abrupt onslaught of pain bowls me over. This is agony I have never known, tearing at me from within. As if my insides were being rearranged in the relentless furnace of a metalsmith's forge. I dig my nails into my palms. I scratch my legs, claw at my neck, stuff my fingers into my mouth and bite down on them until the metallic tang of blood coats my tongue.

I cannot detach myself from the torture wracking my body.

Maybe only a second has passed, or maybe a minute or two. By the time Ilam comfortably settles himself inside me, I am so weak and vulnerable that I don't even have the strength to sit upright. I just lie there, splayed on the floor, breathing heavily. Ilam takes up a lot more space now—my entire head is saturated with his presence. I grit my teeth, adjusting myself to this new sensation, and the headache that splits my temples ebbs into a dull throb. I gain enough focus that I can observe my surroundings. The bite wounds on my fingers have already closed over. I marvel at the sight.

That's just a fraction of what you can do, Ilam says with glee.

He's everywhere, rummaging through my thoughts like one pawing through a cluttered room of lost belongings. But I cannot contain him any longer—he's simply too large—and I don't have the energy to wall him off.

Tomorrow, I think.

My vision is pulled into darkness.

I am wading through a bloodred fog. I attempt to flap the smoke away, but the fog only thickens with each passing second. In fact, it feels as though I am clothed in it. I can barely see my fingers. Goose bumps prickle all over my arms. There is a familiar atmosphere here that I cannot place.

My brows crease together as I try to figure out where I am. But it's as if the fog has seeped into my head, clouding all my thoughts and tucking them away.

"My dear Binsa," a melodic voice abruptly rings out. "How you have grown."

A chill snakes up my spine. I know that voice, but I cannot remember to whom it belongs.

"Don't be afraid, Binsa. It's me."

The fog pulls apart, revealing a figure right before me. She is tall, regal. Despite her well-worn clothes and her tangled hair, her beauty is so dazzling that she could be a goddess. Sharp cheek bones and a high nose, large, expressive eyes, and full lips.

She reminds me of Ykta.

I suddenly remember who she is.

An involuntary gasp escapes me. I need to run. I need to hide. But hide where? She controls this fog. And my legs are frozen in their position.

Her eyes start to glow red, the colour of the fog. She smiles, revealing teeth stained in red. Blood seeps throughout the white cloth of her kurta, starting from her belly and spreading to her entire torso.

"Why do you look so afraid?" my mother says. "Don't you miss me?"

"Go away," I whisper. "You're dead."

"Didn't I tell you I would be with you always?" she laughs. "You took my soul, Binsa. And now our blood is forever bound."

"No. No." I clap my hands over my ears. "You're dead. Go away. You're dead."

She takes one step closer to me. Her fingers ghost over the yellow sapphire at my throat; I clamp down on my lower lip, as if the pain can jolt me awake. Nothing happens. "But am I truly dead, when I live in you? When my spirit lives on?" Her red eyes pierce straight into my soul. "You chose this path. You can never be rid of me, especially now that you are welcoming blood magic into your life."

"No. I'm different from you!"

"Really, my Rakhti?" she says, taunting. "You could have chosen to drop the act, but you didn't. You could have chosen to be truthful, but you didn't. You love power too much."

"Quiet." I fight tears in my voice. "You're dead. You're dead."

"I know you, Binsa. I know you better than anyone. You're just like me." She throws her arms open, as if ready to pull me into an embrace. Her smile is so wide that it nearly cleaves her face in two. "You are my daughter."

"You're dead!" I scream, the noise ripping through my throat. "I killed you myself!"

My muscles awaken, jerking forth from their stupor. I pounce on my mother and wrap my fingers around her throat. There is no fear in her eyes; she merely laughs.

"We are truly the same, Binsa. Can't you see that?"

6

The Foreigner

I jerk awake with a gasp. Cold sweat soaks my clothes, and my blankets are tousled all around me. I grit my teeth and suppress a groan, tentatively shifting an arm. It's so heavy to lift. I let it flop back down with a muffled thump.

I try to recall what happened. My mind is a cesspool of muddied thoughts. The only thing I can clearly see is Ilam lounging about, his presence overshadowing all else. And the taunting echoes of Kavita's words ringing in my head.

The nightmare returns to me with full force.

Pain lances through my temples, and I wince. All of a sudden, I am acutely aware of everything, of how a cricket has just landed on my windowsill, of the grainy texture of the kurta against my skin, of the slight creaks my mattress makes whenever I move. Of the whispers that fill the air—so dense that they are suffocating.

Whispers that sound familiar.

The voices draw closer, hammering and clawing at my mind. The door swings open, and Jirtash and her handmaidens march into my room. Too loud. They're too loud. Their breathing, their footsteps—every sound is too clear, too bright.

They drag me to my feet and go through our routine. They stay silent as they bathe and dress me in an unassuming daura-suruwal, yet their voices plague my ears, all the same.

I'm so sleepy, someone thinks as they yawn.

I wonder what's for breakfast today, another girl thinks.

When will I be able to serve the new Rakhti? Jirtash's matronly voice rings in my mind.

This must be the outcome of Ilam's amplified magic. I feel as though my skull were about to crack at any moment. To think that Kavita had endured this all the time; I cannot imagine the toll it must have taken on her body. Perhaps I too would have gone mad if I had to listen to other people's thoughts all day.

However, I don't have the luxury of going mad. I need to find a solution to this. Fast.

The problem, Ilam says, *is that you see it as a problem. You just want your mind to be fixed. But minds are such fluid, indefinite entities, my dear Binsa. You cannot fix a mind.*

Cut the philosophy and just tell me how to stop this incessant headache, thank you very much, I reply dourly.

I've already given you the answer, Ilam laughs. *Kavita picked up blood magic far faster than you did, that's for certain.*

As unhelpful as always. I go through the rest of my morning routine overwhelmed by the sensory information fed into me. I barely notice as I'm led into the cleansing hall, and I almost forget to straighten my posture when Rashmatun is "summoned." By the time I enter Rashmatun's room to get dressed, it's a miracle that I am still standing upright.

I consider playing sick. But for a Rakhti *and* her successor to not attend to their people on the very first day after the Selection? An inauspicious sign.

I cannot afford any more fuel for gossip.

The goddess's room is cavernous, large enough to fit three elephants. The beady yellow eyes on Anas's ten heads shadow me wherever I step, his golden serpentine bodies breaking the monotony of the red furnishings filling the space. My own room—or "Binsa's" room—is a paltry shed compared to Rashmatun's room. However, no one is allowed inside the room save for Rashmatun herself; aside from one hour every morning, the place is left empty.

The maidservants go on with their duties, draping me in Rashmatun's jama—its fabric red for the creativity and wisdom of the married woman, and its hems gold for wealth and good luck. Every thread of the richly embroidered fabric is secured in place, one half of the clothing knotted over the other before a scarlet sash binds the waist. The bangles and earrings and four necklaces go on; the maidservants coil my hair into a tight yet comfortable topknot.

All the while, they are oblivious to how their internal chitter pelts at me like a hailstorm. Something heavy is affixed atop my head; I sway on my feet and stumble sideways.

A shriek tears through the air. The whisper of metal kisses my ear.

I regain my footing and turn around to see what has happened. Medha's half-Dennarese sister stares at me from several paces away, her face as white as the uniform she wears. Her fingers quiver violently, clasping tight to a hairpin that has a heavy trail of golden flowers on one end.

Scattered images surface before my eyes: Nali attempting to weave a pin through my topknot and headdress. Rashmatun taking a step to the side, the abrupt movement causing Nali to misjudge the angle of the pin.

The tip of it nearly stabbing my ear.

"The insolence!" Jirtash screeches at Nali, pulling me out of my shock. "How dare you nearly cause harm to Rashmatun!"

My ears ring from the sudden clamour. I clench my jaw and set my features into stern lines. "The girl did not intend it, Jirtash."

"The Namuru decrees that one who injures another must receive penance, whether the act was maligned or unintentional."

Ah. Right. That particular excerpt from our holy book: *And to those who draw the blood of a brother or a sister, they must receive the appropriate penalty. For all our bodies are a temple in itself to the Forebears, and to wound it is to deny the sovereignty of the Forebears.* Nowhere does it mention that all acts that caused bodily harm *must* be severely punished. It simply dictates that proper penance be paid.

Still, the blood of a Rakhti is sacred, and anyone who injures her must atone for their sin.

"No blood has been drawn, Jirtash," I say.

"Blood *could* have been drawn." The matron's expression twists into rage. "The *urvas* deserves to be punished. If not because of her mistakes, then at least let it be a reminder of who she serves."

Urvas. The label given to Dennarese immigrants. It simply means "unbeliever" in Ritsadun, the archaic form of Aritsyan, but decades of accumulated derision and mistrust have been compressed into that single word, representing an entire people's scorn towards an empire that has tried to conquer us multiple times—and very nearly succeeded. It doesn't matter that not all who are under Dennarese rule subscribe to the Empire's beliefs. The only thing that matters is that they bear the name of our enemies.

Nali catches the word, and her ears flare pink. She drops to the ground and prostrates herself before me. The inaudible musings of the handmaidens continue to congest my head, both mortified and delighted by this fresh piece of gossip.

But nothing comes from Nali.

She is a void, dark and empty and silent. As if the entire world has caved in on her.

"Nali Yankaran, is that right?" Years of practice enable me to summon the authoritative voice I need. "How did you come to be born into a kishari's family?"

"My mother was a refugee of the Ritkar genocide," she answers. I'm surprised by how she maintains composure. Perhaps she has provided this answer so many times that it smoothly rolls off her tongue. "My father, Ranjit Yankaran, was kind enough to take her as a second wife so that she may forget her bloodied past. I grew up in Bakhtin my entire life."

"How did one of Dennarese blood come to worship the Forebears?"

"How could I not believe, when the goddess Rashmatun herself stands before me?"

Of course she'd say that, one handmaiden thinks.

It's not like she can deny the goddess Rashmatun right in her face.

What an excellent liar.

"Silence, all of you," I snap. Blank confusion overtakes the handmaidens.

Much better.

Even then, nothing comes from Nali.

She's either dense or she's trained herself to put up mental walls, like you did, Ilam drawls. *Or she is a blood shaman herself.*

Both of the latter suggestions rattle me in a way that I haven't experienced ever since I killed my mother. I do not know why this upsets me—more so than the prospect of being replaced by a new Rakhti or losing my power.

I didn't predict this, and I do not like it.

Just like how I didn't foresee that Medha would pass the Selection.

I recall Adarsh's polite smile as she nominated Nali to stand in as company for Medha. Does Nali being half-Dennarese have anything to do with the decision? What does the Yankaran family hope to accomplish through this? They went so far to deceive Harun and Nudin of the fact that their family isn't purely Aritsyan.

There must be a reason for her presence here.

"You flatter me by forsaking your gods, Nali Yankaran. Rise, and look at me." She obeys, albeit with stiff limbs. "As punishment, and as reminder of who you serve, you are hereby assigned as personal attendant to Binsa for the rest of her tenure, second only to Jirtash. You will not be allowed to visit your sister until she is crowned Rakhti."

Her eyes bulge.

Is that a punishment or a reward? the handmaidens think.

"Silence!" I growl through the sharp pinch at my forehead.

Everyone stares at their feet.

"Are my instructions clear enough?" I tilt my head; the head-dress doesn't throw me off balance this time.

"Very, my goddess," Nali replies. "Thank you for your mercy."

Jirtash opens her mouth, a protest heating at the tip of her tongue. She swallows it and remains silent.

What is the goddess planning to do? she thinks.

None of your business, I scoff internally.

"Now leave me be." I flick my wrist. "I must sanctify this body once more."

The handmaidens filter out without another word. Nali casts a glance over her shoulder before being jostled forward by the other handmaidens. She'll certainly be subjected to interrogations and cruel words from her colleagues, but it is none of my business.

For now.

I allow my focus to completely spill, the unbrokered force of blood magic wracking throughout my body. My chest tightens, and my knees go weak. I stumble against the table for support, gritting my teeth against the pain. Gods. How am I supposed to go through the entire day like this? I barely survived this morning.

Not bad, Ilam purrs. *Separating the siblings in case they have diabolical plans in store for you? Unless—that's what they were planning all along.*

Ilam, I heave. *Please. I can't go out like this.*

Your body isn't strong enough. It doesn't matter what I teach you. You won't be able to handle it.

Every breath is heavy; my lungs are filled with gravel. *No. I can. Please. Ilam.*

He laughs.

What else was I expecting from a demon? They dislike weakness.

Kavita. How would Kavita handle all this?

"It's all in the will and soul," she would say. "Your mind is always stronger than your body."

My mind is stronger than my body.

The mind is an ocean of limitless power—reality is only limited by your imagination. I suddenly recall Privindu's opening words in his book. *When does a falsehood become truth? Very simply, when you believe it to be true.*

A falsehood becoming truth . . .

I have the power to stop Ilam.

That's it, I snarl.

And completely shut him out of my mind.

Perhaps it is frustration. Perhaps it is rage. But whatever emotion has been building in me bursts forth and slams straight into Ilam, forming a barrier between us. I do not know if this action will risk his anger—all I know is that I do not hear him.

My breathing slows, and my senses gradually return to me. My head throbs, but it is mostly clear.

I cannot feel Ilam at all.

Panic clenches me. Then the feeling passes. This is only temporary, after all. I just have to make it through the day, then I'll deal with Ilam.

An indescribable emptiness permeates my mind as I proceed through the rest of the day. Usually, Ilam will be there *somewhere*, his presence like the cold, inky sensation of an eel slithering through my hands. Having nothing accompany me the whole day feels odd.

I do not know if I should be grateful or apprehensive about this. On one hand, I'm glad that Ilam's power will not reduce my brain to mincemeat, but on the other, I'm dreading the consequences of abruptly slamming him off.

I idly leaf through the book before me, eyes glazing over its pages. I discard *Theories and Principles of Aritsyan Magic for Beginners* in favour of lighter reading today: Thaget's *Collection of Folktales*, an anthology of various myths and stories passed down among the tribes of Aritsya. Privindu's words triggered my current predicament, after all, and I'm not sure if I can pore over his book without my mind constantly wandering towards Ilam.

My attempt to distract myself doesn't seem to be effective, however. Worry still closes my throat.

"Binsa, what's wrong with you?" Ykta sets his lizard automaton down with a loud clang against the wooden table. I jump in my seat. "You look tired."

"I'm fine." I look up from the book. It is opened to "The Tale of Tashmi," a legend from the Rulami tribe about a wandering entity who impersonated the faces of the gods, all to win the love of the people. "I'm...stressed, I suppose. There's a lot going on."

Ilam. Nali and Medha. Kavita appearing in my dreams again, although I've been doing my best to forget her.

My brother's expression softens. "Is there anything I can do to help? Take care of Medha, perhaps?"

I shake my head. "I assigned her to read the Sacred Scrolls. The words of former Rakhtis *should* drill some good etiquette into her head. How not to bite her tongue off to get something she wants, for instance."

Ykta releases a bark of laughter. "What about Nali—the half-Dennarese sibling?"

"She got into minor trouble with Rashmatun this morning." I pick at the hem of my sleeve. "She was assigned as personal attendant to Binsa, and she is never to see Medha until the Shira-Rakhti takes the Scarlet Throne."

Ykta's brows knot together. "Are you sure you don't want to try and investigate her? I'm sure her stepmother had good reasons for placing her in the temple."

"Give her time to familiarise herself with the temple. We don't want to strike prematurely and risk her raising her guard around us."

My brother nods his head in stately agreement. "And the goats?"

There were three new cases today, two of them involving headless ones. "I don't know what's going on." I sigh in defeat. "But I'm sure I'll find a way."

Ykta fidgets in his seat, buzzing like a bird whose feathers have been plucked. He keeps his mouth shut, though.

"What do you want to say?" I needle him.

"Binsa, you may not like this, but"—he drums his fingers against the desk—"are you sure you want to continue being Rakhti?"

I am so stunned that I can do nothing but stare at him.

"They may call you Rashmatun, but you're only fifteen years old, with no inherent magic or power or money." Ykta folds his arms across his chest, the corners of his mouth downturned. "You're taking so many unnecessary risks—and all for what? So you can pretend to rule over people? I know Kavita pushed you to be in this position, but you—"

"Kavita has *nothing* to do with my decisions," I snarl. "I'm going to continue to be Rakhti because I want to."

"You may want to continue being Rakhti, Binsa, but should you?"

His words leave me speechless. Shouldn't wanting to do something be enough? But I think of little Medha and her straightforward answer during the Selection. Wanting to become Rakhti is not a strong enough reason for someone to ascend to the position. I understand Ykta and where he is coming from. Naturally, I look delusional to him, so desperate to remain Rakhti that I'd sacrifice life and limb.

Yet a spike of my own anger rises. Is he aware that if I am no longer Rakhti, our bond will be severed? That we will no longer be able to see each other, and we will have to live the rest of our lives pretending we do not know each other? He knows that a retired Rakhti is never to see anyone from the temple ever again.

Besides, *I* am Rashmatun, not him. I am the one who will truly lose everything if I am a goddess no longer. He graduated from the University of Dahlu as one of its most eminent scholars. He has an adoptive family to support him. He will be able to find a path for himself even if I'm not around.

Without my position as Rakhti, I am nothing.

"Saran," I whisper.

The name slices through the anger clouding his mind, dissipating it.

"Trust me, Saran," I implore. "You are my brother. I can't afford to lose you. I don't know what I will do."

Fat tears plop onto my suruwal. Soon, I am heaving with sobs. Whether they are genuine or an exaggeration of my feelings, I cannot tell. Perhaps it is a mixture of both. Years of switching between masks have left me unable to tell which thoughts are mine and which are my persona's.

"I'm sorry, Binsa," he says, so hastily that it feels like he is trying to plug a hole in a dam. "I shouldn't have said all that."

I do not supply an answer. Tears continue to roll down my cheeks.

Ykta places a hand on my head, smoothing my hair. "There, there," he coaxes me. "I'll continue to be by your side. Don't worry. I'm just...concerned for you, is all."

"Haven't you been with me long enough to trust me?" I choke out.

"Of course I trust you. It's just—" I think he swallows a sigh, and his brows crease in frustration, but the action is so minute that the next time I blink, he's back to playing the caring and overbearing older brother. "I am part of your life. You don't have to shoulder all your burdens yourself, all right? Think everything through carefully. Talk to me if you have any worries."

I stay silent, and he does not attempt to fill in the quiet.

We remain like that for a while. I imagine that I am not Rakhti, and my brother is not my tutor. I imagine that we're free from our secrets, that we can declare that we are siblings to the outside world—that I don't have to pretend to come from a kishari's family to stay alive. I imagine that we were never separated—that we're children again, huddling against each other during the darkest, coldest nights in our ramshackle shed.

But we are not children anymore.

I wonder how long this bond will last.

I jolt in shock at my own musings. My heart thunders against my chest. I have to believe that Ykta will remain loyal to me. I have only gotten this far because of him—I certainly cannot doubt him now.

"Binsa?" Ykta finally speaks.

I look at the shelves of scrolls and tomes beyond Ykta's figure. Reading a thousand books wouldn't give me the wisdom to handle my brother. I have to appease him first. Give him a task that can make him feel like he is doing substantial work while distracting him from my larger schemes.

"I can help you look into the goats," Ykta suggests. His response makes my stomach jump. "If it helps you, of course." Then with some of his usual humour: "I *am* an expert in creating replicas of them."

My lips twist into a wry smile. A retort builds in my throat. Goats...his goat automaton among the other carcasses during the Selection...headless goats dropping across Bakhtin...I sit still, whatever I was going to say slipping out of my mind.

Ykta pokes an experimental finger at my arm.

"Hold on. Yes. You can look into the goats." I place my elbows on the table and bury my head between my hands, threading my thoughts into a cohesive piece. "Shadow the priests in Bakhtin. Especially the boruvindas. They might lead you to something interesting."

"All of them?" he asks incredulously.

I lift my head. "All of them."

"How are they related to the goats?"

I chew on my lower lip. "The Rakhti Selection."

Ykta's lips part in shock. "They needed the goats, so no one would bat an eyelash at their purchases." Then after a pause and a frown: "But Uruvin's case was presented before they officially announced the Selection."

I shrug. "Best to keep an open mind."

"All right." He strokes his chin, thoughtful.

Not bad, I can almost hear Ilam speaking.

A shudder runs down my spine. I force my lips to twist into a grin. "Thank you. That'd be a great help."

My brother gives a brittle smile and goes back to his automaton. I do not know whether he has accepted my goal to remain Rakhti, but at least he will be temporarily occupied.

Since I cannot be seen anywhere else except the library at this hour, I continue reading "The Tale of Tashmi." It is one of my favourite stories, one that I return to time and time again for comfort despite its morbid ending. The final page has an illustration of a faceless figure impaled by Nardu's spear. Notably, the figure is completely white, whereas the gods that surround it are painted in bright, esoteric colours.

> When the gods found Tashmi, they lashed out in rage. They banished Tashmi to Duna, where everything was a mirror of our world, and thus everything was reversed. They bound the false god to the top of a mountain—but the mountain was upside down, and its tip pierced through Tashmi's belly. The Nameless

One was forgotten by the people who had once loved them, their existence forever steeped in pain and anguish, for this is the retribution of the gods they had tried to impersonate.

My lips curl sardonically at the corners. I will not be forgotten, even if the gods exist only to bring retribution upon my head.

7

The One in Control

The night crawls into existence, shadows creeping over the sun and swallowing the land into its belly. I place my hands on my windowsill, gripping the frame so tightly that my knuckles turn white. Usually, I take comfort in the darkness; tonight, it is a poison that upsets my stomach and squeezes my heart in an iron grip.

I take a deep breath, mentally preparing myself for the onslaught that will surely come when I release Ilam—

Agony tears through me, as if I am being hollowed from inside out. I clench my teeth to contain my screams. Smoke steams off my skin. I watch, in a mix of horror and fascination, as blood drips from my hands and trails onto the floor. Is this happening because I've kept Ilam trapped for too long?

A shape coalesces before me. I register the sinewy tail, the soft, furred paws, and the glowing silver eyes. Ilam. He's here. In the physical world.

"Hello, Binsa," he greets me, fangs flashing.

Where he had only reached halfway up my calves before, he is probably as large as a young leopard now. He walks on air, his steps finding invisible footholds. Purple smoke trails off his body and clouds my eyes.

The pain doesn't relent.

"Do you know what you've done, dear Binsa?" he purrs.

My heart nearly stops at his tone. It is completely amicable, and if anything, he sounds good-humoured, no trace of malice or anger in his tone.

I'd much rather he raised his voice instead.

"You know it is impossible to master a demon." Ilam circles me in slow, deliberate steps. "Yet you tried to erase me while I was still tethered to you. If this happened to a lesser demon, I would have been gone already. Fortunately for you, I am not a lesser demon. Unfortunately for you, I am *not* a lesser demon. And I do not take such treatment very kindly."

I scarcely notice the pain anymore. Only white terror fills my veins.

He pauses, drinking in my fear. His muzzle curves in a way that makes him look as if he were smiling. "Why did you do it?"

"I—I didn't know what I was doing," I sputter. "All I knew was that it was too much, and I needed to find a way to stop it."

He laughs. Its musical quality reminds me of Kavita's.

I wrap my arms around myself, trying to stop myself from trembling. "Please," I whisper, hating how weak I sound. "Please believe me."

"Do you know why I served Kavita? Because she did not fear death. Yet she feared me." Ilam's voice is carried upon the circling wind. "And she was powerful—far more so than you are. She could easily slip into minds and manipulate them. She knew the hearts of men, and she knew how to pull them to her bidding."

Despite the panic coursing through my veins, I cannot help but be intrigued by his words. Was Kavita truly capable of manipulating minds? Everything had always seemed to fall into place so easily for her.

"You asked for power, I gave you power. It is your fault, and your fault alone, if you are too weak for it," he continues. "It was interesting, watching you go through the entire day without me, constantly worrying, worrying, worrying."

He stops, his muzzle still curved in an impersonation of a smile. "Clearly you need to be taught a lesson."

I swallow a sob.

"How shall I go about this?" The pupils in Ilam's silver eyes are razor slits, almost invisible. It makes his gaze seem even more otherworldly. "Oh, I have an idea..."

He blinks once, then he is back inside me.

His presence shutters all other thoughts. Yet he is outside, sitting on his haunches, staring at me. This is unlike anything I've ever experienced before. I've never had Ilam within and without me at the same time. My vision tunnels; all I see is myself and Ilam. I try to regulate my breathing, the way I used to whenever I had to face my mother's wrath.

Ilam clamps down on me, as though he were furiously stamping out a small flame. I attempt to fight back, struggling to wrest control away from him. But he is too strong, and I am too weak. I can only watch as my arm lifts on its own. Ilam laughs, gloating at my despair.

My will is being suffocated, and there is nothing I can do about it.

My arms press down on the windowsill. One leg clambers onto its surface, then the other. Before I know it, I am standing on the sill, the comfort and safety of my room behind me, a yawning chasm of darkness before me. A strong wind loosens a few strands of hair from my braid. *How does it feel, Binsa? To be unable to breathe, to be unable to be yourself?* Ilam's voice comes from everywhere, echoing inside me and reverberating throughout the atmosphere.

I cannot answer. My body is not my own.

This is what you tried to do to me. This is what it feels like to be trapped within yourself—to be aware, yet powerless to do anything.

My attention is pinned onto the jagged rocks below. They look like the maw of a dragon, jaws unhinged and ready to swallow a man whole. The drop is so steep that the cliff stretches on for an eternity. There is a small landing between the Bakhal and the cliffs, but the space is narrow enough that one misstep ascertains death. The handholds on the wall Ykta had risked his life to carve mean nothing if I am unable to latch on to them in the first place.

I wonder if my mother's spirit haunts the abyss down there.

My hands withdraw from the sides of the sill, and I am balancing on my two feet. The wind howls stronger than ever; if I lean ever so slightly, I will pitch out of the window and into the chasm. I do not know what is more petrifying—Ilam, or the sheer drop before me.

I can keep you alive, you know, even if all your bones were broken and your organs crushed, Ilam whispers. *I can keep you alive even if you want to die, even if your body is in so much agony that you want to give up. I am that strong.*

Fright slithers throughout my body like snakes wrapping around my limbs.

Ilam, I quickly decide, is more terrifying than death itself.

Isn't the view here magnificent, Binsa? Ilam says conversationally. He edges my toes over the sill. I try to fall backwards; he keeps me standing ramrod straight. *Why don't you look at it more often?*

My vision narrows towards my feet, which are coming dangerously close to stepping through air.

You should look up sometimes, instead of fixating on what is below you.

He wrenches my gaze upwards and forces me to behold the view, at the grey mountains that slope towards the basin, at the sky that is a still, deep blue. The vast expanse of the various districts in Bakhtin, the contrast between neat, clean layouts and haphazard dumps of buildings highlighting the difference between rich and poor districts. The shadows that drape over them, a dark curtain that kisses sharp and jagged edges, softening the silhouette of the city.

I am so entranced by the sight that I nearly miss how my leg is moving forward.

A silent scream tears from my throat when my foot finds no purchase. I pitch over, and my gaze snaps back to the cliffside. The wind sweeps around me, a jeering howl that laughs at my moment of carelessness. I am unaware of anything save for the chasm and the horror latching on to me. My body tumbles down—

I am suddenly yanked backwards. I fall onto the floor of my room, backside sore. Ilam is gone—no, he is there. Still in my mind but no longer controlling me. I subconsciously release a cry of relief.

Only control what you know you can control. Ilam is savouring my fear, though at the same time there is a hint of reservation in his voice. Perhaps I am imagining things now. *If you cannot control it, find another way.*

I clap a hand over my mouth, bile rising to my tongue. The accumulation of pain and fear and Ilam's control is too much, and what little food I ate spills onto the floor. Coughs wrack my frame, and my fingers tremble, although I cannot feel them.

And always respect those who give you power, Ilam tacks on, any trace of doubt from before gone.

I am still mute with fright. I can only nod in response. Ilam is not a friend, not an ally—simply a creature who helps me because he finds me useful.

A demon.

Will you ever try to control me again? Ilam asks.

I convulse with dry coughs.

Ilam reemerges into the open. "Weak and foolish. How did you ever hope to be able to summon rain in this state?" The line of his muzzle morphs into a sneer. "You can barely maintain a clear head for five seconds. Privindu was far stronger than you."

My brows draw together. "Privindu?" I say, wiping spittle from the corner of my mouth.

"A slip of the tongue. I meant Kavita."

"Did you have a connection to Privindu?" I press on, excited despite my exhaustion. "You must have. Otherwise you wouldn't have mentioned him—"

"Have you already forgotten your lesson?" Ilam says, quiet.

I bow my head.

"Good. I tell you what you need to know, and no more. Remember that." He emits a derisive snort. "Until you become stronger you have no right to question me."

"Then teach me how to wield your power," I say. "Tell me how to use it effectively."

"Like I said, no amount of instruction will strengthen your body to summon rain in a week's time." His silver eyes are twin halos, blinding in the darkness. "I need more soulstream."

He paws his ears nonchalantly, the motion resembling a normal feline's. I stay silent, considering the implication of his words. "You want more blood," I say at last. "From others."

He bares his fangs. "Excellent deduction."

"And how, exactly, should we go about this? Walk up to a priest and ask them if they want their blood drained by a demon?"

"No need to be so prickly." His tail swishes lazily. "Of course you can't use a priest. In fact, you cannot use anyone within temple grounds. I dislike their scent."

I wait for an explanation as to why. It doesn't come.

"There's Nali," I suggest. "She's a newcomer."

"I'm not too keen on Dennarese. Besides, no one will notice a missing drunkard or two from the slums."

Horror rings throughout me. "You want to *kill* people?"

He cocks his head. "You've already killed once. Why does it matter if you kill twice or thrice more? You are already a murderer."

My mind flashes back to *that* moment. My mother's body on the floor. Me kneeling over her, scrubbing and scrubbing and scrubbing, trying to get her blood off my hands, till my skin peeled and there were bloodstains on the floor. The moonlight filtering in through the window; the sheer silence smothering the air.

"Murder is not the only solution," I say, struggling to maintain indifference.

"Maybe not. But it is the fastest solution. You wanted power? Here you are. Did you really think your womb was all I needed?"

I place my hand over my abdomen. I do not know if it is still there, or if Ilam has taken it already.

"The womb was a mere exchange for my power—to seal a transaction. I still have to *sustain* said power," he continues. "And that is near impossible with your pathetic body."

I clench my teeth, my head still light. I should have considered the offer more carefully, lay down the specifics. I feel like a fool now. So much for being the goddess of wisdom and foresight.

"If I refuse to do as you say?" All my courage and defiance rush out in that one sentence.

"You may do as you please," Ilam laughs. "But what would your own people think if their goddess failed them? Who would they blame? The goddess? Or the girl whose past is shrouded in blood?"

"Don't. Please," I whisper. I don't want to remember anymore. I do not want to recall the day of my Selection, the Bloodbath of Shiratukh, the girls who dropped dead beside me while I sat unharmed. I do not want to recall the days that followed after, the fear that shadowed my every move.

I do not want to recall the day of Kavita's death, and how a void has carved my insides since then.

"It's up to you," he says. "I only act as far as you allow me to."

My throat tightens. He already knows my answer, yet he continues to dangle choices before me as if I truly have an alternative.

For a moment, I wonder what would have happened if Rashmatun actually existed. If Kavita's strange and cruel rituals had worked and the goddess magically came to me. Could I truly be rid of Ilam? Would I maintain my position without bloodshed? Or would I still concoct desperate schemes to ensure that Rashmatun stays with me?

I look at my hands. These are the hands of a murderer. Ilam is wrong. I haven't killed only once. I've killed ten times already.

What's one more count to the list?

My heart thrums against my chest, a loud, ferocious rhythm that may burst forth at any moment. I touch the yellow sapphire at my throat, its crude edges giving me comfort.

"I'll do it."

8

The Holy Guard

It is easier to slip out of Ghanatukh than I thought. I use the hidden passage tucked at the back of the library—the same route Keran always takes to see me. The Dennarese was the one who discovered it, along with many other tunnels that web throughout the temple. I reckon these were emergency escape routes during the Age of Strife, when Aritsya had not yet been united and various tribes were still at war with one another. I find it amazing that no other temple denizens have found these passageways, but it is to my advantage. The temple has been here for centuries, and many of its secrets have been lost to time.

The passage is eerily dark and uncomfortably cramped; apparently my enhanced senses are little use if there is nothing for me to sense in the first place. As I toe my way forward, keeping a hand against the moss-coated wall, I wonder how Keran has managed to slither through here for the past three years.

At the end of the passage, I shove against the stone before me. It slides open easily. A small, square space is revealed, depictions of the Forebears and the lesser gods and goddesses painted all over its walls. A mural of Rashmatun, seated on her Scarlet Throne, reigns over all, her limbs unusually long and her curves unnaturally smooth. Even in the shadows, the red-and-gold colour scheme of her jama has a jewel-like quality, its vibrancy highlighting the darkness of her fierce eyes.

Though I do not believe in her, a shiver runs up my spine.

I've ended up at a small temple at one of the cardinal points of Bakhtin. I tread out—ensuring that the opening is closed behind me—and survey my surroundings. The Yaborun range is far to the north; Ghanatukh's sprawling complex is but a speck in the distance. The summer night is cool, quiet. Nothing but the singing of cicadas accompanies me as I continue to make my way forward. The footsteps of a nearby Holy Guard patrol come down the corner, and I bypass them. There's no telling what they will do to a girl who's wandering the streets alone.

It is just as Keran had once said—the passage leads to the Eastern District. Near where I had lived as a child. I continue pacing, hoping that my unassuming kurta and suruwal help me blend in. The white and yellow is the most inconspicuous set I have in my wardrobe. Black would have been ideal, but black is the embodiment of evil, and Rakhtis can never clothe themselves in it. Jirtash personally ensures that not a single piece of black clothing is present in my wardrobe. Even I find it difficult to completely forsake cultural superstitions, although I wish to believe them to be untrue.

I stumble—more than walk—my way down the streets, only vaguely aware of my surroundings. It is difficult to recognise the area, when night masks the buildings in shadows. Then, as if my body remembers, it twists and turns and takes paths I would never take. Hazy memories surface in my mind. There's the blacksmith's shop. An old woman sold her gloriously sweet yomaris down that corner. There's the artisan street, and there's where Ykta and I ran away from a furious textiles merchant, from whom we swiped an entire bolt of fabric to make ourselves new clothes.

Nostalgia overcomes me. I realise that this is the first time I have truly seen my city in a decade, and its alleyways and uneven paths, while familiar, are also foreign to me now.

Don't forget what you're supposed to do, Ilam reminds me.

How could I?

Soon enough, I arrive in Dharun. The difference between settlements is stark. One moment, I am walking past clean, if dusty, houses. The next turn down the street reveals broken pots of clay and ramshackle houses crudely moulded out of mud. The district is named after a lesser character in one of Rashmatun's legends, a poor fisherman who traded his last fish for coin that was offered to the Forebears. In turn, his act of devotion was recognised and Rashmatun ensured that his nets were full for the rest of his life. Unfortunately, the only similarity the people of Dharun have to the folktale figure is that they are poor.

Flickering gas lamps line the streets; I stick to the shadows as much as possible. The air hums with the quiet activity of tired people returning home after work and of scattered groups whispering and laughing over alcohol. A few stray residents sprawl on the streets, wooden bowls placed in front of them. Most of them have a missing limb or two; all of them sleep on ragged cloths.

I resist the urge to hug myself and shy away from them. I have to look as if I belong here, unperturbed by these sights.

Something in me snaps into place—I become the girl from Dharun, whose only worldly possessions were the clothes on her back. I am small, hobbling with a slight hunch, indistinct among a sea of faces. Yet my eyes are alert, always on the lookout for a tiny morsel of food or an opportunity to swipe something away.

A life of constant poverty, the fear of starving or being beaten to death engraved in my bones.

I recall how it all changed when my mother became strong enough to host Ilam, and we somehow moved into a kishari's mansion. She started out as a servant, but eventually she won the kishari's affections, and he took her as his third wife, and me as a daughter. I'd been nominated as a Rakhti candidate under the Gopal family name. If Kavita hadn't wiped the entire family out after I was selected as Rakhti, I would have had a place to return to if I retired.

I recall Ilam's earlier words, when he mentioned that Kavita was powerful enough to manipulate minds. Had she manipulated everybody at the Gopal mansion, twisting their emotions so they were oblivious to her machinations?

An involuntary shiver travels down my spine. I shove the speculation aside for now. I have to focus on my task.

Ilam's power isn't as overwhelming as it is in the day, as there are far fewer people here. Most of their drifting thoughts involve fleshly temptations or gambling debts; others are too addled to listen to clearly. A few deign to look my way. If their interest in me increases, I quickly slip down another path.

Still, it's too crowded for me to murder anyone unseen. Although drunken brawls are frequent, murder is rare, and the holy book of Namuru specifically dictates that it is the one sin that propels you straight into the fire pits of Duna. I doubt the residents will take kindly to a child stabbing a grown man to death and having a demon drink his blood.

Ilam is growing impatient. *Calm down*, I tell him. Then I latch on to an alcohol-riddled mind some hundred paces away from me, trusting Ilam to guide me towards them. It is easier to find a victim whose mind is clouded—to pretend that they do not have a name nor a life, that they do not have fears and ambitions of their own.

It turns out that though their mind is blank, the drunkard still moves like water. They stream between streets seamlessly; my untrained legs find it difficult to keep pace.

At long last, the person slows. Then stops.

I cautiously inch forward and peer around the corner of the wall. It's a man, his shoulders broad and strong. He staggers, then falls over into a heap of rubbish. He groans, lying motionless for a while.

My breath hitches. This is the perfect opportunity. I do not know who this man is, who he was, or the friends or family he will leave behind. All I know is Ilam's gnawing hunger, scraping ferociously at the back of my head.

I slowly unsheathe the small kukri at my waist, tucked beneath my kurta. Its wicked, curved blade glints like the fang of a dragon. My feet make no noise as I creep forward. The man has not made a single sound for at least a minute now. Perhaps he is drifting off.

Good. That makes my work much easier.

Then I am standing above the man, the point of my kukri above the nape of his neck.

My hand trembles. I hold my breath, willing my body to listen to me—to be calm and focused, to strike with the fearlessness of a goddess. My left hand closes over my right, steadying my grip. It is for the good of Bakhtin, I tell myself. This one man will be a sacrifice that will grant the city prosperity in the years to come. What is one man in the face of many?

I raise the blade.

"I wondered when you were going to show yourshelf."

Before I can react, the man flips over and sweeps my feet beneath me. I land on the ground, rump sore and hand still holding on to my kukri.

The man hauls himself onto his feet. His jawline is unevenly shaved, and the crinkles around his eyes—a result of smiling or laughing a lot—are weather-beaten, weighing his rugged handsomeness down with lethargy. He regards me with an unfocused gaze, yet there is a hawkish light in them that makes me shiver.

"Who are you, O attempting assasshinator of the great—*hic*—Gurrehmat," he says, speech slurred, "former member of the Holy Guard?"

I stare at him. It is impossible for a Holy Guard to have fallen so low.

"Aha! I see that you are confusion. So ish many when I tell them I am former Guard." He pounds his chest proudly. "But look at me! Can you not believe it when I am sho strong, sho tall, sho handsome? Do I not look like a warrior?"

He is, in fact, wearing an extremely tattered daura-suruwal—and his kurta is worn inside out.

"Of coursh you don't believe me. No one ever does!" he wails.

My grip around my kukri tightens. My knees shift into a more comfortable position.

I lunge forward.

The kukri is twisted out of my fingers. I startle and release a cry of pain. The man—Gurrehmat—throws me over his shoulder and slams me onto the ground. My head cracks against stone; my vision spins. I struggle to breathe, and I can't feel my limbs.

"For a trying assassisinator, you're not very good at it." Gurrehmat crouches beside me, raising his brows. He plops onto the ground with a resigned sigh. Perhaps he is indeed a former Holy Guard. Only someone of their ranks would be able to move like lightning even when intoxicated.

Wrong target, I hiss internally.

Or a good test to see how determined you are, Ilam laughs.

I struggle to refocus. The kukri is on the ground, right beside Gurrehmat. It's probably an arm's length away from me. If I just reach out—

No. He'll react faster than I do. I have to think of something else.

"Maybe ish good that an assass—sassinator is after me," he chuckles dourly. "What do I 'ave to live for? I 'ave nothing. I gave my life for Rashmatun, and what'd I get in return? Nothing! Not just that, everything was taken away from me. My Guards, my family—*everything*!"

He releases a bellow of laughter, its echoes filling up the space around us. The stink of alcohol and rotten meat wafts through the air. I wrinkle my nose, trying not to consider how long it has been since the man has taken a proper bath.

"What happened?" I ask, curious in spite of myself.

Wrong question to ask, as he immediately bursts into sobs. I push myself to sit upright. Either he is unaware of the motion, or he is allowing me to move so long as my actions do not threaten him. Most probably the latter.

"They—they dishcharged m-me. Without honourably," he gasps between sniffles. "Me and all the Guards on duty with me that day. They dishgraced me and turned—*hic*—me away from the courts in Aritsya, shtripping me of all my privileges. And then my wife and my daughter—they abandoned me. After all I did for them! Shaid I was a fool and delu—delush—"

"Delusional," I supply the word.

"Thash it. Delushion." He smiles at me as though I were an old comrade. "Can you believe it? Me! Gurrehmat! Delu—delushional! *They* are the foolsh. All of them—my fam'ly, Rashmatun, all the prieshes. They couldn't recognish blood magic and told me to stop blaming others when ish my fault."

I frown. "What involved blood magic?"

"Are you a fool too?" Gurrehmat rolls his eyes at me—the nerve. "The Shelection, of course! Anyone with a pea for a brain could figure it out. But they all didn't believe me, even when I told 'em th-that there was no other way the girls could've been poishoned unless it was blood magic. Gods, if they 'ad properly inshpected their bodies, they would know—know that it was all unnatural. Their bodies were unnatural. Becoming rotten like that—that'sh not right."

A chill snakes throughout my limbs. The image of the nine other girls sitting alongside me that day comes unbidden to my mind. Their bright, beautiful faces brimming with the hope and excitement of being chosen as Shira-Rakhti. The same faces contorted in agony when decay spread over their skin—

"You should have reported it to the Council of Shamanism, then," I say, stopping myself from thinking any further about those girls. I hope Gurrehmat doesn't notice the tremor in my fingers.

"Bah! You're just a kid, sho you wouldn't know, but"—he leans in conspiratorially—"the Council is ushless. Plenty of my former colleagues tried reporting sushpected cases of blood magic, but what does the Council do? Nothing! Tell us they'll come back with news shoon, only they jusht sweep the case under the rug and make everyone shut up about it. I'm telling you, they don't do their jobs at all."

My ears ring. So there have been other cases of blood shamanism throughout Aritsya. And the Council does nothing about them? Why have I not been informed? What does this mean? What are they planning? There must be a reason why they've been suppressing news about blood shamans.

Then my heart skips a beat. If Gurrehmat had been blabbing to everyone about blood magic being used to kill the girls at my Selection . . . does that include Harun and Nudin and the rest of the priests?

My head goes light with the implication. If Harun and Asahar are communicating with each other, and if Harun is trying to forcibly remove me . . . does that mean they know already?

It's suddenly hard to breathe.

"Foolsh, all of 'em—and you too," Gurrehmat continues. "All told me it was imposshible, and that they would've known if it were blood magic. The eshpression on their faces when I told them what I sushpected! Looking at me ash if I'm too absorbed in child-hood tales."

"So...they really didn't believe you? At all?" I prod.

"Thash what I just said!"

I purse my lips. I'm not sure how much I can trust Gurrehmat's words, considering his drunken state, but it's always better to err on the side of caution. I have to assume that Harun and his priests know of my blood magic. On the other hand, if they know I have a demon, why haven't they tried to expose me? Why allow me to continue to rule for so long?

None of this is making sense, now that I think more carefully about it.

"What else do you remember about the Selection?" I ask.

"That and my punishment, of coursh!" he barks, a little too loud for my liking and ignoring my question completely. "Well. They always say that ash a Holy Guard you reap great rewards and resheive greater punishment."

But I've never heard about the punishment dispensed upon the Holy Guards before. Then again, I never gave the Holy Guards much thought, as they are—for the most part—an autonomous group that only heeds commands from their leader, the Rakhta of war. Had Chandri been the one to order his punishment? Had she done it herself or had Rashmatun been possessing her—

My mind snaps back to Gurrehmat, who wipes his snot off with the hem of his kurta.

"Stupid people! How dare they belittle the great Gurrehmat!" he resumes howling. He emits a burp that reeks of cheap raksi. "I shwear one day I will prove them all wrong! I will bring the truth and justice into light! Wait, was that phrash right? Never mind. Anyway, I shwear I will get out of this good-for-nothing dumpster and find the blood shaman and tear them into pieces..."

I pretend to continue listening to his rambles while my hand inches towards the hilt of the kukri. My senses are clear and heightened with fear egging me on—Gurrehmat knows too much. Leaving him alive is dangerous. Who knows if he shares his theories with everyone even when he's sober, and who knows if some of them believe him—no matter how nonsensical it sounds.

I have an excuse to kill him.

"Cut them and carve them into slices." He starts making a morbid song out of his fantasies. His singing voice is jolly, an odd contrast with his violent, made-up lyrics. "Smash them and bash them and feed them to mices—"

I grab the kukri and bring the blade up.

He slaps the kukri out of my grip. But he doesn't see my second blade—a smaller dagger forged in the Dennarese fashion, sheathed beneath another sleeve. I slash at his throat. His eyes widen in shock when he realises it is too late to bring his arm up in defence. The tip of my blade kisses skin—

And he twists. My dagger strikes air, though the blade has managed to open a shallow cut on his neck.

I snarl in frustration and lunge at him.

This time, he is ready for my attack. He seizes my arm and contorts my wrist, forcing me to drop the second dagger. A slow, understated fury broils in him.

Oh no.

"Gurrehmat doeshn't give second chances, you know," he drawls. "And if shomeone hurts Gurrehmat, you can be sure he will not rest until that shomeone ish dead."

Cold fear sinks into my bones.

He easily pins me onto the ground, placing his knees over my elbows. No amount of kicking and screaming does me any good. He may have been disgraced for ten years, but he was a Holy Guard. I can never hope to physically match him.

He twirls my second dagger between his fingers. "What's this? Looks Dennarese."

He spits into my face.

"How should we deal with a Dennarese dog?" Gurrehmat draws a finger over the edge of the blade. He is a totally different man from the blubbering, sobbing mess earlier. "Before I wash a Holy

Guard, I wash a soldier in the army, where I made a living by kill-ing your kin. In hindsight, I should have served Nardu instead of Rash—matun. The god of war would have rewarded me better for my deeds."

"Nardu dislikes mindless warriors such as you," I snap.

"Oh? Shays the weak, untrained boy who tried to kill a former Holy Guard!" He howls in laughter, the sound of a predator toying with its prey. Impossible. This shouldn't be happening. This man is still inebriated, his mind muddled and slow. "I will show you, then, what a mindless warrior can do."

He drives the blade into my thigh.

An anguished scream rips from my throat. Tears prick at the corners of my eyes. Gods—it hurts so much. And I can't do any-thing about it. Then what? The great goddess Rashmatun falls to a mere drunkard? The thought enrages me.

I am not the only one who is enraged.

Ilam roars to life, splitting my head with a terrible shriek. My body burns—not from the stab wound, but from the demon. His power gushes forth like water from a broken dam, surging from the recesses of my mind and out into the world.

Purple fog clouds my vision. Gurrehmat rolls off me, yelling in terror.

Ilam is out in the open, his silver eyes gleaming with vengeance.

9

The Land of Waking Spirits

For a moment, everything stops. A suspension in the flow of time, as man and demon regard each other. Fear hangs taut in the air, so thick I can almost taste it. And there is anger—pure unbridled wrath. The fury of a beast provoked, and the madness it is about to unleash on its prey.

"No one," Ilam growls, "bleeds my vessel unless I say so."

He pounces forward and clamps his jaw around Gurrehmat's neck. The man's skin shrivels and cracks. The colour from his cheeks fades, until nothing is left but a greyish cast. His eyes are still wide open with shock, their glassy gaze staring into nothingness. I wonder if he is glad his theories of blood shamans existing among us are true.

A frightened gasp rings out from behind. I turn around. It's a young woman, her spindly arms nearly as thin as mine. I only missed her because I had been busy struggling with Gurrehmat.

She takes off like a deer fleeing from a tiger.

I swallow a curse and grab the Dennarese dagger. Ilam continues to feast on Gurrehmat, preoccupied with drinking as much soulstream as he can. I sprint after the woman. The wound in my thigh drives spikes of pain every time I take a step, but adrenaline fuels me.

She cannot escape. I cannot allow her to tell anyone about a demon in the city, or the child who was with said demon.

I narrow my focus towards her mind, tailing her through the maze of alleys in Dharun's underbelly. My thigh no longer hurts; my body does not seem my own. I push forward, willing myself to go faster, to close the distance between us.

But despite the alarm flooding my veins, my pace starts to lag. She runs farther, faster, her mind a speck disappearing into darkness.

No, no. No. No. I have to kill her. I must kill her.

She wheels into a narrow alley, her steps slowing. Terror emanates from her. She's run into a dead end.

With a grim determination, I speed up.

I spot her just as she tries to slip out of the mouth of the alley. I reach out and snatch her arm. She doesn't stop. I leap forward and use my momentum, driving the blade into her side.

She sputters in surprise as we both crash to the ground. Using Gurrehmat's method, I pin her arms with my knees. The woman whimpers, her eyes glazed with tears.

Yhadin, someone's voice rings out in the woman's mind. *You must take care of yourself.*

"I'm sorry," I say.

I cut her throat. She emits one final gag before her limbs slacken. Bright red blood gushes from her wound. My eyes fixate on that one colour—the colour favoured by Rashmatun, the colour of wisdom and fortune, the colour of fertility, and the colour of death.

Another person dead. Because of me.

"I'm sorry. I had no choice," I whisper, even though she— Yhadin—can hear me no longer.

A few people nearby have heard the commotion and are heading in my direction. I quickly kick my dagger to the side. Using what little strength I have left, I heft the woman's body up, wrapping one of her arms around my shoulders so that it looks like I am supporting her. Fortunately, the alley is dimly lit, and the woman's head lolls forward so that her hair conceals the wound on her neck.

The people step into view. Three of them. All men. All intoxicated.

"Come on, let's go back already," I say, tilting my head towards

Yhadin—no, the woman's corpse. It's easier to refer to her without using her name. "See—you're so drunk that you wore Mama's clothing instead!"

I hold my breath. Cold sweat beads down my neck.

The men stare at me and the body for a heartbeat. Then they decide we are not worth their attention; they wheel around and continue down the main street, chatting loudly of the pretty women they want to bed.

I release a breath and drag the woman's corpse into another alley, dumping her body on the ground. Her eyes are vacant, and several strands of her hair are matted with blood. I had felt the warmth leaving her body, her frail frame leaning heavily against my own.

I hunch over and retch into a corner.

Purple fog drifts into view. With it comes Ilam. I stare at him, wiping vomit from my mouth. He bares his fangs; they drip with Gurrehmat's blood.

"Two people," he says. "Good work, Binsa."

I give a curt nod.

Ilam prowls towards the woman and sinks his teeth into her throat. I head back into the other alley and retrieve my dagger. I wipe the blade on my kurta; the blood stains the pure-white cloth a grotesque red. My suruwal is also bloodied from my wound. I'll have to discard the clothes later.

"It's time we go back," Ilam says.

I force myself to look at the woman's body. It's gone—nothing but ashes are left where she lay. Even her clothes have disappeared.

A shudder runs through my bones. I had carried her just moments ago. Now she's gone. As if she had never existed.

It's for the best, I tell myself. Their lives were meaningless anyway.

"Your kukri," Ilam continues, dropping the weapon right by my feet. "You were careless."

"Thank you." I pick it up and sheathe it.

His form dissipates into purple fog, seeping into my body. His renewed strength courses through me. It is not a bright, roaring fire, loud and crackling and arresting, but the strength of an ocean—quiet and gentle on the surface, but filled with dangers lurking in its unfathomable abyss.

Unlike the power that tore me apart from the inside a week ago, this is calm, contained, ready to explode if triggered.

The wound in my thigh closes in an instant.

Let's go, Ilam says.

I go back the same way I came. Everything blurs past me— people, critters, the symphony of the night. My head is numb, completely blank of thoughts. If anyone finds the sight of a child traipsing through the streets in bloodied clothes strange, they certainly don't show it.

I eventually find the temple and stalk back through the passage, before slipping out of the library and ribboning through the Bakhal like a wraith. All is quiet. No one has noticed the absence of their Rakhti.

In my room, I peel off my clothing and change into a looser-fitting daura-suruwal. The kukri and dagger are stowed into the hollowed square of a wooden block, painted and carved to resemble a book on the outside. The block returns to the shelf, and I check my hands for any remaining speckles of blood. There are a few drops here and there on my fingertips; I scrub them away at the basin, then toss the water and refill the container. Drawing upon Ilam's magic, I burn my bloodied clothes and scatter the ashes outside my window.

With that, I fall onto my bed in a tired heap, exhaustion permeating into my bones.

I dream of the night I killed Kavita.

It was a typical summer night, thick and humid. A night like any other. I just celebrated my seventh birthday; the temple was soaked in a merry atmosphere the whole day, and the chefs had whipped up a mind-boggling array of Aritsyan delicacies. My devotees wished me well and sang my praises; the priests prostrated themselves before me and expressed their gratitude profusely.

It was supposed to be a happy day.

I would have been happy, if my mother hadn't forced me to throw all the food away, saying that they might try to poison me. I would have been happy, if her voice hadn't been literally ringing in my head and telling me what to do.

Now she stands before me, her smiling face concealing the fury radiating from every pore of her body. I bow my head. I do not know what mistake I've made today, but it's best to keep a deferential posture around Mama.

"Could you be any more slow-witted?" she says, her tone so saccharine it makes me shiver.

"What have I done, Mama?" I ask.

She slaps my face.

I can feel my cheek swelling and blood trickling down my nose, but I do not make a move to nurse them. I do not cry, I do not scream. It's as though I am a lifeless doll, to be used and abused as and when my mother likes.

"Today was the perfect opportunity to try to summon Rashmatun," she continues. "You were all alone in the cleansing hall. You should have cut yourself before her statue to show her your devotion."

"I did that today, Mama," I reply. "Just like what I've done all the months before."

She snatches my wrist and pulls my sleeve down. My arm is free of blemishes—Kavita always takes care to heal me before the handmaidens can see my wounds. She had done just that earlier, but she might have forgotten—she always conveniently forgets her actions when it is time to blame and punish me.

Her expression darkens. She releases my arm. My muscles tense, preparing me for the next blow.

"Ilam," she says.

The demon slips out of her body. The brilliant plumage of a regular peacock is replaced by shadows, yet its form is tangible and real, as though black-feathered peacocks truly exist in this world. I force myself to stay still, to not hiss at it or cower from it.

"I cannot delay this any longer," Kavita mutters. "I must

transfer him to you. Maybe with his power you will be able to find Rashmatun."

Before I can react, she draws a kukri from under her sash and slices it across her palm.

She grabs my wrist again and cuts my palm as well and holds our wounded hands together. Needles tingle my limbs. I jerk involuntarily; my mother tightens her grip. Ilam's body dissipates into smoke that billows towards our entwined fingers. Kavita's eyes start to glow red; her veins become visible beneath her skin.

My stomach lurches. I've seen the way the demon feeds on her. The cruelty he's brought to our lives through her.

"No, no!" I cry, trying to pull myself away. "I don't want a demon! Get away!"

"To find Rashmatun and kill her, to give me the power to conquer men—these are the terms of our contract," Kavita says. Either she is in a trance, or she is electing to ignore my screams. "I sacrificed my heart to you, and it is with this sacrifice that you will continue to fulfil your contract."

I can feel the demon inside me, writhing through my body and slithering through my head. It is a sensation I have never felt before—one that fills me with terror. "Stop it!" I sob. "I'll do whatever you want, just don't make me host a demon. I don't want a demon. I don't want your magic!"

"With my soul bound to yours, you will serve your new host," Kavita continues. "I draw upon your true name—"

"Stop it!"

My mind goes blank with dread. I cannot take her demon. I cannot become like her.

I lunge for the kukri with my free arm. Kavita is so engrossed in the ritual that I snatch it from her easily—too easily.

I stab her in the side.

She gasps, finally releasing me. Ilam does not leave me, although his presence weakens.

With a feral cry, I rush forward and bury the kukri in her stomach.

She falls, an uncharacteristic, understanding smile on her face.

My chest heaves; the kukri clatters onto the ground. Blood blooms around her wounds, the red resembling a blossoming flower against a white canvas. Her face is ghastly pale, frozen in death. Yet I cannot tear my eyes away.

"You are just like me," she laughs all of a sudden.

I startle, and I am no longer little Binsa. I am the Rakhti who has ruled over Bakhtin for the past ten years, the vessel who has done her best to survive.

I am not the daughter she knows.

Colour returns to Kavita's cheeks, and she blinks, a red glow emanating from her eyes. "I am proud of you, my dear Binsa," she croons.

I try to wrench my eyes away from the gaping hole in her abdomen, but fail. "Even though I was the one who killed you?"

"I love you, my daughter. And that is why I allowed you to kill me. I knew it was a sign of your inherent strength." Her grin widens into an unsettling curve. "My sacrifice was not in vain, for you have chosen to tread the path I have walked."

"No—no. I'm done. I won't have to kill anyone anymore. I just need enough power to summon rain."

"The path of blood demands more blood, my child. It takes, it takes, and it takes." She pauses, and the wrinkles on her face smooth out, her cheeks plump with youth. "And one day, you will become just like me."

"No!" I back away from her. "I will *never* become like you. You killed innocent girls for your own benefit!"

"My benefit? They were for you, dear Binsa. A cheap sacrifice for the wonderful life you lead now."

"You should have killed me too," I say, my voice cracking.

"No. Never." She sits up. I take a step back. "You were born for greatness, my daughter. To be anything less is to defile the gods."

"The gods don't even exist. Where was Rashmatun when I needed her?"

"You have read stories of the Rakhtis of old—of how they summoned storms and fire from the sky and shifted the mountains to their will. The miracles over the past century are on a far smaller scale, of course, but just because they are smaller does not mean they are any less significant." She gets up onto her feet, blood dripping from her wound. "Rashmatun exists. And that's why I wanted you to become Rakhti—to obtain her power. But you were too weak to find her."

"Even if she does exist, was it worth murdering those girls? They didn't do anything to deserve it."

"Did Gurrehmat deserve it? Did Yhadin deserve it?"

"Shut up. Go away. Stop haunting me!" I cry, throat hoarse.

"We are here because of you, Binsa," a chorus of voices ring out instead, rasping in horrible synchrony. I know instinctively that they belong to the girls of the Bloodbath, as well as Gurrehmat and Yhadin. "You are responsible for our souls."

"No. Please forgive me," I beg, squeezing my eyes shut. "I had no choice. I didn't want any of this. Please—"

"You are responsible for our souls," they continue to chant. "Our blood is on your hands."

"Stop it." I clamp my hands over my ears, trying to pretend I cannot hear them. "Stop, stop, stop. You're all dead. Why are you here? You're all dead!"

"Our blood is on your hands—"

"*Stop it!*" I scream.

My eyes jerk open. Jirtash's concerned face hovers over me. She dabs at my forehead with a cloth. A sheen of cold sweat coats my entire body. "Binsa, are you all right?"

I cautiously push myself to sit upright, massaging my temples. My mind is still stuck in that nightmare—a memory I thought I'd be able to forget. With great effort, I manage a somewhat convincing smile. "A dream," I say. "I'm fine now."

Jirtash's brows knit together in a mixture of concern and suspicion. "You have a slight fever, child."

This girl . . . In spite of what Rashmatun is saying, I do not think the gods are with her.

I slap a hand to my forehead, trying to ignore the sting of Jirtash's unbidden thoughts. I am heating up a little—nothing some water and a good amount of undisturbed sleep won't cure. "I'm fine, Jirtash," I insist. I can't afford to be sick. Not now. Not ever. "I haven't been sleeping well lately. But I'm all right."

She releases a long-suffering sigh. "That's what they all say. Lutna, Chandri—the Rakhtis before you. For some reason they all succumbed to stress towards the end of their tenure, as though all the anxieties and burdens they carried throughout the years finally caught up to them." Then in a soft voice: "I hope they're all right now."

My eyes widen in surprise. This is the first time she's talked about what the former Rakhtis are currently doing.

Before I can ask her more, she pats my shoulder and readjusts the blanket over me. "Get some sleep, my Rakhti. I'll inform the priests that you need rest today. Leave Medha to me as well. I know she's comfortable with you, but she can't be secluded forever."

I spring up to sit on the bed. "No! No…" I say, scrabbling for an excuse to keep Jirtash away from Medha. The little brat's tongue is not healed yet. "Let me continue to look after her. I can do at least that much. Otherwise I cannot bear to call myself a Rakhti."

She lifts her brows and laughs. "I've never seen you so excited over someone before."

That's because her antics give me a heart attack, I think. "I like her, and I want to make sure she's able to acclimatise to life here properly."

"Well, if you can sit up so quickly, you're well enough to watch over Medha."

I flash her a rueful grin.

"I'll send some food and water." She gets to her feet and makes for the door. After everything that has happened, her presence is a calming pillar I can lean on. While the world shifts and flows with the passage of time, Jirtash has remained unchanged all these years.

I don't think she knows I am a blood shaman. Else she would've done something long ago, with her righteous personality.

"Thank you, Jirtash," I say.

10

Introduction of a Future Goddess

I spend the rest of the week in relative peace, as few handmaidens are allowed to attend me as I recuperate. Though they find it strange that I am so insistent on looking after Medha still, they do not voice any of their questions, and bury their puzzlement using various reasons—I've grown attached in the brief time I've been with Medha, as I have not had such a companion since my mother disappeared; Rashmatun has ordered me to keep a careful eye on little Medha, to begin preparing her for the life of a Rakhti.

When I am in the right mood and there aren't too many people around me, it's quite interesting to listen to their thoughts.

Eventually, I learn how to narrow my radius of focus to filter through the sensory input, much like how one learns to block out unnecessary noise at a rowdy gathering, only paying attention whenever one's name is called. Rather than an extension of my senses, Ilam's power *becomes* my senses. I give up on trying to contain the wealth of information brimming my head, instead allowing it to stream in, as though my mind were an ocean linked to several rivers. As much as I hate to admit it, Ilam was right—the problem with my newfound abilities is that I see them as problems to solve. The shift in perspective allows me to adjust better to Ilam's presence.

Yet as much as I've improved, it isn't enough. I am still weak, still inadept at blood magic. The ability to hear thoughts is handy, but I am unable to pick out useful thoughts, and am capable of listening only to musings at the forefront of one's mind. If I try to dig deeper, I am met with a lancing headache and dark spots dancing across my vision. I need more power. Fast. Shira-Rakhtis are usually promoted to Rakhti a month after their initial appointment; with Medha's injuries presenting a setback, my plans to obtain more information from her and her sister are delayed. Starting to take three meals a day—albeit in limited quantities—to compensate for all the years of starving myself is not enough to help me take in more of Ilam's magic.

You can kill more people to obtain more power, a voice in my head occasionally suggests. And each time, I recall the way Gurrehmat and Yhadin died—how their bodies had been so thoroughly consumed by Ilam that not a trace of their existence remains in this world. My stomach roils in disgust every time I remember that I am using the same blood magic Kavita used to make others suffer.

I won't have to kill anymore, I comfort myself. *I just need to summon rain.*

To which Ilam responds with an amused cackle.

But no matter how much my skin crawls at the notion that my power comes from Gurrehmat and Yhadin, there's nothing I can do to bring them back. By the fourth day, the initial discomfort weighing down on my lungs fades into a dull numbness.

Since Jirtash has personally avowed that I need to take a break from Rakhti duties for a while, I extend the leave as long as I need to for Medha's wounds to heal. Fortunately, Ykta's sutures—though a little uneven—were excellent for someone whose only experience involved sewing a dead rat's splattered guts together out of curiosity. Three days after Medha first injured herself, we removed the stitches. Another three days later, Medha has regained most of her vitality and is eager to explore the sprawling temple grounds.

The day of Medha's first public appearance in the temple starts like any other, except that quite a few of my maidservants are gone. They are attending to her, I presume. Nali and Jirtash flutter around me as they towel my body dry and drape me in clothes. The latter noticeably glares at the half-Dennarese from time to time.

When they are done, I spin around and grin at Jirtash. "I've never felt more eager to return to my duties."

"A prolonged break does wonders for the mind," Jirtash agrees.

I make my way towards the door, the smile lingering on my face.

"My Rakhti," Nali blurts, "may—may I ask you something?"

I whip around. Jirtash's cheeks puff. "How dare you speak to the Rakhti without being spoken to first!" she snaps. "Don't think that just because you received Rashmatun's mercy means you can act however you like. Apologise, now!"

"Jirtash." I lift a hand. "It's all right. Let's listen to what she has to say first. Make it quick, though, Nali. Rashmatun awaits."

Jirtash closes her eyes, frustrated; the other handmaidens gather behind her in a timid huddle, not a single sound escaping them. But their verbal silence doesn't translate to their minds.

I focus on Nali. During the week she has attended to me, her mind has remained as empty as a blank slate. Whether she is panicking, joyous, or sad—I am unable to hear anything. She unnerves me. She is frightening.

She is someone I need to treat carefully.

Nali drops to her knees before speaking. "My Rakhti, if it does not trouble you to share this with me, how is Medha doing?"

I lace my fingers before me. Of course she would ask about her half sister, if the both of them had been deployed to Ghanatukh to uncover its secrets together. The question is, am I truly the only barricade standing between them? Are they unable to contact each other through other means?

Most importantly, what do they want from me?

"You can see for yourself later," I say, tone light. I turn back towards the door. "Rashmatun may not have granted you permission to meet your sister personally, but that does not mean you are disallowed from seeing how she is faring."

We walk towards the courtyard in the Bakhal, where Medha is already waiting. She bounces around the dried fountain in excitement. The golden jama she wears lends an evanescent quality to her features, and a red hairpin secures her topknot in place. The rising sun peeking over the Yaborun range washes over her, setting the natural glow in her skin aflame. I hear Nali gasping in relief behind me.

I do not know if it's because of Ilam's power, but Medha seems brighter than usual, and her appearance is striking. Envy twinges in me. The one thing I never inherited from Kavita was her looks; I wonder if my life would have been easier if I had a beautiful face—one that truly befits a goddess.

I press my lips together and shove my musings aside.

"Are you ready?" I ask.

"Yes, my goddess," she replies reverently.

"I'm not a goddess right now," I say, a wry smile twisting my mouth. Someone's stare is pinned onto my back, and I cannot help but feel that it is Nali. My awareness of every move I make and every rise and fall in my intonation is heightened. I place a hand between Medha's shoulders and steer her forward. "I'm still Binsa."

"Oh! Forgive me." She inclines her head. "You look like Rashmatun herself."

"I am Rashmatun's vessel, so in a way, I *am* Rashmatun." I frown at my own words. Then I frown at how this cheeky little brat has just complimented me in an off-handed manner. "Let's go. You have much to learn."

"Yes, Binsa!" she exclaims happily.

We walk side by side towards the cleansing hall, Medha *oohing* and *aahing* at the temple sights. Her mind is equally exuberant, darting from one thought to another so quickly that trying to follow them gives me a headache. I settle for allowing her thoughts to stream past me without trying to latch on to any of them.

As we weave through the central courtyard, Medha suddenly takes off into the distance.

I stare after her, stunned. It takes a few seconds before I recover and stride over, holding myself back from breaking into an indecorous sprint.

"Medha Yankaran!" I shout, the tips of my ears reddening from both rage and embarrassment. All my maidservants are here to witness this; they will be more than happy to gossip about how the current Rakhti cannot even keep her successor on a leash.

The little brat does not stop. She scurries to the side of the courtyard and fawns over a cluster of rhododendron bushes, their red petals resembling a blanket of fire. The sight is beautiful, but hardly worth her tramping off like a wild goat. I take a deep breath, trying to calm myself before I close the distance, lest I slap her to death in anger. I have to remember that Nali is watching.

The first thing that hits me is the scent of blood.

It is not the metallic tang of fresh wounds; it is a deep, rotting stink that worms its way through my nostrils and is impossible to dismiss once you notice it. I've seen plenty of bodies in Dharun, stuffed into alleyways and left there to decay till the stench of corpses becomes a permanent fixture in the air. The smell here is not as apparent, but my enhanced senses now have enabled me to snuff it out.

The closer I am to Medha—and the rhododendron bushes—the stronger the stench. I cover my mouth and nose with a hand and swallow a gag.

Why would there be such a horrible stench in Ghanatukh Temple, of all places? Where is it coming from? My eyes sweep over the clusters of rhododendrons, their petals spilling over the ground like fresh blood. The subtle, gentle fragrance of the flowers must have been used to mask the stench. The stench of what, exactly? It smells like carcasses to me. But what carcasses? And why here?

I would have to dig beneath the rhododendron bushes to find out. Not exactly a viable option at this moment in time.

I slowly tread over to Medha's side, trying to not keel over from the stench. I will find a way to deal with this later. Now it's time to deal with her. My voice comes out razor sharp: "What do you think you're doing?"

Medha's fingers stiffen over a bunch of rhododendrons. Fear washes over her as she realises her mistake. She turns towards me and ducks her head. "I'm so sorry, Binsa," she says. "I got excited when I saw them. They remind me of home."

"Oh?" I arch a brow. "How so?"

"My mother grows them. They were my sister's favourite flower." Medha's lips curve into a polite smile. *Were?* I wonder. Before I can press her, she continues to jabber away: "But the ones in my house wilted already. How do you grow them during summer, Binsa?"

"Magic, Medha." I trail my fingers over the rhododendrons, still pondering over her use of the past tense in relation to Nali. I hope the half-Dennarese isn't close enough to overhear our conversation. "The priests' magic keeps our gardens blooming all year round."

"Will I get to see lightning?" she gasps, eyes wide with anticipation.

I stare at her, confounded by her sudden switch in topic. "Our priests don't summon lightning. They have no need to."

She pouts. "But Rashmatun would be strong enough to summon lightning, right? You too!"

I inadvertently recall my early days as Rakhti, when I tried to summon Rashmatun—when being crowned as her vessel didn't bring any changes to me. How at some point I gave up on believing in Rashmatun, even though my mother continued to rage at me.

If Rashmatun did exist, I'm sure she wouldn't have ignored my plight.

"Rakhtis do not simply abuse their goddess's magic," I chide Medha. "Why are you so curious about lightning, anyway?"

Her eyes sparkle. "Doesn't it sound fun?"

The girl sure has a perverse idea of fun.

"It'd be incredible to wield magic, though. Like the Rakhtis of old," Medha continues to chatter.

You have read stories of the Rakhtis of old—of how they summoned storms and fire from the sky and shifted the mountains to their will.

The words of Kavita—or Kavita's ghost—from my last nightmare echo in my mind.

Lies. Ridiculous folktales the people of Bakhtin have conjured to give them something to believe in.

"Enough dawdling." I snatch Medha's hand and grip it firmly, dragging her back to the centre of the courtyard. The maidservants smother their snickers. "If you dare to run off without notice again, I'll confine you to your room for a whole day with no meals!"

Medha withers in defeat and trudges alongside me. I wonder again about her true purpose here.

Still suspicious of her? Ilam says. *She's but a child.*

So was I when I first came here, I reply.

Only Jirtash and Nali—who are my official personal attendants—are allowed into the cleansing hall. Harun approaches us with an uncharacteristically wide beam on his face, clad in his orange-and-white robes. An inverted seven-lobed leaf is painted on the middle of his forehead, representing the fruits of Rashmatun's wisdom being passed on to humankind. Meanwhile, his son tags after him like a taller, more sallow-looking shadow of himself. Although Nudin lingers in the background like usual, I find my gaze pausing on him for a few seconds. Will he remain quiet today, or will he burst into an unusual fit of emotion once more?

"Shira-Rakhti," the chief priest greets Medha, his arms thrown wide as if he were going to wrap her in an embrace. He settles for placing his hands on her shoulders instead. "It is an honour to finally lay my eyes upon you."

"You examined me for the virtues," Medha says, puzzled. "We've met."

"It's my first time seeing you as our future Rakhti." The chief priest's eyes gleam with elation.

He thinks he's won—that he's successfully installed a new Rakhti, that he's already overthrown me. Him addressing Medha first is testimony to his confidence.

I cannot wait to tear that confidence down.

Harun proceeds with the morning ritual after instructing Medha to stand aside. I wear a demure smile on my face as I kneel before the statue of Rashmatun, masking the rage that continues to bubble inside me. The cold water the priests douse over my head does little to cool that internal fire.

After Harun paints the star on my forehead, I hold myself tall, becoming Rashmatun. The priests fall to their knees. In my peripheral vision, I spot Jirtash pressing Medha against the floor to kneel.

"Rise," I command.

"My goddess," Harun says in return, clambering to his feet. The rest of the occupants in the hall do the same.

"Are there any more incidents with falling goats today?" I ask, tone frosty.

"There are indeed a few devotees who have arrived to see you about that issue." Harun keeps his chin low. "Some of the goats are headless, in fact."

I expected no less, coming from Harun. It cannot be coincidence that an exorbitant number of goats were used for the Selection, and that goats are also dropping all over unsuspecting citizens—all in accordance with the Prophecy of Geerkha. Now the next question is, where and how would the carcasses be buried? I am still waiting for Ykta to confirm that only Ghanatukh has acquired a large number of goats in recent weeks, but it should be obvious enough if the priests are indeed behind the falling goats. They would—theoretically—need to be within close proximity to me to be able to perform magic.

My mind drifts towards the rhododendron bushes in the courtyard, recalling the stench, recalling how the blood-like blossoms spread over a space large enough to bury several bodies—

The goat carcasses. My nerves buzz with cold realisation.

Ilam merely laughs.

They wouldn't be so bold, right? To hide evidence of their crimes right under my nose?

Then again, why wouldn't they? Harun was already bold enough to attempt to remove me without even informing me of the Selection. He was already bold enough to speak of the Prophecy of Geerkha in my presence.

Fury starts to broil in the pit of my belly as I observe the chief priest, the robes immaculately wrapped around his frame, the tray of paints and brushes he's holding. I think about the stench in the main courtyard, and how the priests could have possibly dropped goat carcasses from the sky.

"Harun"—I jab a finger towards the tray in his hands—"teleport the brushes to the outside of the Paruvatar. Nudin can help you, if you require assistance."

The chief priest nearly drops his tray. "What is this for, Rashmatun?"

"Medha Yankaran here wishes to see a demonstration of magic," I say.

The little girl emits a gasp of delight.

Bewildered looks from everyone in the hall needle me. Their thoughts are a clanging jumble of confusion and acquiescence. Harun nods at Nudin, who steps forward to take one side of the tray, alongside his father.

"*O Great Goddess of Wisdom, lend us your strength,*" they chant together in Ritsadun. "*Give us the power to carve the space between spaces, to manipulate the existence of a being.*"

The yellow sapphire I wear grows hot against my chest.

Odd. It feels like this has happened before. Was this pendant a gift from Kavita? But I cannot imagine her passing a gemstone so raw and unpolished to me. Or was it from Chandri—

I blink. The brushes on the tray are gone.

And are now on the floor beneath Jirtash's feet.

Paint has also been splattered over her kurta.

"I don't recall asking the two of you to dye Jirtash's clothes," I comment. The matron tries to laugh it off, but she is upset about having one of her favourite kurtas ruined. She slaps Nali's hand away; she was trying to wipe the stains off with cloth.

Harun's face reddens. *What was the point in doing that?*

I needed to confirm the capacities and limits of your magic, I think. Aside from registered shamans in the Holy Guard, only priests who have been specially anointed by one of the ten Forebears have access to magic, where their strength is tethered to the respective Forebear. That is the reason why the priests of Gha-natukh have claimed to only be able to cast magic when I am around. Individually, they have little power, but if Harun were to lead and coordinate all of them . . . it might be feasible to drop goats from the sky.

Perhaps with just the two of them, their powers are more unpredictable.

But I have no conclusive evidence of all this either. I cannot tell everyone that I smell carcasses in the courtyard when no one else can. I cannot accuse one of Rashmatun's priests of dropping goats from the sky. They'll just see me as a madwoman, someone to be removed from the Scarlet Throne immediately.

There is also one snag in my theory: If I do not possess Rashma-tun, where do the priests draw their power from?

"My goddess, perhaps we should return our attention to matters at present . . ." Harun simpers.

I click my tongue in annoyance. "What compensation are the victims asking for?"

Harun jumps, finally breaking his unflappable composure. "No-nothing much, Rashmatun. Just—"

"Give them their compensation. I do not wish to see them today."

Harun's frog eyes bulge. "My—my goddess, wh-what brought about this hasty decision?"

I cast him a contemptuous side glance. "There are other citizens of Bakhtin who require my attention. I cannot waste my time on such fanciful folktales."

"Why would common citizens conspire to create such a fantastic tale, m-my goddess?"

Despite the nervousness, Harun's mind is a quiet hum. Not the sheer emptiness that is Nali's, but a faint whisper. It's as though he has trained to protect his mind against prying eyes.

I try to dig deeper into the chief priest's mind, throw all my focus towards him.

My breaths grow shorter.

Don't bother to strain yourself, Ilam says. *Not now, at least.*

How am I supposed to manoeuvre my way around him if I cannot read his thoughts? I reply.

You were doing just fine manipulating people without my help. The demon yawns. *Just because you have my magic doesn't mean you can afford to be lazy.*

Again, although it grates me, Ilam is right.

Harun clears his throat. "My goddess, I still think it is wise to see all your citizens with pressing issues. It will never do for the people of Bakhtin to think that their goddess is sweeping their problems aside."

"Are you the goddess of wisdom, or am I?" I retort. "Are you the one who knows what is best for my people?"

"Of—of course not, my goddess," Harun stammers. "But the goats— Perhaps you have accidentally done something—"

"If I were to choose an animal, it would certainly not be a goat." In legends, Rashmatun was famously jilted by Nardu, the god of war and passion, who rides an armoured ram into battle. He deemed her too clever for his liking, and promptly decided that he would rather be alone forever than have her as a lover. "And do you think I am so foolish to not know what I or my vessel has done?"

He finally shuts up; I revel in his cowering expression. If Harun is acting this way, he wouldn't know that I don't hold a goddess, right? Otherwise he would be more confident, quicker and wittier in his responses.

Then why is he planning to oust me from my throne in the first place? Does Asahar have anything to do with his plan?

"Rashmatun, in addition to these matters, the Trial of Divinity is scheduled to take place the week after next," Harun says after he recovers. "I have already sent invitations to the other Rakhtas and made the necessary arrangements to receive them."

My stomach drops to my feet when I hear those words. I had completely forgotten about it, what with my problems concerning Ilam and Medha.

With all the Rakhtas slated to convene in Bakhtin...Asahar will come.

Perhaps Asahar has been supplying the priests' magic all this while. Yet that is also impossible. Asahar has not visited my district for the past five years; the last time I saw him was during the decennial meeting between the Rakhtas and the king of Aritsya.

The only fact I know for sure now is that the priests are responsible for dropping the goats on my innocent people. Even then, the truth is uncertain until I obtain solid evidence. I wonder what Ykta will think of my discovery, since he was supposed to investigate this matter.

I shoot a cutting glare at the chief priest. "You did this without consulting Binsa?"

"My goddess, I did not wish to trouble your vessel any further, as she was looking after the Shira-Rakhti for the past week, all while being overwhelmed with her own duties," Harun answers. Nudin watches on, placid. "Do not worry. I have seen to many Trials before."

I contemplate revealing Harun's crimes right here and now, just so I can get under his skin and remind him of who is truly in power. But the only witnesses are the priests—who are all complicit—Jirtash, Nali, and Medha. Bursting out now does not change anything about my circumstances.

"So be it," I say, wheeling around and stalking out of the cleansing hall. I cannot push Harun too much, lest he chooses to bites back.

He'll be forgiven—for now.

Medha takes a while before she catches up, scuttling alongside. "Why can't you just...stop the goats?"

"You walk *behind* me, not beside me."

She slows her pace. "So, why can't you stop the goats?"

"Because I did not create them," I snap.

She goes silent for a while, sulking at my unsatisfactory answer. It doesn't take long for her to jabber away again: "Are all the stories true? The legends? The tales where you outwitted demons into giving you their greatest weapons?"

Is there no end to her questions? I suspect that some portion of my splitting headache may be attributed to her ceaseless talking.

Yet some part of me empathises with her—that incessant nagging at the back of the mind, wanting to ask why things are the way they are. Unlike her, I never voiced my sentiments aloud, keeping them bundled and locked in an airtight box inside my mind. The consequences for me were dire if I didn't play the part of the perfect Rakhti, calm and kind and demure.

I continue to make my way towards Rashmatun's chambers without entertaining her. "It's time to get ready, child."

11

Words of Wisdom

The rest of the morning passes by uneventfully—save for Harun's dismay at my order to offer more than ample compensation to devotees affected by the falling goats. His immediate thoughts are that he will not be able to afford buying extra ornaments for his room this month, unless he docks the other priests' allowances instead. Too bad for him.

After we've cleaned up and had our lunch, I introduce Medha to daily lessons with Ykta. She likes Ykta; I can tell from the way she immediately bombards him with a thousand questions, her eyes brightening at the sight of a somewhat familiar face. Whether Ykta enjoys her attention as much . . . that's up for debate.

He's impressed by her, though. She takes to the lessons like a duck to water, her quicksilver mind eager and always ready to learn. As Ykta introduces her to the basic subjects of religion, history, math, and science, I leaf through Privindu's *Theories and Principles of Aritsyan Magic for Beginners*. There hasn't been anything substantial so far—as expected.

But I must keep looking. Privindu's words helped me contain Ilam, even for a brief moment. There must be hints about blood magic somewhere else. I just have to look harder.

We continue in peace for a long while, interspersed with Medha's occasional odd question. Then halfway through a brief overview on the history of Bakhtin, she suddenly asks Ykta, "Are you going to be my tutor? Or do I have to change tutors?" Her words break my concentration on Privindu.

"You can retain me if you like, Shira-Rakhti," Ykta replies. "It is entirely up to you. If you find me to be satisfactory, then it would honour me to be your tutor. If I am not up to your standards, it is your right to select another."

"Oh! Good. I like you," Medha declares happily. "You actually teach stuff. You aren't like the old men who used to tutor me. They always tried to keep me in the house, but they're so *boring*."

"You didn't attend the Ghushnayets?" It's Ykta's turn to ask, out of surprise. I'm surprised as well. The Ghushnayets are renowned as public spaces of learning, where the brightest talents are identified and nurtured. Even sons and daughters of kisharis attend them.

"Papa and Mama prefer me to stay with them..." Medha takes a sudden interest in the table. Her mind goes quiet.

Interesting, Ilam murmurs.

Care to pry further?

I cannot pry what refuses to be opened.

I swallow a frustrated sigh. Why do I have the ability to hear thoughts when I can't even put it to use at crucial moments?

"I want to know more about the lineage of Rakhtis," Medha abruptly declares.

Ykta shifts in his seat, taken aback by the change in topic. "All right. Let's start with Rala," he says, "the first to receive the goddess Rashmatun's blessing."

"Can't we start with Chandri?" Medha asks.

"We could." Ykta grows more bewildered. "But we usually study history in chronological order."

"I want to learn about Chandri."

"All—all right. Her segment is incredibly sparse, though."

"I don't think so. There's the Bloodbath of Shiratukh."

Ykta looks as though he wants the gods to strike him where he sits right now.

"Why are you so interested in such strange things, Medha?" I chime in. "First, lightning. Now the Bloodbath of Shiratukh."

She wrinkles her nose. "Is it wrong to be interested in such things?"

"Not wrong, no. But...it's unusual."

"I want to know," she insists.

I want to be Rakhti. Her first words in Shiratukh Temple ring in my head, as clear as a cloudless dawn. Spoken with so much confidence and determination, just like now.

"Why?" I ask, tone quiet.

"It's tragic," she says simply. "Nine girls dying on what was supposed to be an auspicious day...But also, isn't it strange?"

Another person's voice overlaps hers—deep and feminine, like the matured tone of a middle-aged woman. A thin, angular face surfaces in her thoughts—Adarsh, her mother. "Do not forget why you are entering the temple," Adarsh tells Medha. There is no trace of affection in her tone, as if Medha were a servant and not her flesh-and-blood daughter.

Could it be...Had Medha's mother drilled her to ask about my Selection? Does her family suspect something? "No stranger than innocent folk getting murdered by lawless bandits on the roads," I reply.

"Binsa, you were there that day. Didn't you feel that anything was amiss?"

I part my lips under the pretence of mild confusion. My fingers curl into fists under the desk. "I was too young to remember anything. I'm sorry I can't satisfy your curiosity," I say, pulling on an apologetic mask.

Lie. I remember everything about that day—every single detail. The exquisite necklace that hung around one girl's nape, woven with glass beads; the elaborate knots another girl had on her head; the mixture of anxiety and excitement fluttering across their features. The way the chief priest—Harun's father, a thin, sallow man with a listless smile named Baryak—scoured his eyes over the line of girls and poured out the purifying wine in tiny wooden bowls for us to drink.

I remember watching as each of the girls lifted the bowls to their lips, one by one, sip by sip, until their bowls were emptied.

Gurrehmat's face flashes before me—his drunken confidence in the idea that the girls were killed using blood magic. How the Ghanatukh priests and the Council of Shamanism swept his opinions aside—or so he thought.

Gods. They all had ten years to come after me about the Bloodbath. Why are they all popping up only now? I am supposed to retire soon anyway; what use is it investigating me? Why can't the dead just rest in peace? Why can't I be allowed to forget?

Why is everything insistent on haunting me?

"Do you think Chandri knows what happened that day?" A huge grin is plastered on Medha's face. "Some parts of the Sacred Scrolls were really strange. Maybe she has the answers!"

I almost forgot about the Sacred Scrolls; the words of my predecessors have evidently done little to tamp her capricious nature. With a sigh, I push Privindu's book aside and intertwine my fingers on the table. "One: If Chandri knew the truth of the Bloodbath, she would have done something about it." I speak in a slow, patient voice. "Two: What is so strange about the Sacred Scrolls? Do you doubt the wisdom penned by our previous Rakhtis?"

"No! Of course not. But . . ." she says, frowning. "I didn't understand what she was saying."

"What part did you not understand?"

Truth is, I cannot remember the Sacred Scrolls anymore, the words I had learned through rote memorisation long forgotten. It's as though my memory of them has faded, along with my memories of Chandri. Frustration wells in me, as it always does when I try to remember my predecessor but fail to do so. I'm sure that the Sacred Scrolls were a significant part of my time spent with her. But what—

My attention snaps back to the library—Medha flaps her arms angrily. "You just have to believe me—there's something strange about them! I'm old enough to tell when something is off!"

I stare at her, like a mother would a mischievous child whose antics stretch on for too long. Ykta shakes his head in sympathy.

"I would tell you to go see Chandri about this, but a Rakhti is officially cut off from the temple she served after she retires," I say. "That means she can never step back into Ghanatukh, nor can she see anyone working for the temple. She can also never meet anyone who *used* to work in the temple."

Medha's eyes widen with puzzlement. "Why?"

"Temple traditions," I answer shortly. My brows furrow. Why is it that I've never questioned these rules? If I could see Chandri, I would get my answ—

The crease between my brows smooths out. I give Medha a placid look.

Dissatisfaction broils in the girl, so intense that it singes my skin.

"Fine," I relent. "I'll look through Chandri's Sacred Scrolls. Happy?"

Her temper quickly dissipates. She beams at me, the cheeky little brat. "Thank you, Binsa! If you want to, I can recite everything for you now."

Ykta and I regard her with surprise. "You remember *everything*?" my brother asks.

She nods. "I only had to read through them a few times. It's easy enough."

I seethe internally at her flippant, careless tone. There are dozens upon dozens of those scrolls. I need to work hard over the span of a few weeks to recall the contents of one book, and she just... remembers everything.

I rein my irritation in. She does not mean any harm by it. To others, it is her gift. To her, perhaps it is normal.

"No need. I'll read it myself." I clear my books and prepare to leave the library.

Ykta raps his knuckles against the table. "It's time to start studying, Shira-Rakhti. I expect you to be able to recite the exact order of the Rakhti's instalments and the years of their reigns by the end of the week."

"You're joking," Medha gasps.

"You asked for it."

Medha releases a dramatic groan. I catch Ykta's eye and flash him a grateful smile. He answers with the smallest of nods, then fully focuses on Medha's lesson.

As I make for Medha's room to fetch the scrolls, Ilam cackles at me. I sigh.

I've been utterly beguiled by a little girl.

While Medha is occupied with her lessons, I line up the ten Sacred Scrolls written by Chandri in chronological order. I need to do this in front of the little girl to prove that I am taking her seriously. Her attention briefly flickers towards me, but a scolding from Ykta quickly draws her back to her work.

I emit a quick huff and skim through the first scroll.

Something invisible slams into me.

I gasp for air. I can't. Whatever has slammed into me is holding me down. My vision blurs at the edges.

I look down. I am holding a quill in one hand.

And these hands aren't mine.

In fact, my entire body isn't mine. It's stronger, sturdier, my skin smoother and less pallid. I draw in a deep breath and expel it before pressing the tip of the quill against paper.

> The twenty-first of the month of Burlak, the spring of the 499th year of the Age of Steel.
>
> The duties of a Rakhti are taxing, but I am glad I took on this burden. I am certain that the Rakhtis coming after me will find this sentiment true as well. The goddess in me is real—and she has the power to shape our world. It is an honour to partake in this, and you will also achieve many great things with Rashmatun.
>
> Fret not if the goddess's voice is overbearing. Fret not if the weight of being Rakhti seems too heavy to bear. Remember this—Rashmatun chose you for a reason. These are my first words of wisdom to you, the Shira-Rakhtis who come after me: You are stronger than you

know. Your identity is intertwined with Rashmatun's, but that does not mean you are not your own person. Trust in your own judgment, and trust in your own discretion. If all else fails, look to Anas's eyes for guidance.

There is little hesitation in my writing—every stroke is broad and sure, and I do not scratch anything off.

"I wonder if she will understand everything one day," I murmur. This voice isn't mine. It's too lilting, too refined, too *kind*. It sounds too familiar.

Chandri.

Just as I make the connection, the world spins before me.

Then I am back in my own body. I inhale, savouring every breath. I lift my arms, check my fingers, my clothes. They are all mine—Binsa's.

What just happened? I ask Ilam.

How am I supposed to know? he snarls.

My muscles freeze in shock. Ilam is hostile, his anger a glowing ember at the back of my mind, about to spark and set everything on fire.

Why is he so agitated?

Keep reading, Ilam instructs me.

My hand hovers over the next scroll. I grit my teeth; I cannot allow fear to overtake me at this point. This is my only connection to Chandri right now—and I need to know what went on in her head while she was writing all this.

I grab the scroll.

The same sensations wash over me—something punching me in the gut, my vision blurring before sharpening. I have Chandri's hands again, and the air is warmer, brighter. I look outside the window. The pale blue of the spring sky envelops my city in a gentle embrace.

I turn back to the empty parchment before me and begin to write.

The twenty-third of the month of Burlak, the spring of the 500th year of the Age of Steel.

It is a well-known secret that the life of a Rakhti is frequently envied, for it promises riches and blessings beyond
comprehension. However, the path ahead is treacherous,
and it will take and take and take from you. Take courage, nevertheless. Know that you have sacrificed the life
you were promised for the good of our people.

Where does this courage come from? It lives in your
heart. Rashmatun's strength lies within us as well; if you
do not know where to find it, look to the snake's yellow,
discerning eyes.

I pause at the last stroke of the final letter. My arms are heavy.
With a sigh, I set the stationery aside. A breeze tickles the backs of
my ears.

A tear slides down my cheek.

The vision fades, and I am back in my own body. I lift a hand to
my cheek; it is dry. Yet my limbs are shaking. Ilam is still seething.
I became Chandri, but I did not know what she was thinking. I
could only physically experience what she had done. What magic
is this? Is it only channelled through the Sacred Scrolls?

Or perhaps I am shaking because this is the closest I've been to
her ever since she left.

I recall the warm touch of her hand as she guided me to first read
the Sacred Scrolls. I recall her face, calm and beautiful and perfect,
growing stern when I failed to recite a passage.

"You must remember all the words of the Rakhtis before you,
Binsa," she had told me. "Especially mine."

For once, her memory does not slip away from my grasp.

I sit still for a few seconds, stupefied. It's as though a fog has been
lifted from my mind. I remember Chandri. I remember the lilt of her
voice, the way she could coax and command at the rise and fall of a
tone. I remember how she had braided my hair and woven flowers into
it, marvelling at its length and silkiness. I remember her poised demeanour, her measured movements—a mannerism befitting a goddess.

I study the words before me. Each of them is now so dear and
familiar, as if I had found a long-lost friend.

All this while, I could have remembered her if I looked at the Sacred Scrolls again.

This begets another question: How did I forget her in the first place?

Who would want you to forget Chandri? Ilam suddenly says.

Gooseflesh prickles all over my arms at his sinister tone. *Kavita?*

He hums in answer.

But why? What benefit would she have if I forgot about Chandri? She treated me like a sister, and she had been so kind to me—

Realisation strikes me cold. It is precisely because Chandri treated me like a sister that Kavita couldn't allow me to remember her. My attachment to Chandri had been so strong that it would have affected my loyalty to Kavita. In the long run, it would have diminished my fear of her.

She could easily slip into minds and manipulate them, Ilam had said of Kavita.

Anger and discomfort churn in my belly, creating an indiscernible mess that turns my world upside down. I had an inkling that she manipulated other people—but her own daughter. She manipulated my mind. She forced me to become her puppet, a stepping stone for her to obtain power. How much of my memories of her are true, and how much are false? Is the reality I know a falsehood constructed by her hands?

When does a falsehood become truth? Privindu had written. *Very simply, when you believe it to be true.*

I curl my fingers on the desk, nearly crumpling the Sacred Scrolls.

A chortle escapes me. Ykta and Medha shoot me curious glances; I wave a dismissive hand and ignore them.

Lies. So many lies. My position is built upon a lie. My own memories were a lie.

I've never been happier that I killed Kavita myself.

Why did Kavita's enchantment break now, of all times? I ask Ilam. *Is it something to do with the Sacred Scrolls?*

Every armour has its chink. Likewise, every enchantment has its undoing, the demon replies, surprisingly straightforward. *Mind manipulation can only be done at the cost of attaching a weakness to it—and the stronger the manipulation, the easier the illusion will fall apart once it's discovered. More precisely, touching an object of significant importance to the target will make them recall their real memories. Since you hadn't touched the Sacred Scrolls since Chandri left . . .*

I forgot her, I complete the sentence.

He allows me to sink into a grieving silence. Chandri was gone from my life for so long that not all my memories of her are back—they trickle in like the remnants of a thunderstorm dripping down a roof. But with what little I know, maybe I can find out more about the truth of the Rakhtas—and the gods that are supposed to sit behind them.

Me becoming Chandri is clear evidence of magic.

Magic I need to learn, even if I do not know its nature.

I return my attention to the scrolls. Chandri had told me to remember her writing. I need to find out why. I trace my fingers on the letterings of the first scroll. I do not fall into her body this time; are there hidden conditions that Chandri placed to trigger the enchantment? There's only one way to find out.

I read the rest of the scrolls.

Each time, I fall into her experience. Her chest weighs heavier with each scroll she writes, and even though her words appear confident, the tremor in her hands indicates anything but. Strangely, I understand her less and less as I read more of her words. The last scroll, in particular, is so dissonant from the others that if I didn't see the world through Chandri's eyes, I would have scarcely believed she wrote it.

The fifteenth of the month of Sarthek, the spring of the 500th year of the Age of Steel.

The yellow sapphire, the holy stone of Rashmatun, is widely regarded as a gem that channels the energies of wisdom and vitality. It is no coincidence, then, that I am writing this in Sarthek, the month of the great star of Nuris, which ancient tales prescribe as the origin of the yellow sapphire itself, believing the golden stones to have fallen from the brightest light in the night sky. The goddess Rashmatun herself also favours this stone, although her reasons are lost upon me.

However, looking at the gem itself, I think I have gained an inkling of understanding as to why it is coveted by the goddess. There is familiarity and warmth in its multifaceted depths; shamans claim that it enhances feminine energy, and that is possibly why we vessels of Rashmatun are drawn to it. If you happen to be in possession of a yellow sapphire, do not ever lose it.

As Chandri, I lean back in my seat and gaze up at the ceiling. My shoulders slump—in relief or despair, I cannot tell. "Is this enough?" I whisper.

My hand drifts towards the yellow sapphire hanging around my neck. It takes me a while to realise that it is I, not Chandri, who is touching it.

Now I remember that it was Chandri who gave me the pendant towards the end of her tenure, when I was soon to be crowned Rakhti. "Do not ever lose this," she had said. "The goddess will bless you through it."

No wonder it has always brought me great comfort.

But why dedicate an entire scroll to this subject? I am aware that the yellow sapphire is Rashmatun's favoured stone, and it is embedded in all reliefs and sculptures of the goddess. But what does this have to do with "taking courage" or "trusting oneself," or any other virtue of a Rakhti? And why is she speaking of Rashmatun as though she actually exists?

Is there something I'd missed somewhere?

I prop my elbows on the table and massage my temples.

Quite an interesting piece of work, your predecessor, Ilam comments. His uneasiness ripples throughout my body.

Have you any idea of what she is trying to say?

No response.

I suppress a sigh. The somewhat helpful demon from earlier is gone. Of course. I should have expected this.

I must find a way to contact Chandri—ask her what her words mean in person. But no temple dweller is allowed to see former Rakhtis. Not even Ykta, who is considered an outlier here. Who can I get to help me?

An idea stirs in my head: Keran, my only true connection to the outside world.

I rebind the scrolls and set them aside. I get up, the legs of my chair scraping against the floor. The noise breaks Medha's focus. She sneaks glances at me, excitement radiating off her in waves. I try to block her musings from my mind and disappear into a secluded corner of the library.

"Ykta, there's something here!" I holler.

"What is it? Let me see!" Medha cries out instead.

My brother scolds her, and she silently goes back to events and dates. His footsteps scuffle towards me.

"I tried following a whole host of priests," he reports unprompted. "Nothing. But I checked around the city for recent purchases of at least a dozen goats. The only transactions of the sort lead back to Ghanatukh Temple. To the Selection."

I gnaw on my fingertips. Right. The goats. Which I assigned him to investigate.

"Did you manage to see the receipts of those transactions?" I ask.

He draws a stack of slips from his pouch and waves it in front of my nose. "You didn't need to ask."

I take them and sift through the receipts. They're not originals, but copies signed and stamped by the vendors. "Good work, but this isn't enough evidence."

"Well, the problem is, I'm not sure what other evidence we can get. Since the goats seem to drop at random and their corpses are burned almost immediately, there is hardly a trace we can follow— it'd be harder still to try to link them to the Ghanatukh priests."

"Check the rhododendron bushes in the main courtyard," I say.

He stares at me. "Why?"

"Just trust me. You'll find the goats."

His brows furrow. "You knew all along?"

I pause before answering: "I just found out myself."

"How?"

I open my mouth, but no plausible excuse comes to mind. I can tell him that I smelled the stench, but considering how everyone else around me didn't seem to notice it, he wouldn't be able to detect the rot either. Then he would ask how I developed such an unnaturally keen sense, and maybe—just maybe—he would remember how Kavita too had unnatural senses, and always knew where to find us even though we always changed our hiding spots and made sure to cover our tracks.

Who's to say your magic doesn't come from Rashmatun? Ilam suggests.

You . . . really want me to tell him that? I reply in disbelief.

He may have been witness to Kavita's blood magic, but he does not know its intricacies, Ilam scoffs. *He's in no position to question you or where your power comes from. Besides, it will be far easier for you to pass off any future instances of when you tap into my power.*

If you say so . . . Though I am reluctant, Ilam is right. Magic is the one topic I will be able to successfully bluff my way through with Ykta.

"I think Rashmatun's magic is returning to me," I say, keeping my cadence meek, unsure. "She hasn't appeared to me yet, but I can now use traces of her power. I used it to sense the goat carcasses around Ghanatukh Temple."

His countenance stills. "When did you discover this?"

"Just before we learned that Harun was organising a Rakhti Selection."

Ilam cackles, amused by how the lie slips out so easily.

Why did she tell me to investigate the falling goats, then, if she was planning to do everything herself? Ykta thinks, both miffed and confused. *I could have devoted my time to doing something else. And how did I not realise she has magic? Gods. I'm such a dimwit.*

It leads to a despondent train of thoughts: *Maybe that's why I feel like she's not telling me everything. Maybe that's why she isn't listening to me. I haven't fully earned her trust yet.*

I'm truly a fool.

My heart twists in my chest. I lace my hands behind my back and cast him a pleading look. "I need another favour, though. There's only so much my magic can do." Hopefully this will make him feel involved.

I need to give him a reason to continue working for me.

His gaze is full of doubt. "What is it?"

"Get Keran to find Chandri."

He quirks a brow. "Now you want to seek her out? What about all those times I asked you if you wanted to find her before?"

Had he? Maybe my recollections of his offers also faded, since they're connected to Chandri. But I don't have the energy to deal with his overwhelming bitterness. I cannot help him sort out all his unresolved regrets. "There's something else I need to ask her about." I fold my arms across my chest. "It's about the Sacred Scrolls."

"You could share them with me," he says. "I could help you decipher them."

I shift on my feet. He's right. Having Ykta read the Sacred Scrolls would make my life so much easier. Yet trepidation seizes me.

Ykta recognises my hesitation, and questions flood his mind, knotting his thoughts into an ugly tangle. *Why didn't she try to look for Chandri earlier? Does she actually want to remain Rakhti? And if she's had magic for a while now, what else is she not telling me?*

I'm sorry, Ykta, I think. *I have to do this. For you and me both.*

"You're a big enough help by contacting Keran," I try to assure him. He mirrors my posture and folds his arms.

"Whatever helps you, Binsa," he mutters. "My life is devoted in service to you."

"Thank you." I flash a grin; I hope he doesn't notice the tension in it. "Your services will not go unforgotten."

He tries to remain upset, but I am still his little sister, he thinks. He needs to be a reliable elder sibling. "I expect two months' worth of bonuses," he says. "And extra allowance for alcohol."

12

A Gathering Storm

The temple bustles with activity three days later, more so than usual. Instead of being carted to the cleansing hall to summon Rashmatun, I am clothed in a pale yellow jama, its hems embroidered with gold. The handmaidens dress me with an air of unusual reverence; Jirtash braids and pins my hair into a topknot with a stoic expression. Nali stands to the side after being explicitly ordered by Jirtash to not serve me at all, lest her touch brings me bad fortune.

It is the day I am to summon rain.

Today, I ride on the palanquin by myself; Medha marches alongside the small procession surrounding me. We are to make our way towards the base camp of the Yaborun range. From there, I will make the ascent alone.

Harun had raised his concerns to Rashmatun, if her vessel would be able to survive the hike with her frail body, without an entourage to accompany her. In return, Rashmatun silenced him with a question—if she wasn't able to protect her own vessel, would she be able to protect everyone else?

In truth, I need to be alone so that Ilam can work his power without any witnesses.

The sure, steady pace of the palanquin bearers falters as the flattened ground beneath them gives way to an unpaved, rocky path. Each step between them requires extra effort to push forward in synchrony. Even though we are in the dead of summer, a cold wind from the direction of the mountains gusts past us, biting my cheeks.

After nearly half an hour of walking, we arrive at the base camp. I exit the palanquin, my bare feet finding hard, jagged purchase beneath. I look at the mountain range, regarding the sight in awe. Its tallest peaks almost seem to graze the sky, their tips still glistening with white despite the sun beating overhead. Historians recorded that Aritsyans traditionally worshipped objects of nature before the Forebears came to walk among mortals. It's not difficult to understand why.

I wheel around to face the procession. It's a small one compared to the enormous fanfare that escorted me through the streets of Bakhtin on the day of the Selection. Only the boruvindas—the highest-ranking priests of the temple—and Medha have been allowed to accompany me.

"Well," I begin, projecting the image of a girl unused to making eloquent speeches, "I'll be off."

She couldn't have found out already, right? How else could she be so confident? Nudin suddenly thinks. His expression remains as immovable as the mountain. *Oh well, I'll find out soon enough.*

What on earth does that mean? I want to ask.

"May Rashmatun bless your journey," Harun says.

Collectively, the priests press their palms together and mutter incantations. The chanting swells into a rich, sonorous note. The air around me shifts, its temperature rising. An invisible cloak of warmth engulfs me like a second skin. The yellow sapphire I wear grows warm. Just like how it always has when the priests use their magic, I now remember.

"The priests of Ghanatukh wish you all the best, Binsa," Harun says. "May Rashmatun succeed, for the sake of Bakhtin."

I hope the climb won't kill her. His only thought amid the quietness of his mind—and a stark contrast to the palpable excitement of the surrounding priests.

I wonder if the rest of the priests truly agree with his schemes, or if they are all unwitting pawns. Not like it matters; in the end, if they partook in Harun's plan to drop the goats, they are also complicit in the murders of several innocent people.

More importantly, they are also complicit in turning against me.

Outwardly, I give him a nod and a smile. Then I turn around and begin my trek.

My entire body burns; my lungs heave for air. My pace has slowed considerably, but I know that I have barely climbed for five minutes. I continue to push myself forward, desperate to put as much distance as possible between me and the procession.

Get out of sight, Ilam hisses. *With the way you're moving, it'll take an entire year before we reach the peak.*

Easier said than done, I retort. Still, I duck behind a large boulder, huffing and panting. It has grown colder, yet sweat films all over my body. I want to rip off the spell that the priests had cast over me. It protects me from the cold and suffocates my breathing at the same time.

Enough dawdling, Ilam snaps. *We don't have time to waste.*

He engulfs my mind.

Dark smoke wreathes out of my body, and adrenaline rushes through my limbs. My power is raw, unbridled, like a wild horse galloping free through untamed plains. I instinctively *know* that I can leap up to the peak of Aratiya in a single bound. And if I wanted to, I could probably run the entirety of Aritsya.

But this body is mine no longer.

Laughter escapes my mouth—Ilam's. My limbs crackle with unstoppered magic, as if they were on fire. An image flashes in my mind: Kavita, cackling over a mangled body, her hands stained with blood, eyes glowing red, and smoke curling over her frame. Fear clenches my heart—fear of blood magic, of what it is capable of doing and what it turns the shaman into.

Yet a trill of excitement runs through me as well.

"Are you ready?" Ilam asks, using my voice.

Yes, I answer.

He brings his magic to a searing heat that gathers in my core. My body is not strong enough—it cannot hold his magic. Sooner or later, it will disintegrate or collapse upon itself and burst into flames.

That doesn't happen. Ilam is controlling his power. Enough to push the boundaries of my capacity, but stopping just short of destroying me.

An odd sense of comfort blankets me when Ilam crouches and springs towards the sky.

The wind roars past my ears. The chilly mountain air permeates deep into my bones, yet I do not feel anything. I am weightless, soaring upwards; a mountain eagle glides above my head, and I yearn to fly past it. The world is beneath my feet, and everything that happens down there—the people, their lives, the disputes that are inevitable between them—is all insignificant. From up here, they are nothing.

A laugh escapes me, the sound carried away by the wind and dissipating into the atmosphere.

It takes me a moment to realise that the laugh is mine, not Ilam's.

We leap our way towards Llaon, the abandoned prison that had been dismantled during Chandri's reign. It was a storehouse for extremely dangerous criminals. Murderers, traitors, and the like—people who cleaved themselves off from society.

If I am ever convicted of my crimes, the people might just demand the reopening of Llaon to throw me in.

The prison itself is a cluster of crude and unpolished buildings, carved on a small plateau halfway up the mountain. Yet it remains one of the most prominent architectural accomplishments of Bakhtin; the various holes blasted into the mountain face extend into a web of tunnels that run deep into Mount Aratiya. A thin layer of snow covers the plateau, lending a sense of evanescence to the scene. I would have marvelled at the sight if I didn't know the history behind it.

We turn away from Llaon and face the open sky. It is strange to have Ilam and myself moving as one. Even though he has taken over my body, I too am controlling my frame. All this time, I feared the potential of blood magic. I cautioned against its side effects, afraid of the madness that slowly overtakes blood shamans, and how dearly it costs everyone around them.

But in this moment, I can understand why Kavita was intoxicated by her own power.

And I can see everything.

I see the procession, still waiting at the base camp above Ghanatukh. I see the temple itself, its red-and-gold roofs shimmering like dragon scales under the sun. I see my city, the masses of buildings that are so closely sequestered they seem like beehives. I see the basin that holds my city, a series of jagged teeth that ring the buildings, and I see the rivers that flow into Bakhtin, ribboning through the arteries of the city, before pooling at Lake Minya to the south.

This is the view of a deity, standing high above the world.

Ilam lifts our arms. His power surges through me once more. Purple smoke coalesces at my fingertips.

"Now," he says, "we become a god."

My pulse quickens. Ilam's smoke curls into the sky, beckoning the clouds to come. Here I am, standing above Bakhtin, Ilam's power thrumming in my veins. This is it.

I am about to use blood magic to summon rain.

There is no turning back after this. No more room for repentance nor regret.

"Binsa, whatever happens now," Ilam says, as though responding to the sudden influx of worries clogging my head, "know that it is your choice."

That's right. This is my choice. I chose to stay on the Scarlet Throne for as long as I could. I chose to kill Gurrehmat and Yhadin.

I chose to become a goddess.

"And whatever you do," Ilam adds, "do not give in to the pain."

What pain? I want to ask.

A surge of fire overtakes me before I can voice the question.

A choked cry escapes my throat. Tears stream down my face as pure, distilled torture strangles my insides. The agony I'd experienced when I'd first struck the contract with Ilam is nothing compared to this. The skin at my fingertips begins to peel off, blackening and cracking in decay. The rot spreads to my hands and snakes down my arms at a horrifying speed.

The same rot that killed the girls at the Bloodbath.

The rot of blood magic.

Please, I think. *Make it stop.*

Ilam flares his magic instead.

Slowly but surely, my mind sinks into an abyss, numbing itself to the pain. Yet the magic that courses through me pounds a relentless rhythm, refusing to loosen its grip, cresting higher, higher, higher—

Then I sense it—just as surely as Ilam has. The scattered threads of our magic latching on to something, reeling it in and twining it all together.

Clouds, I surmise. Or water droplets, at least.

Ilam stretches our arms and makes a dragging motion that resembles a fisherman hauling his catch. Through the fire that smogs my consciousness, I sense his magic growing tighter, tauter—as if it were a tapestry being woven with a million different threads, each a different thickness, a different length. He fumbles with the threads, grabbing random parts and attempting to bind them.

As the tapestry grows bigger, so does the torture afflicting my body.

Endure, I tell myself, even as my peeling skin gives way to bright red blood flushing out of the wounds. Endure, even as my body feels as though it might crumble into dust.

In fact, it *will* crumble to dust if Ilam doesn't finish the job soon. His knowledge—now my knowledge—slaps me cold.

Help me bend the clouds to our will, he says. *If you do not wish to die here.*

Determination reignites in me. I do not know how, but I help Ilam search for his threads and braid them into intricate loops. *Do my bidding,* I tell the clouds, pouring all of my will and ambition into them, as if they can hear me and succumb to my resolve.

Come to me, I call out to them. *Obey your goddess!*

And obey they do.

Ilam flares our magic in one last burst. I scream as the rot spikes up my arms.

It is the push needed to knot the final piece in place. Ilam retracts his magic just as quickly as he had released it. My knees buckle under me.

The frost of the mountain winds spears deep into my marrow. The cloak of warmth that the priests had cast over me provides some relief, but is little protection against the cold. I double over, both gasping for air and heaving in pain, huddling into myself automatically in an attempt to shield against the treacherous mountain weather. Coughs start to wrack my frame.

Something dribbles out of my mouth. Red spots bloom on the snow beneath me.

Ilam, I cry in dismay.

Get inside the prison. You need to rest before we can make the descent.

Despite protesting muscles, I manage to drag myself into the nearest building, slipping through an archway and taking cover behind the wall, the wind breaking over my head.

The coughs do not subside; more blood spurts out my mouth.

I grossly overestimated your body's capacity, Ilam remarks.

Can't you just heal me?

I already did. Look at your hands.

And there they are, my skin repaired and smooth and unmarred, a sharp contrast to the decay that spread through them earlier.

Healing you requires more of your soulstream, Ilam explains. *The more I take from it, the more I'll destroy your body.*

That doesn't make sense. You heal me, but destroy me at the same time?

Why do you think the strongest blood shamans are those who have remarkable vitality or an infinite supply of soulstream? Ilam snorts. *Blood magic is a contract, Binsa. A give and a take. You cannot create something from nothing.*

I wrap my arms around myself, shivering uncontrollably. This is how Kavita managed to conceal all her ugly sides from the world; one night I would see her skin greyed out and peppered with black splotches, and the next morning I would see her hale and hearty and glowing. How much soulstream had she consumed to maintain that power? How long would she have survived, if I hadn't killed her?

What would have happened to me if I'd tried to summon rain without killing Gurrehmat and Yhadin?

Their faces suddenly flash before my eyes. Gurrehmat's horrified expression as Ilam unfurled before him. The confused glaze over Yhadin's eyes as I slashed my dagger across her throat.

I remember Kavita's face, the smile she wore even as I stabbed her, her life rapidly bleeding out of her.

I pull my knees in tight, banishing those images from my mind.

Gurrehmat and Yhadin sacrificed their lives for this—for rain that would bless Bakhtin and make its land thrive once more. I must remind myself of that. They didn't die for nothing. Their lives meant something, unlike the millions of meaningless names that came before them.

The coughs gradually die down. But my head is still light, and my limbs are as heavy as logs. Fatigue cocoons me, a cool yet comforting blanket that drags me into a void—

Fool. Ilam's voice jerks me awake. *Do not fall asleep.*

I blink my eyes blearily. I remember stories about unfortunate hikers who aimed to conquer Aratiya, about how their excellent physical condition was little use against the constant cold pervading the mountainous region. Instinctively, I clutch the yellow sapphire through my kurta.

I take solace in its familiarity, knowing it is Chandri's last gift to me.

I need to find out what she meant in the Sacred Scrolls, and how she implanted her memories into them. I need to understand why Medha is so intent on Chandri and the Bloodbath. And above all, I need to prove my worth to the people of Bakhtin. To accomplish that, I cannot die on this mountain, stuck in an abandoned, dilapidated prison.

Let's go back, I say.

Are you sure your body has recovered enough? If he weren't a demon, I might think he is genuinely concerned.

It'll just grow worse the longer I stay here.

I cannot deny that, Ilam concedes.

I lean against the wall for support as I stand up. Every inch of me screams, begging to lie down and take a nap. I force myself to remain upright, my posture squared and dignified—the posture I use as Rashmatun.

Ilam's magic fills my veins once more.

The descent is far less exhilarating than the ascent. I am completely spent, and my senses are clouded. I barely register the uncomfortable burn throughout my limbs, the buzzing in my ears. We flurry down the steep mountain face, which slopes into a more gradual incline.

Before I know it, we've arrived at the same boulder I had hidden behind before we ascended Aratiya. "You'll have to return to the camp alone," Ilam says as I rest against its pocked surface.

Of course, I reply.

"Can you do it?"

In spite of my exhaustion, I manage a snort. *Who do you think I am?*

Ilam laughs. "Don't die, Binsa."

He retracts his magic. I crumple onto the ground, coughing up more blood. I wipe my mouth with the back of my hand. My skin comes away stained with scarlet. I quickly wipe off as much blood as I can against the boulder.

Get up, I tell myself. *You can't stay here forever.*

I grit my teeth, forcing myself to my feet. One foot forward, then another. I trudge down the slope, nearly slipping and tumbling a few times. The air grows warmer, to my relief. I keep my eyes pinned on the speck of buildings in the distance, and the people flittering around it.

Eventually, the priests spot me as well. They huddle together near the start of the trek, forming a semicircle. They do not help me down.

I am the Rakhti of Bakhtin. I need to make this descent to prove this to them.

One last push, I think. *One foot before the other.*

Then they are right before me, little Medha at the centre of the semicircle. Her bright, eager eyes are widened in amazement and wonder.

"It is done," I declare, fighting to keep the fatigue out of my voice.

Thunder rumbles in the distance.

I lift my chin. Dark, grey clouds have amassed near the peak of Aratiya. From the direction of the wind, the clouds will make their way towards the city itself. They are heavy, filled with the promise of rain.

They were created by me.

I am proud of you, daughter dearest. Kavita's voice tickles my ears, though maybe it is a trick of the wind.

"Rakhti Binsa," the priests chime in unison. They press their hands together in reverence and bow their heads.

Harun's conflicting feelings clang through the fog cloaking my head—relief at my safe return, and confusion.

What does Rashmatun want? he thinks.

I smile at all of them. "Rashmatun has brought her blessings upon us."

I pitch forward into darkness.

13

Days Long Past

I settle into a long, suffocating dream. Snatches of half-forgotten memories play in my head. Saran and I running through the streets of Dharun. My mother rankling over the debts Papa left us after he died. The day she struck her first official contract with Ilam, the demon's tiny peacock form somehow menacing and overwhelming in our ramshackle house.

Then my head is cradled in her lap as she gently smooths my hair. Our room is small, its rough clay walls the only place we can call home. A scrawny boy squats in a corner, using a stick to poke the fire beneath a makeshift stove. A lullaby hums in the air, its tone oddly melancholic, uneasiness wedging between its intonations.

"When will the Prophecy of Geerkha come to pass, Mama?" I ask.

"No one knows," she replies. The lullaby still sings in my ears. "Shamans and seers alike have tried to predict its occurrence. None have managed to unravel its mystery."

"Do you think Rashmatun will know?"

She laughs. "Of course. Rashmatun is the goddess of wisdom, who knows all and sees all. That is why you must become her Rakhti, Binsa. So she can answer all the questions you pose."

I nibble on my lower lip. "What if Rashmatun does not choose me, Mama?"

Her strokes against my hair stiffen. "You *will* become Rakhti, Binsa." Her tone is soft, but there is a surety in her words that leaves no room for defiance. "I will make sure you do."

I turn around. Her face is mostly obscured by the shadows, but the little light in the room highlights her sharp features—once proud and beautiful, now too angular to be considered attractive. She's been working herself to the bone ever since Papa died, and my chest tightens.

"I'll help you, Mama," I say. "So I'll always listen to you."

Her touch turns gentle again. "Good girl."

The scene fades. I am transported into Kreyda Gopal's mansion. Kreyda himself is a lower-ranked kishari, born into a formerly illustrious line of advisors who all claim to be descendants of Guphalon, the fifth Forebear and the god of luck. The Gopal family had been well-respected until one of their members was caught in a corruption scandal a few decades ago; now they live simple lives compared to the opulence they once enjoyed. Their residence feels like a palace to me, nonetheless.

I wander down the hall. Heat clings to my skin, and the scent of roaring stoves fills my nostrils. I am then peering at Kavita at the entrance of the kitchen, observing as the head chef snaps at her for messing up the dishes again. She presses her lips together, seething, yet not making a sound.

The head chef flings a bowl of gravy at her.

She flinches; still she does not say anything.

"Only the gods know why our master hired you," the head chef snarls. "You cannot clean, you cannot cook, you cannot sew. What good are you as a woman? No wonder your husband died—perhaps he found it better to depart from this world than to be confined to a wretch like you for the rest of his life!"

Her frame trembles. She remains silent.

In a split second, we are whisked into our quarters. It's an upgrade from our previous residence, with its walls free of cracks and sturdy, simple furniture filling the space. Kavita is combing through my hair, unravelling its knots before retying it into an intricate braid.

"Mama, why are we here?" I ask.

"Because we need to survive, Binsa," she answers quietly. "Because we need a kishari."

"Why a kishari, Mama?"

"A kishari will be able to vouch for your eligibility for the next Rakhti Selection."

I frown. "But I'm not a kishari's daughter."

She yanks on my braid; a yelp escapes my mouth. "Hush now," she murmurs. "You promised you would help me, right? You said you would always listen to me. So listen to me now, Binsa."

I puff out my cheeks. Then I remember seeing her in the kitchens earlier that day, how she endured the bullying. A poor nobody from Dharun, the servants had whispered among themselves—someone who did not even deserve to step foot inside this mansion.

I have to help Mama. So I nod my head in acquiescence.

A richly embroidered jama suddenly replaces my plain daura-suruwal, its skirt full and heavy. I am no longer in the servants' quarters. Instead, I am in a spacious room that is larger than our entire house back in Dharun. Grandiloquent furnishings and intricate tapestries occupy the area.

Kavita stands before me. The gauntness that had haunted her in Dharun is gone, and her skin seems to glow from within. Her lips are painted red, as full and luscious as scarlet rhododendrons.

There is a boy of about twelve years old in the room. My brother. He hangs by the sides, as if he has always wrapped himself in shadows. His face is beautiful and handsome at the same time—Kavita's face, but with a distinct tinge of masculinity to it.

"Binsa, you know what you must do," Kavita says. A cage appears in her hands. Inside, there is a yowling cat, its feet bound in ropes.

She puts the cage down and extracts the cat, placing it at my feet.

I stare at the animal before me, its feline form coated in black, its eyes a hideous yellow.

"Binsa," Kavita says. I look up. The handle of a kukri has been thrust towards me. I gingerly take it from her grip. The weapon is heavier than it looks, and I almost drop it.

My hands shake. I take a deep breath, trying to steady myself.

I raise the knife above the cat, its tip aimed at the creature's throat.

Do it, I tell myself. *Do it for Mama.*

Saran dashes forward and wrenches the kukri out of my hand. He wheels around and glares at Kavita, fury radiating from him. "Stop it!" he yells. "Can't you see that she doesn't want to do it? She's *crying*!"

I am. Tears are streaming down my cheeks.

She sneers at him, as though his very presence defiles her. "What do you know? She is destined for great things, Saran. Far greater things than you could ever accomplish. Do not forget that you are only here because she likes you."

"And do not forget that *you* only managed to marry Kreyda Gopal because I helped sow distrust between him and his wife," he says darkly.

"Upon my orders," she scoffs. "You know nothing, fool boy. Stand aside."

"No," he snaps, planting himself firmly between me and Kavita. "Isn't this enough? You're married to a kishari. You're no longer shunned. Aren't you satisfied?"

"My ambition and Binsa's extend far further than Bakhtin," she replies, her eyes glittering. They almost glow red. "Far beyond the imaginings of vermin like you."

Saran recoils, evidently stung by her words, but doesn't remove himself. "I'm your child as well, aren't I? I just want us to be happy!"

"Weak. Foolish. Just like your father." Kavita sighs, as if she were tired of a plaything. "Step aside. Or else."

"Or else what?"

She backhands him. The inhuman strength in her arm sends him flying across the room and crashing into the wall.

"Saran!" I shriek.

He slumps against the wall, his gaze unfocused. Blood seeps through his kurta and pools into a small puddle on the floor. He opens his mouth; no words come out. Kavita walks over to him. Rather than check on his injuries, she plucks the kukri from his grip and saunters back towards me.

"If you want me to heal him, do it," Kavita commands. She flexes her fingers, purple smoke wreathing around them.

I swallow a sob, taking the kukri from her again. I have to help Saran. I have to help Mama.

I approach the cat.

Someone is calling my name in the distance. *Binsa, Binsa, Binsa.* My first instinct is to block the voice out and try to sink back into sleep. I am so, so tired. Why can't they let me rest for a while longer?

The voice grows louder, more incessant. My mind is reeled out of a slush; my eyelids flutter open. I stare up at the ceiling of my room, its corners—in spite of Jirtash's best efforts—raided by spider-webs.

I blink once. My eyes are damp.

"She's awake! Thank Lithari," someone gasps. Jirtash, I recognise groggily. Had I been asleep for that long, for her to invoke the goddess of disasters and healing? "Binsa, do you hurt anywhere? Why are you crying?"

Why am I crying? Did something happen to me while I was asleep? Did Kavita come to haunt me again? Wait—yes, it had something to do with Kavita. I try to recall what exactly happened—

As if there were some part of my mind trying to protect me, I stop myself.

I shake my head, and my neck spasms. My bones ache. I move around experimentally. It hurts to even twitch a finger, so I just lie there, as still as a frozen lake in winter. I open my mouth to ask about what had happened; only a prolonged groan escapes.

"I'm not done," another voice rings out, soothing and husky, like the sound of a setting sun. "Her internals are still bleeding."

"Hurry up, then," a deeper, authoritative voice snaps.

"The healing cannot be rushed. I am merely helping her recover at a faster pace."

Only now do I notice a deep pool of warmth emanating from my belly. It possesses the same soothing quality as the woman's voice, a balm to relieve any wound. Then I notice that I am not on my bed—I am lying on the floor instead, a woven rug slipped beneath me.

Heat flows throughout my body, returning life to my limbs. I flex my wrist and raise my arm, splaying my fingers and peering at the ceiling through the gaps in between them.

"What happened?" I croak. My arm falls to the side.

"You were unconscious for three days," the deeper voice answers. Harun? But the timbre of his voice is different. "The physicians could not find a cure for your deteriorating health after they examined you, so *she* offered to help."

I blink, my gaze slowly sidling towards the figure kneeling beside me. It's Nali, her dark hair pulled into a severe knot at the nape of her neck. A sheen of sweat coats her forehead. She doesn't stop to wipe it away, keeping her hands hovering over my stomach.

Faint blue light glows from her palms. I spring upright, startled.

The sudden movement strains my muscles, and I collapse back onto the floor. Choked cries escape me.

"What did you do to her?" the man demands sharply. Enough of my focus has returned for me to see that it is Nudin. No wonder his voice sounded familiar.

What's he doing here? I wonder. *Where's Harun?*

"She strained herself," Nali replies. "Her body is not used to movement yet."

"Binsa, just lie down, all right?" Jirtash says.

Whatever Nali is doing, it's repairing my battered body. My senses return to me. I hear Jirtash's unsteady breathing, Nudin's disgruntled muttering. The rug beneath me is soft, woven with a sure and precise hand. Rain splatters against the walls, its erratic, subtle rhythm lending an air of tranquillity to the atmosphere.

Rain...

Elation sparks in me. I did it. I brought rain upon Bakhtin.

Then why are Jirtash and Nudin so glum?

"There. You can try to get up now, my Rakhti," Nali says.

She keeps a hand pressed to my back, helping me sit upright. My bones creak, but I do not wince in pain.

I scan my surroundings. There is a chalk circle drawn around the rug, a series of unrecognisable symbols lining its circumference. The characters vaguely resemble the strange writing of the Dennarese, with its broad, criss-crossing strokes and circles and squares. Only Jirtash, Nudin, and Nali are attending to me.

The sky outside is a still, mirror-like grey; I cannot tell what time of day it is.

"Can someone explain this"—I gesture towards the circle—"to me?"

"It's hadon, or Dennarese magic," Nali explains. "It's an ancient art that dates thousands of years—"

"Which we only permitted because the Shira-Rakhti vouched for it," Nudin interrupts. "Please forgive us, my Rakhti. We wouldn't have allowed her to use Dennarese magic if the circumstances were not so dire."

"The physicians declared that you would never recover—not unless they got a shaman from the capital city," Jirtash further clarifies. "But it would take at least a week for them to arrive, and by then..."

"I would have been dead," I fill in the blanks.

The initial excitement I had at the sound of rain is replaced by an encroaching gloom.

I look at my hands, recalling the decay that had spread through them like wildfire. What would Ilam have done with me if I had died? He fulfilled his end of the bargain; our contract never stated that I needed to be alive by the end of it.

I was aware of that, and I climbed up that mountain foolishly, driven by the hunger to maintain sovereignty at all costs.

Was it worth it? I do not know. Was I prepared to throw my life away? Certainly not.

I did it, nevertheless.

My fingers curl, clenching into fists. What's done is done. What matters is that I've summoned rain, as promised.

Ilam? I ask.

He unfurls himself, as if he has only just awakened. *I'm here.*

I shouldn't be taking solace in a demon's presence, yet I do.

I shake my head. "Why haven't I heard of hadon before?" I ask Nali. "Is it permitted in Aritsya?"

"Strictly for medicinal purposes, my Rakhti. There is a community of Dennarese who migrated here after the civil war. Some of us are hadon users." She keeps her eyes pinned to the floor. "It's kept a secret from the general population, though. All Dennarese who have legally registered themselves under the census must declare if they have hadon, and the Council of Shamanism will strictly monitor us thereafter. While we aren't restricted from using it, it's advisable to limit its use to emergencies."

My brows crease together. She hasn't quite explained *why* hadon is kept a secret from Aritsyans; it does not help that I cannot crack her mind. The Council of Shamanism—the congregation of legal shamans in Aritsya—must be quite effective at their job, being able to clamp down on news so tightly that not even I have heard of it. I've never dared to involve myself with them before, afraid they would be able to immediately recognise my blood magic. Fortunately for me, they have no relations with Rakhtas.

I wonder if Keran has known of hadon all along. No, of course he has. He was born and raised in Dennar.

Then why has he kept it a secret from me?

"You must be a skilled practitioner," I comment, returning my focus to Nali, "if you were able to bring me back from the brink of death."

"It—it was nothing, my Rakhti."

"My Rakhti," Nudin interjects, "if you have no more business with her, may she leave?"

His disapproval is as pronounced as the pouring rain. And briefly I'm able to see into his mind. He is angry at Nali. Angry that her family had hidden her existence. Angry at Harun for allowing the Yankaran family to nominate Medha for the Rakhti Selection. Angry that his father had accepted the mountain of gurisi the Yankarans presented, and completely disregarded the fact that one of their daughters was a victim of the Bloodbath.

A distinct chill seizes my body. The Yankaran family has a dead daughter?

They were my sister's favourite flower, Medha had said of the rhododendrons.

"If you'll excuse me, my Rakhti," Nali says abruptly. My gaze drifts towards her. "Oh, and please do walk around more often. It will help you recover faster."

Then she is gone. Jirtash clucks and fusses over me, helping me get up and sit on a chair. Nudin observes us impassively from a corner.

My fingers curl into fists. They knew. Harun and Nudin knew all along—that the Yankaran family should have never nominated a daughter of theirs, that Nali and Medha were never supposed to be here.

That they had a sister who was at the same Selection as me.

I take deep breaths, forcing myself to calm down—to think. No one knows what happened that day—all witnesses are dead, save for me and Chandri. And I've not heard hide nor hair from the latter for nearly ten years.

My secret is safe. For now.

"It has been raining for the past three days, Binsa." Jirtash's voice jolts me out of my thoughts. She beams at me. "Rashmatun watches over us."

It takes a while for me to reimmerse myself in the present. "Where's Harun and Medha?" I ask, tone quiet.

Jirtash and Nudin exchange a quick glance.

"Where are they?" I repeat.

"Thiravinda Harun is with Shira-Rakhti Medha in the Paruva-tar," Nudin answers.

"In the worship hall?" I lift a brow. "Why?"

"Thiravinda Harun thought to prepare her to take over your position, in case anything happened."

Rage throbs in my veins. I temper my anger, telling myself to wait, to strike at the perfect moment. If I want to win in this game that Harun has orchestrated against me, I have to play the right cards, knowing when to be bold and when to be cautious.

Now, it is the time to be bold.

I slump forward, head hanging low, appearing dejected.

Ilam. Lend me your strength.

My power is yours, Binsa.

Jirtash takes a cautious step towards me, her hands hovering uncertainly. "My Rakhti?"

I suddenly straighten myself. My posture is tall, unwavering, my head held high and chin lifted. I do not hide the furious glint in my eyes. Ilam's magic courses through me. I pray that my skin doesn't decay from his power.

"I am not the Rakhti," I say, the cadence of my tone deep and booming.

14

An Exchange of Information

It sounds strange, hearing myself speak in a voice that is not mine. It is deeper, radiating with authority—even more so than the voice I use when I am sitting on the Scarlet Throne. It is unnatural—the voice of a demon. It creates the intended effect, though. Jirtash flinches, and Nudin's stoic, unflappable expression gives way to pure shock.

They drop to their knees. "My goddess, forgive us," Jirtash pleads.

"What is there to forgive?" I cross one leg over the other, curling my lips in disdain. Ilam's enjoying this too; I do not know if this elation is mine or his. "I have granted mercy many times. Yet all of you take it for granted. Did Binsa not fulfil her duty? Have I appointed Medha as my vessel already? You know that I see all and hear all. Still you dare act upon your foolish human wisdom!"

Jirtash's hands tremble; Nudin's mind goes blank, confusion overtaking his senses.

I'd already planned to make Rashmatun appear unsummoned. Harun's boldness has only pushed me to take this leap a little earlier; I must assert my authority before he oversteps his boundaries.

This is what it means to be a blood shaman, Ilam laughs. *This is the power you can wield.*

"My goddess, it is true we have taken your mercy for granted," Nudin continues, a slight tremor in his words. "But please forgive us once more. We had no choice. We feared the worst—"

"Enough." I push myself off the rug and stand up; the coldness of the floor seeps into my bare feet. Jirtash and Nudin stare at me, goggle-eyed and jaws slack. "I will see Harun. Now."

"My goddess," Jirtash protests, "you cannot allow your feet to touch tainted ground—"

"I will walk wherever I please." I am dressed in yet another white daura-suruwal, no sash of red to mark my sovereignty. It is clothing unfitting of a goddess; I hold myself like one, nonetheless. "Take me to the Paruvatar."

"Rashmatun, wait," Nudin says, an unusual bite in the way he calls upon the goddess's name. "You can't go—"

"Are you telling me what to do?"

He gulps and bows his head. *So that's how she summoned rain? Gods, but she can't do this. If Father finds out—*

Pure terror wipes all other thoughts from his head.

Is it so strange that Rashmatun is indeed helping me summon rain? I think.

Jirtash appears with an oblong straw hat in her hands, nearly as long as I am tall. An item usually worn by common folk to protect themselves from the harsh weather. "My goddess," she says, "will this do for you?"

"It will serve me fine." Jirtash fixes the hat on my head, adjusting the straps so that it stays on firmly but isn't drawn too tight. She also procures another two hats for herself and Nudin.

Nudin leads the way, his shoulders hunched against the wind. It is a long walk to the Paruvatar from here; the temple grounds are a sprawling maze of smaller shrines and complexes, and the Rakhti is usually not allowed to step out of the Paruvatar without strict supervision. This is a welcome change of scenery for me, although most of the scenery is clouded under rain. The storm shrinks into a baleful patter by the time I step out of the building.

Ilam's magic is a dull pulse in my chest, warming me from within. He is using the bare minimum to protect me from the weather; Binsa alone will not be able to walk around like this in the rain, especially when she has just recovered from a near-death experience. There is an odd sense of camaraderie between us, as if he is finally acknowledging me as an equal in his contract, and not a poor, foolish human desperate for power.

What do you know about hadon? I ask him, suddenly bold.

It draws strength from the earth and manifests in forms that are very much attuned to nature. It only started making its appearance in Dennarese armies over the past century. That's as much as I know about it.

Then why did Nali say it dates thousands of years back?

I only know what all my vessels know, he snaps.

Really? But you are far older than I am, with a wealth of knowledge and experience that the greatest scholars of the world can only dream of, I say, teasing. *I'm sure you are smarter than that.*

I thought you should know better than to question my intelligence now, Ilam says, a quiet warning in his tone. It's as though his claws are closing around my head. *If I say I do not know something, you remain silent.*

And that's the end of our conversation. I do not understand why Ilam is so defensive about the topic. It's not like I am asking him to talk about his past, which he never does.

Patience, I tell myself. Perhaps he will deign to tell me his secrets if I become powerful enough to earn his respect.

Ilam emits a cynical snort.

It takes approximately twenty minutes of walking before we enter the main courtyard. The rhododendrons bloom a pure, distilled scarlet, stark even against the downpour, and the stench of blood is somewhat masked by the rain. Outside the Paruvatar, a stream of devotees are lining up, apparently oblivious to the storm pouring over their heads. Excitement rolls off them in palpable waves. I slow my pace, sweeping my eyes over the people. Some old, some young; some wealthy, some poor. Each of them reflections of the various communities that form Bakhtin.

Nudin and Jirtash match my deliberate steps. I cut past the crowd, heading straight for the entrance of the worship hall. Murmurs of dissent fill my ears when they notice that I haven't bothered to join the queue.

"Hey! Wait your turn!" Someone slaps a hand on my shoulder and jerks me backwards.

I turn around to face the person who accosted me, wearing a mask of utter contempt. "Are you telling me what to do, child?" I say, Ilam's voice infused with mine.

The man's face blanches. Gasps of shock echo around him.

"Do tell, why is it that I need to wait to enter my own worship hall?" I continue, revelling in the way each word creates minute shifts in his expression, until nothing but terror remains.

"N-no, my goddess. P-please forgive m-me," he stammers. "I— I didn't know—"

I wheel around and resume making my way forwards. The news of my arrival quickly ripples through the crowd. Some fall to their knees, muttering fervent prayers for forgiveness. Some thrust baskets of offerings towards me. Their limbs tremble in awe. This is their goddess. This is the all-knowing Rashmatun they worship with all their hearts and all their minds.

My chest swells with pride, and a small smirk plays at my lips. It was worth it, after all—killing Gurrehmat and Yhadin, putting my body through so much torment, resorting to blood magic to bring blessings to them.

I've won their love and respect.

Medha and Harun are at the end of the hall, seated right before my throne. The former is dressed in her lavish Shira-Rakhti uniform, silently accepting the offerings that my devotees place before her.

The pride that had inflated my chest dissipates. I clench my fingers, then release them.

One of the priests near the entrance startles at my unceremonious arrival. "Hold on. What are you—" His eyes widen in recognition. "My—my Rakhti. You've recovered."

"I am not the Rakhti," I announce, ensuring that my voice echoes throughout the crevices of the Paruvatar. "I am Rashmatun."

The chatter that filled the air abruptly dies.

I continue down the carpet, my hat still dripping wet, my feet soiled with dirt. No one makes a sound of protest. Panic notably emanates from the chief priest. Meanwhile, Medha's surprise quickly gives way to a blinding smile. She leaps to her feet.

"Binsa!" she cries. "You're awake!"

She pommels straight into me and wraps her arms tightly around my waist, knocking the wind out of my lungs. Her tiny frame quivers, though I do not detect any trace of fear in her.

It takes me a while to realise she is crying out of relief.

I stand there for a few seconds, at a complete loss. Then I remind myself that I am Rashmatun, who is impartial towards all—even towards strange yet fascinating little girls. I wrench myself out of her grip.

"Control yourself," I chide her.

She stares at me with doleful eyes. But she takes a respectful step backwards and murmurs a quiet "Sorry."

Harun has also risen from his seat. He strides towards me, disbelief written all over his expression. "My...goddess," he says. "Your vessel recovered."

"What else did you expect my vessel to do?" I retort.

"The physicians— They said there was no way to save her—"

"But she is saved, is she not? By the *half-urvas*, no less." Harun flinches at my tone. Good. I want him to remember this—the shame of being ridiculed by his own goddess, that even a half-Dennarese proved to be more faithful than a descendant of a noble line such as him. "What were you doing here, Harun?"

I must inform Rakhta Asahar of this, he thinks, the words clanging in my head like a bell.

Interesting. Nudin had panicked when I'd become Rashmatun, thinking about his father. Now Harun intends to report this to Asahar. But why? Although Rashmatun usually only takes over her vessels during the summoning ritual, there is no specific mention in any official religious texts that she *cannot* appear unsummoned. Why, then, would this be worth Asahar's attention?

My fellow Rakhtas are due to arrive for the Trial of Divinity by the end of the week, assuming that three days have indeed passed since I summoned rain. Would Rashmatun's appearance change whatever plans the Rakhta of war has in store for me?

No matter. I will prepare for him in due time. Now, I will savour my moment of victory as the Forebear of wisdom.

"We were receiving your devotees, my goddess," the chief priest simpers. "An influx of your worshippers wished to present their gratitude to you."

I arch a brow. "This couldn't have waited until Binsa was better?"

"In all honesty, my goddess, I feared the worst for her." At least he has the decency to look embarrassed. "In case of anything, I thought it best to instruct Medha—"

"That is Binsa's responsibility, not yours," I cut in. "Your responsibility, in case you have forgotten, is to oversee the temple, not to meddle in the affairs of the Rakhti and the Shira-Rakhti. Do not forget the privilege granted to you by virtue of your bloodline, Harun, and the boundaries you must adhere to."

He dips his head. "Yes, Your Holiness."

If only he were not a direct descendant of one of the most powerful—if not *the* most powerful—families in Bakhtin. His forefathers served Rashmatun as her chief priest without fail for centuries. Otherwise, I'd be more than happy to strip him of his title.

No. I must be careful. Harun maintains his power in many other inexplicable ways as well—including colluding with Asahar, apparently.

I turn my gaze towards the long line of devotees, at the eyes who look at me with hope and joy. I smother a smile. "I will see all of them," I announce. "Medha will remain by my side as an observer. Harun, go with the priests and sort out their offerings."

A servant's job. If I cannot strike Harun down today, I can at least make him suffer. "Yes, my goddess," he says, clenching his teeth.

I take my place on the Scarlet Throne, still sopping wet. My appearance doesn't matter—not when my people have already seen my power, when they have witnessed what I can do.

Today, I have truly become Rashmatun.

The devotees come and go in a blur. I receive lavish praises, prayers muttered in fervour. Some even burst into tears at the sight of me. All of them bear gifts—coin, gold earrings, a family heirloom. I receive each offering with a detached inclination of the head.

When we are done, I step off the Scarlet Throne and fall into the role of Binsa. The priests all scrutinise me, as if they are trying to determine whether it was truly Rashmatun who spoke to them earlier, not the scrawny girl who can barely look anyone in the eye.

I am escorted back to the Bakhal in a proper palanquin. In my room, a hot bath awaits me. The handmaidens are surprisingly gentle when they scrub my skin and help me dress, as if I might shatter into a million pieces with a single touch.

Later, as I study myself in the mirror, I understand why they handle me with such care. The three days of unconsciousness have hollowed out my already sallow cheeks, and my frame is paper thin, ready to topple over from a gust of wind. My eyes are narrower, haggard, as though I have not quite woken up. My entire countenance is heavy, my shoulders slumped with an unseen weight.

Perhaps this is another reason why Harun is working so hard to discard me. How can a living goddess be as unsightly as I am?

I shake the thought out of my head and dig into the meal on the table, inhaling the entire tray. It is a relief to be able to eat freely after spending so much time depriving myself. My stomach still pinches with hunger after I'm done; I'm tempted to order an extra portion of roti from the kitchens. A memory of Chandri drifts into my head: She sneaks me an additional portion of sel roti during one of our tutoring sessions, avoiding the watchful eye of her stuffy, patronising tutor by passing it below the table. I happily shove the deep-fried, ring-shaped snack underneath my kurta, ignoring the oily mess it would leave.

Subconsciously, the corners of my lips lift.

"Why can't I see her?" Ykta's voice rings outside my door.

I bolt upright, stunned. Ykta has never publicly visited me in my room before.

"The Rakhti has just recovered from her illness," Jirtash explains wearily. "And she went walking around in the rain. Do you really think she's well enough to see you?"

"I need to talk to her about something," he insists.

"Whatever it is, it will wait till tomorrow." Irritation tinges Jirtash's tone. "The Rakhti will see no visitors today."

"Did she issue such an order?"

I do not need Ilam's magic to know that Jirtash is bristling. "What right have you to see her with such urgency? In her own room, no less! Have you no shame? Just because you are a Dahlu graduate doesn't mean you can go about and expect everyone to worship the ground you step on. You're not a Rakhta. *She* is."

"I know you're worried about her." Ykta softens his tone. "So am I. That is why my message is of immediate importance."

"Tell me, and perhaps I shall consider how important your message is."

"It concerns her education," Ykta replies briskly. "Which has nothing to do with a handmaiden. However, as her tutor, it is natural for me to—"

A sharp crack pierces through the wooden door. I imagine Jirtash releasing her pent-up frustration on Ykta, throwing all her weight into a slap across the cheek.

"What good will her education do her once she's no longer Rakhti?" Jirtash snarls. "She won't even be in a position to use it! Once she steps into society she will be expected to marry and have children. Do you think she has time for all this? All you're doing is feeding her head with nonsense!"

My chest clenches in pain.

I recall the faces of adoration I saw today in the Paruvatar—faces of people who see me as nothing less than a goddess. Faces of people who will forget my existence, if I am ever replaced. They love Rashmatun, not Binsa.

And I am reminded once more of why I must remain Rakhti.

I stalk towards the door and edge it open. Jirtash and Ykta turn towards me in surprise. A throbbing imprint of a hand lashes across my brother's cheek. "It's okay, Jirtash," I say. "I will see him."

"Are you sure? You must be tired." Concern etches deep, anxious lines into her face.

I smile at her. After all she's said about my education, I know she's only doing her best for me. As someone who never married and has remained in service to Ghanatukh for all her life, she understands the harshness of the world towards young girls. "It's all right. I'm sure Ykta wouldn't want to see me unless it's dreadfully important."

I gesture for Ykta to enter the room. He enters, his head bowed respectfully. I flash a reassuring grin at Jirtash and duck back into my room.

"What is it?" I ask softly, guiding him towards the corner farthest away from the door. Jirtash's seething aura still lingers outside, and I do not want to risk her eavesdropping on us.

"How do you feel? They said you collapsed right after you descended Aratiya. I—" His voice cracks here. "I didn't know what to do. They wouldn't even let me see you. And the number of physicians going in and out of Ghanatukh— Gods, Binsa, if only you had seen it yourself."

"I'm fine, as you can see." I open my arms and wave them. "No need to worry."

"Did Rashmatun's magic make you become like this? But it shouldn't be that way. She's a goddess. Her magic shouldn't drain you of your strength."

It actually sounds similar to blood magic, Ykta thinks.

"I'm just not used to her magic yet," I say hastily. I reach out and close the gap between us, taking my brother's hand in mine.

The colours of my room abruptly fade, as if my vision were folding upon itself—only to be replaced by other colours. The wellcrafted, if unassuming, furniture common in Kreyda Gopal's mansion sprouts before me. My physique shifts, taller, stronger; I do not feel my braid weighing down my back.

A figure is kneeling on the ground before me, her kurta a pale, dirty yellow. She keels over, violent coughs wracking her frame. When the coughing subsides and she removes her hands from her mouth, splatters of dark blood stain her palms.

Horror rings throughout me. "Mama!" I cry, my voice caught in the awkward hoarseness between childhood and adolescence. I rush over to the woman's side.

She lifts her head to look at me.

It's Kavita.

"Mama, why is this happening?" I ask, almost bursting into tears. It twists my heart to see her like this—weak and broken and vulnerable, when the world outside is ready to swallow her at a moment's notice.

"I'm fine, my boy." She smiles at me, extending an arm to pat my head, only to retract it after remembering that it's covered with blood. "This is the price I pay for us to lead a better life."

"I don't want this!" I cry, throwing my arms around her. "You've grown so weak ever since we came here. I don't want to see you like this, Mama. Please. I'll work hard and earn a living. You don't have to do this."

"I have already struck the contract with the demon," she answers, tone soft. "I must follow through."

The backs of my eyes burn. "Can't you just break it?" I plead. "It's not worth your life."

"Saran, I'll be fine." She adjusts herself so that I'm forced to release my grip on her. She tilts my chin up, casting me a gentle, affectionate smile—the one she wears to sing me to sleep. "Just promise me that you'll take care of Binsa, all right? Be a good boy and help me. Promise?"

I think about my little sister, small even for her age. I think about how she always hides behind me whenever she does something wrong, or how she would weave flowers into a necklace for me. I think of her smile when she is delighted, the innocent joy radiating from her expression.

I think of how my mother might not have long to live, and how my sister will have to grow up without her.

"Promise," I whisper, a tear sliding down my cheek.

The scene collapses. I am whisked back into my room in Ghanatukh Temple. I stumble, as though someone struck my head. Ykta grabs my arms to steady me. "You're still so weak! Do you need a physician?"

I extricate myself from his grip and shake my head. "No, no. I'm fine," I say, struggling to suppress the tremble in my voice.

What was that? I ask Ilam.

You slipped into your brother's mind, the demon replies smugly. *Congratulations. This is proof of a mutual emotional connection. It's the first step to manipulating his mind.*

I stare at the space before me, dazed. It feels like someone had dunked my head into a basin of icy-cold water and poured hot gravy over it in quick succession. I lift my arm and check my hand, just to ensure it is my own, and that it does not have the slimmer, longer fingers that belong on my brother's.

"I'll get someone to help you," Ykta says, taking a few steps towards the door.

"No. Wait. I'm fine," I assure him. "Please, I don't want to worry anyone else anymore."

His brows furrow in concern. "All right, Binsa."

Inside, I'm still reeling. If I want to manipulate someone's mind, I have to be close with them first; what a sick, twisted joke this is. No wonder most blood shamans went insane. Warping your own heart and telling yourself it is all right to hurt the ones you love.

Haven't you been doing that all this time? Ilam drawls.

With Ykta?

Meanwhile, Ykta sighs internally.

When is she going to realise that she cannot keep pushing herself to her limits without telling me what's going on?

If I didn't know better, I'd say that there is dissent in him.

At first, I am horrified. But I think about his behaviour towards me, the way he kept interrogating my decision to remain Rakhti. His reluctant easiness when he'd agreed to help me, trying to pacify the tears I'd shed.

Am I hurting Ykta by keeping the truth from him?

No, it is all because of Kavita. It is because he promised to look after me. I just peered into his memory—I became him. Kavita had manipulated him into devoting his life to me, even when she had abandoned him and he was free to leave our family. He wouldn't know if our mother had cast an enchantment on him.

Right?

Didn't I tell you I would be with you always? Her voice rings in my head.

Even after all these years, Kavita still wreaks havoc on our lives, refusing to lie dead.

"Binsa? You still there?" Ykta knocks my skull.

I slap his hand away. "Of course I am!" I snort. If he's in the mood to play around, it means he has forgiven me.

"Thought that Rashmatun spirited your soul away somehow." At my sour expression, he says, "Sorry."

"It's fine." I lean against the wall. If I have to stand anymore I might just collapse from dizziness.

"It's fine," *Mother had also said back then,* Ykta thinks.

I'm not sure if I can continue listening to his thoughts like this, so I try to change the topic: "Have you checked the rhododendron bushes?"

Ykta blinks, then says, "I did. Nudin has been consistently wandering around them at night. I dug around the bushes one time once he left, and found dead goats—their bodies preserved by magic, I believe."

This news is unsurprising; it simply confirms my suspicions. The priests are taking advantage of the prolonged drought to drop the goats and pin it on the Prophecy of Geerkha. However, is there a particular reason why Nudin, of all people, keeps checking on the rhododendron bushes? Did his father assign him to do that, or is he there of his own volition?

I chew on my thumb. He had panicked at the thought of Rashmatun's appearance being reported to Harun, and pure fury radiated from him when he thought about how it was his father who had unwittingly allowed Nali into the temple. Yet Nudin must be a co-conspirator in the plan to drop goats over Bakhtin. Is he doing it out of genuine belief in his father, or is he doing it out of mere duty?

Where does his loyalty lie? I wonder.

"Perhaps Chandri has all the answers," I muse. "Any news from Keran concerning her whereabouts?"

"He'll come by sometime tomorrow," Ykta says. "Though he didn't care to elaborate much on his findings to me. I imagine he wants to keep that an exclusive piece of information for you."

"To extort money from me, you mean?" Both of us grin, and for a while I can imagine that we have grown up together all our lives. "Where should I wait for him, and when?"

"You know his style. He'll come find you, somehow. As he always does."

"Almost as though it were magic," I comment absently.

My muscles freeze when the words fall from my lips. Some Dennarese possess hadon, according to Nali. I am not sure if Keran possesses it too, but the way he weaves in and out of the temples, and the way he chooses the right time and place to appear...

"How does Keran do it? How does he learn his secrets?" I suddenly ask. "How did he know that Asahar once snuck into a gambling den? How did he know that Larvit accosted a handmaiden and gave her money to silence her?"

"All rumours, probably," Ykta grunts.

"Have you heard of our people whispering of such scandalous rumours? If all this information were truly widespread, everyone in Aritsya would have heard of them by now."

"But some of those rumours were confirmed anyway," Ykta argues. "Like the handmaiden who spoke out against Larvit and was found dead two days later in her quarters. It's not entirely impossible to obtain those secrets."

"Still, those are temple secrets. Secrets that no outsider should know. Yet *he* does. How do you suppose he got such accurate information?"

"He has insiders?" my brother suggests.

"That's one possibility. Or... he has something more interesting up his sleeve." I lace my fingers behind my back and turn towards the window, observing the grey haze clouding Bakhtin. "Nali is able to use Dennarese magic—hadon. She used it to heal me this morning. But her magic is a tightly kept secret in Aritsya—and only the hadon practitioners themselves and the Council of Shamanism are supposed to know of it."

Meanwhile, Ykta's brows draw into a furtive line as he connects the dots himself.

"Come to think of it, his eagle has always been able to find me,

even once when I was away in Hyrlvat. I always assumed that creature had a keen sense of direction, but I suppose it could also be
magic," Ykta murmurs. "But so what if Keran has—hadon? Does
it matter?"

"It matters because Nali uses it, and Nali and Medha have a sister
who died in the Bloodbath," I answer dryly.

Shock bowls him over. "So you're saying..."

"I think there is a reason Nali was sent in place of her mother,
and it's connected to her dead sister *and* her hadon."

Ykta takes all this information in; I sense the cogs in his brain
turning, gradually clicking into place. "I know their father," he
murmurs. "Ranjit Yankaran, a prominent philosophy scholar. But
he's been retired for a long time now."

"Did you know he has two wives?"

"The professors' private lives are never spoken of." Interestingly,
relief floods through his veins; he's happy because I decided to
share this with him. "Can't hurt to know more about hadon, I suppose, if you want to know their family. What should we do about
Keran?"

"Prepare two hundred gurisi for him."

His jaw goes slack. "Two *hundred* gurisi? Are you mad?" he
gasps. "That's a Holy Guard's entire year of wages!"

My lips curve into a thin smile. "Oh, don't worry. I intend to
make him work for every last bit of it."

15

Ghosts

The next day, Keran makes an unceremonious appearance during the night, slipping through my window; the only sign of his intrusion is the feather-light thump beside me. I jump, nerves on edge after spending a whole day waiting. It induces an amused grin from him.

"Thought you'd know better than to be surprised by me," he chuckles.

"Thought you'd know better than to vex a client."

"Peace, Little Mantis." He plonks his backside on a chair and props his feet on the table. He's probably trying to rile me.

I can't tell, though. His mind is empty, as uncomfortably silent as Nali's.

Ilam emits a noncommittal hum. *I'd be more surprised if I could pierce his mind*, he says.

I refuse to sit down. "Make this fast. I have an early day tomorrow. I assume you have information about Chandri?"

"Ah, before that, your medicine—"

I raise a hand, cutting him off. "I have no need of that anymore."

He lifts his brows. Then he slips back into his usual nonchalant mask. "Don't tell me you've found another dealer who offers better rates?"

"What I do is none of your business," I reply. "Now, about Chandri."

"I'm a *dealer* of information, Little Mantis," he says languidly. "Since when did I become a charity?"

Sighing, I pluck five gurisi out of the heavy pouch belted to my suruwal. Ykta had been mumbling vehement curses under his breath when he had returned from the bank, exchanging the slips he receives every month for coin.

Keran's grin grows wider, creasing his eyes into half-moon slits. My heart pounds in anticipation, and nervous sweat films over my palms. This is it. I will soon know how Chandri is doing—if she has built a family for herself, if she is still devoted to Rashmatun. I wonder if she still remembers me, and I wonder—

"And that's the escort fee," Keran says as he swipes the gurisi.

I blink in confusion. "What?"

"Just what I said—that's the escort fee. It's high time you stretched your skinny legs, Little Mantis. What say we pay a visit to Chandri's family?"

"Now?" I stare at him, stupefied.

"You can wait till morning, if you prefer," Keran says, sarcastic.

"I paid you for *information*, not for a field trip."

"You can either pretend you donated the five gurisi to me, or you can come along. Don't worry. I promise we won't get caught."

I swallow a hiss. "Am I not paying you enough?"

"Unfortunately, this is one of the few instances where paying me more won't solve all your problems." Keran picks his nails and casts me a sidelong glance. "You either risk coming into the city with me, or you stay ignorant of Chandri's whereabouts forever."

My fingers curl into fists. "Do I at least get a refund if I refuse to go?"

He dangles his pouch in the air. "I'm going to consider this a tip for all the trouble I went through to find your predecessor."

"If you know where she is, why can't you tell me?" I say, my words almost biting into a snarl.

The playful light in his eyes hardens. "You'll know once you find out."

Although I am still irritated, something tells me to not push back so hard against Keran. There must be a reason why he's being so insistent on dragging me out; he knows that both he and I will get into serious trouble if we are caught together outside Ghanatukh.

But I cannot use blood magic in front of him in the event we do get caught. I cannot risk an information broker knowing the truth behind my reign.

You want answers to Chandri's magic, no? Ilam goads me on. *Besides, this won't be the first time you've broken the rules.*

I bite the inside of my cheek.

"I understand your hesitation, Little Mantis," Keran continues. "But you've trusted in my skills for the past few years. You can certainly trust me now."

If only Ilam could read his mind. Then I wouldn't be toyed with like a doll hanging from a thread. I could get the information I want and be done with it.

"Fine," I finally say. "Let's go. But if anything happens, I'm going to say you kidnapped me."

Keran bares his teeth. "I expect nothing less."

"Can't you move a little faster?" Keran whispers, catching my elbow and hauling me over the eave of a rooftop.

"Have you considered that I hiked Aratiya just a few days ago?" I snap, wheezing. Rain pours down from the sky in a steady sleet; what I wouldn't give for one of the oblong hats that Jirtash brought out before. The cloak I wrap around myself does little to stave off the nighttime chill.

"Nothing short of a miracle." Even as shadows and rain obscure most of his expression, I discern Keran's teasing gaze. "Did you actually summon the storm, by the way?"

I lower myself into a squat, trying to catch my breath. I'm cold, wet, and miserable. This is probably as close as I've felt to my hungry days back in Dharun. We've been winding through cramped alleyways and scrambling across roofs, and I've seen more rats in the past ten minutes than fellow human beings. An eagle dips in and out of sight despite the onslaught of rain—the same one that always accompanies Keran. It's been circling us ever since we left Ghanatukh.

I'm sure there must be a connection between the Dennarese and the eagle, but even after observing him closely I cannot see any hint of magic. Nali's hands had glowed blue when she was using hadon, so it stands to reason that Keran should give some sort of indication as well.

Except that he doesn't.

Or could it all just be in my head? What if I've wrongly suspected Keran of possessing hadon?

But...no. There are too many unexplained secrets that he keeps. Secrets that encompass the entirety of Aritsya's courts—secrets that should be impossible for a single person to gather, even if they are the greatest spy in the world.

"Too tired to answer my question?" Keran says, extending a hand towards me.

I stand up without his help, trying not to slip on the tiles. "Would you believe me if I said that some of Rashmatun's power has come to me?"

"I heard from Ykta. If that were true, shouldn't she help with how easily you get winded?"

My stomach flips. Who knows how much Ykta has been telling him on a regular basis? I scowl at him to disguise my unease. "Or we could have just walked. Like normal people. Rather than climb roofs in the rain and announce to the world that we're doing something illegal."

"This was supposed to be the fastest route, though at your speed it might be dawn by the time we get there."

Before I can retort, his arm whips out and shoves my head down. His hand clamps over my mouth as I release a yelp. I struggle, but he holds me flat on my belly. Something warm scuttles over my hand. My eyes widen in horror when I realise it's a rodent.

Keran points towards the alley we just climbed up from. Oh, how I wish I could summon Ilam to tear him apart right now— because there is absolutely nothing down there. I try to kick him, but he pins his knee over my calves. He is surprisingly light, but I am too scrawny to throw him off my back.

Footsteps echo in the distance, slightly muffled amid the rain. Someone yawns—not Keran.

A pair of Holy Guards stroll into the alley. A few rats scurry behind them, but the Guards do not stir, perhaps too used to the vermin crawling through the city at night, or too distracted by the storm to even notice them.

What an awful night to be on patrol, they think.

The Dennarese does not let me go, even though I attempt to gesture that I can stay quiet without his help. It is only a few minutes after the Guards completely disappear from sight that he releases me. I draw in a sharp inhale.

"Save your breath," Keran says. "I know this city better than you do."

I press my lips into a thin line, trying to remain calm. A difficult task, considering that Ilam is also growing increasingly vexed.

Keran saunters across the roof as though he were gliding across water. I feel like a clumsy crocodile clambering after him. "That's what years of trying to avoid being seen does to you," he explains without prompting. "You gain a knack for knowing which people to dodge and which paths to take so you don't get into any trouble."

"What an uncanny sense of intuition," I mutter. I hadn't been able to sense the Guards until they were close enough for me to spot them. Are Ilam's senses dulled in the rain?

The demon huffs indignantly. I suppose not.

"It's a necessity, considering that your people don't take very kindly to Dennarese—especially ones who lurk in the darkness." He turns around; the moonlight makes the scar on his face gleam, cutting through my obscured vision and appearing more grotesque than it would in the day. "I told you that we wouldn't get caught, eh?"

But something about the way he sensed those Holy Guards coming feels off. First, he has his eagle, still swooping around us from a respectable distance. Then there are the rats—perhaps it is simply my imagination, but we have been surrounded by them throughout this mini excursion. I don't remember there being so many vermin flocking to me the last time I snuck out of Ghanatukh.

Coincidence, or hadon?

Nevertheless, it is his "intuition" that gets us safely to our destination. We observe a mansion from another rooftop; it spans two buildings, with one main house and the servants' quarters at the back. Elaborate reliefs of deities—mostly Orun, the deer god of welcoming strangers—hang over door-frames, and the grounds are well manicured and clean, no overgrown bushes or pockets of uneven ground filled with water. As one would expect of a kishari's estate.

Yet its tidy appearance only seems to serve the purpose of hiding *something*, as though the smooth walls of the estate were barely holding the structure together. I focus and scan the area, and notice the lack of gas lamps within the mansion grounds and the chipped tiles on its roofs—details so minuscule that no regular passerby would have paid mind to them.

But I see them—partly because of Ilam's enhanced senses, and partly because it reminds me of Kreyda Gopal's mansion.

"You must have noticed that this family is not doing too well financially," Keran comments beside me, his voice oddly cheery. "Alas, not all kishari families are equal."

"Is this where Chandri stays?" I ask.

He looks upwards and ignores my question. "Should be anytime now."

"What are you talking about?"

"You'll find out where Chandri is in a moment."

Just as the words fall from his mouth, light flickers to life through one of the windows, the unsteady and ephemeral shiver of a candle-flame. Silhouettes shuffle into view. I strain my ears, but I am too far away for even Ilam to pick out what exactly is going on.

The light disappears, then passes through several other windows. The front door to the main house swings open.

My mouth goes dry.

Someone steps into view, the skirt of her sari sweeping the floor. The woman's greying hair turns silver under the moon, and her back is bent over with age. She holds the butter lamp close to her breast, as though it were a precious child. A second figure steps into view—a frail, elderly man who wraps his arms around the woman's shoulders, supporting her, although he could also stumble anytime. They huddle together under the door-frame, shielding their faces from the downpour's spray.

Is that Chandri?

"Come on," Keran says. The next moment, he has jumped down from the roof.

I swallow a curse and follow suit, landing with a squelch on the ground and nearly twisting my ankle. Keran doesn't stop to check how I am doing.

"What are you thinking?" I hiss as he walks straight towards the couple. "Financially troubled or not, that is a kishari's estate—"

"A fine evening this is," Keran calls out, waving his hand. "Good to see the two of you well and healthy."

My jaw slackens.

"Oh, what brings you here tonight?" the woman, to my utter surprise, responds to Keran as though his sudden appearance were the most natural thing in the world.

"I came to offer my respects. And"—he gestures at me—"I brought a little guest today."

My body freezes for a split second before I lumber after Keran, hugging the cloak tighter around my body. I sink myself into a bow first, hoping that the tremble in my legs isn't too obvious. I study the couple's bare feet, then the hems of their clothing as I gradually lift my head. I feel my throat tighten, half-eager and half-afraid to see the truth for myself.

I meet the woman's eyes.

It's not Chandri.

"What's your name?" the elderly woman asks.

"Binsa," Keran says before I can.

The butter lamp drops to the ground. The old man shouts in surprise, but the flame is quickly doused by the rain. I glare at the Dennarese, one word away from swearing at him for revealing my real name.

"Binsa? *Rakhti* Binsa?" the woman says, her voice trembling.

My insides coil. If I get into trouble because of this, I will rip Keran apart, never mind his hadon and never mind how useful he's been to me. Instinctively, I square my shoulders. "Yes, I am Rakhti Binsa, and I am here to see the former Rakhti Chandri."

The couple looks at each other, expressions crumpling, their minds ringing with a sorrow so piercing that it burrows deep into my marrow. Then they look back at me.

"Did he not tell you?" the man says. "Chandri is dead."

I am stunned for a few seconds. "N-no, you're joking, right?" I respond automatically.

None of them attempts to reassure me. They all go as still as statues.

Blood rushes to my brain. The world around me spins.

A memory of Chandri blooms to life: I am standing in my room—what used to be her room—and she pats my head. I jump and squeeze myself against a corner. For any other person, perhaps, it's a sign of affection. But my mother had once squeezed my head so hard I thought my skull was going to crack, and ever since then my first instinct is to cower whenever someone touches my hair.

She approaches me slowly, as if I were a startled cat, wearing a small, comforting smile. I cannot help but balk in fear.

Of course, Chandri could not possibly know all that.

She lowers herself into a crouch and extends a hand. "It's okay," she murmurs. "Everything's fine. No one will hurt you. I promise."

No. She knows. She knows how the girls died, and she is here to exact retribution upon me. I shouldn't have become Rakhti. I shouldn't have gone to the Selection. I should have run away, maybe try to find Saran and start a new life—

Her hand brushes against mine.

I try not to wince, keeping myself as still as possible—even as tremors wrack my body. I anticipate her tightening her grip and snapping my wrist. It does not happen. Instead, she brings my hand closer to her body, until it is hovering over her head. She guides my hand to gently rest atop her crown.

"You can do this to me anytime too," she says, eyes crinkling at the corners.

I draw myself out of the memory. That was my very first day in Ghanatukh Temple, when I was still unsure of my place and gripped with fear in the aftermath of the Bloodbath. Chandri must have been frightened as well, yet she took her time to coax and comfort me. I hadn't trusted her then and there, but it was a start.

A stone lodges in my throat, and my chest tightens.

The couple abruptly wheel around and go back into their house. I lunge after them, but Keran's arm bars me from taking a step forward. "Wait," he says.

A few long minutes drag past. My vision still swims; each raindrop splattering on me adds an infinitesimal weight that grows heavier and heavier and heavier. It takes all my strength to keep myself standing. The old man and woman reemerge, this time with a parchment gripped between the latter's fingers. She thrusts it towards me, a layer of waterproof goatskin protecting whatever is inside.

"Take it and go," she whispers. "And never return. We do not want to see you ever again."

"Hold on. You're her parents, right?" I say, desperate to cling to anything that remains of Chandri in this world. I push Ilam's magic a little further beyond what he normally exerts, attempting to paw through their minds.

All they are thinking is *Only now does anyone pay attention to her. When she has been gone for so long that her name has died on everyone's lips.*

Her—Chandri.

The man picks up the butter lamp from the ground, his joints creaking with the motion. "Yes, and we were about to offer her a prayer."

"How—how did she die?"

The fury that roars inside them takes me aback; black hatred glimmers in their eyes, a deep abyss that seems out of place on a frail, elderly couple. "Of illness, a year after she left Ghanatukh Temple," the woman snarls. "Now leave. And do not ever return here. We do not wish to associate ourselves with your goddess any longer."

Keran places gentle hands on my shoulders and steers me away from them. I nearly crumple the parchment in my hand. I stuff it under my sash to prevent myself from tearing it apart.

My only door to finding out more about Chandri has been slammed in my face. I could return to the lonely estate, press her parents for more information. But something about that last expression on their faces rattles me. I do not foresee myself going back. There are too many ghosts there, of unfulfilled promises and lingering regrets.

I have enough ghosts haunting me; I don't need to involve myself with more of them.

I do not know where Keran is leading us. All I know is that I am grateful when he finds us stacks of discarded crates to sit on. I nearly slip off the edge as I lower myself. It must be exhaustion, I tell myself.

"I'd offer you some good, hot tea right now," Keran says, "but sadly we are too far away from any proper amenities."

"Why couldn't you just tell me up front?" I ask.

"Would you have believed me? Besides, I suspected that you would have wanted to see her parents, if only to give yourself a bit of closure."

I think of the old couple left back at the estate, their gnarled hands cradling the lamp so lovingly, as if that were the soul of their daughter. I think of their devotion, how they still light that lamp and pray for Chandri despite the storm outside. I wonder if they were as kind and joyous as Chandri before she passed away, and I wonder if Chandri turned out the way she did because of them.

The backs of my eyes burn. My memories with her were the only happy thing I had in the world. If I had more of those memories in the first place, perhaps I would have turned out to be an entirely different person.

It was because of Chandri that I was able to live out my one month as Shira-Rakhti in bliss. It was because of her gentle touch that I no longer flinched whenever anyone grazed my skin. It was because of her constant smile and support that, for once, I thought myself worthy to become Rakhti—that I could truly become the living goddess, ruling over an entire province.

Now she is gone.

My grief gives way to anger, the low flame heating in my stomach more familiar than the cold distillation of sorrow. Her parents were right—Chandri died so long ago, yet not a single soul in Ghanatukh had told me. No one had mourned for her. Do they even know that she died? Do they care?

So this is our fate as Rakhtis—to be discarded and forgotten the moment we blossom into womanhood. Perhaps that's the real reason why her parents are furious at me, because I remind them of a system that loved and used and tossed their daughter away.

That is why you must make the goddess your own. Kavita's voice brushes against my ear. *Take her power so you will never turn out like Chandri.*

I startle, whipping my head about. Keran frowns at me.

"What's wrong?" he asks quietly.

I shake my head. A hallucination. That's all it is.

"I understand that it's a lot to take in," he says, filling in the silence. "Take as long as you need to recover. I'll make sure no one finds us."

This is a different Keran from the one I'm used to. Although I appreciate the kindness—as much as Keran can be kind—I cannot help but remember the rats shadowing our path, and the eagle guiding our way forward. And I remind myself that he is a broker, first and foremost, and that he cannot be doing all this for free.

"I hope you don't expect extra payment for putting me in distress," I say.

His lips curl into a sharp grin, and some part of me slumps in odd relief at the sight. "I only mentioned the escort fee just now," he says. "There's another price to pay for receiving your information."

I rest my elbows on my knees, propping my chin on interlaced fingers. I must accomplish my other objective in meeting Keran. "How do you do it? Slip through the darkness before anyone can find you? Predict them before they even make a move? And how on earth did you become chummy with Chandri's parents?"

"Those are trade secrets, Little Mantis," Keran says. "But if you must know, I grew close to Chandri's parents using my unrivalled charms."

Ilam rankles at his arrogance. I roll my eyes. "How about another business proposition, since I do not want your medicine any longer? If you accept, then you will waive this little fee for me."

"Oh?" He quirks a brow. "It must be an interesting job."

I turn my head to face him fully. Luckily I can attribute the wetness in my eyes to the raindrops drizzling down my cheeks. "I'd like you to be my exclusive eyes and ears. At least until I've officially secured my position."

A few seconds tick by before he says, "What, exactly, would this entail?"

"Mainly, to help me dig up more information on Asahar and Harun. Learn what they are planning, how they intend to remove me, and why."

"You could assign me to do all that without keeping me to yourself." He rises to his feet and pivots back and forth, kicking up water with his boots. "You know I am a free man. I do not wish to work for anyone in particular. I just serve whoever is willing to pay me."

"I can't take the chance that you'll go passing along what you hear from me to anyone else, and I believe you have special talents. You were the only one who was able to find out that Harun and Asahar are exchanging correspondence."

"Oh, that? A little bird told me. I was lucky to chance upon that." He waves a dismissive hand.

"You have magic," I say, cutting to the chase. "Your skills are invaluable."

"Little Mantis, what on earth are you talking about? You don't have to make excuses for my immeasurable talents, you know." He grins at me, as if he were entertaining a naive child.

"I can report you to the Council of Shamanism," I say quietly. "For the illegal use of hadon."

The smile on his face freezes.

"Hadon? Never heard of that in my entire life," he scoffs.

"You don't know what I'm talking about? Then I assume you're not interested in a hundred and fifty gurisi up front. I'm sure it's more than enough to cover the costs of taking me to see Chandri's parents."

He runs a hand through his hair, exasperated, but I catch the glimmer in his eye. "Of all the places you could choose to broker such a deal," he says, chuckling. "It's time we put you back in Ghanatukh. Make sure no one finds you missing."

16

The Information Broker

More rats scurry around us on our way back to Ghanatukh, squeezing through gutters and travelling along the roof edges. Keran keeps a constant distance between us, although he occasionally glances over his shoulder to check that I am following.

"Can you heal people?" I ask.

He nearly loses his footing—for once. "I can, though some other hadon users are more skilled. Perhaps I would have learned more if someone was there to teach me."

"You learned hadon yourself?"

He trudges forward, finding the seams of the hidden door in a small temple. "Of course. All the Dennarese here are kept under strict surveillance, remember? There's no way I'd be able to safely contact any other hadon users."

"Sounds like you've been in Aritsya all your life."

His knuckles crack as he pulls a smooth slab of stone aside. "Maybe it's best not to annoy someone you're trying to make a deal with, hmm?"

"Likewise," I say, following him into the tunnel. He closes the hidden door behind me; some of the rats have entered as well, and skitter ahead of us. Water soaks every step I take. "Do you need those rats to see in the dark?"

"Why seek me out if you already know so much about hadon?" he asks, tone dry. "Your circle of informants must be far wider than mine. Only the Council—and the royal family—have any knowledge of its existence."

"I have faith in your abilities."

"I'd appreciate payment now, if I am to answer so many questions already."

"I suppose you can't resist a hundred and fifty gurisi a month after all."

"Two hundred," he argues.

"Done." I unhook the pouch from my waist and fling it towards him; he catches it deftly. "Payment for the first month."

He emits an amused chuckle. "You expected me to say yes all along?"

"You are remarkably consistent when it comes to money."

"How do you know I won't take off with this?" He bounces the pouch on his palm like a ball. "This is more than enough to feed a hundred families for a year."

"Because as unpredictable as you are, I trust that you have strong business ethics."

I don't tell him my other train of thought: I trust that he will not abandon Ykta so easily. I've caught the Dennarese's gaze lingering on Ykta one too many times.

"I see." He raises his hands in mock surrender. "You got me."

"And you can start answering my questions now?"

Keran loosens the drawstring on the pouch and inspects its contents. Once satisfied, he reties the knot and tucks it away. "You're right, clever Little Mantis. The rats are the ones that guide my way. More precisely, I commune with them."

"And that's the same for that eagle always following you around?"

"That's right. Though Qara is a little special." He continues walking down the tunnel. I squint, allowing my eyes to adjust to the darkness. "I was bound to her since birth. She's the only one that will never leave me. The other animals all come and go, and since I'm relatively untrained, I can only hold up to a dozen animals at a time."

"But you can also perform other forms of magic, right?" I press on. "Surely you have some other means of gathering your information."

There must be a reason why I cannot read his and Nali's minds.

"There are energies that we manipulate more easily than others," Keran replies. "For example, some are drawn to flame. Others to the wind. Rare individuals are able to commune with human minds. But so long as the energies are tethered to the earth, we will be able to access them. In theory, this means that—yes—hadon practitioners can tap into all forms of magic."

"Tethered . . . to the earth?"

"Hadon involves siphoning energy from the earth and cycling it into our spells." Keran ducks to avoid banging into a protruding rock; I simply walk under it. "Unlike Aritsyans, we worship the earth itself—and yet, it is not a god to us. You can say that it is simply an extension of our ecosystem, and certain individuals have learned how to tap into its ecosystems and manipulate them."

There is a community of Dennarese who migrated here after the civil war. Some of us are hadon users, Nali had said to me a while ago.

"Not all Dennarese are hadon users," I murmur.

"That's right." Keran draws circles in the air, his gaze turning distant. I frown at the motion. "The earth is part of us. We take from it, and one day, we will return to it. If we treasure it, take good care of it, it blesses us. If we do anything that displeases it, it lashes out against us."

He pauses for a while, hesitation laced in his held breath. "Only a small Dennarese clan known as the Ritkar are actually able to wield hadon. Its practitioners were once feared for their connection to the earth, but more than a century ago, the Dennarese Empire saw value in hadon and began recruiting members of the Ritkar clan into their armies. We also learned that it was highly effective against Aritsyan shamanism then.

"But over the past few decades, as the Ritkar clan continued to rise to prominence, they earned the ire of plenty of other ruling clans. These clans started to impose laws and regulations on hadon, essentially enslaving the Ritkar to the Empire. Naturally, the Ritkar protested. In return, the Dennarese Empire destroyed their city."

I'd heard about the Ritkar genocide that happened around eighteen years ago, but I never knew that magic was involved. The Dennarese government has always been tight-lipped about their internal skirmishes.

And if only the Ritkar clan had access to hadon, Keran would have been one of those affected by the civil war. He's around my brother's age, so he must have fled Dennar and arrived in Aritsya when he was very young.

This might be the first time he's shared this story with anyone.

His steps slow, as though he is lost in memory. "Hadon practitioners who fought in the war all died prematurely, for the earth was displeased that they used their magic for ill intent."

Meaning that he must have lost most of his friends and family. But how am I supposed to respond to that? So I pore over his words, piecing together whatever snippets Keran has chosen to reveal about hadon. "Your 'earth' does sound like a god, though, doesn't it?"

"You Aritsyans are so narrow-minded," he says, some of his usual bite restored. "No wonder your backwards shamanism has little effect on hadon practitioners."

Ilam's agitation reverberates throughout me. "I didn't pay you to make commentary on Aritsyan shamanism."

"You are correct. Anyway, when we do something that poisons ourselves—fight and murder other people, for example—it poisons the earth as well. So there's a severe shortage of hadon practitioners in the army, especially after the Ritkar genocide. Which also explains why the Dennarese Empire has been mounting fewer attacks on Aritsya in recent years—don't tell anyone I told you, though. Consider it a personal opinion."

"Interesting," I murmur. "Does hadon also allow its user to be impervious to magical attacks, since it's so effective against Aritsyan shamanism?"

"Honestly, I'm not quite sure how it works. I haven't actually fought a shaman before, nor am I inclined to." Keran takes a right when we arrive at a crossroads; I cannot track where we are, and I cannot help but marvel at the Dennarese's ability to navigate these tunnels so seamlessly. "The fact that we draw energy regularly from the earth means our bodies are slowly strengthened by its magic, though. Maybe that's part of the reason why."

It doesn't quite explain why I cannot pierce through Nali's and Keran's minds, but...if the earth rejects anything that is "poisonous," it would be natural for it to repel blood magic.

There must be other avenues of information I can turn to—Asahar, the Rakhta of war, for instance, must know about hadon. He's been leading our armies for the past seven years.

I suppress a flicker of irritation. I would rather bury myself under a pile of cow-dung than ask him about the war effort.

"Is that too much to take in for today, Little Mantis?" Keran says.

I hum in consideration. "I assume that you know plenty of other forms of hadon, since you also know healing?"

"In *theory*, I could. But as you can see, I am solely remarkable in communing with animals, and am absolutely lousy in all other fields—though I'd prefer to chalk that up to a lack of guidance rather than a lack of inherent talent."

So all he does to obtain his information and travel through the shadows is...by talking with mice?

Don't underestimate the mundane abilities, Ilam chides me.

He's right. However dull communing with animals sounds, it has enabled Keran to obtain all the information he has today. *A little bird told me*, Keran had said earlier. Clever.

Hadon also sounds remarkably similar to blood magic, Ilam comments. *Demons have an affinity for certain types of magic. We have the power to access everything, but there will always be that one element that comes easier to us than others.*

And yours is the mind? I ask. I do not dare to question why he is offering me this information. Perhaps it's a sign of his growing trust in me.

But of course, he replies, smug.

I reflect on how he does not need additional blood to tap into others' minds, but required sacrifices in order to summon. Even then, we barely managed to summon rain, and Ilam was inept at controlling the clouds. Kavita was adept at mind manipulation because *he* is adept at mind manipulation.

I wonder how much more there is to know of blood magic and hadon.

Keran stops in his tracks. "And we're back at Ghanatukh." He shoves against the stone wall before us; cool air sweeps into the tunnel as the door slides open, tickling the sweat-soaked ends of my hair. "This ends our lesson in hadon."

I do not try to prolong the conversation, and jump back into business: "What happens to the letters that Harun receives from Asahar?"

"He burns them."

I contain a hiss. "Find another way to learn what he and Asahar are talking about, and what they're planning for the Trial."

"I cannot guarantee anything."

"Then what do you have hadon for?" I raise a brow, and his jaw clenches.

"Fine," he mumbles. "Anything else?"

"I'd like you to investigate Nudin as well." He is another suspicious figure, although he seems to act on his own. He has been volatile recently, especially during the moments when I am Rashmatun. "I expect a report in two days. And come to collect your next payment in five."

"That depressing man? Of all the people in the world!" He releases a dramatic sigh. "You could have assigned me to someone more interesting."

"What kind of a spy talks back to their master?"

"What a demanding employer." He sidesteps to allow me to pass, bracing a hand on the small of my back when I stumble. My thighs are burning from the journey, and now that I am back in the temple, all adrenaline has left my muscles. "You truly are going to make me work for every last bit of my pay."

"Yet here you are," I retort.

He shrugs.

I level a stare at Keran. I cannot help but be curious—I had not expected him to agree to my proposition so easily. Throughout the

three years we've known each other, there has been absolutely no
reason for him to help me other than money, and sometimes I'm
not sure if what I am paying is enough to compensate for the risks
he takes by associating with a false goddess.

I am in no position to question his motivations, though. "For
your convenience, you can report to either me or Ykta," I say. "So
long as the information is relayed properly."

"You're surprisingly lenient," he says.

"Have you only learned this now?" I say. In truth, I still am
unable to fully trust Keran. But since he and Ykta seem to regularly swap information, I should be able to keep him in check by
reading Ykta's mind.

I know he will not betray Ykta, at least.

"Apparently so." He dips into a mocking Dennarese bow, his
hands raised into a clasp before him. "If there's nothing else you
need from me, I should take my leave. You have an early day
tomorrow. Best get some rest."

He closes the door to the passageway, and the emptiness of the
temple yawns around me.

An eagle swoops into my room two days later, its feathers soaked
from the rain. Puddles form under its clawed feet as it lands on
my table. A small chit is attached to its leg, and attached to the
chit is a length of sturdy, lightweight rope that holds a bundle of
papers.

Jirtash and Nali have just left me; I wonder if the eagle had been
waiting all along for the perfect moment to pass me the message.
I detach the chit from its leg. Keran had the foresight to wrap the
paper in buffalo hide, so the ink is largely intact. The message is
written in an almost indiscernible scrawl—like Ykta's.

I smooth a hand over the grainy texture of the parchment.

*I managed to intercept a letter from Asahar to Harun. I think
you'll find its contents very interesting. Remember to return this to*

me, though. I cannot have such powerful figures discovering that their letters have disappeared.

As for the chief priest's son, I haven't found anything on his person yet. He seems awfully boring. I can't imagine a person like him harbouring any earth-shattering secrets.

As per our agreement, I shall be seeing you in person in three days. I hope you'll have more payment ready by then.

I hear Keran's voice in my head as I read the letter, as though he were right beside me. I pick up the letter, written on paper too expensive for a commoner and with ink too smooth for anyone below a Rakhta. They resemble the Sacred Scrolls, somehow.

My stomach lurches the moment I read the letter.

Black spots dance in my vision. When they fade, I am sitting at a desk that is not mine. My body is strong, and my arms are corded with muscle. The strokes I press against paper are bold and uncompromising.

We have allowed her to stay on the throne for too long. Rashmatun cannot stay in one vessel for an extended period, as I'm sure you're aware. Do not worry. I have made preparations to remove Binsa. We will test her—or Rashmatun's—magic through the Trial of Divinity. The Shira-Rakhti will have to brave flames conjured by the Rakhtas to pass the Trial.

And I am back in my own body.

I clutch my stomach. The person writing the letter did not speak or look at their surroundings. "Who was that?" I whisper.

The letter is from Asahar to Harun. Meaning...the Rakhta of war has magic similar to Chandri's. This cannot be a coincidence. The Rakhtas must have some form of ability to tie their memories to writing.

Why do I not have this power?

I suddenly recall the parchment that Chandri's parents handed to me. Gods, how could I forget such an important item? I paw through the clothing I wore that night, heart wrapped in an icy grip. Where did I put it? I spot the wrinkled sash and flap it open.

Nothing.

I flip it to the other side and scour its length. Still nothing. I turn all my clothing inside out, to no avail.

There's no way the parchment could have disappeared into thin air. I haven't touched it since that day, and Jirtash only gathers my clothing to wash at the end of the week.

What was I doing that night? Did it drop somewhere while I was undressing myself?

Then I remember Keran's hand on my back when I had stumbled from exhaustion, when we were back in Ghanatukh.

That's ridiculous, I think, just as Ilam gives a short bark of laughter.

I wouldn't put it past him, Ilam says. *Perhaps that was his original intention of bringing you to see Chandri's parents—so you would be able to obtain whatever they were hiding and so he can use that for himself.*

I gnash my teeth. Oh, I will make Keran pay for this.

My fingers wrap around the yellow sapphire hanging from my neck, and calmness washes over me. I can get the parchment back from Keran when I see him in person. Right now, I have to skim through all the possible implications of the letter.

I pore over Asahar's words, scrutinising every detail, the way he phrases his sentences. If the Trial is already planned, and if the other Rakhtas have all agreed on how it should be carried out, does it mean all of them are also conspiring against me? But why actively remove me when I am scheduled to retire? And why does Asahar make it sound like Rashmatun actually exists?

Do you have any idea? I ask Ilam.

What makes you think I'd know something? he huffs.

I remember you comparing me to Privindu once. Doesn't that mean you were around during that time? And if the Forebears were responsible for disposing of Privindu, you would know whether they are real or not.

He refuses to respond, though something simmers in his silence. He *knows* something, but for some reason, he isn't telling me. I swallow a frustrated sigh and continue sifting through the letters. He is too unpredictable—friendly one moment and hostile the next. I won't get much out of relying on Ilam for information.

I return my attention to the letter, and I cannot help but wonder how much longer I will be able to hold my people's sway. As much as I hate to admit it, an older Rakhti is one who is more susceptible to criticism. Even if I never bleed, I will still age. How much value does my youth hold? Why does even Asahar say that Rashmatun can never stay with one vessel for an extended period?

In the legend of Rashmatun, the first human she came into contact with after falling from the sky was a little girl who had picked up her yellow sapphire out of curiosity. Rashmatun remained with the girl for many years, but once the girl started bleeding, her mind, body, and spirit became devoted to earthly matters—her husband, children, and household—instead of focusing on worshipping the goddess. Since then, Rashmatun has only favoured young girls.

Rashmatun isn't the only one with such a story—some superstition is tied to all the Rakhtas to prevent us from holding on to the throne for too long. A leader too long in power is one susceptible to corruption.

But I, unlike the other Rakhtas, have not dabbled publicly in illegal dealings and dangerous vices. Why remove me when all the others are even worse than I am?

I rein my anger in. The only fact I know for sure is that they will strike during the Trial—by forcing me to summon flame along with them. But luckily I have Ilam.

I will not be giving you my magic so long as the other Rakhtas are around, he suddenly declares.

What do you mean? I ask, stupefied. *You won't allow me to use blood magic for three whole days?*

Correct. Your senses will be diminished, and you will not be able to read minds.

The Trial requires me to use magic, *Ilam.* I shake the letter in my hand. Keran's eagle gives me a side-eye, and I put the paper down, checking that it's not crinkled. *How am I supposed to host the Trial if I don't have magic?*

Think of another way, he snorts.

You've never restricted me from using blood magic during Rakhta meetings before. Why now?

You were only performing silly little tricks back then, telling truth from lies. *My presence was so small that it was insignificant. Now I must either completely suppress myself or risk being found out.*

Found out by whom? I huff.

The other Rakhtas, naturally.

Now it's not just Asahar, but Ilam too is making it sound like the gods they carry do exist. *If there is something I should know, I think it's a good time to tell me now.*

He falls silent again.

I resist the urge to drag him out and pommel him until nothing but smoke remains—if that is even possible.

Keran's eagle ruffles its feathers. Swallowing a sigh, I grab a quill and parchment from my study table to pen my reply to Keran.

> *Good work. As per our agreement, partial payment for the month will be ready when we meet.*

Keran's eagle remains calm while I fumble with tying the papers to its leg. When I'm done, it gives me one final golden stare before flapping its wings and disappearing under the cover of the relentless storm.

I pinch the bridge of my nose, fatigue weighing down on my shoulders. I have only one more day to figure out how I am going to summon flame without magic.

PART II

THE FORGOTTEN GODDESS

Cursed is the one who chooses the bloodstained path,
The path wending through the bones of our dead.
Cursed is the one who speaks to the darkness,
The one who shrouds themselves in shadows,
The one whom the gods forsake.

Sleep, little children,
Do not fear the monster.
Though the night fears them,
You are cloaked with light,
And filled with fearful wonder.

Cursed is the one who curses,
Who wears a cloak made of night,
And whose eyes are the colour of our lives.
Cursed is the one who sings this song,
For it is a song never to be sung,
Stolen from the lips without breath,
From the ones never touched by the sun.

Traditional Binyamet folk-song about blood
shamans, from the region of Hyrlvat

17

A Childlike Heart

Rashmatun is not summoned the next morning. I do not even step into the Paruvatar. Medha and I are undergoing preparation for the Trial of Divinity, as—in Harun's words—it is best we drill the entire procedure into muscle memory. We've been practicing for the past few days.

The little brat glues herself to me on the cramped bench. Every fibre of my being screams to push her away, but Harun is right before us, peering over the desk like a benign father. Nudin is the only one among us opting to stand, and the way he looks down his nose makes my bones shiver. I do not know why they elected to have one final discussion in this old, unused study in the Bakhal. The furniture here is so well worn that a sudden movement might send the bench legs cracking beneath us.

Harun opens up the Namuru and recites a verse: "From the teachings of Rashmatun, during the reign of Emperor Mahajarpit. Wisdom does not belong to an individual alone; it is a collective knowledge of people near and far, from past and present. One who possesses the wisdom of a thousand stars will be wise enough not to hoard knowledge, but to ensure it is passed down, its spark kept aflame."

Nudin clicks the beads around his neck, ending the brief prayer. Harun closes the Namuru.

"With that in mind, it is time for the old to pass and the new to come." Harun casts me a deliberate look. *She will not have her way,* he thinks. "Binsa will pass on all she knows to you, dear Medha. But before that, you must also earn the approval of your future colleagues."

"The other Rakhtas will come, right?" Medha bursts out in excitement. "Does Virya really have feet like deer? And does Harmesh have feathers sticking out of his head, like his god Guphalon? Oh, and does—"

"First of all, it's *Rakhti* Virya and *Rakhta* Harmesh," I interrupt her, my head spinning with the sudden influx of unspoken thoughts pouring into my mind. "Secondly, the Trial of Divinity is not a social gathering! Who are you to nose yourself into the other Rakhtas' business?"

Medha's frame deflates and she puckers her lips. If not for the fact that I intend to expel her from the temple, I might find her adorable.

Harun clears his throat. "In case you need a reminder, Rakhti Binsa, it is also up to the current Rakhti to educate her successor in manners befitting the vessel of a goddess."

Don't you think I know that? I grumble internally. "My apologies, Harun," I say. "I will keep that in mind."

"Very good." Harun smiles at Medha. "Now, remind us of what is to happen on the day of the Trial of Divinity."

Medha and I take turns explaining the procedure. On the afternoon the Rakhtas are supposed to arrive, I am to participate in a procession around Bakhtin with them, Medha excluded. After the procession, the Rakhtas will be escorted to their residences in Ghanatukh Temple and have the entire afternoon free. The Trial will be conducted during twilight at the Court of a Thousand Suns, a sacred building that hosts statues of the Forebears and their descendants. The Rakhtas will give us our instructions then; while I am not the one being tested, I will still have to participate in some way.

This is the part I'm worried about.

I still have not thought of a way to conjure flame without Ilam's help, even after spending a sleepless night wracking my brain for possible solutions. And judging from the contemptuous smile on Harun's face, he also seems confident that something will go wrong during the Trial. Although till now I cannot fathom what making me use magic will prove—assuming they still think I have Rashmatun inside me.

"Is there any part of the Trial that is not clear?" Harun says.

"Do you know what the Trial will be?" Medha asks.

Harun laughs aloud; the sound scrapes my skin. "There is a reason why they call it a 'trial,' dear Shira-Rakhti. It wouldn't test you if you knew what was going to happen."

Not that she could do much about it even if she knew what was going to happen. I think of tiny little Medha, being forced to walk through flames to prove her worth. My stomach clenches for some reason at the thought. She's so young and fragile and mortal. Why attempt to break a Shira-Rakhti before she is even crowned?

But I remember her steely determination during the Selection— how she was willing to bite off her own tongue if it meant she could get through it. If she can survive a moving, flame-spitting mechanical goat, she can also survive the Trial.

Wait...a flame-spitting goat automaton?

An idea takes root in my head before evolving into dread. I will have to face Ykta again. We've not seen each other in a few days—he has taken sick leave, and will only return to his duties today—yet it feels like an eternity has stretched between us. The last time I talked to him, he had started comparing me to Kavita, of all people.

I do not know how much longer I can hide everything, and I do not know how he would react to me being a blood shaman if I actually told him the truth. His hatred for Kavita runs lake-deep. Will he come to hate me too?

But I must get the goat automaton from him. There's no other way I will survive the Trial.

"Any other questions about the Trial, Shira-Rakhti?" Harun says, cutting off my train of thought.

"I don't have a question about the Trial." Medha fidgets, and I release her from my grip. I've been holding her too tight, I belatedly realise. "It's about something else."

"Ask away, child."

"What happened during the Bloodbath of Shiratukh?"

The bluntness of her question stupefies all of us.

"Oh, and do the other Rakhtas know what happened during the Bloodbath?" Medha tacks on. "I guess that's two questions."

I jump to my feet. The bench gives way with the sudden motion, a terrible crack splitting the air. Medha shrieks. I grab her arm before she can topple over.

"We need new chairs for the Bakhal, it seems," I laugh nervously.

"Of course, Rakhti Binsa," Nudin says.

"My sincere apologies again about the Shira-Rakhti's conduct." I bow towards Harun and force Medha to bow as well, hand on the back of her head. "I have not taught her well enough. Please forgive me."

"No need to be so worked up. All is forgiven." Harun rises from his seat. "You two may leave now."

I take Medha's hand and drag her out of the room without another word.

Nudin, I notice, is the only one who dips their head towards me.

"Have I mistreated you? Have I taught you something you shouldn't have learned?" I bombard Medha with enraged rhetorical questions once we are back in our quarters.

"I—I'm sorry, Binsa." Tears well up in Medha's eyes. Gods, why is she crying when she is the one who made the mistake? This is why I cannot handle children. "I didn't know. I thought it'd be safe to ask, because you didn't seem to mind—"

"Just because I don't mind doesn't mean other people don't mind!" I snarl. "Have some tact, girl!"

Medha's lips tremble; one second later, she breaks into a full-on sob.

THE SCARLET THRONE   189

She cries so loud it sounds like she is spitting her lungs out. The entire room is filled with nothing but her wailing. I slap my hands over my ears, trying to block out the sound.

Come now, you were a child once, Ilam says. *Surely you can imagine yourself in her shoes.*

I certainly wasn't as insufferable as her.

How would you know? You didn't parent yourself.

I release a low groan. I have plenty of other things to worry about, and I still have to deal with this child?

But Medha's guilt is seeping into me. She has an innocent sincerity, and whatever she does—whether she speaks, plays, or expresses her emotions—she does it wholeheartedly and in a straightforward manner. If there is one mind in this entire temple who I can read without suspicion, it is Medha's. Even if she's here for an ulterior purpose.

So I know her guilt is genuine. I think about all the times I cried when I was a child—when I simply didn't know what else to do.

Once, Kavita would have sung me a lullaby to soothe me. Later, she sang as she beat me black and blue.

I run a hand through my hair, shuddering at the memory. I will not be like Kavita. *I'm different from you,* I'd screamed at her in a dream. And I will keep my word.

You're using blood magic like her, Ilam purrs.

I ignore him. The table has been laid with our lunch—mutton stew with rice today. I walk over and scoop a portion of the rice and stew onto a plate. Then I bring it over to Medha and pat her head. "There now, don't cry. Have some food and feel better."

I'm sorry for yelling at you is what I want to say. But I cannot bring myself to utter the words.

She sniffles; snot runs down her face. "Go wash up first," I say.

She trudges over to the basin while I get my own portion of food. When she sits at the table with me, she immediately digs into her plate. "Eat slowly," I tell her as she stuffs her mouth till her cheeks puff. "Now, tell me why you're still so insistent on learning about the Bloodbath."

"You didn't tell me what you found in those Sacred Scrolls," she says through a mouthful of rice. "And I didn't have the chance to ask you about it recently, so I thought it was a good time just now to bring it up."

"Swallow your food," I say. She gulps. It's amazing how this tiny brat digests everything. "You should know by now that the Blood-bath is *never* to be spoken of."

"I know, b–but—"

The chaos in her mind subsides, giving way to a clear image: a long, thin face hovering over me. For a moment, I think it is Kavi-ta's, but then realise that the eyes are set too wide, and the lips are too thin. It's a familiar face, though not one I immediately place.

Remember your duty, Medha, the woman says. *You and Nali will be able to provide justice for Anju.*

Anju. The name of their dead sister.

My breath hitches as Medha's knowledge slips into my con-sciousness. This is Adarsh, Medha's mother.

Medha's memories do not end there. Her mind darkens, and it takes me a moment to register that it is not blanking out—she is in a space without light. Her limbs tremble as she forces herself to lie down and cover herself in blankets. Dozens of slaughtered chickens surround her, the stench of their blood clogging her nostrils, but she needs to sleep. Her mother will give her a terrific hiding if she emerges the next morning with dark circles ringing her eyes.

As if Medha herself becomes aware of her spiralling thoughts, she jerks herself out of those memories, forcing herself to focus on other things: the glint of the metal plate against the light, the con-trasting textures and colours of the rice and the stew, the soft patter of the rain outside the window.

Soon, her mind reverts to the whirlwind it usually is.

It all becomes clear—why Medha had been so desperate to become Rakhti, the doctrines her mother had drilled into her over and over. The terrible "training" she endured to have a better chance at passing the Selection.

She's just like me, born to a mother who sought ambition not for her daughter's sake but for her own.

My chest tightens in sympathy. If only I were not so desperate to sit on the Scarlet Throne myself. If only I had the courage to step down and retire into a mundane life.

"The Bloodbath was a murder," Medha says in the end. "And the murderer needs to be brought to justice."

If only she knew she was eating with said murderer. "Who told you that, Medha? Your parents? Your friends?"

She keeps her lips pressed in a thin line. For a moment, she considers telling me the truth. Of how Adarsh forced her and Nali to enter Ghanatukh Temple, their intentions in coming here, how she will attempt to learn information from the Rakhti and her servants, how Nali will use her hadon to discover the temple's secrets.

Unfortunately, she does not elaborate on how Nali will use her hadon.

In the end, Medha decides against it. The grip her mother has is an invisible leash around her throat, tightening whenever she lets her guard down.

"It's not right to kill people," she says.

"Of course it's not. But assuming you find the murderer, what are you going to do with them? Will it put your ghosts to rest?"

She blinks at me. The whisper of rain against the rooftops and the wafting scent of food fill the stretching silence. Her mind is— for once—unnervingly blank.

"If you don't know what happened during the Bloodbath, would the other gods know?" she asks at last. "I—I know I'm not supposed to mention it anymore, but...none of you answered my questions earlier." She looks down at her food, expression so forlorn it almost makes me want to do anything for her. "I need to know."

Perhaps she is too young to understand the implications of my words, even though she is wiser than most her age. I pour out water for myself and Medha. "If Rashmatun herself did not know what happened during the Bloodbath, what makes you think the other Forebears have any idea?"

Images of my own Trial suddenly come to mind, released along with my memories of Chandri. I had been apprehensive, afraid that the Rakhtas would find out I was only there because my mother killed the other candidates. Afraid that their gods would see through my lies and deception, and sentence me to a fate worse than death.

But nothing happened. After I became Rakhti, I assumed it was because the other gods did not exist as well.

I furrow my brows. My interactions with my fellow Rakhtas have been few and far between, and each time I see them, I can never tell if they truly host their gods and goddesses. Some Rakhtas are scarcely any different from the entities they channel. Yet sometimes they say something so out of character, so dissonant from their usual selves, that I can almost believe that they have been possessed.

I convinced myself that they're all shams too—but I just never dared to ask them for the truth. And now with Asahar's letter...

I do not know what to think anymore.

"You can't say the Forebears don't know what happened when you've never asked them." Medha's body stills. "Also, you're still not telling me what you thought of Chandri's scrolls. Maybe they have something to do with the Bloodbath. We could just ask her about them too."

I scoop another helping of the mutton stew onto her plate. I want to tell her that Chandri is dead, that no one in the temple even knew about her death, but I cannot bring myself to crush her so mercilessly. "Remember what I said? A Rakhti will cut off all ties with the temple she served once her tenure is over. She must *never* come into contact with anyone there, and is not allowed in its halls any longer. We, in turn, are forbidden from seeing her as well."

Her face crumples in despair. "There's absolutely nothing we can do about it?"

"No. But..." I hesitate to offer her my solution, to lie to a child and give her false hope. But this is for the sake of protecting my secret. "I'll talk to Harun about it again. Perhaps he knows something, since he was the Thiravinda-in-training then."

Medha's expression brightens. Impulsively, she throws her arms around me. "Thank you, Binsa!"

"Wash your hands!"

She gasps, horrified. "I'm so sorry, Binsa." She rushes towards the basin and returns to me at breakneck speed, her wet hands dampening my clothes. "Thank you again!"

I tentatively return the embrace, pleased at how she's returned to her normal energetic self.

And vexed at how I am pleased.

18

Gathering of the Gods

I relieve Medha of her Shira-Rakhti duties for the rest of the day, which would normally consist of lessons with Ykta. But during his absence over the past two days, I've been using the time to rehearse the procedure for greeting the Rakhtas. The little brat has been whinging and groaning every single time I smack her stray hands, or when I tell her to stop slouching, so her eyes immediately brighten when I tell her that she is free to roam around the Bakhal.

"Can I see Nali?" she asks.

I need to tell her that Binsa will help us uncover the truth of the Blood-bath, she thinks.

"You do realise that it's *Rashmatun's* orders that Nali is to never see you while I am still Rakhti, right?" I say.

"I know." Medha laces her fingers behind her back and pouts at me. "But she didn't say anything about *me* visiting her."

The impudence! I should scold her for daring to suggest such a thing, and yet I find myself not having the strength to argue.

She's a clever one, Ilam chuckles. *I wonder what would happen if she became a blood shaman.*

My stomach roils at the idea of innocent little Medha being poisoned by devious whispers and twisted desires—like me.

"It'll only be for today," Medha continues to persuade me. "And I won't see her again until after my coronation, I promise!"

I tilt my head, considering. I've kept the half siblings apart for more than two weeks now. They are probably growing anxious from not being able to commiserate with each other. Would it be wise for me to allow them to see each other this once, so that I will curry favour with them?

Besides, if Medha tells Nali what she is thinking, I will be able to gain the half-Dennarese's trust without even having to lift a finger. Medha is many things, but she is not a liar. What she thinks is what she does or says; if she is unable to speak the truth due to circumstances, she simply doesn't talk about it.

"Fine. Just this once, and no more," I say sternly, folding my arms across my chest. "You are allowed to see her for only an hour, all right? If Jirtash or any of the other handmaidens question you, say that Rashmatun has decided that this will be an exception. Don't mention my name."

"Thank you, Binsa!" Then she is bouncing out of the room and zipping off.

Hopefully this will also encourage Nali to come see me about the Bloodbath. If what Keran has said is true, I will need to figure out her hadon affinity to discern why exactly Adarsh had planted her in Ghanatukh Temple.

Concerns I will deal with another day. For now, I need to see my brother.

I head to the library alone. My chest lightens when I think about getting to see Ykta after these few days, and despite whatever Asahar and Harun's plans are and the Trial I have to oversee tomorrow, despite all the troubles punctuating my thoughts...I miss my brother. I miss being able to exchange quips with him so easily, and I miss the way he comforts and fusses over me.

Yet one step before the door, I stop.

I do not know why the lightness in my chest has balled into a knot. I may intend to ask him for another favour, but it is not like Ykta is not supporting me anymore, and it's not like he has accused me of using blood magic.

Then why am I so uneasy?

I take a breath and push the door open, marching into the library. Ykta is sitting at one of the tables, reading a book this time instead of working on his projects. "Binsa!" He leaps to his feet when he sees me. "You... You look well."

I nearly laugh at his awkward greeting. "Thank you, I suppose." I take small paces towards him. "I'm glad to see you're all right too."

"It was the summer heat getting to me. Nothing to be worried about."

He stifles a yawn, hoping I don't notice the lethargy still plaguing his movements. The workload from the past three months has finally caught up to him, he thinks.

Mostly because of the goat automaton, which he has not finished tinkering with yet.

"How did getting information from Keran go?" he asks as I take a seat beside him. He lowers himself back down to the chair.

"Where do I begin...?" I sigh. "For starters, Chandri is dead."

Right. Keran told me that, he thinks. Still he makes a show of looking stunned. "I'm sorry. She was probably important to you."

A chill runs up my spine. What have he and Keran been up to behind my back?

You cannot trust him, Kavita's voice whispers.

Stop it, I snarl back. *He's my brother!*

Why so agitated, Binsa? Ilam hums.

Forget it. I huff internally and return my attention to Ykta.

"It's all right. I'm fine now." Relief floods my brother as soon as the words fall from my mouth. He has been fretting over how I would take the news, and he also knows that Chandri would have been a vital source of information about the Rakhti's magic. Guilt twangs in him, for not trying to seek out Chandri sooner, even if I never asked him to do so.

"Did you find out if Keran has hadon?" Ykta continues. "And did he agree to become your personal spy?"

How can he sit there so calmly and talk to me as if he hasn't been doing things without my knowledge? How can he pretend to ask all those questions when he already knows the answers?

Maybe he has his reasons for doing so, I convince myself. "Of course he does. Naturally, he wouldn't refuse such a huge sum of money," I say, curling my lips into a sardonic grin. "Hadon is quite interesting. Perhaps you should ask him to explain his magic to you too."

Ykta is perplexed by the harshness in my tone. *Maybe she's not completely recovered from summoning rain yet.*

As if, I snort in my head.

"Anyway, I have something to ask of you," I say, straightening my spine. "Remember how you mentioned that your goat automaton could spit flame?"

This does not bode well, Ykta thinks. "Yes, and what of it?"

"How does the mechanism work? Would it—" I clasp and unclasp my fingers. "Would it be possible to remove the one part that can shoot flames?"

He stares at me. "What on earth is this for, Binsa?"

"Answer my questions first."

"Yes, it's a simple flamethrower installed into the mouth of the automaton," Ykta says, tone cautious. "You'd need to manually push a button to trigger it, though."

"Can I hide it under my sleeve?"

"Binsa!" he cries, and I startle. "What are you trying to do?"

"I need the flamethrower by tomorrow. Preferably before the Trial of Divinity commences." I drum my fingers against the table. "Keran managed to intercept a letter from Asahar to Harun. They say they plan to have Medha walk through flames conjured by the Rakhtas."

Ykta's brows furrow. "If that's the case...why can't you use Rashmatun's magic? Using the flamethrower is dangerous, Binsa. Especially if it's your first time using it."

I cannot tell him that the demon inside me is being awfully stubborn when it comes to using his magic before the other Rakhtas. "I don't have enough control over her magic yet. Please, Ykta. I need that flamethrower."

"Look, I'm sure there's something inside here that can help you." Ykta picks up the book he was reading. Privindu's name blazes across the cover; it's *Theories and Principles of Aritsyan Magic for Beginners*. The same book I've been poring over for weeks.

"You've been reading that?" I ask, stunned.

A flush creeps up his cheeks. "Don't laugh at me!" he protests. "I—I thought I should read up more on magic. So I'd be able to help you better."

It'd be awfully considerate of him—if my "magic" actually came from Rashmatun.

I think about how he communicates with Keran in secret, how he wants me to rely on him but keeps questioning everything I ask of him. And now he is studying magic in secret instead of asking me how "Rashmatun's" works.

"Why are you always doing things without telling me!" I finally explode. "I told you to trust me, but you go off and don't listen to my instructions and challenge all my decisions. What kind of a brother are you?!"

His mind goes blank, then kindles in rage.

"Who are you to control my every single move and make me report to you? Gods, I am trying to *help you*. What's wrong with telling you that a flamethrower is dangerous because you might just torch yourself? What's wrong with trying to understand your magic? I told you that your life is not just yours to lead! I am part of your life! I also have a say in what happens to you!"

Fury sets my body aflame. "Don't think that just because you came back for me means that all my problems are automatically solved. You are not a god. *I* am. I know what needs to be done. I know how to secure my position. I know what's best for me. All you had to do was follow my orders and not involve yourself in anything unnecessarily!"

A shadow falls across his eyes, and I know I have said too much. I reach a hand towards him. "Saran—"

He avoids my touch. "I've been nothing but helpful to you all this while. I'm tired of giving in to you without you explaining yourself properly. I still can't comprehend why you want to be Rakhti."

The backs of my eyes burn. "Ykta..."

He shoves Privindu's book towards me and gets up, stomping towards the door. "Have it your way, since there is no other path for you."

He does not throw a second glance at me when he leaves. I take a shuddering breath as I curl my fingers into fists.

Before I know it, it is the morning of the Rakhtas' arrival.

I stand on the stairs leading to the Paruvatar, garbed in full Rakhti uniform. Today, I will greet my fellow Rakhtas not as Rashmatun but as Binsa, as is customary. Behind me, Medha barely manages to hold herself still as she buzzes with nervous energy. I stare into the rain-hazed sky; not a single drop of water falls upon me. The priests had changed the weather wards this morning so that the barrier enclosing Ghanatukh Temple would deflect rain instead of heat; we can't have the Rakhtas of Aritsya being soaked here.

I search for Ilam's presence to assure me, but he is absent.

I take a deep breath, struggling to collect myself. Compared to before, the lighting in the Paruvatar is dim, and the air is thin. It's as if my world has been dunked underwater, colourless and sound-less and dull. The incessant whispers of people's thoughts are no longer in the background, and I realise how quiet and monoto-nous my environment is without them. My body feels as if it could collapse at any moment—mortal and fragile without Ilam's power thrumming through it.

I am grateful for Medha's chittering now; she attempts to squeeze in as many questions for me before the other Rakhtas arrive: *Are they nice? Do they like goat cheese? Will they start breathing fire?* Each of them is more ridiculous than the next, but I assume it's because she's even more nervous than I am. I do not shut her up.

For good measure, I raise my fingers to the base of my throat, where my yellow sapphire protrudes beneath my jama. *Chandri, please give me strength.*

After an eternity of waiting, the tower bell in the main courtyard clangs nine times, signalling the arrival of the nine other Rakhtas.

Medha emits an anticipatory gasp and straightens her posture. I straighten myself as well, lifting my chin and relaxing the knot between my brows.

I have faced the other vessels without Ilam's help before. I will be fine.

Of course, that was when Asahar wasn't actively trying to dethrone me—for gods know what reasons.

The first vessel enters the courtyard on her palanquin: Rakhti Iridis, vessel of Vashmar, god of law and justice, and de facto leader of the Rakhtas. When her palanquin stops before me, she descends with the aid of her attendants and takes her place on my right. Her bearing is tall and imposing, and the thick kohl lining her eyes adds to the harshness of her features.

The other Rakhtas gradually march in, following the sequence of the Forebears when they first arrived on Eyra. The thick, cloying scent of their mingling perfumes nearly makes me gag, and I am momentarily thankful for my diminished senses. Some are clothed in jamas—like me—while others opt to wear the traditional costumes of their respective regions: chaotic, multicoloured fabrics that hold so much detail I worry that their seamstresses have gone blind; silver sashes slung over shoulders and circling the waist; heavy cloth-threaded necklaces inlaid with glass beads, as if the stars were woven into them. Ornate headdresses adorn their hair, with glittering jewels or parts of sacred animals serving as a symbol of their power.

Then in comes Asahar, the vessel of Nardu, the ninth Forebear and god of war.

He is clad in a green-and-gold daura-suruwal embroidered with intricate motifs of chariots and horses, but it pales against his striking features; he has a perfectly symmetrical face only found in official portraits, and his beard is so luxurious that any man would envy it. Before he had been crowned Rakhta, he was the commander of the Holy Guards of Aritsya, elevated to the status at only twenty. It is not hard to imagine why he is one of the most popular Rakhtas.

"My fellow Rakhtas, greetings to you, and may the Forebears' wisdom be with you," I declare, officiating the beginning of the Trial.

"Greetings be upon you," they return.

I turn my head, careful to maintain my balance with the heavy headdress sitting atop it, to look at Medha. "Shira-Rakhti."

She steps to my side, gliding forward in a manner that we've practiced over and over for the past few days. She caught on to the formalities easily, but the reason why I'd made her repeat the motions several times was to ensure she wouldn't decide that a passing butterfly was worth more attention than the Rakhtas standing right before her. To my relief, she presses her palms together and dips her head.

"My humblest greetings, O Vessels of the Forebears," she says, injecting more grandiloquence into her voice than necessary for a girl barely six years of age. "I am Medha of the Yankaran family, and was granted the honour of becoming Shira-Rakhti by the venerable Rashmatun herself."

"Rise, Shira-Rakhti," Iridis says, her sonorous alto a fitting medium for the god she supposedly carries. "Look at us."

Medha obeys her command, lifting her eyes and smiling politely. The brat can behave well when she wants to. I wonder why she thinks it's appropriate to run rampant when she is alone with me.

That's because you've allowed *her to run rampant.* I can almost hear Ilam snickering.

Iridis scans Medha from top to toe, her gaze resembling an eagle locking onto prey. The other Rakhtas also observe Medha from their spots, their expressions ranging from doubt to grudging approval. Asahar grins at Medha, the two rows of his teeth too white and too perfect. Then his attention sidles towards me, and I deflect my gaze, heart pounding against my chest.

We will test her—or Rashmatun's—magic through the Trial of Divinity, he had written to Harun. *The Shira-Rakhti will have to brave flames conjured by the Rakhtas to pass the Trial.*

Why test my magic? What does he have in store for me? If Ilam were here, I would have been able to scrabble through Asahar's mind to uncover every detail of his schemes, and I would be able to summon flame without worry, since Ykta had so soundly rejected my request yesterday. I need the demon's blood magic. I need his power to survive.

Do you see now, you foolish, stubborn child? Kavita's voice sounds like it's being carried by the wind—as though she were right beside me.

My breath hitches.

At long last, Iridis declares the results of her assessment: "She is of adequate appearance and conduct. As of now, she *looks* fit to be your successor."

"For once, I agree with you," Virya, the vessel of Lithari, comments. Similar to her patron—who is the goddess of disasters and healing—she is known for abrupt mood swings and bouts of cruelty and mercy in quick succession. Keran had also told me that she hoards a collection of gemstones—worth far more than what our salaries can afford. "No one will doubt that she is a Rakhti with her appearance."

She casts me a side glance. I force myself to smile, to inject some plumpness into my cheeks. But two weeks of having three proper meals per day does not compensate for years of malnutrition, and any signs of beauty that I might have had when I was younger have long since faded into my sallow complexion and jutting cheek bones.

Even though I've performed my duties faithfully for the past decade, I am still judged by my appearance in the end.

I hate it—and I cling to the hatred with every bit of vengeance I can muster.

"Indeed, Rakhti Virya," I say, keeping my voice calm. Then directing it towards everyone: "Are there any further opinions, my fellow Rakhtas?"

Murmurs of approval gradually fall from their lips; I clap my hands twice. The palanquins shuffle back into the courtyard, arranging themselves into a single file, snaking down the length of the courtyard like the body of a dragon.

I step forward. "Now then, shall we see the people of Bakhtin?"

The Rakhtas incline their heads and disperse, mounting their palanquins. Asahar is the last to move from his position; he leans forward and casts me a wink. "Your people were quite the sight while I was on the way here," he laughs. "I'm sure they enjoy constantly being soaked in rain."

He wheels around and leaves before I can sputter in rage.

How dare he taunt me when I am the one who brought rain upon Bakhtin, blessing our crops and ensuring we will prosper another year. He does not know what I am capable of. Even stripped of Ilam's magic, I will—

Little Medha tugs at my sleeve. "Binsa, why are you so nervous? It's me who's going through the Trial."

I blink. She's right. I shouldn't be so nervous. Asahar just wants to rattle my nerves. And this is my city. There's only so much he can do here.

Right?

19

Drowning

Half of Bakhtin is flooded.

Torrents of water rage through the lower-elevation districts, sweeping refuse from the drainage systems into a muddied swirl. The only fortunate thing about the flood is that it only reaches up to the calves.

In but a few minutes, the strength I injected into myself at Ghanatukh is gone, replaced by an overwhelming wash of shame. Why wasn't I alerted to this? Why did the devotees flocking to my temple not make any mention of the flooding? Did this only happen last night? Is it possible that Harun purposely turned those with flooding problems away?

Through it all, I think, *I brought this rain.*

I look upwards; the clouds are just as dark and tumultuous as they were on the first day. What were the terms of my contract with Ilam? That in exchange for my womb, he would give me the power to summon rain—

Snivelling Sartas. I never specified how much rain I wanted.

I can almost hear Ilam's dark laughter.

And beneath the ghost of Ilam's mocking cackle, Kavita's voice echoes faintly: *Do not resist him. This is the natural course of your path.*

My gut clenches; my breaths come in shorter, faster.

I want to bury my head in my hands, but instead I square my shoulders, remembering that everyone is watching me in this procession. Ilam's power can't last for that long, I reason with myself—the rain will stop on its own. I just have to wait it out.

Stubborn, foolish girl, Kavita's voice echoes in my head. *Never mind. You'll learn soon enough.*

I clench my teeth. My eyes scour my surroundings, as if they can pierce through the heavy downpour and dissipate the roiling clouds above-head. Harun walks on the right of my palanquin, while his son flanks the left. I find my palanquin oddly empty without Medha by my side. People throng the streets, cheering at the sight of the Rakhtas parading around their city, but even their hollers are muted. Their smiles dim once my palanquin passes by, which brings up the rear of the procession.

Despite my constant self-reminders that this rain is a blessing, that the alternative would have been a relentless, scorching drought, that no one should be able to question my sovereignty as Rashmatun's vessel, my throat closes.

I summoned the storm.

In three hours' time, we manage to go through only the Eastern and Southern Districts, completely bypassing Dharun. All the while, I remain as motionless as a statue. I cannot do anything. Without Ilam, I am nothing. I am nothing but an ornament dressed in heavy livery and magnificent jewellery, with no authority nor voice to truly call my own.

And though the rain roars in my ears, I hear a familiar lullaby being scattered throughout my surroundings if I focus. Some high, some low, some out of tune and out of rhythm. All singing the same song.

> "Red and bright the skies will burn,
> Our offerings mourn, and the ghosts return.
> The skies darken with fear, trembling amidst the goddess's might,
> The fallen stars shatter, and the seas rise.
> At the end of it all, the Scarlet Throne bleeds,

The crown at her head rusts,
The ornaments turn to dust."

The Prophecy of Geerkha.

A chill washes over me—and it's not from the rain.

The people of Bakhtin are clinging to the words of a prophet-ess who died over five centuries ago, refusing to believe the god-dess right before their eyes. And yet I cannot blame them. I would curse myself too, if I were one of those nameless people standing in the crowd, looking at a little girl dressed in Bakhtin's finest fabrics while they are left to shiver outside.

"Hear our song of mourning, O Forgotten Goddess,
Hear our cries of despair!
Go back to whence you came from,
And leave us forevermore.
A sacrifice given, a sacrifice saved.
At the end of it all, a path of blood awaits."

How are you going to maintain a hold on your throne now, Binsa? a lit-tle voice at the back of my mind whispers. *Maybe you should just let go. Maybe you don't deserve to be Rakhti after all.*

I close my eyes, allowing the despair to sink into my bones.

No one says another word to me when we return to Ghanatukh Temple. Not when I am escorted to the Bakhal, not when Jirtash and her handmaidens dunk me into a hot bath. And Jirtash always has something to say.

They all knew about the floods, and they all refused to tell me anything about them.

I study my hands in the bath, their skin wrinkling the longer they are soaked in water. Frail hands that have never done a day's work of hard labour in their life. Hands that should not belong to a goddess.

I curl my hands into fists. The flooding, the procession, the derision of my own people. Even after all I've done, all I've accomplished, I am weak.

After I am hauled out of the bath, I change into a daura-suruwal, but with a shawl layered across my shoulders for more warmth. Jirtash guides me to my table, where a steaming bowl of gwarcha awaits me. I barely manage to swallow one mouthful of soup and beans. All the while, I cannot help but imagine what everyone is thinking of me right now, even though Ilam is not with me.

I can't believe it. She's such a nice girl.

Maybe she was pretending to be polite all along. She was the only survivor of the Bloodbath, after all. There's no way someone who rose to power through such a tragedy can be good.

I no longer recognise her as the Rakhti of Bakhtin.

I force another spoonful of gwarcha down my throat. These are my own speculations, I remind myself. There is no way I can actually hear them.

"Rakhti Binsa," someone mumbles. Nali bows towards me.

It's the first time she's willingly approached me since she healed me. It must be because of what Medha has relayed to her. Can't she tell that I'm too exhausted to talk about the Bloodbath? But I set my food aside. "Leave us," I tell everyone.

They all step outside in a flash. Nali takes something out of the pocket of her uniform and hands it to me. "I was going to just give you this," she says. "I didn't think we had to be alone."

I unwrap the cloth to find a hot, freshly fried sel roti.

I look at her in astonishment. She averts her gaze and blushes. "I'm sorry. I thought this might cheer you up. You seemed down after the procession. I hope I'm not stepping out of line."

My grip around the sel roti tightens. "Thank you," I whisper.

I take a bite. It's warm and sweet, crispy on the outside and fluffy inside. The taste and texture overlap with my memory of Chandri sneaking me snacks during our lessons. The small acts of kindness may not have mattered to her, but they meant the world to me.

Tears roll down my cheeks.

"My Rakhti!" Nali jolts. "Does it taste that terrible?"

"No. It's perfect." I take another bite and wipe my tears away with my sleeve. It's ridiculous; I don't know why I am crying. In front of someone I barely know, no less. "I'm surprised the chefs allowed you to steal one, though."

"I'm the only one among the servants who regularly praises their cooking." Her arms hang awkwardly by her sides, as if she doesn't know what to do with them. "I'm just sorry that this is the only way I can help you."

"Please. You've helped enough. I haven't even done anything for you." I take another bite of the sel roti and smile at her. "I also never thanked you properly for saving my life the other day."

She ducks her chin. "It was my duty."

"Your hadon is a wonderful gift, and I'm glad you were here when I needed you."

Nali's blush deepens. If this coy personality is a façade, it is a convincing one.

Subconsciously, I compare Medha and Nali. One loud and chatty and infernally curious, the other quiet and submissive and keeping as low a profile as possible. Two wildly contrasting characters— each with a different set of strengths and weaknesses.

It's my opportunity to figure out Nali's role in her stepmother's schemes.

"I must repay you," I say. "Tell me what you want. If it is within my capacity, I will grant your wish."

"My Rakhti." Nali presses her palms together and sinks into a deep bow.

"Please. No need to be so formal when it's just the two of us." I laugh. "I am around your age, after all."

Her gaze is doubtful yet eager, reminding me of Medha's. "I think your aid in investigating the truth of the Bloodbath is reward enough, my Rakhti."

There we go. "I assume Medha has already told you everything?"

Nali maintains the slouch in her posture, as if she were trying to shrink herself into the background. "Indeed. She speaks very fondly of you too, and it seems she wholeheartedly trusts you."

The real question is, does Nali trust me? "I'm glad to hear that. I'm rather fond of Medha's company as well."

"A talkative one, isn't she? I hope she hasn't given you much trouble."

I think about my first encounter with her at the Selection, and how she'd bitten her tongue to win her place as Shira-Rakhti.

"Not at all," I say. "In fact, I find her antics most endearing."

"But *we* are going to give you trouble if you do help us with our investigation." She lowers her voice until it is barely above a whisper: "If you permit me to ask, my Rakhti, why are you helping us?"

She is desperate, yet cautious. I wonder if she's aware of the chinks in her armour that she's showing to me. "The Bloodbath is a mystery to me as well," I say, "and Rashmatun has never spoken of it to me."

Nali falls still; briefly I wonder if another hadon user would be able to read her mind. "Now I will ask the same of you," I continue. "Why is your family so interested in learning the truth of the Bloodbath? Most of the families affected by it simply accepted their compensation and mourned their daughters in silence."

I need to get Nali to admit everything herself. Most of what I managed to glean so far came from reading Medha's mind.

She clasps her fingers before her. For a moment, I can read the dilemma tearing her apart. Should she trust me, the Rakhti of Bakhtin and the most prominent figure in the entire city? Or should she keep the important secrets to herself, the way her stepmother would prefer?

But I also know that she has no choice. Nali's stepmother will be able to pay her regular visits once Medha is crowned Rakhti, and she will have to start showing results. If Adarsh is anything like Kavita, she would stop at nothing to get the answers she wants. She might even go so far as to report her own stepdaughter to the Council for illegal magic.

A mother capable of subjecting her flesh-and-blood daughter to psychological torment would think nothing of using a girl who is not her own daughter.

Nali straightens herself, having made her choice. "I had an elder half sister, who was Medha's biological sister. Her name was Anju. She died during the Bloodbath."

"Ah," I say, closing my eyes, as if offering a silent prayer for her dead sister's soul. "It makes sense."

"Thiravinda Harun and Boruvinda Nudin also know of this," Nali says. "My stepmother bribed them to allow Medha to take part in the Selection when they were screening for potential candidates."

Yes, I know all that already. "Your mother must have offered quite a huge sum, for them to flout the Selection's laws just like that."

Nali flinches. "I'm sorry."

Somehow her reaction reminds me of when I would constantly apologise for wrongs that I never committed, back when Kavita was still around. "No, don't. The Bloodbath is a stain upon our history. I understand why your family would be aggrieved." I release a shuddering breath. "I should be sorry, for being the only survivor."

If Ilam were here, he would have approved of this charade I'm putting on. There may be truth woven in my words, but I'm well aware of how I'm twisting and manipulating everything to design a specific image of myself.

It feels nice to have some control again.

Nali shuffles on her feet. "Please, no, my Rakhti. That's not what I meant."

I wave my hand. "Never mind that. I have another burning question to ask. I understand why your parents would be desperate to shove Medha in, but why you? They must have been aware of the commotion that would ensue from nominating a half-Dennarese sibling in place of the Shira-Rakhti's mother."

Trepidation seizes her features.

"I won't tell anyone," I assure her. "I've managed to keep Medha's secrets, and I will keep all of yours. I swear this on the name of Rashmatun. Besides, if I wanted to harm you and Medha, I would've declared long ago that your little sister has been wagging her tongue about the Bloodbath." I pause and pretend to consider. "Is it your hadon?"

"My—my hadon is strictly sanctioned for medicinal purposes, my Rakhti," Nali protests.

"So you're capable of performing other types of magic?"

Her limbs stiffen.

Just a little more.

"I need your full cooperation if you wish for me to help you uncover the truth of the Bloodbath, Nali," I say. "If I do not know the full range of your capabilities, all our effort will be for naught. I have only two weeks left in my position. Help me to help yourself."

Come on, I'm the only person you can turn to in this temple, I try to convey.

Some of her hesitancy dissipates, although she still has a slight stammer when she speaks: "I—I am able to become invisible for brief periods of time. Shadow-melding, my blood mother called it. But my control over it is limited."

My stomach drops to my feet. She could squeeze into the darkest corners of Ghanatukh, eavesdrop on conversations that she has no authority to listen to ...

"Have you done anything yet?" I hope she doesn't notice the tightness in my voice.

She shakes her head. "It's extremely taxing on my body, and I am able to maintain it for twenty minutes at most. Besides, I could be executed if I were to be caught using hadon illegally." Her mouth curves into a sheepish smile. "I'm a coward, honestly. Too scared to make a move because I keep convincing myself that the time isn't right."

I release a sigh of relief inside.

"And what happens after you find the truth of the Bloodbath? Will you be satisfied after that?" I ask, posing the same questions I did to Medha before. "Or do you seek revenge?"

Nali stares into the distance, at the grey haze clouding Bakhtin. "I do not know," she murmurs. "I just know I must atone for my sins—for my existence brought ill fortune upon the Yankaran name. That's what my stepmother told me, at least."

The air grows heavy, stale. As if realising this, Nali tries to clear the air with a nervous laugh. "I'm still grateful for my family, of course."

I cast her a sympathetic look.

"Anyway, I told Medha I would ask Harun more about the

Bloodbath, although honestly...I'm not too inclined towards the idea," I say, changing the topic. "If he's happy to receive hush money for allowing Medha to be nominated in the Selection—not that I'm blaming you—then it's hard to say he wasn't completely involved in the incident."

Nali's eyes widen. "My Rakhti, what you're saying—"

"This is all merely speculation. My gut feeling could be wrong." I polish off the last of the sel roti; it's grown cold throughout the duration of our conversation. "What is a little more viable right now is assigning you to work in his quarters instead. Listen to the other servants working there and observe Harun's behaviour. Then perhaps we can decide what we will do after that."

She pauses a while before answering: "I see. Yes, that would be best."

"In the meantime, do not talk to anyone else about the Blood-bath. And don't use your hadon for a little longer. I'll help with your transfer once the Trial is over." I slump in my seat. "Go ahead with your duties. We don't want Jirtash fussing over you. And I need to prepare myself to face the Rakhtas later."

"You have my gratitude, my Rakhti," she says, falling into a deep bow—one reserved for the most sovereign of elders. "For helping us with this. And for taking care of Medha."

She leaves the room at long last, and the smirk I've been holding back all along spreads across my face.

I may be a Rakhti currently in a precarious position, but at least I have my successor and her half sister dancing in my palm.

20

Trial of Faith

Even taking one step further in winning Nali's trust fails to quell the anxiety spilling throughout my limbs, though. I watch the sky melt from blue-grey hues into the dusky slate of a rain-filled twilight. The Rakhtas will call for the Trial anytime soon.

And I still have no way to summon flame.

Ilam, I call out. *Come on. Can't you appear, even just for a split second?*

But he has retreated so far back into my mind that I cannot sense him anymore. It's almost as though I were no longer a blood shaman. Just a normal human girl wallowing in the face of impending disaster.

I contain a sob. I've already cried once today. I need to keep myself together. Despairing will do me no good here. I remain near the window of my room, taking in the sight of Bakhtin and the rain, steadying my breaths.

The shriek of an eagle pierces through the haze.

I instinctively step aside. Keran's eagle dives through the window like an arrow, landing with a metallic *thunk* on my table.

The sound of metal? My brows furrow as the eagle—Qara, I think, is her name—hops aside to reveal a cylindrical piece of steel, leather straps attached to one side. I pick it up to inspect it; an external tube conceals two mini cylinders inside, which converge into a single chamber in the front. A round button protrudes from the top. It weighs heavier than it looks, despite the fact that it fits in my palm.

Qara flaps a wing to draw my attention. A chit has been attached to her leg. I gulp and quickly unfurl it.

> *You can strap this to your wrist. Press the button on top to trigger the mechanism, and remember to bend your wrist downwards so you don't accidentally burn yourself. The part with an open chamber faces forward. I only loaded two charges inside, but it should be enough to get you through the Trial. Each charge will last you approximately ten seconds. The flamethrower is an extremely dangerous weapon. Use it with caution.*

I could collapse now from relief. There's no sign-off, no greeting, no mention of our argument, but it's definitely Ykta.

He is still helping me.

Not without making you worry and fret the whole day, though, Kavita's voice murmurs.

A knock sounds from my door. "My Rakhti," Jirtash calls out. "It is time to get ready to summon Rashmatun."

I quickly tuck the flamethrower into my bookshelf and toss Ykta's note outside the window and chase Qara off. Luckily the eagle is smart enough that she exits without making a sound.

"Come in," I tell Jirtash.

They dress me in the heavy robes of Rashmatun—the same clothing I used for the procession this morning. The wide, full sleeves enable me to conceal the flamethrower, and my hand ghosts over my right wrist, feeling the metal grooves beneath the layers of fabric—feeling the trigger. The flamethrower is small, but sits high enough above my skin that theoretically I should be able to wield it unscathed. I wonder if I will be able to successfully fool the other Rakhtas with this.

My heart slams against my chest. I will only find out after the Trial.

After we're done at the cleansing hall, I am carted on a palanquin to the Balamat, an enormous tower that stands at least three floors taller than its surrounding neighbours. Its tiled, tiered roofs slope downwards in shimmering yellow, as if gold were pouring down from the sky. Its name—the Court of a Thousand Suns—comes from the thousand windows that surface the walls, allowing natural sunlight to filter in and illuminate the entire place. Although now the weather is much too dreary to showcase the full extent of its beauty.

The interior is larger than what the outside indicates. Statues of lesser gods—the descendants of the Forebears—form an outer ring, while the ten Forebears form the inner ring. Rashmatun's statue helms the centre of the ring, and is the first figure that one sees when treading through its entrance. Today, the bloodred hue of her jama contrasts against the subdued background, and the yellow sapphires embedded in her eyes sparkle with an incandescent light.

As if she were a falling star bathed in blood. Beautiful. Fearsome.

Do you exist, I think, *or do you not?*

Nothing. As usual.

I turn my attention to my fellow Rakhtas, who are seated in a circle in the middle, right before the statues of their corresponding Forebears. Medha is already here, taking up position behind my designated seat. She is dressed in a resplendent purple jama threaded with silver stars, as if the fabric were woven out of the night sky. Jirtash must have commissioned the seamstresses to specially craft this for her—perhaps for the Trial of Divinity itself.

My throat tightens as I take in her appearance; I do not know if it is out of envy or admiration.

I glide towards my position—taking care to not accidentally toe the thousand-pronged star painted on the floor—and settle between all the Rakhtas. They do not acknowledge my presence.

"Let us begin the Trial of Divinity," I declare.

The Rakhtas nod.

"Medha Yankaran," Iridis—now possessed by Vashmar—says. "Why do you wish to become Rakhti?"

A bark of laughter almost escapes me. A coincidence, or an imitation of my question to her?

I cannot see Medha, as she is behind me, but there is confidence in her small voice: "I want to know what it means to be Rakhti. I want to know what it means to govern people and what it means to cry and be overjoyed for them."

She pauses. She knows what she is doing; everyone's eyes are on her.

"And I want to honour Binsa's footsteps," she says. "I want to honour all the Rakhtis who came before and ensure that their legacies live forever."

Silence.

Then a slow clap rings out.

"I'm impressed, Shira-Rakhti," Asahar—or Nardu—says, lips curled into a toothy smile. "Rakhti Binsa has taught you well. Now, let's move on to the actual Trial."

Iridis gestures towards the centre of the Balamat. "Step forth, Medha Yankaran."

I hear little Medha shuffling forward with as much grace as she can muster. She maintains a perfect posture, but even with the Rakhtas seated, they all seem to dwarf her.

"Our test for you will be Trial by Fire," Iridis, or Vashmar, says. "A wall of flame will be conjured near where you are standing. If you successfully walk through it, you pass the Trial."

Through Medha's side profile I see the colour draining from her face. I was lucky during my Trial, I realise.

"Do you understand the Trial?" Vashmar asks.

Medha nods.

"Good. Do you accept this Trial, Medha Yankaran?" Vashmar continues.

"I do," she says bravely, though I've been with her long enough that I know it's all a façade. I know it is how she survived her mother, and how she intends to get through the Trial, even if she has to risk getting burned to succeed.

We're more alike than I'd care to admit, I ponder wryly.

"Rashmatun," Vashmar calls out to me. "We have decided that

you will be the one to initiate the Trial. The rest of us will not interfere."

I swallow so that my voice is not dry when I reply. "I understand."

How did Asahar convince them to conduct the Trial in this manner, so that I alone will have to use magic? But it is custom for the host Forebear to accept whatever the other gods have planned for their Shira-Rakhta, to indicate trust in their judgment. Even though this one was organised with a clear agenda against me.

So I silently raise both hands as Medha turns to face me, left hand hovering over my right wrist. I wear a stony expression, the face of an unfeeling god. But perhaps somewhere beneath the ornate jewellery and the heavy makeup she'll find the face of Binsa—the face of the girl she trusts and admires.

Be brave, I try to tell her.

She sets her jaw. I force myself to breathe, praying that Ykta's little flamethrower is more than enough so that the fire is convincing. I lower my left hand under the pretence of steadying my outstretched arm.

Fire bursts from the chamber hidden beneath my sleeve in an orange riot. The heat that radiates from the flamethrower feels like it is singeing my skin. For a moment, I think I smell charred clothing—or flesh. I hold on, sweat beading on my brow. I do not feel my hand going dead yet, and this is nothing compared to the pain I endured from Ilam.

Medha balks at the wall of flames suddenly appearing before her. I grit my teeth and aim it at her feet so that I don't accidentally torch her. The seconds that tick by feel like hours. The heat, the recoil of the flamethrower juddering up my arm, the struggle to not lose control of my movement.

The flamethrower sputters, and I release the trigger.

I tuck my right hand beneath my left; I cannot check if there are any wounds there now, and I can no longer feel anything on that side because of the searing heat. I maintain my neutral expression and hope the other Rakhtas don't notice the tremble in my limbs—which seems to match Medha's. My gaze sweeps across the Balamat; the Rakhtas' eyes are all pinned on the little girl standing in the middle of the room.

"Medha Yankaran, did you forget the instructions already?" Vashmar asks, tone cutting.

"No, my Rakhta," she whispers.

"Then why did you not take a single step just now?"

She's just a girl, I want to scream. I would be frozen with fear if I were in her position. *Stop torturing her like this!*

"And you, Rashmatun," Nardu says, the deep cadence of his voice now intimidating when I usually find it infuriating. "What are you doing? She may be the successor of your Rakhti, but it does not mean you should go easy on her."

Easy on her? The fire that almost burned me as well?

"I knew that fire was never your strong suit, but I never thought you would be this pathetic," he says, lips curled into a taunting smile. "Or have you spent so much power summoning rain that you don't have enough left for such a simple Trial?"

"Nardu," Vashmar says, a warning in their tone.

"He is right, Vashmar," Virya—or Lithari—interjects. "Rashmatun needs to take this Trial seriously."

"There's more where that came from," Nardu continues. "You don't have to feel shy to demonstrate your power before us. We already know what you're capable of."

My stomach clenches. I have to prove my magic before them. I cannot let them learn that I am not Rashmatun. I cannot let the Rakhtas and the Forebears, of all people, see that a mortal girl has been posing as one of them all this while. If only Ilam were here. Why does the demon abandon me when I need him most?

Ilam, I call out.

No response.

Ilam, I cry as my mind starts to unravel.

"Do it again," Vashmar says. "I hope you're truly ready this time, Medha Yankaran."

They might as well have directed the sentence towards me.

I lift my hand again. It's getting harder to hide the trembling now; my muscles tighten so much they are beginning to cramp. Little Medha stares at me with terror-stricken eyes.

I cannot breathe. Still I push the trigger once more.

Ilam! I scream, and search for him in the darkest, deepest recesses of my mind.

Just as I had forcefully shut him out last time, this round I drag him out in a clawing and shrieking and enraged mess. Maybe he'll choose to kill me now. Maybe he won't. I just know the panic settling in my bones, and that I need his magic. Nothing else. I don't care if summoning fire is not Ilam's affinity. I don't care if I have to wreck my body to use his magic.

The world around me roars to life.

I use Ilam's magic to stoke the flames as I aim the flamethrower at the ground. His power courses through my arm, giving it strength and destroying it at the same time. I release the trigger on the flamethrower. The flame wall grows higher and burns hotter.

I can breathe now, with the comforting lull of Ilam's magic in my veins.

And I can control the flames freely.

Through the flickering fire I spot Medha, completely petrified.

I could use this to get rid of her, I think.

I was fretting over my own fate so much that I completely forgot that the Trial centres Medha, not me. She's the one being assessed, not me. I never thought it was possible for her to fail, though— Trials of Divinity are supposed to be customary, to officially welcome the Shira-Rakhta into the ranks of the other Rakhtas.

But right now, I have the power to make sure she never crosses that wall of flames.

What are you waiting for? a voice whispers in my head.

For a moment, my eyes lock with Medha's.

Her lips thin, and I know she has made up her mind.

Make the flames hotter, my inner voice says. *Make them burn so bright that she can do nothing but stare at them. Or make the wall so thick that she cannot get through it even if she tried to.*

Yes, I should do that. Get rid of her while I have the chance.

And yet, I release my hold on the fire when Medha jumps.

It is only a split-second window, but I make sure the fire is not too hot the moment it comes into contact with her. She charges through before she can falter.

I lower my hand and extinguish the flames. Ilam quickly retreats. I thought he'd berate me on the spot for using his power so recklessly.

Medha lies on the ground, covering her face with her arms, shivering uncontrollably. Her clothes are intact, and her skin remains blemish-free. I made sure the fire didn't catch on her.

"On your feet, Medha Yankaran," Vashmar says, devoid of empathy. "You have passed the Trial."

The little girl pushes herself to stand. I hear a faint whimper from her. When she lifts her face, though her cheeks are still colourless and tears gather in her eyes, she puts on a resolute expression. One befitting an official Shira-Rakhti.

For some reason, my chest swells with pride.

You could have gotten rid of her! a part of me snarls. *Why didn't you?*

Why didn't I, indeed? Now that I have time to retrace my decision, confusion eddies my mind.

"Congratulations, Shira-Rakhti," Nardu says. "And that was a spectacular show you put on, Rashmatun. Simply splendid! I enjoyed every second of it."

What is that supposed to mean? "I'm not sure if you're supposed to 'enjoy' a Trial, Nardu," I reply. "Save your uncouth mannerisms for your failing wars instead."

The reason why I've managed to survive all these years during meetings with other gods is that Rashmatun tends to be of few words. That, and getting on the other Forebears' nerves is a distinctive trait of hers. Lithari had once asked if I was all right when a meeting ended without a scathing remark from me.

A scene surfaces in my mind: The very first Rakhta meeting I attended with Chandri. My predecessor, usually composed and calm, nearly flared up at Iridis, who was possessed by Vashmar. They interrupted her proposals and dismissed her opinions. Chandri wrung her hands together in a motion that looked like she was imagining wringing their neck.

In the end, she settled for throwing a few snide comments at them, infuriating Vashmar so much that Iridis's entire face reddened.

Perhaps the observations I made that day melded into my

subconscious, helping me avoid scrutiny all these years. Now that the memory returns, I try to discern if the one who had been attending that meeting was Chandri or Rashmatun.

I cannot tell.

Just like how I cannot tell if it is Nardu or Asahar speaking to me right now.

"Enough," Vashmar interrupts. "Our vessels require rest. It's been a long day for us."

"Agreed." Guphalon, the god of luck, stretches and yawns. "Call me back when you've got something to show."

He abruptly gets up. He blinks once, twice, and his body quivers. Then he is looking at us as if he were in a room full of talking mushrooms.

"My...fellow Rakhtas?" he says. He is back to being Harmesh, Guphalon's vessel.

Vashmar heaves an irritated sigh. "Always going ahead and ignoring procedures, as usual."

Harmesh, upon realising that he was talking with the Forebears themselves, starts to wheeze in anxiety. Everyone rises to their feet, shaking their heads and rubbing their eyes, as if trying to reorient to their surroundings. I do the same. Medha hurries over to me and clings to my waist, not saying a word. I place a hand on her head, unsure of what to do now.

Asahar is the first to recover. "That was a long day!" He gestures towards the exit. "Come. Shall we all have a proper rest before dinner?"

Did I...pass whatever test Asahar had prepared for me, by asking Rashmatun to summon flame? That should be the case, since he is not confronting me now or making any mention of the fire I conjured—

"Rakhti Binsa." He has traipsed over, his movements so swift and sleek that I don't notice him until he is right by my side. "I know this seems out of the blue, but I have a question for you."

I frown at him to disguise the uneasiness crawling up my spine. "What is it? If they're matters related to your living arrangements while in Ghanatukh, you may ask my chief priest."

"Oh, I wouldn't bother you about trivial stuff like that," he chuckles. "It's something much more serious."

I raise a brow. "Such as?"

"Have you ever gotten wounded before? Stabbed? Slashed open?"

I think of the time Gurrehmat stabbed me in the thigh—and how Ilam shredded him moments afterwards.

"What a strange question you have," I say. "No, I can't say that's happened to me before."

"That's good, right? On the battlefield it's so easy to rack up scars." He sighs and runs his fingers through his hair. "You must live a comfortable life here."

Does he remember my insult to him while he was "Nardu"? "Why are you asking such a thing, anyway?"

"No, no. Don't mind me. I just wanted to gauge how familiar you are with suffering." He grins in a way that may appear handsome to some, but only makes my skin crawl. "And congratulations to you, Shira-Rakhti Medha. I look forward to working with you over the years."

"Thank you," Medha murmurs, burying her head in my skirt. Normally I would scold her for speaking so half-heartedly, but considering what the girl just went through I do not say anything.

"Goodbye for now." Asahar waves, maintaining his grin. Then he leans forward so that our faces are on the same level. "See me at your worship hall at midnight," he whispers. "Alone."

He saunters out of the Balamat.

I know I am walking into a trap. I know that without Ilam, I have no power to try to oppose Asahar. Even the flamethrower is out of fumes now; I tested it briefly when I was back in my room. I cannot turn to anyone for help, so I am alone.

Navigating the darkness without Ilam's magic proves to be an arduous task. I trip over invisible bumps along the path, and my eyes strain to make out shapes in the shadows. Still, I find my way to the Paruvatar, its two-tiered roofs stacked atop each other in perfect, sloping squares, as strong and uncompromising as the goddess it is meant to hold.

I take a deep breath, filling my lungs with the cool night air, and step in.

Asahar is already waiting inside, running his hands over the Scarlet Throne—*my* throne. Anger flares in my blood, but I level my voice as I speak. "What are you doing?"

"Admiring the place. This sculpture of Anas is remarkable." He studies it for a moment, seemingly fascinated by the details in the snake god's scales and fangs, the yellow stones embedded in his eyes. "Who did this for you? It must be wonderful to have some of the finest artisans in Aritsya working for you. *I* wouldn't want to ever stop being Rakhti."

"Are your artisans truly that poor, Rakhta Asahar?" I retort, refusing to be rattled. "I'd be more than happy to lend you a few hands."

"I couldn't possibly trouble you so, Rakhti Binsa," he replies cheerfully. "Especially when you are busy trying to retain your position."

"What are you talking about?"

He lifts his grubby fingers off the Scarlet Throne and turns towards me, a slow, devious grin spreading across his lips. "You really came alone? I didn't think you'd trust me this much."

My fingernails scrape the insides of my palms. *Calm down*, I tell myself. *You have your wits.* "I trust you to have integrity as a vessel of Nardu." I tilt my head in condescension. "Even if you frequently sneak off to gambling dens with the money your people offer you."

His gaze hardens into a glare. He unsheathes his kukri; my insides clench, and I'm sure that my face has gone white. But I force myself to stand tall, to stand firm, to look as though I am in control. "Why so agitated, O God of War?" I laugh. " 'The righteous man does not balk in the face of slander.' Don't tell me you've forgotten the words of our holy book?"

He climbs down from the dais, his kukri held loosely by his side. "Why so quick to jump to conclusions, O Great Goddess of

Wisdom?" he responds in a mocking tone. "I merely enjoy the weight of a weapon in hand. Makes me feel more comfortable."

"Really? Have your weapons helped you slay hadon practitioners from Dennar?"

The tip of the kukri suddenly whips up in a silver blur, its tip grazing the skin under my chin. My attention zones in on that lethal, icy tip, and its cold spreads throughout my limbs. "I shouldn't be surprised that nothing escapes your attention," Asahar says, the curve of his smile taking on a hint of cruelty. "What other secrets do you know, O Goddess of Wisdom?"

"It is my goddess who is all-knowing, not me," I say, still smiling. "Besides, it's you who is being secretive today. What's with all the fuss and the threats and the strange questions? Why do you wish to see me?"

He digs the blade in a little deeper—one slight shift, and my skin will be sliced open. "I'm sure you know the answer very well, Binsa."

The kukri is retracted. I finally take a deep breath; the area around my chin is still numb from the cold. Asahar fiddles with his weapon, but makes no move to sheathe it. Then he is thrusting his arm towards me.

Driving the blade into my gut.

21

The Scarlet Throne

My mind goes blank. I cannot cry out in pain. All sound has been clawed out of my throat. Only pure, hot agony is left.

Asahar rips the kukri out.

I gasp, keeling over and collapsing onto the floor. My hand clutches my stomach. Warm blood gushes out, dripping between my fingers and staining the floor.

Purple fog coalesces at the edge of my vision.

My head spins. Ilam suddenly appears before me. Am I hallucinating? Am I dying? Is he going to claim my soul, just as all demons eventually do to all blood shamans?

The blood pouring from my wound slows; the injury stitches itself closed.

"You dare draw blood from my vessel?" Ilam growls.

Asahar throws his head back in triumphant laughter.

Ilam is still out in the open, his feline form bristling and crackling with magic. Purple fog clogs the hall. My core thrums, and his power flows back into me, sharpening my senses—making me feel *alive*.

Relief is replaced by terror—even colder than the feel of the kukri against my skin. No. Why is Ilam out here? Couldn't he have healed me without showing himself? My brain spins and spins and spins, all my possible next steps, the possible consequences I will have to face rearing to life, turning all my thoughts upside down.

Asahar knew about Ilam all along. That must be it. He was the one goading me during the Trial...the one who pushed me to use blood magic. Perhaps that was how he learned of Ilam's presence. Was he trying to force me to use Ilam's power back then, or was it a coincidence?

No. It cannot be. He mentioned he was trying to remove me as Rashmatun's vessel in his letter to Harun. He must have learned that I have Ilam long before this Trial.

But how?

"Don't blame your demon. He was acting on instinct," Asahar drawls, wiping his blade on his kurta. My blood stains the beautiful green-and-gold fabric. The sight of red jolts me awake, and fury, both hot and cold, lances through my veins.

I push myself onto my feet, clenching my teeth. *Calm*, I think. *Calm. You will go nowhere with a muddled head.* "Did you really need to stab me to prove your theory?" I say. "You already knew that I don't have Rashmatun, isn't that right?"

"Ooh, you figured it out! Not too shabby, considering you don't have her wisdom."

I release a huff; though my wound has closed, the area still feels sore. "What do you want?"

His teeth shine in the darkness. "I'll cut straight to the point. What have you done with Rashmatun?"

I stare at him. That was not the question I was expecting. "What do you mean?"

"Don't play pretend any longer," he hisses. His eyes flicker towards the statue of Anas for a brief moment. "You have a demon inside you, which means you can't hold Rashmatun at the same time. Now tell me—what have you done with the goddess?"

I track backwards, adjusting to the richness of the world that comes along with Ilam. Asahar's mind is a low hum; I won't get my answers immediately. "I do not know what you're talking about," I say. Then after a brief pause: "Rashmatun does not exist."

Even as the words fall from my mouth, I can only half believe what I am saying, though. Does she not exist, or do I want to believe she does not exist? The fact that Chandri and Asahar have similar magic is irrefutable. Is it the magic of the Forebears—magic I was supposed to receive but didn't?

Then why? Why was I not chosen by Rashmatun?

"I've granted you the mercy of not killing you right away, and you dare lie to my face?" Asahar raises his blade. At this point, I do not have the strength to flinch. Ilam snarls, yet makes no move to protect me. His fear stings me like a slush of ice. "What will you do once I tell the entirety of Aritsya that their goddess of wisdom is a *blood shaman?*"

My stomach sinks. No. That would be far worse than getting killed. I cannot accept a lifetime of scorn and humiliation. Is there any way I can get rid of Asahar without risking my position? Is Ilam strong enough to overpower—

Hush, Kavita says. *Listen, and observe. There is more to this story than you think.*

Despite how frightened I am of her voice, I heed her words. I take a deep breath, clearing my mind. I wait, and listen.

"I will ask you once again," Asahar continues. "What have you done with Rashmatun?"

They never suspected you all these years, Kavita says. *Only now are they taking action. Why?*

"What makes you think I've done something to her?" I ask, fighting to keep my tone steady. Ilam's fear is affecting my sense of self.

"Of course you've done something! How else would she not be with you?"

Asahar still has not made a move to end me. Strange. He stabbed me to draw Ilam out, and with the power of a god, he could have easily killed me the moment he saw the demon. But he didn't.

Which means that whoever or whatever Rashmatun really is, she is important. And he and the other Rakhtas need *me* to find her.

"Why should I return Rashmatun to you?" I say, folding my arms.

Asahar puffs out his chest; he glances at the statue of Anas again. I can hear the erratic pounding of his heart. "Your lack of control over your demon flooded your city. Your own people wish to see you off the throne. You have failed them, and you ask me why you should return Rashmatun?"

"Really? From the way I see it, you're willing to go soft on me if it means getting your so-called goddess back."

"You insolent—"

"Of course, you could just kill me right here and now. Get a head-ache out of your way." I lace my fingers behind my back and pace around him. "All your dirty little secrets will die with me, along with the secret of Rashmatun. Or you could negotiate a little more."

Asahar grips the handle of his kukri, clearly attempting to regain some semblance of control. He walks back up the dais, stroking one of Anas's heads. Why is he so obsessed with the snake god? "I do not like negotiating on uneven grounds, Binsa."

Asahar tears the statue down.

A terrible crack splinters the air. The ten heads of Anas come free in Asahar's hand, and a gaping hole now sits behind the throne. Dust plumes the area; I raise my hand to stifle my coughs. Asahar flings the statue aside, the impact creating further cracks in the floor. He reaches an arm into the hole and pulls Ykta out.

I can only stare at my brother, stunned.

"Did you plant this intruder here as witness?" Asahar grabs the collar of Ykta's kurta and shakes him; the Rakhta is a head taller than my brother, whose wiry frame is a poor match for the other man's battle-hardened figure. "I do not appreciate your little games, Binsa. I've been forthright till now. I expect the same from you."

Briefly, my eyes meet Ykta's. Time slows as the full weight of his horror crashes over my head.

He saw Ilam emerging out of my body, saw the demon roaring in rage as Asahar pulled the kukri out of my abdomen. The truth has hollowed him into shock—I have been a blood shaman all this while, following in our mother's footsteps. He recalls how he met Keran just yesterday; they convened under the cover of darkness, somewhere outside Ghanatukh Temple.

Asahar will be visiting her tonight, Keran said to him. *Observe them. I think you'll find something interesting.*

Rage snaps me back to my senses. That Dennarese bastard. He had known all this would happen. He simply withheld the information from me to help Ykta. But of course. I should have suspected something more when his eagle brought Ykta's flamethrower to me. I should have thought it strange that Ykta commissioned Keran, of all people, to deliver the weapon to me.

If that's the case, Keran knows of my blood magic as well.

I'll skin him alive next time I see him.

You truly are a fool, Kavita laughs. *I told you that you cannot trust your brother.*

I keep my eyes pinned forward, holding myself tall.

"You tell me where Rashmatun is now." Asahar whips out his kukri in a fluid motion and holds the blade against Ykta's throat. The sound of Asahar's pounding heart gives way to my brother's, a thrumming roar that deafens my ears. "Or he dies."

I inhale, channelling Rashmatun's indifference into my veins. The only way to keep the two of us alive is by remaining nonchalant. "Go ahead," I say. "I'd be more than happy to testify against you before the lawmakers. In fact, we might as well make use of Rakhti Iridis's services while she is here."

Asahar's muscles still. "You do not care for him at all? Are you that heartless?"

Perhaps he expects me to grovel on my knees. My lips curl into a sneer. "Why should I be afraid when you are willing to serve your own head on a platter? 'And to those who draw the blood of a brother or a sister, they must receive the appropriate penalty.'"

"The blood shaman dares quote the Namuru against me!" Asahar releases a howl of laughter.

"The rules hold for any citizen of Aritsya."

He levels a contemptuous stare at me. "Fine. State your terms, blood shaman. I'll see if they're worth considering."

"I'll hold on to the throne for another two years. At most. No one is allowed to interfere in my reign. None of the Rakhtas are allowed to question my decisions." I pause for a while, enjoying the tension in the silence. "Then I'll tell you where Rashmatun is."

He presses his lips into a thin line. "Two years is a long time."

"It's not *unreasonably* long." I straighten myself, smiling warmly. "You've tolerated me for seven years since you ascended the Bladed Throne. What's another two?" After a while, I add, "Rashmatun is fine. You'll get her in two years."

He presses the kukri into the skin of Ykta's neck, drawing a thin line of blood. My brother whimpers.

I remain as unflappable as stone.

"Will this man blabber about what happened today?" Asahar asks.

"He will not." Ykta casts me a desperate, wild look. I wrench my eyes away from him and focus on Asahar. "If he does, I'll kill him myself."

Asahar cackles. Perhaps he would have liked me better if I had shown this side of myself in the first place. "Fine. You can have him back. His blood is weak anyway."

He drops the kukri and shoves Ykta forward. My brother stumbles to the floor, chest heaving, fingers checking his throat. I make no move to help him. "So we have a deal?"

"You give your word, I give you mine. I'll let everyone else know what happened. Those bastards couldn't believe you were a blood shaman, even though I tried to convince them. Then again, they could barely accept the fact that Rashmatun is gone." Asahar sheathes his blade once more. "We can wait two more years. I expect you to release Rashmatun then."

"Remember to tell Harun about this. I've had enough of him breathing down my neck," I say, voice dripping with disdain. "Were you the one who gave him the idea of dropping goats on my people?"

Asahar shrugs. "It seemed the only way to properly convince your people that you're losing your sanctity as Rashmatun's vessel. And at the time, I wasn't aware that you were a blood shaman. I only knew that you have indeed stayed on the Scarlet Throne for far too long."

That doesn't answer all the questions raging in my head, but it'll do for now. "And I assume you will not have any objections if the current Shira-Rakhti were to suddenly be rejected?"

"Just ensure that her manner of departure is not too scandal-ous." Asahar releases an audible sigh. "The Forebears have already approved of her."

"Done." I incline my head towards him. "Pleasure doing busi-ness with you."

He stomps past me, shoulders squared. "I hope I will never have to strike a deal with you again."

He exits the Paruvatar.

My knees go weak and crumple beneath me. I support myself with my arms, hunching over the floor, sweat beading at the tip of my nose. Ykta is still lying down, as though he were smacked into a stupor. I crawl over to him and shake his shoulders. "Ykta, are you okay?" I ask, struggling to keep the tears and relief and terror out of my voice. "Please. Tell me you're all right."

He slaps my hands away and recoils in disgust.

No. Not my own brother. Not the only family I have left. I reach out to him again. He dodges my grip and sits upright, shift-ing backwards. Silver streaks down his cheeks, highlighted by the faint glow of the moon. "How could you do this, Binsa?"

"I had no choice. He would have used my affection for you against me. That's why I had to—"

"Not that. *That!*" He points at Ilam, who is resting on his haunches and licking his paws. The demon looks up, seems to real-ise he is in physical form, and merges back into my body.

My mouth goes dry.

"I trusted you, Binsa. I trusted you," Ykta sputters, choking down sobs. "All these years, you could have told me. Instead of leaving me in the dark like this!"

I can feel the betrayal tear at his insides. Memories of Kavita surface in his mind. The cruel smile twisting her lips when she successfully banished Kreyda Gopal's wives out of the family. The sadistic gleam in her eyes when she drained the life out of the poor women, until nothing but husks remained of them. The utter lack of sympathy when she turned my brother out, leaving him on the streets with nothing but the clothes on his back when winter was approaching.

I fight to contain my emotions. Why did Ykta have to find out this way? Why couldn't he have remained blissfully ignorant? Why couldn't we have continued our lives like a normal family? Now deep, irreparable cracks are running throughout the precarious bond that he and I have worked so hard to rebuild over the years.

My only brother in the world—gone, just like that.

Ykta pulls himself onto his feet when I don't answer. "Don't worry about tonight. I have no intention of revealing what I know," he says. "And I'm sorry. For not being able to help you enough, even though you asked me to."

He wheels around and leaves me alone in the Paruvatar.

You have become just like me, Kavita whispers.

I whip my head around. No sign of her. "Stop it," I hiss. "Stop talking to me!"

You can trust no one, love no one. Even your dearest brother hates you. It will be you and you alone till the end of this path, Binsa.

"No. Stop." I fight to hold back the sob building in the base of my throat. "I don't want to be you."

You will perish if you do not accept yourself. Look at the darkness inside you—and bask in it.

Why is she speaking to me? I ask Ilam, desperate.

Who?

Kavita is talking to me! I shriek.

This is between you and me, daughter of mine. Ilam cannot hear me, Kavita says. A dark chuckle rings in my ears, then her voice fades away.

My breathing evens out; a sheen of cold sweat has filmed over my entire body. I re-collect myself and look towards the Scarlet Throne—at the decimated statue of Anas beside it, and at the ominous hole behind it. Miraculously, the throne itself has survived the mayhem unscathed.

I get up and stagger towards it, stroking the grooves carved into its armrests, the gemstones embedded into the rhododendron reliefs.

This is what I'm fighting for—a life without fear, a life where all love and respect me, regardless of who or what I am.

I rest my head against the throne and finally allow my tears to spill.

22

Growing Webs

Everyone—the priests and Rakhtas included—react to the destruction in the Paruvatar as poorly as I expected. All colour drains from their faces when they behold the hole and the fallen statue of Anas. Although I cannot read their minds—Ilam has retreated once more, cautious as ever around the gods' vessels even if they know of his existence—their panic is clear as day, showing in their frightened trembles and murmurings.

Asahar shoots me a pointed look as he leans against the wall.

I walk to the front of the crowd. I do not say anything, but a path empties out before me. Then I am standing before the dais, scanning the destruction—a single bronze head of Anas that has split off from the main body stares at me, his yellow eyes gleaming under the sun.

"Harun, no one is to visit Ghanatukh Temple today. Not even to seek blessings from the other Rakhtas," I announce, voice firm. "Call for Ykta and ask him to fix this."

The chief priest dips his head. "Yes, my Rakhti."

"Rakhti Binsa!" comes the furious voice of Iridis. "You cannot mean to sweep this under the rug!"

"Allowing word of this to get out will only further stoke panic."

"You do realise that the Prophecy of Geerkha is—"

I whip around, glaring at Iridis. She staggers backwards in shock, despite her imposing stature and broad shoulders. Despite the fact that she has a god, and I don't. "Would you like to be the Rakhti of Bakhtin?" I say, a single note away from snarling. "You seem to have plenty of suggestions on how to carry out my duties."

All the Rakhtas' eyes go wide, and their lips part in astonishment. Even Harun and Nudin, so used to my docile temperament as Binsa, look as though lightning just struck them.

Only Asahar is unfazed. His lips take on a feral curve.

But I cannot deny the truth to Iridis's words. I have pushed the implications of the Prophecy of Geerkha aside for far too long, content to dismiss it as fuel to forcibly remove me from my position. The end of the prophecy's first verse plays in my head:

> At the end of it all, the Scarlet Throne bleeds,
> The crown at her head rusts,
> The ornaments turn to dust.

I run through all the evidence piling up against me. "Our offerings mourn" refers to the falling goats, "the skies darken with fear" to the storms clouding Bakhtin, and "the Scarlet Throne bleeds" to the wreckage in my worship hall now.

So far, everything that has happened has been decidedly human-made. Yet each of the events is chained to one another—from Harun and the priests dropping the goats, to my summoning rain in a frenzied bid to stave off rumours of the Prophecy, to Asahar destroying part of the Scarlet Throne. All according to the sequence listed in the Prophecy of Geerkha. Perhaps it is all happenstance, since all these events seem to have occurred separately, with little relation to one another.

Yet a strange feeling settles into my bones—as though the future I am hurtling towards is preplanned. I think of the fallen stars spoken of in the Prophecy; they're the only part I cannot find a real-life connection to. I furrow my brows, trying to grasp at *something* brushing at the edge of my mind.

Realisation hits me like cold water being dumped over my head.

Chandri referred to the yellow sapphire as a fragment of Nuris, the northern star, in one of her Sacred Scrolls. It was said that Rashmatun leaped forth from the segment of Nuris that had plummeted to the earth.

I clutch the yellow sapphire around my neck. *Do not ever lose this*, Chandri once said. *The goddess will bless you through it.*

Now that reminder takes on a different meaning. If the "fallen stars" are connected to Rashmatun, and if Rashmatun is connected to yellow sapphires... Does this mean Rashmatun's disappearance has something to do with the Prophecy of Geerkha? Is the yellow sapphire Chandri gave me also connected to the goddess's absence? Maybe they are two completely different issues, but the fact that the mysteries of Chandri's yellow sapphire and Rashmatun's whereabouts are surfacing together... Can I believe that it is all a coincidence?

My mind is a convoluted mess. It all makes sense, and at the same time doesn't. Voices mumble in my head—Kavita's, Chandri's, Asahar's, intertwining in a thrum that threatens to split my head into two. Rashmatun. Vessels. Gods and goddesses. The world that I know is turning itself inside out—the hierarchy of the Forebears and their Rakhtas, the traditions that bind us in place. I cannot quite place the notion, yet I just know that something is wrong, as though everything I had been taught up until now is a lie.

"*Rakhti Binsa.*"

I return Iridis's glare. "What is it?"

She sucks in a breath. "I was *saying*, there's also the matter of you summoning rain without our consent. You know that this is not your issue alone—it concerns the entire nation."

"It was not me who summoned rain," I reply, tone placid. "It was Rashmatun."

Oh, Iridis is livid. Her eyes practically bulge from their sockets, and her lips tremble with rage. "You know what I mean!"

"My people were suffering, Rakhti Iridis." I try to stifle a laugh. "Is it so unwise to have presented a solution for them?"

"No... But how did you have the power to summon rain?"

"You can ask Rakhta Asahar about that." I gesture a hand towards him. "He'd be more than happy to explain everything."

The Rakhtas shoot him simultaneous looks. He shrugs and smiles. "Rashmatun knows what she's doing with her Rakhti."

"There you go," I say. "Any more questions?"

"Still, you should not have done it," Iridis presses on. "It is because you do not know how to properly bend the skies that your city is drowning. If this continues, Bakhtin will fall due to your incompetence."

"My city is doing just fine."

"Did you not see your people yesterday? The way they were looking at you with utter scorn," Iridis says. "You can be as clever and strong as you'd like, but if you do not have your people's favour, then there is no point in being Rakhti."

Now she's making it personal. I struggle to not let anger get the better of me. "Perhaps," I say, my gaze travelling towards Asahar, "if the Aritsyan army were more competent, and did not rely on the precious grain from my province, Rashmatun would not have been so desperate to ensure that we yield a bountiful harvest."

The Rakhta of war stiffens.

"You should know why we do this," Virya jumps in. She does not bother to hide her contempt. "This is more than a simple expansion of power."

"All I know is that our fruitless war efforts do nothing but starve our nation."

Everybody goes speechless. My secret is out. I have no reason to be nice to them. The only thing stopping me from directly insulting them is Medha, who is hanging at the back of the crowd, watching me with doleful eyes.

"Now, now. It's too early in the morning to argue with one another," Asahar says, clapping his hands. "Rakhti Binsa is only trying her best."

"I'm glad you understand." I flash a toothy grin at him. "We could all do with some food. Harun, I assume that their meal has been prepared in their quarters?"

The chief priest jolts. "Y-yes, Rakhti Binsa."

"Please escort the Rakhtas there. I'm sure they must be hungry after all this fuss."

Iridis grits her teeth so hard a muscle works in her jaw. Virya picks at her sleeve, probably wondering why they haven't gotten rid of me yet. Asahar maintains a mask of nonchalance, while the other Rakhtas display various emotions, from disdain to indifference.

"This way, my Rakhtas." Harun bows his head and walks outside. One by one, the Rakhtas trail after him. Good. The longer I look at them, the more I want to smash their faces in.

Medha lingers in the Paruvatar. I lift a hand and gesture for her to come over. She scuttles forward, and I rest my hand on her shoulder. She retreated into her room after the Trial and did not emerge until this morning. I'm glad to see she is physically well, but the energetic hum of her mind has been dampened. "You should go eat with them," I say. "It'd be good for you to get along with them."

She frowns after the Rakhtas' silhouettes. She cannot help but remember the gods that possessed them yesterday, how they all scrutinised her as though she were a cockroach to be squashed. She remembers the fire, burning right before her. She remembers the spike of heat tickling her clothes when she jumped through the wall, only for it to ebb. *It must be Rashmatun's blessing*, she thinks.

It was me, I think. I protected her. Even though I would have gained more by allowing her to fail the Trial.

Why did I protect her again?

"Do the Rakhtas not like you?" she asks, turning back towards me.

"That wasn't the case, Medha. They were just shocked at the destruction here."

"But they sounded angry at you. Almost like they hate you."

I forget how perceptive children can be sometimes. I chuckle and pat her head. "It's a natural reaction. Why shouldn't they be upset after this?" My gaze slides towards Anas's statue; the priests are still mourning the wreckage and mutter prayers under their breaths. "Go on now, Medha."

She shakes her head. "I'd rather be with you."

"Don't worry about me." I smile at her. "I need to stay back to organise repairs. Don't be afraid of the Rakhtas. The Forebears may be frightening, but their vessels are all human."

"But I want to stay with you."

I sigh. There's truly no convincing this girl once she's made up her mind. "Fine. But let me handle everything, all right?"

She clings to me in answer; the warmth of her tiny frame seeps through my kurta.

Perhaps this is the reason why I held back at the last minute.

I stroke her hair, trying not to think of how Kavita used to pat mine.

I finish dispensing orders before Ykta arrives. The priests' movements are sluggish; they take my instructions with a disdainful curl of the lips. If Harun knows I am harbouring a demon, the other priests should be privy to this information as well. But then again, I imagine that they would have immediately resigned from their positions if they knew the truth.

To what extent are they involved in Harun's schemes?

Nudin escorts me and Medha back to our rooms; the dour-faced man is even quieter than usual. He does not respond to Medha's prompts or questions, as though he were carved out of rock. Only when we are right in front of my room does he finally say something: "My Rakhti, I noticed you frequently holding the yellow sapphire you wear. Has the chain loosened?"

My eyes flicker downwards, then back at him. "And why does this matter to you?"

He shakes his head. "I was merely making an observation, my Rakhti. I could help you fix your current chain, or find a new one if you wish."

"My necklace is fine, thank you," I say with a snap to my words. I cannot help it; even if Harun does not share all his plans with his subordinates, he must have at least shared them with Nudin.

"Understood, my Rakhti." He presses his palms together. "Allow me to take my leave. I hope you and the Shira-Rakhti will be able to rest well."

After he walks off, I see Medha to her room before resting in mine. The quiet of the world subsides, and noises and colours and scents fill the emptiness. Ilam surfaces from the depths of my mind, and his yawning presence clogs my head. I tense myself, ready for the full breadth of his wrath to be unleashed on me.

It doesn't come.

Save your strength, he says. *You revealed my presence to them already. Threatening you wouldn't make a difference.*

He is being surprisingly magnanimous. *Why didn't you appear earlier, then?* I ask.

The Rakhtas were still nearby, Ilam answers in a tone that is not to be questioned.

The clattering thoughts of my handmaidens drill my head. I grit my teeth. "Everyone, get out. Except for my personal attendants," I say. Then I remember that I am meek little Binsa, not commandeering Rashmatun, and add, "Please."

I wonder how she will retire in glory at this rate, someone thinks.

But all of them are more than happy to abandon me. Jirtash heaves a sigh in their absence. "I'll give them a scolding later," she says. "How can they be so disrespectful?"

Were they? I didn't notice. I just wanted to stop hearing their nonsensical speculations for a minute. Exhaustion sinks deep into my bones. I am tired. I want nothing more than to lie on my bed and wait till the next Rakhti coronation is over, and maybe once I wake up, all my problems will be solved.

I may have outmanoeuvred the Rakhtas for now, but time is still against me. I need to deal with the rain and my citizens' increasing doubts about me. I need to devise a way to smartly and soundly get rid of Medha.

But do I actually want that?

I shake my doubts from my head. Of course I do. It's what I've been setting out to do since the beginning. I cannot allow my heart to be swayed by her impetuous nature and quick mind. I must not see my younger self in her, for if I do, then I will never be able to remove her from Ghanatukh Temple.

Even if it means I will never see her again.

I steel myself. I'll deal with little Medha later. For now, there is her problematic older sister.

"Jirtash, I have a favour to ask of you." I place my hands over hers as she removes my kurta; her skin is gnarled from the decades of hard work. "Can you transfer Nali to the Yharuda?"

The matron stares at me as though I have dropped a boulder on her head. "Why on earth would you do that, child? Serving *you* is the greatest honour the half-Dennarese will have around here!"

"I believe that her unique set of skills will make her more suited to serve a priest," I say. "She is well-versed in the Namuru and great Aritsyan literary works. She has many talents that will only go to waste here."

Jirtash rears upon Nali. "What are these 'talents' that Binsa is referring to?"

"I can translate between three different languages: Aritsyan, Dennarese, and Shurran," Nali replies promptly. "And I dedicated a good portion of my education to studying the tales and legends of Aritsya. I believe I can contribute greatly if Ghanatukh Temple comes across any foreign texts that concern the Forebears."

I certainly did not expect her to play it off so well. Had the flushing, stuttering maidservant been an act?

Jirtash raises her brows. "You do realise you serve Binsa because *Rashmatun* ordered you to, no?"

There is no ulterior motive to the matron's phrasing; she is genuinely concerned about disobeying the goddess's orders. It is a small comfort that she is not part of the priests' conspiracy against me. Perhaps if I wasn't harbouring a demon within me, I would not have held her at arm's length all these years.

"Rashmatun gave me permission to make the transfer," I murmur.

The matron's eyes flicker between me and Nali. Then she releases a defeated sigh. *Perhaps the goddess is accommodating the whims and fancies of a retiring Rakhti.* "Fine. I shall make the proper arrange-ments," she says. "She will report to Harun starting tomorrow."

"Thank you, Jirtash," I say.

Nali's eyes close in relief. I'm surprised by how she handled the impromptu decision. It was just a guess that she is well read; half-Dennarese or not, her father is a scholar from Dahlu, and the fact that Medha used to have private tutors means their family is well educated. I just did not expect her to be so intellectually accomplished.

I remember the time Nali nearly stabbed me with a hairpin. Was it truly an accident? Did the half-Dennarese botch the murder attempt out of fear, or was she trying to get my attention?

An idea sparks in my head. If someone is found guilty of mur-dering another, they will be immediately sentenced to death, no questions asked. And the relatives of that person will be discharged from whatever duties they have, as being associated with a mur-derer means that either you failed to counsel them, or you will be influenced by them eventually.

That's it. That's how I'll be able to rid myself of both Medha and Nali.

The half-Dennarese flashes me a grateful smile. *Thank you,* she mouths.

If only she knew what I am planning.

The pouring rain is a taunt, each drop like invisible acid on my skin, each thunderclap a slap to my face, the wind a jeering howl.

I bolt upright on my bed and throw off the coverings, then walk towards the window. Ilam's vision enables me to catch the nee-dles of silver streaming down from the starless night sky. The wind shifts, and some of the rainwater sprays onto my face.

I should be happy with what I managed to glean from Asahar, as now I know for sure that my position will not be questioned by the other Rakhtas. Yet emptiness hollows out my chest. Iridis's words from this morning haunt me: *You can be as clever and strong as you'd like, but if you do not have your people's favour, then there is no point in being Rakhti.*

Although I still seethe when I recall those words, she is right. It's all because of the rain. I must stop it, in the very least. Show my people I still have Rashmatun's power, for I cannot rule Bakhtin without its people submitting to me.

You already predicted this would happen, didn't you? I ask Ilam.

I had to secure a way to obtain more soulstream, and it was your fault for not clearly stating the terms of the contract, he says, placid. *You can let your city drown, of course. Your people wouldn't be able to do anything against you.*

I cannot do that, I say. *You know that.*

Do not resist him, Kavita's voice murmurs in my ear, echoing what she said during the Rakhta procession, when I first learned of the floods. *This is the natural course of your path.*

I swap into a less conspicuous daura-suruwal, gathering my kukri and Dennarese dagger and strapping them beneath my sash and my sleeve. The temple bells chime twelve as I slip out of my room.

Ghanatukh is deathly quiet, with only the light showering of rain filling the atmosphere. I breeze through the hallways, weaving my way towards the library.

Someone is waiting inside.

I clench my teeth and push the door open. Ykta lounges on one of the chairs, apparently studying a stack of papers. Yet his attention isn't on his notes—he's been anticipating me.

"What are you doing here so late at night?" I ask, tone light. I expected him to confront me again, but not like this.

"To stop you from doing whatever you're going to do," he says. He places the papers onto the table and levels a stare at me. "I overheard some of your conversations this morning. Rakhti Iridis was pushing you, manipulating you to believe that no one will follow you if you do not stop the rain. You know it."

I scoff. I'm the one who can read minds, not him.

He leafs through the papers; upon closer inspection, they are essays. Theories for his automatons and mechanical formulas that he must have been thinking of submitting to the University of Dahlu. My ears buzz. Even now, he flaunts his accomplishments before me, flaunting his life outside Ghanatukh Temple.

A life outside of me.

"Get out of my way, Ykta." My fingers curl into fists. "Don't you dare stop me."

"Or what? You'll break my arm? You'll ram my head against the wall and patch me up, just like Kavita did?" he snarls back. "You know the consequences of blood shamanism, Binsa. You were right there with me when we suffered it!"

Tears abruptly well in his eyes; he blinks them back. "Do you know how much my heart ached every time I thought of you while I was away? While I laughed and ate with my new family? Because I knew that Kavita would be torturing you while I was sleeping. I knew that she would be breathing threats down your neck while I was attending the Ghushnayets. I knew that with every day I studied and played, another piece of your heart would be gone. That's why I promised myself that I would work hard enough to be by your side once more.

"But you? You betrayed me. You betrayed *yourself.* Blood magic tore our family apart, and now you're doing the same to others!" He takes in a deep, shuddering breath, stepping from behind the table to stand before me. "I won't let you, Binsa. You can't. This isn't you. Remember the little girl who loved playing with cats and weaving necklaces out of flowers? What happened to her?"

I press my lips into a thin line. He has every right to lash out against me—I was the one who first betrayed him. His mind no longer rings with the clarity of a temple bell; instead it is a dull thrum, only evident if I listen closely. Has he trained himself to block some of his thoughts from me?

No. His attachment to you is not as strong as before, Ilam says. *You will find it harder to listen to those who have closed their hearts to you.*

That sounds awfully convenient, I say. *What about my handmaidens? They seemed plenty guarded around me.*

They are not actively cautious around you, though.

I don't understand.

I don't control how my magic works, all right? Ilam snaps.

It sounds more like he does not understand how his own magic works. Before I can question Ilam any further, Ykta extends a hand towards me. "We can go back to the way we were, Binsa. You can stop using blood magic, and I'll forget everything that ever happened. We will figure out a way forward together."

His pleading tone does not reflect his wary thoughts. Thorns prickle my heart; he just wants me to play the role of an obedient and appreciative little sister. A kinder cage than Kavita's, but a cage just the same.

I cannot allow him to stand between me and my goals.

"That little girl is long gone," I answer, tone quiet. "Did you really think you could fix everything? That you could use all the pretty theories you learned in university to lecture me? That you can save me with a snap of your fingers?"

I take a step towards him, lips curled into a sneer. "You're dead wrong."

He staggers backwards, as if he has just been slapped.

But it is the truth. He thinks he can help me, and that I am foolish for not telling him everything. He questions why I want to continue being Rakhti without truly understanding me. He thinks of himself as the responsible older brother, the saner, more righteous one between the two of us. But he is the fool here. His saviour complex is written all over his heart, his actions—in the way he wedges himself into my plans, in the way he carved the space behind Anas's statue and how he had been the one to find Keran. His pride has been there all along.

I was just too naive to see it.

That's right, Ilam murmurs.

"You weren't here when Kavita orchestrated the Bloodbath," I continue, closing the gap between us. "But I was—and I remember every bit of it. She manipulated a priest into pouring poison into the purifying wine. To prevent me from being poisoned, she made me ingest her blood every day for an entire month. I remember how horrible it tasted, how it seared my tongue and scorched my insides.

"I remember the wine being served to each of us before Chandri came in. Then Chandri arrived, and the girls started dropping dead, one by one. Blood frothed from their mouths; their skin began to blacken—spreading from their fingertips to their entire bodies. They were screaming in pain the entire time.

"Chandri—or Rashmatun—did not know what to do. By the time she came to her senses, the screaming stopped, and all that was left were charred corpses, as though they had been burned alive."

I close my eyes, hating that I am reliving memories that should be forgotten, hating that I am allowing Kavita to live within me, even though she is dead.

When I open my eyes, Ykta's face has gone white from horror and guilt.

"This is the legacy she left me, Saran," I mutter, holding my hands up. They are clean, but phantom blood stains my fingertips and drips to the floor. "The Bloodbath, the demon—everything. Do you know why she did it? So I would survive. So I could protect myself against a world that was never mine to begin with. Do you think I never struggled with this power? That I never thought about a life that could have been, if I were not a blood shaman?"

I lift my chin. "But this legacy is my responsibility now, Saran. The people of Bakhtin are my responsibility. I started the thunderstorm, and I will put an end to it. So if you have any regard whatsoever for the bond we once had, I'm telling you to step aside now."

His entire mind crumbles; the image of the smiling, laughing girl weaving necklaces out of flowers is gone. It is now grey, cracked, like a wasteland of grief—and Ilam gleefully basks in it.

"You know it won't end here," Ykta whispers. "The demon—it'll tell you to do more things, kill more people. You *will* suffer at the end, Binsa. And the only one who will profit is the demon."

"If you really wanted to help me, you wouldn't be saying all these things. Make sure that Keran sees me tomorrow evening as scheduled, if you wish to atone. I want to have a heart-to-heart with him. I'll also return your little flamethrower then." I stride past him, heading straight between the bookshelves. "I told you that I am prepared for the day I am replaced as Rakhti, and that I have my own plans for it."

Ykta stares after me in dazed horror. *I don't know her anymore,* he thinks, his mind a tumble of emotions that roar and rage along with the storm.

I take the hidden passage and do not look back.

23

The Making of a Blood Shaman

Dharun is completely flooded.

Water reaches up to my chest; I struggle to wade through the debris and the rain that sprays my face with the wind. The gas lamps are little use in illuminating the way, merely acting as checkpoints to orient oneself in the darkness.

And the people? Launched into chaos. Those who are alive scrabble onto roofs with all their worldly possessions on their backs, huddling together in pitiful masses. Those unlucky enough to be asleep when the rain overflowed the river float along with the raging waters, their limbs bloated and lifeless.

I accidentally bump into one such corpse, its flesh so cold and loose it scarcely resembles a human. Bile rises in my throat, and I quickly trudge away before I can study it any further.

I recall how the palanquin bearers from yesterday avoided the Eastern District—how they all chose to completely ignore the stain upon our city.

Of course, nobody cares about Dharun anyway.

I cling to my yellow sapphire for comfort, my limbs shivering in the cold. This was the life I could have led if Kavita had not fought to get us out of here. I would have been at the mercy of storms and earthquakes and the nastiest of humans, and denied help when I needed it most. I could be killed with my entrails dragged through the streets, and not a single person would have blinked an eye.

No. This is no time to be ruminating about what could have been; I do not have the luxury of standing around and allowing my sympathy for the people of Dharun to get the better of me. Moral righteousness is a privilege reserved for those who do not have to fight and claw their way to survive.

I will take only the lives of true sinners, I tell Ilam, resolute. *If I am to kill people, I might as well get rid of vermin.*

Ever the benevolent Rakhti, he snickers.

I do still have a conscience, Ilam.

Do what you like. Blood and flesh taste the same, no matter the good or the sins they have done.

The human minds around me are scattered, drunk on pure terror, and it is difficult to pin a single one down without getting washed away by their distress. In the distance, a voice sings, the deep, gravelly quality of the tone grounding the lilting rhythm with harshness:

> "*Hear our song of mourning, O Forgotten Goddess,*
> *Hear our cries of despair!*
> *Go back to whence you came from,*
> *And leave us forevermore.*"

The Prophecy of Geerkha again. It is like a curse that refuses to be dispelled. I cling to a nearby gas lamp for support as my foot catches a jutting stone. Interesting that there are believers even in the dirtiest dump in Bakhtin, though, where no existing gods would deign to cast their eyes—where all would prefer that its problems fold in and collapse on itself.

> "*A sacrifice given, a sacrifice saved.*
> *At the end of it all, a path of blood awaits.*"

I focus my attention on the direction of the voice. The man's mind is completely unguarded, and his memories fill my head as though they were mine: He was once a kishari's servant, but got into trouble when he accidentally spilled tea all over his master's clothes. His master promptly cut off his salary for the entire year, and in a fit of drunken rage, the servant attacked his master's wife, forcing himself upon her.

Naturally, he was thrown out of the estate after that. With nothing to do, he ended up in Dharun, working odd jobs and spending every bit of his gurisi on alcohol, occasionally dragging a woman to bed if they were unfortunate enough to be within the vicinity. Now his entire life flashes before him, regret drowning him whole. If only he had accepted his punishment without complaint, if only he could be given a chance to start all over. Perhaps the gods brought this flood to punish him for his transgressions—as penance for the women he wronged.

What a miserable life, Ilam laughs. *Entirely self-induced, of course.*

Wicked yet pious. An interesting juxtaposition, I say, clenching my fists. The horror on the women's faces are fresh in my mind; I cannot imagine the terror and humiliation they'd experienced, and this man just uses his drunkenness as an excuse. *He does not deserve to live.*

Ilam's strength surges through my limbs. I hop onto a nearby roof and traipse my way towards the man, unsheathing my kukri. He stops singing the Prophecy the moment he notices my presence.

I crouch and look at him, at the pockmarked skin beneath dark, hollow eyes. Rikshi is the man's name. He gurgles in surprise. "Hush now," I murmur, offering a smile but not bothering to disguise my disgust. "It'll be over soon."

I slit the kukri across his throat.

He doesn't even have the strength to fight me. As life bleeds out of him, Ilam emerges, wreathed in smoke and blending in perfectly with the shadows. He sinks his fangs into Rikshi's arm; his skin blackens and cracks into decay.

A new rush of energy sweeps throughout me. I haul myself onto my feet, savouring the crackle of Ilam's magic—my magic. Experimentally, I push my hand to the side; a small bubble of water forms, and not a single drop of rain falls through it. Creating the bubble makes my fingertips blacken, and my body singes with the slight flare of power. The same sensation I'd felt when I first summoned rain and when I called upon flame. I wonder how strong Ilam's affinity to read and manipulate minds is; will my body literally break down if I start digging deep into everyone's head?

But I no longer panic at the sight of my decaying skin. In fact, it is exhilarating to be able to utilise different forms of magic.

Laughter erupts from my throat.

More. I want more. It doesn't matter if my limbs split and crumble—I want a power so great that I become more than a god. So that all will fall at my feet, and that the wicked will receive their due penance.

"Good. Hold on to that ambition." My mother's voice brushes against my ear.

I startle and whip my head around. There's no one nearby, save for me and Rikshi's body. I subconsciously reach a hand to my ear. While I've always heard her voice in my head, this time is different. Her breath whispered against my skin, and the melodic quality of her voice was rich and corporeal.

No. I cannot give up my claim on the Scarlet Throne simply because I am fearful of my dead mother—not when I've sacrificed so much already.

Anyway, I'm not here to wipe out the entire city of Dharun. I am here to gain enough power for Ilam.

How many more do you need? I ask.

Three more should do nicely.

He's truly revelling in this. But it's fine. Keeping a demon satisfied is no easy task, and this is only to be expected. I have to keep telling myself that. There is no room for doubt or hesitation—I must forge a path before me with a ruthless determination.

"Just like me," Kavita whispers.

My heart skips a beat.

No, do not think about it, I tell myself.

Rikshi's blood easily washes off my kukri. I focus my attention on the surrounding area, listening to the minds encased in my radius, picking those who have committed unforgivable sins—individuals so vile that getting rid of them is like getting rid of pests. People for whom no one would grieve.

Their goddess has come to declare judgment upon them.

By the time I return to my room, the rain has stopped.

All the lives I consumed in Dharun made that possible—Rikshi, Manisha, Tyag, and Aditya. I wonder if there will be a point where I stop counting and remembering their names and faces. Where I merely see them as a supply of soulstream for Ilam.

I sink onto my bed, draping an arm over my face, exhausted yet intoxicated from the rush of adrenaline. I have been holding so much power that my insides feel like they are about to explode. If I were stronger, I would be able to contain even more magic without feeling overwhelmed.

An unnatural chill crawls over the skin of my forearm. Frowning, I remove it and open my eyes.

A face stares at me. Long and pale, with bloodred eyes and lips, dark hair framing the cheeks.

She smiles.

A scream tears from my throat.

And the face is no longer there.

Cold sweat drips down my forehead, and my limbs shudder. I stare at the space where the face had been. I scrub my eyes and blink several times. It is completely gone.

I put a hand to my forehead and slowly sit upright. There is no trace of a fever. A shiver runs down my spine. I tug my blankets closer around myself.

I saw Kavita, I tell Ilam.

Really now? he replies dismissively.

Didn't you see her?

No.

I release a resigned sigh. That was Kavita's face, though, no doubt about it.

More specifically, it was the face she had when she died.

I fall back onto my bed and steady my breathing. She's dead, I remind myself. Maybe she's back to haunt me now that my blood magic is stronger, but it doesn't change the fact that she is gone, a corpse buried deep in the chasm beside Ghanatukh Temple.

I remember staring at her body, limbs sprawled in unnatural angles. I remember the horror of what I did creeping up on me, twisting my insides and making it hard to breathe. How I hauled her limp body across the room, how her blood left messy stains on the floor. I remember being so desperate to get rid of her—to erase every trace of her existence and every bit of evidence against me. Somehow, although it should have been impossible for a scrawny girl of seven years old, I hauled her corpse and shoved it out of my window, watching her tumble down, down, down into the chasm.

After that, I spent the whole night scrubbing the stains out of the floor and cleaning every speck of blood—on her kukri, on my clothes. I snuck into her room—which was adjacent to mine—and gathered all her things and tossed them out of the window as well.

Ilam must have helped me somehow. The bloodstains disappeared, as though Kavita had never existed in the first place. And it should have been impossible for me to kill an adult and get away with it. Or maybe I was so overcome with rage and resentment that I could have overpowered a tiger then.

But she had Ilam too. At that moment, the demon's power belonged to both and neither of us.

Perhaps that is why I maintain so little control over Ilam. He was never mine to begin with. As much as he professes that demons belong to no one, he truly belonged to Kavita. He would bend to her every whim and fancy, and would go to any lengths to get a drop of her soulstream.

If Kavita had control over Ilam, why didn't she use blood magic to stop me? Or why didn't she use it to heal herself, the way Ilam closed the wound in my thigh when I was stabbed?

I love you, my daughter. And that is why I allowed you to kill me, her voice had whispered the night I killed Gurrehmat and Yhadin.

Ilam, why did you enter a contract with Kavita? I ask the demon, lying flat on the bed and folding my fingers on my chest. I am risking his anger, but I cannot contain the question any longer. *You told me she was powerful. How?*

Shouldn't you be trying to sleep?

Answer my question, I reply. *Please.*

For a moment, my muscles tense as I anticipate the abrupt closing of my throat or pain erupting through my limbs. But Ilam only heaves an exasperated sigh. *Fine. You want to know so badly? I was born into her bloodline*, he snaps. *I do not know how or when, but an ancestor of hers bound me to this family.*

I frown. *What does that mean?*

It means—I can almost hear him rolling his eyes—*unless the original terms of my first contract are broken, I cannot be bound to someone outside your bloodline.*

Does this explain why you always threaten to kill me? I say jokingly.

He merely snorts.

I do not know why I find his response amusing, but I suppress a chuckle. Then I sober myself and ask in a sombre tone: *How did you come to be bound to our bloodline? Are all demons required to devote themselves to a single lineage?*

Of course not, he scoffs. *We follow whoever is strong enough, and whoever offers us power.*

You still haven't answered my question. How were you bound in the first place?

He remains silent for a long while. I think he is about to either explode or completely withdraw himself, but I sense an uncharacteristic discomfort in him. *I do not know. I cannot remember.*

You cannot remember, or you don't want to tell me?

You know how it felt when Kavita wiped your memories, Ilam snarls. The hairs on my skin stand on end when he flares his magic. *You would know what it's like to have an entire portion of your history emptied out.*

My mouth goes dry. *Then who do you remember? Which blood shamans were you bound to?*

I only remember Kavita.

My brows knit together. He remembers Kavita...and someone else. He'd mentioned Privindu's name once before.

For the first time in my life, I wonder what his true nature is. I wonder which blood shamans he previously served, and why his memories only started from Kavita.

She summoned me. There is a faint sigh in Ilam's voice. *And I was awakened.*

His answers only bring on more questions. Who erased his memories in the first place? Why didn't any other ancestor of mine try to summon him?

Sleep, Ilam says, more of a command than a suggestion.

His rage is a string that is coiled tight around my heart, ready either to snap or to slice me into pieces. I've reached the limit of my questions for today. But now I know the reason why he sticks with me, even though I assumed we were never quite bound together in the first place.

I heed his words and allow fatigue to completely take me under. Blissfully, no unwanted ghosts appear as I drift into slumber.

24

The Meeting of Shadows

The next day, the Rakhtas gather in the Balamat one last time. As I glide into the hall and take my seat at the centre point of the circle, I ignore the pointed gazes of my fellow Rakhtas, wearing a tranquil smile and holding my spine tall. Medha tails after me, settling on a cushion placed near my back.

Sunlight streams in through the thousand windows of the Balamat, bathing the hall in the resplendent glory of its namesake.

"Rakhti Binsa," Iridis begins, "would you care to explain how you stopped the rain?"

"I didn't stop the rain." I dip my head. "Rashmatun did."

She opens her mouth to retort, then presses her lips shut.

"Let us simply give thanks for Rashmatun's grace upon Bakhtin," Asahar interjects, "for a bountiful harvest is sure to be had this year."

The vessel of Vashmar's cheeks puff in rage.

"I hope to see you again soon, my dear," Virya suddenly says, directing the statement to Medha. "It is difficult to find one so young yet so wise, and one who has the bearings and beauty of a goddess too—such as you."

If I have to listen to Virya's subtle jabs about how my looks cannot compare to Medha's one more time, I might just tear her throat out myself. Entertaining the thought brings a genuine smile to my face, at least. "Thank you for your kind words, Rakhti Virya. It is my honour to be her mentor."

"Now that the Trial is officially over," Asahar says, cutting through the tension, "I believe our provinces sorely miss our presence. We will take our leave, Rakhti Binsa. Thank you for being such a generous host."

"It is my pleasure to receive such honoured guests," I return. *Snakes, all of you*, I think. *Scheming snakes who would not hesitate to strike with fangs glazed in honey.* I slowly get up on my feet, inviting the others to do the same. "May the gods' blessings be upon you, and I wish you a safe and speedy journey."

They press their palms together, a final farewell before they set out for their provinces. Their respective retinues are already waiting in the main courtyard, palanquins and servants at the ready. This time, Medha will join the procession as well, a signal that the other Forebears and their vessels have endorsed her.

One by one, the Rakhtas exit the Balamat, the hems of their suruwals sweeping the floor. Medha clings to my arm; her sweat seeps into my sleeve. "Is it over? Truly?" she whispers.

I chuckle and pat her head, taking care to not disturb her top-knot. "Of course. Congratulations, Medha. You are officially Shira-Rakhti now."

"The Trial was so scary, but I'm glad it's over now." She releases an exhausted sigh and leans her head against my forearm. "Did you have to go through something like that too?"

"Her Trial was easy, apparently. All she had to do was answer some questions. Isn't that right, Rakhti Binsa?" a deep, masculine voice cuts in. My stomach drops to my feet. Asahar. Why hasn't he left the hall yet? "But you were very courageous, Shira-Rakhti. You are more than equipped to face the arduous years ahead."

"Rakhta Asahar!" Medha gasps, quickly dropping her head into a bow.

"Do you have anything else you wish to say?" I ask, forcing the corners of my lips to curve upwards.

"Oh, nothing much. Just don't forget your promise to us, Binsa," he replies, casting a flirtatious wink. With that, he wheels around and marches out of the Balamat, a thousand rays of sunlight bathing the brocade draped over his shoulders in golden opulence.

I grit my teeth in annoyance. I hold on to my yellow sapphire, reminding myself that Rashmatun exists.

And finding her will give me leverage over the other Forebears.

"He *does* like you!" Medha exclaims, yet keeps her voice low.

"What on earth are you talking about?" I say, bewildered.

"I was observing you two since the first day. He paid you so much attention. That means he likes you, right?"

"What do you mean by 'like,' Medha?"

She purses her lips as she contemplates her response. "'Like' as in...something Mama and Papa do?" Her eyes brighten with excitement. "So tell me, does he like you?"

I almost release a scoff; it comes out as an amused chuckle instead. "Far from it," I reply. *In fact, he stabbed me right in the stomach.*

"Oh." She blinks at me. "Do *you* like him?"

I'd rather be stabbed again than have that become reality.

"No, I do not," I say, as gently as I can manage. "And I've never 'liked' anyone, Medha. In case you were curious."

"Oh," she says, confused.

I shake my head and steer her out of the Balamat. "It's all right. You don't have to understand right away."

"Okay." She is still puzzled.

I help her mount the palanquin before getting on it myself. The temple bell rings ten times, every strike sending a deep reverberation through my bones. The palanquin bearers hoist the litter onto their shoulders and march forth, descending the stairs that lead to Ghanatukh Temple, the city shimmering under the glow of the sun, the scent of rain still thick in the air.

When the procession ends and I see the Rakhtas off at the borders of the city, Ilam's magic returns, and the world grows brighter, sharper. My limbs awaken with renewed vigour, as if they had been dead all this while and I've been moving around with strings tugging at my joints. The demon laughs.

Good riddance to all of you, I think as the Rakhtas' silhouettes fade from view.

I relish in the peace the absence of the Rakhtas brings to me in my room. I plunk myself onto a chair and wait. I do not know if Ykta listened to me. I do not know if Keran would even dare to show up, if he knows I am livid. But if he does not come, I will hunt him down myself.

The azure blue of the summer sky blushes, pinks and purples kissing its edges. The sun dips beneath the mountain range, and the world is plunged into darkness. Flickering lights glow throughout the city, like fireflies about to be snuffed out. My food is served, and still no sign of Keran.

Perhaps he has his own timing. I wait a bit longer.

The temple bells chime in the distance, once, twice, thrice—one for each hour that has passed. I finish my food, and Jirtash collects the utensils. I look out the window. I do not hear the song of crickets or the hum of wildlife.

I was expecting too much from him. I get up and walk along the bookshelves, running my fingers over their crumbling spines.

Something scrapes the floor behind me. I take a sharp breath and whip my head around. It's Keran, completely nonchalant. He takes a seat and leans back like a lazy cat, as though he owns the entire place.

My blood boils at the sight; Ilam's warning hiss steadies me.

"Are you unsatisfied with your salary?" I ask.

"Not at all, Little Mantis," he replies, grinning. "In fact, I find it most comforting that my stomach will be filled with fine food for the rest of my life."

"Then why did you sell me out to my own brother?"

Keran maintains his crooked grin; I want to rip it from his face. "You did say that I could answer to either you or your brother. But nowhere did you mention that both of you had to be on the same side—"

Ilam rushes out, his form of smoke and claws a distillation of fury. He knocks Keran over and pins the Dennarese against the ground, his fangs whispering against the man's throat.

"You seem to forget who your real benefactor is," I say, returning his smile.

Keran gulps; it is gratifying to see him go pale for once.

"You may think yourself clever. You may think yourself cunning and resourceful and slippery. And perhaps that is true." I get up from the chair and stride over to him; the corners of my lips curve upwards at the sheer terror in his expression. "But do not forget this: However terrible you are, I can—and always will—be worse."

He takes slow, deep breaths. "You—you can't hurt me," he protests feebly. "My hadon—"

"Is useless in the face of a giant cat who can tear your throat out at a moment's notice."

His expression crumples.

Can't you twist his mind somehow? I ask Ilam. *Manipulate him to reveal his secrets?*

Can you fix a broken clock in the dark? the demon retorts, sarcastic.

Looks like we'll have to settle for more brutish methods, then. "Tell me, Keran," I say. "Can a hadon practitioner heal themselves?"

"I—I— Of course," he stammers. "B-but—"

"I remember you mentioning that you are somewhat familiar with the healing arts?"

His eyes go wide with horror. "I—"

"Let's test and see just how strong your hadon is." I tread closer to him, tearing off a scrap of cloth from his kurta and stuffing it into his mouth. That isn't enough to completely shut him up, but Ilam's magic will be able to ward off sound as well. "We must punish his hands. For they are greedy hands, so eager to snatch up every bit of coin they see."

Ilam moves in a blur, his head whipping from Keran's throat to his left hand. In a split second, the hand is within Ilam's jaws, blood dripping from where it's been torn off.

The scent of charred flesh hits my nose.

Ilam drops the hand onto the floor, sticking out his tongue.

Bright red stains paint over his muzzle. "I knew he would taste terrible."

The Dennarese thrashes beneath the demon's weight, but to no avail.

"Instead of moving around so much, you'd be better off trying to heal yourself," I say, unable to stop the smile spreading across my lips. Delight bubbles in my chest; the sight of his suffering is a cathartic release for all the anger and tension I've accumulated over the past few days. "Ilam has no intention of getting off you. If you don't do something about your wound, you'll bleed to death."

Keran's eyes are bright with agony and rage. He releases another muffled scream, but he soon turns his attention to his hand, brows knitted in concentration. Cold sweat beads across his forehead, and a strange aura sweeps across the room—my vision tilts, as though the very earth were shifting beneath my feet. In fact, it feels like I am being pulled towards Keran, all my energy and focus gravitating towards his wound. A faint yellow glow covers his bloody stump, and gradually, I see his skin growing—raw pink flesh folding over the wound and stopping the bleeding.

Ilam recoils, fangs bared in pain. His discomfort permeates my bones, and bile rises in my throat. I quickly wave a hand. He sees the signal, and rips Keran's wound open once more.

The Dennarese releases another muffled scream. The golden light disappears, and the world is no longer tipping itself upon me.

"Ilam," I say, taking deep breaths. The demon places a paw over the newly opened wound, tendrils of ash winding around the stump.

The tendrils slither and attach themselves to flesh and bone, knotting outwards until they form the bones of a new hand. Layers and layers of muscle grow next. Then skin stretches from Keran's arm, melding over the frame; nails and wrinkles appear, until even I cannot tell the difference between the old hand and the new.

Satisfaction wells in me. This is a creation of my power. A reminder of the wrath of a goddess for Keran.

Ilam steps off Keran, and I pluck the cloth out of his mouth. His entire body trembles. He eventually pushes himself upright, raising his new hand, inspecting it from all angles. His lips quiver, and his chest rises and falls at a rapid pace.

His eyes drift towards the mangled hand by his side—the one that had been his.

He inhales through his teeth—

"If you even think about screaming, I'll make sure it's not just your hand that is made anew this time," I cut in before he can do anything. "Am I clear?"

The lump in his throat bobs up and down, and he nods his head. I pat his shoulder. "Very good," I say.

I straighten myself and walk back to the table, retaking my seat and gesturing for him to do the same. He obeys my silent command, albeit with shaky breaths and shivering limbs. He nearly stumbles twice, but manages to steady himself against the back of the chair. I notice that he does not use his left hand for support.

"Is there anything else I should know?" I ask, picking my fingers.

He gives me a blank stare.

"You must have had something to placate my rage, since you knew you were going to betray me." I lean forward and place my elbow on the table, resting my chin on the crook of my palm. "If you have nothing, you no longer have any use to me as a spy."

Ilam prowls forward; Keran immediately throws his hands up. "I have something for you."

"Good to know that you still have your wits about you. Tell me."

He reaches inside his pouch. His movements are so sluggish that I am tempted to snatch the satchel and dig through it myself. He produces a sheet of paper. I take it from him and recognise the parchment he stole from me the night we visited Chandri's parents.

"Why are you giving me something I should have in the first place, hmm?" I say, throwing the parchment onto the table.

"You can't blame me for being an opportunist. Any amount of leverage I can get to survive—"

"Save it. I'll decide what to do once I've read it."

I unfold the parchment. *Dear Binsa*, the first line reads.

My vision spins—the same sensation as being pulled into a Rakhta's memory. I am not fearful when my body becomes Chandri's.

But unlike before, she is weak.

Her skin is so thin that it is translucent, and the tips of her fingers are an alarming grey. Her hand trembles when she lifts it. Her body is as frail as paper; it feels like it will collapse upon itself anytime soon.

She coughs. Something wet and metallic rises in her throat. Drops of blood stain her palm.

Her movements painfully slow, she grabs a cloth at the edge of her table and wipes her hand on it. Its original fabric has been stained a deep red.

"I must do this," she whispers—to herself, most likely. "I don't have time."

She picks up a quill and forces herself to write.

Dear Binsa,

If you have found this letter, it means you have realised that something is wrong. Rashmatun is missing, and you want to know why. You are desperate enough to break temple rules and find me. How can I deny you the answers, then, if you have gone this far to search for them?

The letter ends there.

But I am not pulled out of the memory. Confusion fills me.

Then through Chandri's eyes, I see her recalling something.

She is in Ghanatukh Temple, back when her body was strong and healthy. She carries a heavy tome in her arms, and her eyes dart about as she traverses through the Bakhal's courtyard and out of it, under the cover of darkness.

Someone steps into view, the figure dimly lit by the temple lights. Chandri jumps, then lets out a sigh of relief. Wordlessly, she passes the book to the figure. I catch a glimpse of the book's title before it's shrouded in shadows again.

The Origins and Workings of Blood Shamanism, by Vharla Privindu.

The person taking the book is Nudin.

And the memory ends.

I gasp as I am thrown back into my own body. I grip the edge of the table, feeling every groove, anchoring myself in its rich mahogany colour. *I am Binsa, I am Binsa,* I remind myself.

Yet horror gnaws my bones. That was Chandri. Her parents had mentioned that she died of illness, but I didn't expect her sickness to have started before she left Ghanatukh Temple.

More memories of her trickle in. She was always exhausted after hosting Rashmatun, with her unsteady gait and her unfocused eyes. I thought it was due to the stress of being a goddess's vessel.

What happened to her?

More importantly, what was she doing with a book on blood shamanism?

"What is it?" Keran asks.

I put the letter down and conceal my trembling hands beneath the table. "Didn't you read it already? If you were looking to gain leverage over me, you would have opened the parchment before handing it to me."

"Guilty as charged. Though I don't see why you're so shaken up after reading it. She didn't leave any clues behind to find your goddess, right?"

So the magic that Chandri possessed is something only I can access. I exhale, relieved that Keran did not see the most important part of the letter. "She was someone very dear to me," I say. "It should not be surprising that I am a little emotional after reading something personally addressed to me. You're not the recipient, so you wouldn't understand."

He bows his head. "Fair enough."

I hate how composed he is for a man who had his hand torn off a few minutes ago. I unhook the pouch tied to my suruwal and fling it at Keran. "Your payment for the month. At least the information you brought to me about the Trial of Divinity was correct. This will be the last time I give you money."

He studies the pouch in his hands, then scrutinises me. "You know, this blood magic..." His gaze inches towards Ilam, who is sitting on his haunches, silver eyes glowing bright even during the day. "You know that it destroys your body and your mind."

"I do not want to hear the comments of an urvas. Now leave."

He rises to his feet, shoulders tense. "I'm twenty-five years old. I escaped from Dennar when I was seven—when the Ritkar genocide happened," he suddenly says. I'm baffled by his unexpected revelation, but although anger still sparks in me, I do not interrupt him. "I was young, but also old enough to remember everything that happened. The bodies. The cries of my people when they were slaughtered by the same soldiers they once fought alongside.

"The only person who could stand against them was my older sister. She accomplished many great feats on the battlefield, although she was only eighteen, and was considered one of Dennar's strongest generals. She alone rallied what little was left of my clan after the Empire's first strike, and managed to hold the enemy troops off for about a week.

"But as powerful as she—and her hadon—was, she was the only one of her calibre. The Dennarese forces chipped away at the weaker Ritkarans, and slowly our defences crumbled. Before they completely conquered us, I was smuggled away to find refuge in Aritsya. I later heard from other Dennarese that my sister died after fighting three days nonstop, so overcome by exhaustion that she missed an arrow aimed straight for her throat."

He pauses for a while, still refusing to look at me. I wait for him to gather his thoughts. "She fought valiantly and she was powerful, but she was alone. No one could match her brilliance, and no one was strong enough to live and fight beside her," he continues, voice almost a whisper. His catlike gaze finally penetrates mine, sharp and unreadable.

"You reminded me of her the first time I met you."

I raise my brows and fold my arms across my chest.

What is he trying to tell me, exactly? That I am strong and brilliant and powerful? That I am alone and doomed to die?

"I'm not your sister," I say, wondering how much he is aware of—how powerful he thinks I am, exactly.

"I know." With that, he slips out the window.

I sink into my seat like a melted puddle of yogurt.

"You're going to let him go? Just like that?" Ilam asks, slinking towards me. "Are you not worried he will reveal your secrets?"

"He's a Dennarese. Even if he screams them out in the streets, nobody will believe him." I eye the bloodstain on the floor and walk over to it. I wipe my palm over the stain, and it is gone in an instant. "I'm sure he's smart enough to keep his mouth shut, with that much money at stake."

Ilam does not comment further, brushing his tail against my legs as I pick up Keran's mangled hand. It is still warm. Purple fire abruptly plumes around it, and it disintegrates into ashes; my body burns and cools off along with Ilam's magic. "What about Nudin?" the demon asks.

I close my eyes and sort out the puzzle pieces in my head. Nudin... He's always been thrumming in the background. But his presence lurks in the corners of my recent memories like a shadow. I recall his outbursts and how they seem to come untriggered— most of them directed at Harun. Now that I think about it, what do I know of him, exactly? That he is a devoted son? But a devoted son would not be so upset with his father all the time.

All this while, I had been more focused on Harun. Perhaps I had the wrong target in sight.

My mind drifts to Nali, and Nudin's resentment towards her, partly because of her foreign heritage, and partly because of her dead sister. Nali, who is now placed in the Yharuda, in the priests' abode.

Nali, who is determined to unearth the truth of the Bloodbath at all costs...

"Nudin's been working hard lately," I murmur. "It's time he's given a little surprise for his devotion."

25

The Heist

I no longer have any time to waste. With the Rakhtas' endorsement of Medha, and with her coronation due in just over a week's time, I have to put my plan into motion. So I summon Nali to my room. Jirtash immediately pulls a disapproving expression, but airs none of her thoughts aloud.

Nali's footsteps barely whisper against the floor as she slips through the door. I nod at Jirtash, who takes this as cue to leave. Then only the maidservant and I are left here; a noticeable gap stands between us.

"How's the Yharuda?" I ask, trying to ease her into conversation. "I hope they haven't been working you to death."

"It's all right," she replies quietly, dipping her head.

"Are you allowed in the library now? I'm aware that they only allow certain trusted servants inside. Or are you at least in charge of cleaning the priests' quarters?"

"I'm only assigned to sweeping the courtyards and scrubbing their latrine buckets," she says, tone dry. "A lot less exciting than when I was under your care, I assure you."

I tamp down a hiss. Of course they don't trust her enough to allow her into the more restricted areas of the Yharuda. Looks like it will be a bit harder to get access to Nudin's book.

Oh well. Time to put my backup plan to use.

I wear a mischievous smile and shove my irritation aside. "By the way, I didn't know you were such an intellectual. You should have told me you were multilingual! I could have gotten you to teach me Shurran."

"But you have a tutor, my Rakhti," she says.

"Please, call me Binsa when it's just the two of us. And Ykta is lousy at languages," I chuckle. "Honestly, all his brain is good for is..."

My voice trails off when I remember my brother. As much as I tell myself that I don't need him, our broken relationship is a raw wound that stings.

"Anyway, Ykta doesn't matter," I say. Nali lifts her brows at my uncouth comment. "I didn't mean it like that."

She doesn't reply.

"What's important is you, though! Don't you feel that your talents are wasted as a mere servant in this temple?" I continue. "You could be sitting alongside the best professors in Dahlu! You should be deciphering texts and consuming more knowledge."

"Binsa, being a servant of this temple is never a waste. How could you say that?" she says. "And the University of Dahlu does not accept women, anyway."

I rub the back of my neck. "I'm sorry. I—I suppose what I'm trying to say is that I...found something. I will help you, but you must also do your part."

Her eyes brighten. "What is it, Binsa?"

"How familiar are you with Aritsyan literary texts?"

Her brows furrow. "Quite familiar?"

"Good. Even if you're not that familiar, you will be soon. I will try to help you get a temporary position under Nudin. You, in turn, must prove your mettle to the priests. I've heard from Ykta that they are quite strict on the standards they impose for their scholarly work."

The crease between her brows deepens. "I don't think I follow. What exactly do you need me to do?"

"Once you are placed under Nudin, you will help search his

quarters and his office. Wherever it might be possible for him to hide something."

"What is it? Why Nudin, and not Harun?" she asks, unable to suppress the suspicion underlying her words.

"He possesses a book by Vharla Privindu, famed heretic and rumoured blood shaman of the last century," I say. "The title: *The Origins and Workings of Blood Shamanism.*"

Her eyes grow as wide as twin full moons. "Are you sure? How did you find out?"

"Just a rumour, but...it's worth exploring." I rub my chin between my fingers. "Better than sitting around and waiting for something to happen, at least."

"But my hadon," she protests feebly. "I do not know if it's strong enough to conduct an extended search."

"I'll help you create an opportunity. Don't worry about being caught using your magic. Just leave the distractions to me."

"How would I even get assigned to Nudin in the first place?"

I had no idea she was such a pessimist. I stride over to my bookshelf and pluck out a book: Thaget's *Collection of Folktales.* "Tell the priests that I assigned you to translate this from Aritsyan into Shurran, in hopes that it may be disseminated to Shur, and that relations between our nations will improve. They'll have to allow you to work in their library because it's an order from a Rakhti. You will automatically be under Nudin, since he handles religious texts from Shur."

Childlike excitement washes over her features, yet caution threads her demeanour. The polarity between her moods takes me by surprise. "This book...My birth mother used to read this to me when I was young. She used this as a reference point to learn about Aritsyan customs."

"Oh? You're familiar with it?" I hand the book to her. She nearly snatches it, and her eyes rake over its every angle, as if it were worth a mountain of gemstones. "That makes your job a lot easier."

Her grip on the book tightens. "I hope so."

"What is your favourite folktale?"

"'The Tale of Tashmi,' from the Rulami tribe," she answers without hesitation.

Did she use hadon to peer into my mind? I try not to stare at her in disbelief. Ilam snickers at me.

"It's such a bleak tale, though," I comment, keeping my tone light. "There are far happier endings in other stories."

"I did share your sentiments when I was younger, but over time I came to appreciate how Tashmi was written." She lightly strokes the cover, smiling. It's the first time I've seen her at ease. "Their end may have been tragic, being punished by the gods and doomed to be forgotten by all who once loved them, but they tried their best while they were still alive. Despite being born without a name and without a face, they fought to help the people who had shunned them. Despite their lies, they wanted only one thing: to be accepted and remembered."

"Do you think the gods should not have punished them?" I ask. "They may have helped others, but they also impersonated the gods and used deceit to win favour."

Her cheeks flush, and she hunches her shoulders, as if just realising the weight of her words. "My apologies," she murmurs. "I have no intention to slander the gods."

"Do not apologise for what you think is true." I run my fingers over the book's cover as well, its rough, grainy texture surprisingly soothing to touch. "I can understand why you would develop an attachment to Tashmi, being an outsider in this land."

Her blush deepens, and her eyes are glued to the floor.

"Don't worry. My favourite story is 'The Tale of Tashmi' as well," I laugh. "It makes for interesting discussions, no?"

She presses her lips together, and suddenly, I fear I've gone too far—that I've misjudged her temperament, and that she will be on her guard against me.

"I'm sorry." I pat her shoulder. "I shouldn't have scared you like that."

She shakes her head. "No. I should have watched my words more carefully."

I shrug. "We must all walk carefully here. You help me find the book about blood shamanism, and you may be one step closer to uncovering the truth of the Bloodbath. You've spent a bit of time in the Yharuda already, right? You should have a vague idea of Nudin's routine. Memorise the complex's layout too, so you know where to search."

"Will this really work?" Hesitancy laces her voice.

"Do we have a choice?"

She closes her eyes, takes in a juddering breath. "You know, I've been thinking about what you asked me the other day. About what I would do once I discovered the truth. I have no answer to that, and I fear that Medha is worse. Her mother has done nothing but train her to become Rakhti and to seek justice for Anju, but what happens after that? What is her life if she is removed from the shadow of her sister?"

I hum in contemplation. I have to strike at the core of her reluctance before it completely consumes her. "I don't think you need to worry too much about Medha. She's a smart one. She understands her responsibilities and how to fulfil them, but more importantly, she's always curious. She'll be fine."

I wanted to be like that when I was younger, I do not say aloud.

"Perhaps you're right, my Rakh—Binsa." Her last-minute correction induces a grin from me. "I'm underestimating her. But as her half sister, and as the older sibling, I suppose it is natural to fret over her well-being. She may be smart, but she's so young."

Did Ykta feel that way too? Is that why he still wanted to take care of me, even after all the years we were separated? Is that why he felt like he always needed to watch over me, questioning all my decisions?

But he went behind your back, I can hear Kavita saying.

"What about you, Nali? Will you be fine?" I ask.

She emits a forlorn laugh. "I do not know. I can only hope so."

I close my fingers over hers, wrapped around the book. She doesn't pull away. "I...must admit that I am being selfish, Nali, asking you to do this. It is not just you I seek to help, you see. All these years, I've felt so guilty about living when all those girls could have been alive too. Why me? Why not another girl? I kept questioning my fate, asking the gods why they did not kill me as well." I take a deep, shuddering breath. "I want to find the truth. Do you?"

Her lips part in reluctance.

One final push, Ilam mutters.

"This is the only lead we have," I whisper. "Are you going to let this chance slip by just like that?"

Her expression crumples. Inside, my heart sings with glee.

Her grip on the book tightens. "All right. Let's do it."

"Binsa, why hasn't Rashmatun made an announcement yet?"

Little Medha clings to my hand as we tread towards the cleansing hall; I've tried several times to pry her fingers off, but she keeps a stubborn grip on me. I sense Jirtash's admonishing stare behind me, and the accompanying maidservants chitter at our unseemly behaviour. But I know Medha simply misses my presence. She and I didn't interact much throughout the Trial of Divinity; now that the Rakhtas have left for their provinces, she is able to spend as much time with me as she wants.

Although I tell myself that her attachment to me is a wonderful sign of her complete trust in me, my stomach still cannot help but churn.

She will come to hate me one day.

"Patience, Medha," I laugh, my slippered feet sinking slightly into the damp soil. The skies remain clear, the dark, grey clouds leaving a subdued blue tint in their wake. "Rashmatun knows what she is doing."

"Of course. I don't doubt Rashmatun." Her grip around my hand tightens. "It's just..."

A muddle of emotions washes over her, a swirl of excitement and melancholy, curiosity and fear—each emotion palpable in their individuality, yet eddying into an incomprehensible mess. Her thoughts are so numerous that I marvel at how her skull hasn't exploded yet.

"You'll be fine," I assure her as we near the cleansing hall, the

familiar sight of its small, homely frame a welcome respite from the
overwhelming grandeur of the Balamat. "Remember what Chandri said in her Sacred Scrolls? 'Trust in your own judgment, and
trust in your own discretion.'"

"I know," she says, sighing, unable to string her scrambled
thoughts into a cohesive sentence.

We step past the final patch of rhododendron bushes, the vibrant
red blossoms still as beautiful as they were when spring first began.
The rotten stench of goat carcasses lingers in the air, though it has
diminished of late. I wonder if it's because the rain washed the
scent away, or if the priests finally realised that it was foolish of
them to store the dead goats here in the first place.

My gaze slides left, where a mini complex of buildings stands,
contained within their own compound like a temple within Ghanatukh Temple, their brown walls bare and their rectangular windows inlaid with rigid latticework. The Yharuda—the priests'
place of residence, and the place where the main library of Ghanatukh is situated.

Where Nali should be.

It's been three days since we made plans to steal Nudin's books.
Two days since she was officially assigned translation duties and
received permission to work in the priests' library, much to the ire
of everyone else. It was difficult to convince Harun to allow her to
utilise their premises and equipment, but he cannot defy Rashmatun's order—even though he knows I am only playing Rashmatun.
I made sure to talk to him in front of the other priests in the worship hall. So Nali had a grand total of one day to finish her initial
survey of Nudin's routine.

A hasty plan. But one that is better than nothing.

I deliberately slow my pace; Medha tries to rush ahead, but I tug
her back. "Once you become Rakhti, you cannot scamper everywhere as you please," I chide her.

"Which is why I should scamper as much as I can now!" she
retorts, a cheeky grin on her face. Alas, I cannot deny the truth in
that.

My steps continue to grow smaller, slower, and even though

Medha is clearly itching to dash off, she remains by my side, casting surreptitious glances at me. Meanwhile, my eyes are pinned on the distance, at the entrance of the Yharuda. My throat tightens. Will Nali come? Or will she pull out due to cowardice at the last minute?

No. I do not have time left. She has to come today.

Just ten paces away from the entrance to the cleansing hall, we see a tall, lithe figure clothed in white appearing near the Yharuda's gates. With Ilam's magic, I discern Nali's pasty skin despite the distance and the intricate six-threaded braid she wears down her back.

Nali dips her head and disappears behind the wall.

The coldness gripping my throat eases off. *Here we go,* I tell Ilam.

Time to have fun, he replies in singsong.

A sudden wave of pain smacks into my head. I keel over, gasping, pulling Medha down with me. The little girl yelps and releases my hand. Jirtash and the handmaidens react a split second slower, crying out as I curl into a ball.

I grit my teeth, cold sweat beading down my neck. I have endured worse, yet tremors run throughout my body, and my vision swims.

"What is going on?" a bellow pierces through the fog in my brain. Harun rushes out of the cleansing hall, Nudin and the other priests all following right behind him. Quickly, I take count of the total number—twenty. Good. All the officiated priests are here, about to head to the cleansing hall as well; whoever is left in the Yharuda should only be insignificant acolytes or servants.

Now to flush all of them out.

I catch the closest arm I can find—Medha's. "Please," I say, wheezing, "please."

All colour has been drained out of Medha's face. Jirtash plucks her up and sweeps her aside in a single, fluid motion. The matron hurriedly places her palm on my forehead, only to retract it instantly. She turns towards Harun. "She's burning!" she cries. "She needs to be bathed in cold water."

The chief priest narrows his eyes. Another wave of pain slams into my head; this time, it feels like burning rocks are striking my skull. I dig my fingers into the ground, scrabbling around like a rabid dog. I open my mouth, only to manage a few low groans.

"Thiravinda Harun!" Jirtash yells, gently helping me sit upright and cradling my head in her arms. "We will have to use a room in the Yharuda. There's no time."

I smother a smile when I hear the blessed word.

Harun remains silent for a moment, quietly considering if my illness is a hoax. The priests behind him shift with nervous energy. "Thiravinda Harun," one of the older priests says. "The Yharuda is the closest building of residence."

"Whose room is the closest?" Jirtash asks.

"The Thiravinda's," someone answers.

All of them go silent.

"All right," Harun says through gritted teeth. "Bring Rakhti Binsa to my room. Summon the physicians. And the urvas, for good measure."

Oh gods, no. That can't happen. "Do you distrust our physicians so much, Harun?" I say, coughing up phlegm in my throat. "So much so that you'd rather use foreign magic?"

What is she up to? he thinks. "Fine. Just summon the physicians." He waves his hand at a few priests. "Go!"

One of the younger priests carries me, and everyone scurries towards the Yharuda. Through bleary eyes, I see patches of red and white blooming amid a neat row of green, and hear the merry singing of a fountain. But the beautiful sights and sounds are gradually overtaken by chaos, as more and more personnel flood the place, all eager to take a look at what has befallen their Rakhti.

Five minutes, Ilam tells me.

Amid the cacophony, Harun's fury burns nearly as hot as Ilam's magic. *Go back to work, all of you!* he is about to bark.

"The goats!" I suddenly shriek, thrashing in the young priest's arms so violently that he drops me. I fall onto the ground with a solid *thump*; I do not take heed of the new injuries. "The dead goats! I see them! They're everywhere!"

The crowd quiets for a while, then their mutterings—both

internal and external—fill the air. *Has she gone mad? I've never heard of a Rakhti going into hysterics. Perhaps Rashmatun is showing her the truth?*

"I can see them!" I continue to scream, slapping at the hands that attempt to grip me. Then I scrabble onto my feet, chest heaving. "They are close. So close!"

I shove everyone aside and stalk back towards the exit. Abruptly, a strong pair of arms wrap around my waist and lift me into the air. From the stillness of his mind, I know it's Nudin. I kick and screech, clawing at his arms. "Let me go! I can see them. They're right there! Right beneath the rhododendrons!"

Nudin's arms stiffen. Harun's rage flares brighter, like the sweltering flames of a forge.

Everyone's confused murmurings about me turn into confused murmurings about the dead goats.

"Rashmatun is showing them to me," I say, my voice cracking into sobs. Tears stream down my cheeks, and everybody falls onto their knees, terror seizing their bodies. For the first time in the past few minutes, I thank Ilam for the genuine pain he is inflicting upon me. It makes for a very convincing show.

A sign of ill omen, they think. *If she is talking about the falling goats, she must be speaking the truth.*

"Her fever is still unnaturally high," Nudin says, gently placing me on my feet once I've calmed down. "We will investigate the dead goats later. For now, she needs to be treated."

"The goats," I murmur. "The goats will run away."

Several servants come scurrying with a stretcher. They lay me atop it and take me to the residence complex in the Yharuda. Ilam sweeps his magic across the entire area to check for people; everybody has been so alarmed by the commotion that no one is left in the buildings.

Good. I just hope that Nali is brave enough to finish her task.

As chief priest, Harun has an entire building to himself, single-tiered and built in a style oddly reminiscent of my Bakhal. Usually, his entire family would take residence here, but his wife and his other son died long ago—before I entered Ghanatukh.

Despite my spinning head, I discern the intricate sculptures and the exquisite furnishings, the numerous tapestries lining the wall in vivid, gem-like colours, the occasional flash of gold or silver. The faint scent of incense floats in the air, sandalwood fused with a sweet floral scent—most likely a rare perfume from Shur included in the annual tributes we receive from them.

Even though my room is not shabby, its furnishings are pale compared to all these. At least I know what he is spending all his money on.

So much for "a life of simplicity and removal from earthly desires," I think.

As promised, Harun allows me to use his room. The servants help me onto the bed, and Jirtash springs into action, ordering everyone to bring in basins of water and bowls of turmeric powder. Meanwhile, the chief priest and his son pin their attention upon me, not daring to divert their gazes away for a split second.

Ten minutes, Ilam says.

I snatch Jirtash's sleeve as she is about to place a wet towel on my forehead. "The goats," I groan. "You have to get them. They're in so much pain. It hurts…"

She pats my hand. "Of course, Rakhti Binsa. We will find the goats."

"You don't understand. This…this is punishment…for allowing such sins to transgress this temple." I take slow, shuddering breaths. "You have to bury the goats properly."

Jirtash casts a worried glance at Harun. The chief priest pinches his nose between his fingers.

"Fine," he relents, at long last. He wheels around to face the entire retinue of twenty priests, whose faces have gone pale from my blatant accusation. They were involved in the summoning of the dead goats, and now guilt tangles their guts. "Go check the main courtyard. *If* there are goats there, dig them up, and Rakhti Binsa's illness should subside."

"Yes, Thiravinda Harun," they murmur before shuffling out of the room.

The physicians arrive soon after and diagnose me with some

nonsense illness; I can hear them thinking that this is unlike any-thing they've seen before. The fussing and groaning persist for another few minutes. A stream of servants enter and exit with basins of water mixed with turmeric powder. I emit the occasional prolonged moan, as Ilam's magic continues to flood my body with agony.

Regretting your plans now? Ilam asks, revelling in this more than I would have liked.

Of course not, I protest weakly. *I just . . . didn't expect Nali to take so long.*

Do you require an additional push to keep you going?

No, thank you. I writhe on my bed as Jirtash wipes me down as best as she can without removing my clothing; Harun and Nudin have insisted on staying here. The physicians are useless; some of them claim to go out and fetch a few herbs to relieve fever and stress, while the rest stand to the side and bark pointless orders at the poor servants. *But is it really necessary to put me through real torture?* I accuse Ilam.

The best falsehoods are crafted from truths, he snorts.

An abrupt clang shatters my thoughts, and water pours over my face. I sputter and bolt upright, reflexively scrubbing my cheeks. "What do you think you're doing?!" Jirtash screeches. "You are here to help our Rakhti, not create more problems!"

"I'm so sorry," Nali's soothing voice rings out. My initial irrita-tion gives way to relief. "I'll bring a new set of clothing."

She kneels on the floor, an emptied basin in her hands. Her breaths come in fast, shallow, as if she had rushed through the entire temple complex to arrive here. For the briefest of moments, her eyes flicker upwards to meet mine, and she gives a small nod of the head.

You're supposed to be sick, remember? Ilam reminds me as my lips are about to break into a smile.

I cough a few more times for good measure.

"Go!" Jirtash barks.

Nali scrambles to her feet and ducks out of the room. I flop back onto the bed, my chest still heaving. Inside, although Ilam continues to hammer me with pain, my stomach flitters with ecstasy. I did it. I have obtained Privindu's book.

As the servants scrabble around in a panic, as the physicians try to find a cure for a disease that doesn't exist, and as the priests linger in the main courtyard of Ghanatukh, confused, wondering how Rashmatun found out about the dead goats, I continue to savour the taste of victory.

One step closer to my goal.

26

The Forbidden Book

I allow the pandemonium to continue for another twenty minutes, taking utter delight in how I've orchestrated this chaos.

All the while, Harun and Nudin keep wary eyes on me—only averting them when Nali brings a fresh set of clothing for me to change into before whisking my old set away.

What is she planning? they think.

Then Ilam eases his magic off, and the pain subsides. I wait another few minutes before sitting upright, claiming that I have recovered, and that the dead goats have been cleared. The priests return upon my orders, praises of Rashmatun on their lips. Concerned thoughts echo through their heads: *How did she know the goats were there? Why has she only chosen to speak now?*

Good. Stay confused. With Jirtash's help, I get off the bed and walk outside, where most of the servants and acolytes have amassed, although Harun had yelled at them to return to work once or twice. It seems that human curiosity wins out over obedience, in the end.

At my appearance, they immediately duck their heads and scatter back to their posts. Harun has deemed me unfit to receive devotees today, so I head back to the Bakhal. There, the maidservants prepare a meal for me, plain dhindo paired with a plate of salted vegetables. As I consume the bland food, my stomach coils in anticipation. Medha has been resigned to her room due to the unprecedented change of routine, so I am alone.

The cutlery is cleared once I've finished eating, and the maid-servants leave me to rest. I pace around the room instead, my limbs still abuzz. My throat itches for water even though I've drunk plenty. Ilam's own exhilaration pulses through me; it's the first time I've seen the demon so thrilled about something.

Why would a manual on blood shamanism excite a demon, though? Wouldn't he already understand his own nature?

A knock on the door interrupts my thoughts. It is Nali, a neat pile of folded clothes carried in her hands. "My Rakhti," she says, "I've come to return your clothing."

I am unable to stop the grin splitting my face into two. "Thank you." I jerk my chin towards the table. "Put it there."

She obeys my orders. "I cannot read archaic Aritsyan," she suddenly says. "I hope you can."

"That won't be a problem for me," I answer.

She bows and exits the room without another word.

I paw through my clothes. A thick tome bound in goatskin is bundled under the layers, and the title of the book is embossed in gold lettering across the cover: *The Origins and Workings of Blood Shamanism*.

I sit down and open it. In spite of the dog-eared edges and the yellowing paper, it is in excellent condition for a book that must be nearly a century old. I flip to the front section and begin reading.

My hand melds into the page.

It is a world of white and yellow. Grotesque creatures skulk around me, but they either do not see me or are ignoring me. The ground trembles when an elephant with the head of a tiger stomps past me, and the winds whip my hair when storks with beaks lined with fangs cut through the air. They are magnificent, yet terrifying.

And the strangest thing is that they all look like they've been drawn from ink.

Their silhouettes are marked in black outlines, and their bodies are colourless. The strokes that give them shape are harsh, chaotic, as though they had been drawn by a furious artist. When they move, the ink smears along with their momentum. It's like...they are illustrations come alive.

What is going on? I ask Ilam.

I do not know, he says, tone quiet.

In the middle of the canvas, a small black dot appears. It grows and grows, stretching outwards till it engulfs nearly the entire background. The beasts roar and snarl and screech, and they all rush through the black hole.

The black hole fades. New forms start to emerge. Humans. Working the fields, sharpening wooden tools, cooking over fires. Then the same black dot from earlier hovers over them and expands; the beasts pour forth from it. The humans' mouths gape open in soundless screams. The beasts pounce on them, shredding their stomachs and throats open and pecking their eyes out. The fields and tools and fires are left untended. Wild grass grows in place of wheat, the tools break down and meld into the soil, the flames die off and leave ashes in their wake.

A new group of humans appear. They brandish crude weapons at the beasts. Spears, makeshift clubs, unfinished bows. The creatures bite past their weapons and tear those humans into pieces.

Another group of humans come in. They hold no weapons, yet they boldly walk before the beasts. Before they can be shredded, they prostrate themselves.

The beasts pause their assault and look at one another. One of them steps forward, a fearsome boar with tusks twice as long as my body, with claws for hooves and a barbed tail. The humans send their own representative forward, a wiry man garbed in simple clothes. The man bows before the monstrous boar. The creature does not maul him to death, like I would have expected, but instead shakes its head, as though it were talking to the man.

The human draws a short knife from his pocket and slashes his wrist.

The boar stomps in approval and drinks dark, inky blood from the man's wound. Seconds later, the monster's body dissipates into smoke that merges into the man.

The other humans and beasts quickly follow suit. Soon, none of the beasts are left in physical form, and the humans writhe on the ground, clutching their stomachs and clawing their own skin.

The first contract between humans and demons. The origin of blood shamanism.

Then I am pulled backwards, and the scene fades into the distance. When I blink my eyes, I am back in my room, hunching over Privindu's book. My skin breaks out in cold sweat. I trace the words before me, written in Ritsadun, just as Nali said. For once, I am grateful that Kavita had forced me to learn the language, although it has been long dead.

I take a page between my fingers and prepare to flip it. But they tremble so hard that I cannot control them.

What is this book, exactly?

We must go on, Ilam says. *If we want answers to the questions we have.*

I steel myself and turn the page. Nothing happens.

I skim Privindu's writing. *None know where or when demons first emerged and crossed into our world, only that they are malevolent creatures that inflict pain upon others to satisfy a primal part of their beings.*

Perhaps you only get visions when you come upon new information, Ilam suggests.

No choice but to move forward, I say, and turn to the middle section of the book.

My vision tunnels and brightens.

Unlike the white-and-yellow canvas before, this world is vibrant and full of colour, but seems to mesh multiple scenes together. In one corner I see a woman summoning flame into her hand; in another I see a soldier dressed in full armour riding for battle, too easily cutting down anyone who dares stand in their path. I see a man moving mountains aside, and a girl who is surrounded by people, their faces lit with joy.

But I see the cracks on their skin, the black decay spreading from their fingertips. The woman loses control of her flames and shrieks as they consume her. The soldier suddenly collapses in battle, and an enemy stabs him through the throat. The man is unable to hold the mountains in their position, and they crush him in between them.

And the girl—her face suddenly contorts in agony. She clutches the temples of her head and screams and screams and bowls over. The people leave her, one by one, until she is alone.

Chills creep up my spine.

The scene ends, and I am thrust back into my world. *No two demons are identical*, Privindu writes, *but they all share one thing in common: their territorial nature, which induces them to be extremely protective of their vessels.*

I skim through the chapter. The most common type of demons are those aligned with nature and physical attributes, who have the ability to bend elements to their will or to grant the blood shaman the strength of a thousand people. Like the woman, the soldier, and the man I saw. Then there are odder, abstract-type demons— demons of love, demons of war, demons of bad luck.

Mind demons are included in this category.

Entities that can sift through memories and listen to one's innermost thoughts. Entities that latch themselves on to others, tricking them into a bond and bending and twisting their minds till they cannot tell north from south, right from left, or their own will from the demon's. The longer a mind demon stays in a person, the stronger the bonded pair becomes—and the more fragmented the blood shaman's sense of self.

The girl who was at first surrounded by people, only to be alone when she started suffering from the demon's power.

A bead of sweat rolls down my nose and drops, staining the corner of the page. Discomfort trickles down my spine at the mere thought of becoming like them—like Kavita. I saw how she slowly lost her grip on reality, her mind fracturing and splintering further the more she tapped into blood magic.

But I have been relying on blood magic as well, and I've been doing fine.

Right?

Are you afraid of me now? Ilam asks, his voice a gentle whisper.

Of course I am, I reply. *It's one of the first things you taught me, isn't it?*

He chuckles, although it is absent of venom. I am not unnerved by his amicability. A calm acceptance has washed over my heart, dissipating any uneasiness I had felt.

We continue sifting through the book; the further in the chapter, the sharper the visions, and they are no longer drawn in ink. In fact, they seem so real that they could all take place in reality. Throughout all these later visions we see a common face—a man with an angular jaw and piercing eyes. Handsome if not for the constant sneer on his face.

We watch him meditating. We watch him going about his daily activities. He is a commoner when talking with the marketplace vendors, a dignified lord when mingling among the members of court, an enigma with a terrifying smile when he kills someone.

We see him examining a yellow sapphire under the sun. The rays of light catch the arrow-like inclusions and the brilliant colour of the gemstone. *Gemstones are pure conduits of magic,* Privindu writes in explanation. *As they are pressurised minerals formed underground, earthen energy—or hadon, according to the Dennarese—constantly passes through them and leaves sediments of raw magic. If used correctly, this raw magic can be used to store or tamp down on demonic power.*

Through it all, we see his demon—a tiny, harmless-looking weasel that scampers around his legs when summoned. He is completely unlike me, confident and uncowering before the demon.

I instinctively know that's no ordinary demon. And I know that this is no ordinary blood shaman. It's a knowledge engraved deep in my bones, like I was born to recognise them.

The blood shaman is Privindu. His demon, Ilam.

If Ilam had been bound to Privindu, does that mean...?

Yes, you're related to Privindu.

Ilam's confirmation makes me go still. I am hovering between two worlds—my own, where I am sitting with my fingers pressed against a page, and Privindu's, where his memories and illustrations literally mesh along with the text.

But how could Ilam forget that he once served such a powerful blood shaman? If what Ilam said before is true, that a chunk of his memories are missing, who would be powerful enough to override his magic? Another demon? Why did Ilam only regain consciousness when Kavita summoned him?

Questions upon questions. Answers leading to more questions. Questions that even Ilam cannot answer.

Maybe it's all somewhere in this book, Ilam murmurs.

Maybe, I say as I turn a page.

Compartmentalisation techniques are especially useful for blood shamans contracted to mind demons, though they can be applied by anyone, Privindu writes. *One mentally sections their personalities into various "rooms" within one's mind. Between these rooms, one can create contradictory information, and only draw upon information in one room when necessary. This offsets the depravity that comes from hosting a demon, and is also useful for maintaining guises in various circumstances.*

Ilam shifts in my mind. *Remember how you walled me off from your thoughts, before our new agreement? I suppose that's one form of compartmentalisation.*

Is that a backhanded compliment from him? I ignore Ilam and continue reading: *Compartmentalisation also has applications in forcefully severing a contract with a demon. Another technique involves hadon, which is explained in the next chapter.*

I raise my brows.

We watch as Privindu approaches another blood shaman. He holds a red gemstone in one hand and a bowl of dark liquid in another; it is filled with blood, I realise. With inhuman strength, he breaks the gemstone into several pieces. I count ten fragments.

> To sever a contract, one must first weaken the demon enough. Through compartmentalisation, we separate the demon's various energies within ourselves. By gradually siphoning their energy, they will not be able to detect how they are being sealed off until it is too late.

Privindu puts the bowl of blood before the other blood shaman. A demon taking the shape of a bear emerges out of the blood shaman. Privindu holds a hand towards the demon. Purple smoke coils out from his arm and wraps the shadowy bear in tendrils. The demon cries. Sharp cracks split the demon's body. Some parts of the demon somehow shrink and disappear into the gemstone fragments.

Privindu tears the skin off his thumb by biting it. I flinch, yet he remains unperturbed, as if he has been doing this all his life. He smears his blood over the fragments that contain the demon's body.

The blood shaman fades away, while Privindu remains. Seconds later, the same blood shaman reappears. But he looks like an empty husk, with his greyed skin and thinning hair and sunken eyes. If I hadn't seen him moments before, I would have thought him a completely different person.

Privindu extends a hand towards the blood shaman again. This time, he pulls the demon out of the blood shaman's body and forces it inside the remaining gemstone fragments.

The blood shaman gives a great shudder, then collapses onto the floor.

It is a slow and painstaking process, with the ritual to be repeated ten times before the demon can be fully sealed off, one month between each ritual. Each time, the blood shaman must use their own blood to coat the gemstone, as each shaman's blood has a distinctive "scent" that deters other demons from disturbing the sealed fragment.

Even with all the precautions in the world, though, if the blood shaman makes one wrong move and the demon realises their intentions, they will be killed immediately.

I stop reading there. Such a complicated ritual. And to stop being a blood shaman, one must sacrifice more humans to offer their blood to the demon and bait them into coming out. What irony.

Ilam laughs—a blustering cackle that is concealing his nervousness.

Sometimes, I can almost think of Ilam as human.

Focus, Binsa, he hisses.

But the more I understand the details of extracting a demon, the less I understand why anyone would want to do it. As parts of the demon are slowly being siphoned away, the same goes for parts of the blood shaman's mind and body. Privindu estimates that the lifespan of a blood shaman after successfully extracting and sealing a demon is a maximum of a year.

That was why the blood shaman whose demon Privindu sealed away just . . . collapsed.

I release a heavy sigh. Who on earth would go through all that trouble just to rid themselves of a demon? The price is ridiculously high, and the returns so low. I play with the yellow sapphire around my neck, mulling over the information.

A memory of Chandri suddenly comes to me. She sits on the Scarlet Throne as Rashmatun, then she gets up and her feet touch the ground. She topples forward, her face paling in an instant. It's why I always make sure to act weak after "Rashmatun" leaves my body.

My fingers stiffen around the yellow sapphire; my breathing almost seems to stop. Time slows. A yawning churn of possibilities and what-ifs engulf me. A terrible idea strikes, its implications so earth-shattering that it turns me inside out.

Her parents told me that she died a year after stepping down from the Scarlet Throne.

And the gods usually do not emerge unless summoned…Harun and Nudin had been shocked when Rashmatun appeared out of nowhere. I recall Harun scrambling to inform Asahar of that. After that, Asahar was trying to expose the fact that I am holding a demon to the other Rakhtas.

Which means they only learned of my secret when I "summoned" Rashmatun.

I jump to my feet and tear through my bookshelf, scrambling for the Sacred Scrolls. I unfurl every single one of them until I find all ten of Chandri's. As I scan through the cryptic lines, the implications click in my head.

I saw Chandri's memories when reading her Sacred Scrolls and her letter to me. I saw Asahar's memories in his letter to Harun. Privindu's book is chock-full of his own memories. Perhaps this is a coincidence, though I doubt it.

If you happen to be in possession of a yellow sapphire, do not ever lose it.

I gulp for air, leaning onto the table for balance. With a forceful jerk, I tear the yellow sapphire away from my neck. Is it truly burning on my palm, or is it merely my imagination? Is there a shadow darting beneath its shimmering facets, or is it a trick of the light?

No, no. It cannot be. But it is. Everything lines up. Why Chandri gifted me a fragment of the precious stone and told me to never lose it. Why she died so soon after retiring. How the gods are never supposed to appear without notice; on paper, it is because there is a contract between the gods and humans, in order for the gods to rule over humans while balance is maintained. I know now that in reality it's because their power will overwhelm their vessels and destroy their bodies.

Chandri had always been exhausted after hosting the goddess, just like how I am exhausted whenever I use Ilam's magic for extended periods of time . . .

Rashmatun is a demon.

27

The Confidant

My mind blanks out.

Kavita's soft, mocking laughter echoes all around me. *I told you so*, she says. *I told you, dear daughter, that there is power in being Rakhti.*

My fingers are quivering as I set the scroll down. I clutch my kurta, taking deep breaths and pacing around my room. I finally stop in front of the mirror, gripping its frame. My hair is slipping out of its braid. My cheeks are not as hollow as they once were, although the circles that ring my eyes seem to have become a permanent fixture.

How? How did Chandri hold a demon and not succumb to its power, the way I did? No—how did all the Rakhtis who came before me hold demons? Did the goddess ever exist? Or has Rashmatun always been a ruse?

Ilam is strangely silent. *Did you know all along?* I hiss.

I had my suspicions, he says. *Ever since you peered into Chandri's memories.*

Why didn't you say anything back then?

I didn't know. I didn't dare to confirm anything, not until I knew for sure. Ilam's tone is surprisingly soft, yielding. *I've never come across such magic before, but its scent reeked of blood magic.*

You're a demon! Can't you recognise another demon?

My power has been suppressed for too long, he says. *My knowledge is limited.*

I plunk myself onto a chair, burying my face in my hands. I want to shriek at him. Drag him out of my mind and pummel him to death. But it is impossible, and I cannot blame him for his reluctance to admit his ignorance. I might do the same if I were in his position, being an entity so powerful, yet so hapless about his origins and purpose.

Ilam squirms in my head. *I gave Kavita power on only one condition: that she find Rashmatun and take her power for me.* His speech is staccato, as though he were considering pulling his words back. *I helped her enter Ghanatukh Temple. I told her how to manipulate the Gopal family, how to outmanoeuvre everyone in the temple so that she could control you, the goddess. Yet she never managed to fulfil her end of the contract in her lifetime.*

I dig my fingernails into my palm; the yellow sapphire in my grip digs into my flesh. *So her contract is also extended to me?*

Yes and no.

It's not an answer, but it's fine. I don't want to know for now. *Does Rashmatun being a demon have anything to do with the strange terms of that contract?* I ask.

Perhaps, he says shortly.

Laughter rises from deep within my throat, like the torrent of an avalanche that grows and hastens as it draws closer to you. It is high and grating—sounding entirely unlike my own. I laugh and laugh and laugh, throwing my head back, my hair slapping my back.

I had been pulled into this long before I knew anything. For all my previous denial of Ilam, my avoidance of blood magic, I could never have avoided this.

Gods. No wonder Asahar was so intent on recovering Rashmatun—and no wonder he didn't dare to do anything to me. No wonder he was intent on keeping this a secret.

If Rashmatun is a demon, does that mean all the other Forebears are demons as well? Does that mean every single god in Aritsya's pantheon is a demon? Asahar's actions and motivations make even more sense now.

Because if I had somehow found a way to remove Rashmatun, I could potentially remove all the Forebears as well.

My laughter dies down. I know that the Rakhtas found out I was not holding Rashmatun because I "became" her once, when she was not summoned; in reality, her appearing too many times would have taken too much of a toll on her vessel's body. But how did they assume that I had Rashmatun before, when I did not have her magic?

I stare at the yellow sapphire cradled in my palm. If Chandri had truly sealed Rashmatun away, this must be one of the fragments that contains a part of Rashmatun.

And if the yellow sapphire contains a fragment of Rashmatun, that means that other demons would be able to sense her presence—meaning the nine other "Forebears" have always linked Rashmatun's power to me, and that the priests still had a source of magic to draw from.

Ilam, didn't you detect anything amiss about this stone? I ask.

I can't, he retorts. *Did you not read the book? Privindu said that your blood literally deters demons other than the one you are contracted to. I physically cannot even touch your stone.*

Then how are the Forebears able to sense the power in the yellow sapphire?

They are greater demons, Ilam says. *A completely different breed from the demons you know.*

I turn my attention back to the accursed book.

Chandri gave Nudin this book for a reason.

I bundle it into the same clothes Nali had wrapped it in, holding it to my chest and stomping down to the courtyard of the Bakhal. The maidservants cluck in surprise when I shove my way past them, ignoring their heated protests.

"Rakhti Binsa!" Jirtash roars just as I take my first step through the archway. "What do you think you are doing? You cannot saunter out of the Bakhal whenever you please!"

It doesn't matter, I want to tell her. All their rules and regulations and traditions do not matter when they've been worshipping a demon all this while.

But I don't.

"Binsa!" Her hurried footsteps draw closer; I quicken my pace. "Stop right there!"

I am so focused on getting away from her that I run headlong into someone. He stumbles backwards and falls to the ground.

"Boruvinda Nudin!" Jirtash gasps, catching up to me. "My gravest apologies. I—"

"I need to talk to you," I blurt.

Nudin hauls himself onto his feet and gives me a peculiar look, still cautious from the morning's chaos. "Perfect timing," he says, his voice infuriatingly polite. "I was about to look for you as well." He turns towards Jirtash. "My apologies. I know she is not supposed to step out of Bakhal grounds during irregular hours, but I need to borrow Rakhti Binsa for a while. It's rather urgent. Please consider it a supervised excursion."

She grits her teeth. "Of course, Boruvinda Nudin."

True to his word, he leads me outside the Bakhal and towards the Namuru archives, an entire building in the Yharuda that houses all written transcriptions of the holy book, as well as legends related to the Forebears and the gods. It is three storeys tall, with exquisite motifs and patterns adorning the entire length of its walls. According to the history of Ghanatukh, it is the oldest standing building on these grounds.

I've been inside only once before, many years ago when Harun had taken me on a strictly supervised tour of the temple grounds. That had been when I first started out as Rakhti, and I have not been permitted inside since.

Nudin leads the way into the archives. The interior steals my breath away—rows and rows of bookshelves fill the enormous space, stretching on far longer than my little library. The scent of ink and paper perfumes the air, and the hasty scratchings and scribblings against parchment create a low hum of activity. Everyone inside immediately turns their attention towards me when I enter. However, they do not speak a word of protest, and merely bow their heads and press their palms towards me. I spot Nali, relegated to the darkest, dingiest corner of the place; she gives me a small smile.

The chief-priest-in-training weaves his way around the book-shelves, eventually stopping before a door tucked towards the back. It swings open to reveal an office, surprisingly cluttered for a man who I always assumed to be the paragon of perfectionism. He closes and locks the door behind us and sidesteps a teetering pile of books to get to his table. Papers are scattered across its surface, with only a bronze inkwell holding them down.

"Apologies for the mess, my Rakhti," he says, dumping his scrolls on the desk. "I've just had a new set of manuscripts imported from Shur. Apparently they can offer more insight into the Forebears' deeds during the Age of Fire."

"Why would a country that worships only one god have any-thing worthy of the Forebears?" I raise a brow and carefully manoeuvre my way through the books.

"We did conquer them at one point. Their history and culture will always be relevant to us." Nudin sits at his table, a frown creasing his forehead. "Speaking of Shur, why did you instruct the half-Dennarese woman to translate the *Collection of Folktales* into their language?"

"I think it could be useful to share our culture with another country. Help them improve their understanding of us."

"How practical of you." He shoves the scrolls to one side, as if that would eliminate the mess. "But I digress. Let us talk, my Rakhti. You can rest assured that no one will listen to us here."

Indeed, none of the priests seem to be very interested in eavesdrop-ping on us here, as a quick sweep with Ilam's magic concludes. I still do not like how composed Nudin is. I clear my throat; the unusual dryness clogging it does not dissipate. "How are you so sure of that?"

"The priests here are scribes, not spies. I trust them." He folds his arms across his chest. "I believe we wish to discuss the same thing, so speak, my Rakhti."

I study him, the relaxed line of his brows, the dark circles ring-ing his eyes that are similar to mine. "You got upset when Rash-matun appeared out of nowhere," I say. "I also remember how vehemently you protested when Rashmatun said she would bring rain to Bakhtin. Why?"

"I was simply concerned that the goddess felt pressured to bring miracles, even though they were not necessary."

"Even when people were suffering from the drought? Even when Thiravinda Harun threatened to replace me?"

"I knew you never had the goddess."

I hug the book tighter; my knuckles turn white. My lips must have also turned pale from shock.

"At first, I didn't know how you were going to manage to summon rain," Nudin continues. "But you proved me wrong, and I knew there were only two possible reasons. One: You are actually a shaman, but chose to keep your magic secret for some reason. Two: You have a demon.

"Either way, you did not have Rashmatun. I wanted to keep that a secret, but you pretended to be the goddess and waltzed around, flaunting your power. It was then I realised that you were a blood shaman. Regular shamans do not have such overwhelming magic."

For the first time ever since I first met him, he grins. I do not know how to respond to that.

"I also found my book about blood shamanism missing after your bout of illness today." He gestures towards the bundle I hug to my chest. "You're going to return it to me already?"

"Why didn't you say anything about it before?" I whisper, perplexed. "That I didn't have Rashmatun?"

He grabs a clay pipe from his table and stuffs kobir leaves down its bowl, lighting it up and taking a long drag. "I promised Chandri that I would watch over you. But you should know that Harun and Rakhta Asahar were planning to get rid of you anyway. Ten years is far too long for a vessel to remain in power. If you had Rashmatun, your body would have broken down anytime. If only you stayed quiet and chose to retire peacefully."

His patronising tone scrapes against my skin. "Why are you telling me all this?"

"You have a right to know," he says, releasing a puff of smoke. The sickly-sweet scent clogs my nostrils, and I cough. "It must have been difficult for you to survive all these years."

I narrow my eyes at him. How much does he know? More

importantly, can I trust him? Is he out to oust me, just as his father is?

Only one way to find out.

"Let me guess, you worked with Chandri to seal Rashmatun away," I say. "That's why you told her that you would watch over me. And that's why you have Privindu's book."

The condescending light in his eyes dims. Unexpected sorrow wells in him, a fathomless abyss as piercing as an endless night. Chandri's face surfaces in his mind, bright and radiant with energy, her smile like the blush of dawn lighting the night sky.

He takes another puff of his pipe. Perhaps he's smoking it to ease the inevitable pain. "Yes," he replies shortly, before taking a deep breath. "The knowledge of Rashmatun's truth is passed down the line of the chief priests of Ghanatukh. And of course, the Rakhtis themselves. So far in Bakhtin, only my father, you, and I know about this. Only I helped Chandri seal Rashmatun, though."

"None of the other priests know what you did?"

"Of course not."

"Why did you do it?"

He heaves a long sigh. The lines under his eyes deepen. "You know that I once had an older brother." He pauses, and I nod. "Only official heirs to the chief priests are allowed to learn the truth of Rashmatun. By the time he died and I became my father's successor, I was around your age. Before that I worshipped Rashmatun with all my heart and soul, and followed the Namuru faithfully without question. Perhaps at that time my intentions were not so pure either. I was trying to get my father's attention by playing the perfect son. But no matter how perfect I was, my older brother was better.

"But once I learned the truth, I...couldn't take it. I had the one thing my life was devoted to taken away." He taps his pipe against the table. "One day, when I couldn't hold it in anymore, I asked Chandri if the so-called goddess was indeed a demon. She confirmed the fact.

"I was devastated, but she gave me new hope. She told me she wanted to banish the demon and asked for my help. I did things she could not do—go into libraries, scour the city for books on blood magic. Eventually, I gained access to the University of Dahlu's archives."

"And you found Privindu's book," I murmur.

He nods. "It wasn't very difficult to smuggle it out of the university. The scholars are all so fearful of blood magic that no one dares to even check that section." He emits a withdrawn exhale. "In contrast, it was difficult to seal Rashmatun. But we had one advantage—she would only appear whenever she was summoned. Any more than that, and the vessel's health would be at immediate risk. Rashmatun's power is so great that no mortal can withstand her presence for prolonged periods."

I was half-right. I assumed that the Forebears cannot appear unsummoned because they would slowly harm their vessel's bodies. But it seems that their power is beyond my imagination—so much so that they need to monitor the times when she is summoned.

"So aside from the moments when she was summoned, Rashmatun would not appear at all?" I ask. "Not even as an entity living inside the Rakhti's head?"

"No. At least, that's what Chandri told me. Whatever we planned, whatever we did, whatever Chandri thought—Rashmatun wasn't aware of at all."

I remember how my skin felt like it was being seared amid icy winds on top of Aratiya. I remember how black decay had coiled around my fingers when I used Ilam's magic to stop the rain in Dharun. How I burned, both hot and cold, when I trudged through Ghanatukh Temple as "Rashmatun" in the rain. If Ilam alone is capable of making my body almost crumble into ash, I cannot imagine the pain of bearing Rashmatun.

I am not a lesser demon, Ilam growls.

"What of the instances where Rashmatun emerges?" I continue. "Wouldn't she have complete control over Chandri?"

"That's where 'compartmentalisation' comes in handy. You've read about it in Privindu's book, I presume." For a moment, I wonder if this is what it feels like to be lectured in a class, to have a stern professor sneering down upon you as he imparts his knowledge.

"By walling her thoughts in a space within her mind, Chandri managed to keep all her plans hidden from Rashmatun."

I emit a low hum. "How did you manage the ten human sacrifices?"

A shadow falls over his features. His eyes flicker from side to side, a nervous contrast to his usual calm, contemplative stares. "We..." he starts, then trails off.

Images flash in his mind. A blur of faces. Aratiya, its snow-capped peak scraping the sky and towering over the entirety of Bakhtin. Pure, undiluted horror stifles his thoughts. A subtle tremor runs through his fingers.

"The prisoners of Llaon?" I speculate.

His eyes snap back towards me. "How did you know?"

"Lucky guess." Of course Chandri would have used the dregs of society for her ultimate plan—ones who would not be missed if they were sacrificed. Just like how I had used people from Dharun. If I had remained in Dharun, would she have killed me? Perhaps. Was she that cruel? She was the type to look after an injured cat that wandered into Bakhal grounds.

I somewhat understand her, though. She had a goal, a purpose. She could not let anything stand in her way, because it was for the sake of Bakhtin.

Yet I remember the gentle, soft-spoken Chandri.

She killed a murderer without hesitation, Ilam reminds me.

That was according to law, I argue. *And Rashmatun was the one passing judgment, not her.*

Murder is murder, whether it is lawful or not, Ilam purrs. *How can you be so sure that she had no influence over Rashmatun's decisions?*

I clench my jaw. *Whatever it is, she did the right thing.*

Or are you making excuses for her because she sounds like you?

I stay silent.

"What frightened me the most was how *easy* it all was," Nudin says, a quaver in his voice. "Llaon was officially used as a prison, but its true purpose was to extract soulstream for Rashmatun's use. No one suspected Chandri whenever she entered Llaon in the months leading up to the next Rakhti Selection. It was her regular routine, apparently to counsel and educate the prisoners there.

Only the chief priests know that the vessels go there to consume blood."

No wonder Chandri closed Llaon towards the end of her tenure. With Rashmatun gone, there was no need for human sacrifices.

But what had they fed Rashmatun before Llaon? It was built over a century ago, and Rashmatun must be far older.

A century ago . . .

More than a century ago, the Dennarese Empire saw value in hadon and began recruiting members of the Ritkar clan into their armies, I recall Keran's words. *We also learned that it was highly effective against Aritsyan shamanism then.*

You should know why we do this, Virya had said. *This is more than a simple expansion of power.*

"The wars," I say, trying to piece my thoughts into words. "They were all for the Forebears. Human sacrifices in battle. They craved blood, so they sought blood."

Nudin flashes a sardonic smile. "Why do you think Chandri hated Rashmatun and her legacy so much?"

No wonder the Rakhtas had always been insistent on fighting the Dennarese Empire, no matter how much we lose.

"Your father seems to be fine with Rashmatun being a demon, though," I say.

"He's only interested in whatever gives him power," he says, a bitter undertone laced in his words.

"But Chandri sealed Rashmatun, right? No one should be able to tap into her magic."

"A fragment of Rashmatun resides within that yellow sapphire you wear," he says, pointing at my neck. "The priests draw on that fragment every time they exercise their magic. Since we were bound to Rashmatun before she was sealed, our magic operates on the same 'resonance' as hers.

"However, the power we can draw from her is limited, and that which we draw from a fragment cannot be replenished. That's why our magic has been dwindling this past decade. Your particular gemstone is the 'mother' of all the stones, and contains the largest fragment of Rashmatun."

"And that's why you dropped goats on innocent people, because of your 'dwindling magic'?" I say.

"We didn't expect to kill anyone in the process. You know that our magic is unstable." He casts his gaze upwards, as if he were staring at stars that lie beyond the known universe. But his core is burning with a hatred so fierce it could almost match mine. "And my father coerced all the priests in Ghanatukh upon Rakhta Asahar's behest. We didn't have a choice."

Whatever words I wanted to say die on my lips. Nudin knew everything, yet he chose to do nothing. He let those innocent people die. He left me to suffer alone—to fight my way with nothing but my own wits and the demon my mother left for me.

All this while, he could have helped. He could have done more than play the part of the perfect successor to his father.

Does it matter? Kavita whispers. *As long as he proves his worth to you?*

I purse my lips. She is right. Nudin is clearly a valuable asset, if he assisted Chandri so much and still kept it all a tight secret throughout all these years. Now, where is his weakness? Where will he truly prove useful to me?

"What kind of a demon is Rashmatun?" I ask.

"Is it really not obvious to you?" Nudin retorts.

"I was trying to make small talk."

"A terrible way to make small talk, if you ask me." Nudin continues puffing away on his pipe. "She's a mind demon."

Like Ilam.

The demon churns inside me.

"What happens next, then?" I lift my chin and hold Nudin's gaze. "If I'm dethroned, the next Rakhti who takes my place will be without Rashmatun as well. And she may not be smart enough to play along. Your ruse will fall apart, sooner or later."

He presses his lips into a thin line. "It doesn't matter. Whatever happens, Rashmatun *must* be kept sealed."

"*Whatever happens, Rashmatun* must *be kept sealed,*" someone else's voice echoes in his head—Chandri's. Then I see her, holding the final fragment of the yellow sapphire, the cold winds of Llaon whipping her scarf about and pulling her hair free, allowing it to halo her head as if it were a glorious black crown.

In his memory, Nudin takes in a shuddering breath—let Chandri attribute it to the cold, he hopes—and he places his hands over hers, protecting them from the frost. "I promise," he whispers. "I will honour your last wish till my dying breath."

Chandri's mouth curves into a sad, beautiful smile. "Thank you. For all you've done."

Nudin's heart pounds in elation at the recognition, for this is the first time she has personally thanked him. But it also aches, as he knows the end is nigh.

The image fades. He holds on so strongly to the memory of my predecessor, even though she was a blood shaman, even though she sacrificed people for her goals. He would do anything to protect her then; he would do anything to protect her legacy now. It is a single-minded devotion, perhaps impossible for someone other than him.

I can use this against him.

"In order to keep Rashmatun sealed," I say, "*you* must be chief priest. Only then would you have the power to honour Chandri's legacy."

"My father is only forty-two years old, while the previous Thiravinda passed away at seventy." A humourless grin twists his lips. "He will live for some time to come."

"You know you cannot keep this up forever. Harun will one day find out the truth, even if you get rid of me."

"I know that!" Nudin bellows.

I jump in my seat.

He stares at me as if I were the one who suddenly yelled at him. He takes a long drag out of his pipe, and his breathing evens out. Sweat beads on his forehead. "I know that," he murmurs. "But even if I become chief priest, he will find ways to control me. He will ensure that he makes all official decisions, and that all the Ghanatukh priests are loyal to him."

"He didn't order you to seal Rashmatun away," I reason with him. "You made that choice."

"You do not understand. I will always live under my father and my dead brother's shadow."

I do understand. I know what it is like to live under the grip of someone else, to constantly watch your words and control every move, every slight shift of the body. I do not think he will accept my comfort, though, so I say, "A devoted son and little brother, aren't you?"

"Is that your demon talking?" He laughs in a way that is eerily similar to mine. The sticky residue of the kobir leaves he has puffed on suffuses the room, and my head feels dizzy. "I hate them. *I hate them*. My brother, for taking away everything from me when he died. My father, for cheating on my mother with a Dennarese woman not long after they lost my brother and driving her to suicide!"

His breaths are short and heavy. We stay in silence for a while, until he finally sets his pipe down and runs his fingers through his hair. "I spoke too much," he says, body stiff. "My apologies, my Rakhti."

This is all I'm getting from him today. I rise to my feet. "Thank you for entertaining me, Nudin," I say, projecting a confidence that is only present when I'm Rashmatun. The clear divide between personas draws a frown from him. "I hope you'll continue to consider how much we could accomplish together if I remain Rakhti."

"I'll escort you back to your room" is his only reply.

The knowledge of the truth looms over me for the rest of the day, thick and suffocating. It does not lift, even when I tell myself that I can possibly take Rashmatun's power for myself and permanently become Rakhti. Even when I remind myself that scarcely anyone in Bakhtin is privy to this truth.

Even when I think about the possibility of finding Rashmatun.

In fact, I am so absorbed in my thoughts that when I lift my head to the world, Ykta is in my room, poring over several automaton blueprints. I look out the open window; the sky burns a luminescent orange as the day folds into night. He must have climbed in here, since Jirtash made no ruckus.

"It's rude to not knock," I say.

Ykta's eyes snap up from his sketches. "You were very focused. I did not want to disturb you."

I heave a tired sigh and set Privindu's book aside. "What do you want, Ykta?"

"I . . ." He releases a huff and ruffles his hair; I have the urge to replace every strand in its rightful place. "I'm sorry, Binsa, that I couldn't be there for you when you needed me most. I'm sorry you have to shoulder everything yourself. And I'm sorry for everything."

I'm sorry that Kavita ruined your life is what he wants to say.

I close my eyes. It's too much. I cannot look at him when he is like this—I cannot stand the sincerity in him, the honesty that pervades his marrow. How can he be so clever yet so naive? We may share the same past, but our paths have forked. He came back for me, but we could never stay together for long.

He should have known by now.

"I hear that Dahlu is planning to open admissions to female students in five years," he continues. "According to my professors, quite a few talents have been found in the Ghushnayets. They will want someone like you, Binsa."

Too late, too late, I want to tell him. *Ten years too late for me.*

"I'll think about it," I say. He knows it's a lie.

His lips part. Possible answers fleet past his head; none of them are spoken.

He is weak, Kavita whispers. *But you are strong.*

He gets up and stuffs his papers into a satchel. "I see." He inclines his head towards me. "May Rashmatun's wisdom be upon you."

He takes the cue to slip out the window without another word.

PART III

THE GODDESS WITH NO NAME

This is a story so old that its origins have been forgotten. Its characters, older still. For this story is set during the Age of Fire, when the gods walked amongst us and humankind prospered in their presence. This is the story of a being, its true name and face forgotten to history. And this is the story of the nameless and faceless being taking other names and taking other faces. And how over time, over countless retellings passed on from mothers and grandmothers to their children and grandchildren, the being was given a name, so that storytellers may give life to it—Tashmi, meaning "the nameless one."

Yet, in spite of the belittling name we have bequeathed it, we have already granted honour to Tashmi. For this is the story of a nameless being who only wanted to be remembered.

Excerpt of transcription of "The Tale of Tashmi," told by Privitha, an elder of the Rulami tribe, northern Vintya, circa Year 450 of the Age of Steel

28

Threads

I perform my duties as Rashmatun the next morning, if only slightly crankier and more irritable than my usual unflappable demeanour. The devotees admitted today do not complain once about the rain, or lack thereof. They come to me with common-folk problems: missing cattle, cheating spouses, stolen wares. Problems I frequently attended to before the drought began. Problems that seem so menial and insignificant now.

Still, I provide solutions. I draw their thoughts out with words and read their conscience. I create comfort by granting them assurance, by dressing my practical advice with elaborate livery. Not a single thought of the Prophecy of Geerkha crosses their minds.

Satisfaction wells in me.

After the designated twelve devotees per day, Harun and Medha come before me, dipping their heads. I narrow my eyes at the former.

I will not allow her to have her way, he thinks.

If he were truly following Asahar's instructions, he wouldn't think of dethroning me. Yet there is evident dissent brewing in him as he kneels. I swallow a scoff.

He has had *his* way long enough.

"Medha," I say, turning my attention towards the little girl, "how do you find the duties of Shira-Rakhti?"

"Pleasant, Your Grace," she replies, speaking in a demure manner. Not unlike mine when I am just Binsa.

I am stunned by the uncanny imitation, recovering my wits a heartbeat later. "Do you think you are prepared to receive me?"

"I...believe so, my goddess," she says. After a moment of hesitation, she adds, "But I do not mind waiting either, Your Holiness. Everything can happen in your time."

My plain, unmade face appears in her mind—hawkish and outright unattractive. Yet there is an unmistakable adoration bubbling in Medha. She recalls the time we have spent together—the meals we shared, the scoldings she received regarding proper etiquette, the moments of respite in the Bakhal, when we leaned against each other and talked.

I want to be with her a little longer, she thinks.

My lips quirk into a slightly pained smile. "You are certainly a far cry from the tempestuous rascal who first arrived in Ghanatukh. You are fit to be Rakhti."

"Thank you, my goddess," she murmurs.

"Harun," I say. The priest snaps to attention. "We will hold the coronation next week, on Jhokti. See to it that the proper preparations are made."

He stares at me, goggle-eyed. Medha's gaze snaps upwards as well, her expression crumbling in disbelief.

What is she thinking? their voices echo simultaneously.

"My—my goddess, are you sure?" Harun stutters.

"Have I ever been unsure, Harun?" I retort. "Binsa will pass the title to Medha next Jhokti. What part of that is not clear?"

"I...It is clear, Your Grace."

He clenches his jaw; a slight crease forms between his brows. *But she holds power. She is the only one who knows where Rashmatun is. And Rakhta Asahar agreed to let her rule for another two years. Why would she do this?*

I smother a grin as panic seeps into his bones—the slow, torturous sensation of watching everything slip out of your control, and being unable to do anything.

Just like what he and Asahar did to me.

"Medha?" I say.

"Thank you, my goddess," she says.

She does not betray the dread spiking through her.

Good girl, I think approvingly.

"What in the name of *thrice-damned Verumal* are you thinking?" Nudin hisses as he steps into my room. He requested to see me as soon as Jirtash and the other handmaidens finished bathing me.

"Inappropriate words for a Thiravinda-in-training," I comment. "I doubt your father would be pleased to hear the name of a demon prince on your lips."

He gnashes his teeth in frustration and marches over. "What are you planning?"

"Planning? Why would you think I'm up to something?" I pick my fingers nonchalantly. "Unless *you* are the one who has something in mind."

"Give me a good reason why you should continue being Rakhti."

There we go.

"Nudin, Rashmatun just announced that Medha is to be inaugurated next week," I say, flapping a dismissive hand. "There's no way I can continue to be Rakhti. Your secret will be a little harder to keep from now on. But I'm sure you can manage with Medha."

She's pushing me into a corner, he thinks, seething. *She's telling me to make a decision.*

That's right, I think.

"Enough with the games," he snaps. "What do you want?"

Beneath his rage, panic crawls through him, like water crashing through thin layers of frost. It seeps through the cracks in his mind, and for once his thoughts flood my head. *Can I keep Chandri's secret forever? I was lucky with Binsa. What if Medha is unable to play the role? Gods, can I trust Binsa? She's competent, yes. But is she trustworthy?*

Nudin wrestles with his dilemma, frustrated.

"I think you know what I want," I answer coolly. "But first, I need to know if your father took bribes from the Yankaran family."

He immediately straightens his back at the mention of the Yankaran name, agitated. "What will you do with this information? Threaten my father so he supports your reign?"

"No, no. I just wanted to know if you were in agreement with him."

"You know how much I hate him." Nudin clenches his fingers into fists.

I clear my throat; it has been strangely dry the whole day, no matter how much water I drink. "Do you hate your father so much that you want to be rid of him?"

"I always imagine what my life would be like without him," he says. He stares at his hands. "Sometimes...I imagine killing him. Sometimes the scars he gave me are bearable, but sometimes they sting so badly that I just want him gone."

It's like my hatred towards Kavita.

"What would you do then?" I ask softly. "If he were gone?"

"I would not allow an urvas within our temple grounds, for starters. Even if she is half-Aritsyan."

Ah, yes, the mistress was Dennarese, Ilam murmurs.

"Yet you did not do anything to stop your father. You allowed a tainted family on sacred grounds."

"I cannot do anything while he is in power," he protests.

"Chandri would have wanted you to remain true to yourself. You dishonoured her memory once." He prickles, but he does not object. Every word of mine drives more cracks into his walls—because I know the Chandri who lives in his memory is kind and strong, and I know that his Chandri would have been disappointed in him. "If you allow the truth to get out, you would be breaking your promise to her. Imagine if she were alive. What would she say?"

His head hangs low. "How can I trust you when you've done nothing but deceive others all these years?"

"I'm not very trustworthy, I admit. But I am just as interested in keeping this"—I tap the yellow sapphire at my throat—"a secret as you are. Think about it. It won't just be Medha after this. More girls will come. More questions will be raised. Will you be able to handle all of it alone, without any help?"

He releases a low sigh; his shoulders droop. He is in a tight spot, and he knows it.

It makes me wonder what he's been doing all these years, still trapped in the memories of when he was happy with a girl long dead. He could have used his brains to carry on Chandri's legacy. Instead, he spent them harbouring pent-up rage against his father, for gods know what reasons.

It doesn't matter. His story doesn't matter unless it serves my purpose.

"Good girl," Kavita suddenly says.

I catch the fabric of her white jama in my peripheral vision.

"How do you plan to dethrone a Rakhti who has not yet even been crowned?" he asks.

"The 'urvas' you despise. She could be useful."

"How so?" He leans forward, suddenly interested.

" 'And to those who draw the blood of a brother or a sister, they must receive the appropriate penalty,' " I say. " 'For all our bodies are a temple in itself to the Forebears, and to wound it is to deny the sovereignty of the Forebears.' "

"What are you talking about?" Nudin asks, perplexed.

"The gods will never approve of someone who has blood on their hands." I level a stare at him. "Do you have any family heirlooms? Treasures so great that the penalty for stealing them would be close to death?"

"There is a statuette of Rashmatun that was crafted during the Age of Strife. Perhaps you might have seen it in my father's room, when you suddenly 'took ill.' " He frowns. "Why do you ask?"

Harun has so many ornate statuettes in his place that I do not know which one Nudin is referring to. Not that it is of any importance. I grin at him. "In order to set up a perfect crime, we must first create a perfect villain."

29

Two Lives

Thirst claws my throat in the middle of the night—the same one that ailed me throughout the day, now amplified tenfold. I toss and turn on the bed, trying to sleep. But it eludes me, and in the end, I kick the blankets away and roll off the mattress, then walk to the window. A half moon smiles over Bakhtin tonight.

My body trembles. I press a palm to my forehead; my temperature seems normal. What's going on, then? Why do I feel unwell?

I frown, straining my ears. Whispers float in the air, unidentifiable murmurs that blur around me. I grab my kukri and follow them, my footsteps light and cautious.

Before I know it, they have led me to Dharun.

I blink, jerking to my senses. The streets are empty, save for the people sleeping on them. The flood that had ravaged the neighbourhood has been drained. How did I end up here? I take a step forward, feeling every piece of gravel, every rock beneath my feet. I look down. I hadn't even worn my slippers. I vaguely remember passing through the tunnel, trudging through Bakhtin until I found my way here. All the while, the hunger for *something* continues to churn within me.

The whispers still fill my ears.

"What's happening?" I mumble.

Ilam unfurls himself from the corner of my mind. *I don't know about you*, he says, yawning, *but I'm very much craving soulstream right now.*

Then I realise why I am trembling even though I do not feel weak, why I am shivering even though I am not cold.

I need blood.

How long has it been since I last killed anyone? Not too long—about five days ago. I should have been able to hold out longer. It's not like Ilam is weak. Then why...?

You've grown used to it. That's why. Kavita's voice cuts through the whispers. Silence follows in her wake.

What do you mean? I ask.

"You know very well what I mean," she answers, her voice too tangible, too corporeal. I whip my head around. Nothing. I return to face forward.

There she is, standing less than ten paces before me, right next to a figure sprawled on the roadside. She is dressed in a plain, loose-fitting jama—the last thing she wore right before she died. My kukri is within her grip, and she twirls it carelessly.

I check my sleeve. Then my eyes snap up in disbelief. How? Wait, no—

"Allow me to help you with your cravings," she says.

She plunges the kukri into the sleeping figure's throat.

The person's memories pour into my mind: a simple washer-woman who always prayed to the gods three times a day and helped to feed her neighbour's children. Until the day she could no longer afford to rent her small, dilapidated room, and she was kicked to the streets. Still, she dreamed of a better life—one where she could have a small farm of her own and hire children from Dharun.

Now that dream is no more.

I stifle a gasp, stumbling backwards as I sense the woman's life flickering out. No. This can't be happening. This must be a figment of my imagination. There's no way the body in front of me is real. There's no way the blood pooling beneath it is real.

Ilam emerges into the physical world and lunges for the fresh blood.

I crumple to my knees. "I–Ilam?" I stammer. "Is this real?"

"What are you talking about?" he retorts. He has grown larger since I saw him last; where he had only reached up to my waist, now he is hulking over my shoulder. "I wouldn't be outside otherwise, right?"

"B-but, the kukri— I—I wasn't even holding it—"

"What nonsense. Look at your hands."

I cast my gaze downwards.

The bloodied weapon is within my grip.

I swallow a scream.

"Confused now, aren't you?" Kavita laughs.

There she is again, standing some distance away, next to another body, my kukri in her possession again.

I roll my sleeves up and shake my hands. Nothing there. But I had been holding on to the blade. Why does Kavita have it now? What is she doing? What is happening? Ilam will be of no help, since he's oblivious to her presence.

While I'm trying to figure everything out, Kavita murders yet another person.

And another. And another.

It goes on until the street is filled with the blood of innocents, people fighting to get out of Dharun, people who were wronged by others and ended up here. And children—children like me, born to a life they didn't choose, forced to scavenge and steal to survive another day. Their blood floods beneath my feet, a dark, liquid mass that resembles a smooth mirror. It stains my suruwal and seeps into the hem of my kurta.

My muscles are frozen. I can only stare in horror as Kavita continues her killing frenzy, and as Ilam devours all of them, one by one. They laugh and cackle in delight, each seemingly preoccupied with their own mischief, unaware of the other's presence.

Why is this happening? I should be in control, not them.

But what can one little girl do in the face of a ghost and a demon?

I clap my hands over my mouth as I burst into laughter. What was I thinking, that all this power belonged to me? No, it was all borrowed in the first place. I was never in control. I was never the master of my own mind. Kavita had been the first to break me, then Ilam. I never had free rein over myself. How could I, when I am so small and weak and insignificant without them?

I am nothing.

I am nothing, but I want to be something.

I am nothing, but I want to be something, and so I draw on their power.

And there is nothing wrong with that, a voice whispers in my head. My own.

You will do whatever it takes to become a goddess, correct? my voice asks, her cadence a strange mixture of Binsa's and Rashmatun's.

Soulstream fills my limbs, little by little, and the thirst begins to die off. Energy courses through me, and I feel as though I were born again—as though I can leap up mountains and wash floods away. As though I can conquer the world and have it bow at my feet.

This is what it feels like to be a goddess, my voice continues. *You want this, no? This feeling of absolute power.*

Yes, I answer without hesitation.

Before I know it, Ilam has returned to me, and Kavita is gone. I blink.

The street before me is empty, wiped clean of the blood that had coursed through it a few moments ago.

Sleep finally comes to me when I return to my room, strong and swift. I dream of unwanted children, their mouths dark voids as they screech and cling to me; I dream of myths and figures of legends, grand chariots being pulled by fiery horses and figures throwing lightning with their spears.

I dream of the black cat Kavita placed before me, to test my resolve before I entered the Selection. Its pale yellow eyes were wide and baleful as I approached it, kukri in my grip.

A bloodred fog suddenly engulfs my vision. The kukri disappears from my hand.

"Why are you coming back after all these years?" I ask.

The fog coalesces, taking the shape of a human. Its colour saturates into scarlet, and in a few seconds, Kavita stands before me.

"What is the first rule of any contract with a demon?" She deflects the question with another question.

"That you sacrifice part of yourself to it," I reply automatically.

"Correct. And what do you think this entails?"

"You become part of that demon?"

"Indeed." She takes deliberate steps towards me. "And that's why I'll always be with you, dear daughter."

"I don't understand. Why now?" I press on. "Why have you started appearing before me only recently?"

"You should know this already: The stronger the blood shaman, the stronger their connection to the demon," she says. "That is the second rule of a blood contract."

"What are you saying?" I snap.

She reaches an arm out and caresses my head; it takes every fibre of my will to not recoil. "Poor child. You've already figured it out, but you still want me to spell it out, don't you?" she croons. "The part of you that you sacrificed to the demon becomes your tether to them. Think of it as a conduit between you and Ilam's magic. But what happens when you tap into his power more? You become connected with more parts of him, and these other parts are also made of the blood shamans he once partnered with."

My hand hovers over my stomach, where my womb had once been.

"You've only just begun to tap into Ilam's true power. You've only just begun to bond with him," she says. "The more you draw strength from him, the stronger I will become. Perhaps one day we will see the blood shamans contracted to him before us. We are all linked, dear daughter. Through our blood and Ilam's."

"Then why isn't he aware of you?"

She flashes a hideous smile. "Are you sure that's the case?"

My body stills. But Ilam wasn't lying when he said he could not sense Kavita; I would have known.

"Really?" Kavita says. "Can you claim that you know everything about him?"

"Do *you*?" I retort.

"Of course not," Kavita laughs. "I thought you'd know better than to assume his nature just because you've read Privindu's book."

A flush of anger creeps up my cheeks. "How can I be rid of you?"

"You cannot. I am part of you, and you are part of me," Kavita says. "If you wanted to avoid this, you should have thought things through before striking such a reckless contract with Ilam. Understand how he works and what he wants."

I reflect on how I had struck the contract with Ilam without hesitation, unaware of the sacrifices I had to make along the way. Kavita is right. I should have been more cautious with Ilam. I should have remembered that from the very beginning.

And yet, I don't think I would have done anything differently.

"What are you here for, then?" I ask.

"To be your mother," she answers. "To ensure that you have only the best in life. To ensure that you will stay seated on the Scarlet Throne forever."

I give Kavita a cautious look. "You wish to act like a real mother? After you've died? After everything you did to me and Ykta?"

"We will talk about this some other time, sweet child." She presses a kiss onto my head; I hold my breath. "Now it is time for you to wake up."

I sense someone's palm, warm and small, pressed against my shoulder. It's shaking me. I rub my eyes and open them blearily. Little Medha is right beside me, her pretty face drained of colour.

My stomach flips. Does she know that I killed people tonight? Why is she here?

"I can't sleep," she murmurs. "I...keep thinking about Rashmatun's announcement."

I sit up and release a sigh. "That's no excuse to sneak around at night."

Ilam snickers.

"I'm sorry. I just wanted to see you," she says.

"How did you even get in here?" I remember I locked the doors to my room.

"There were holes in the wall outside." Medha points to my window, which is left ajar. "It wasn't difficult. I used to climb trees all the time back at my house."

She—*what?* The handholds Ykta carved outside my bedroom. The chasm yawning right below the narrow ledge. "Medha!" I pat all over her body. "Are you hurt anywhere? Gods, don't do something so stupid and dangerous again!"

She pouts. "I'm sorry, Binsa. I'm fine, I promise." She clutches the sleeve of my kurta. "Can I stay with you for a while, please?"

I run a hand through my hair. Why do I have such a difficult child as Shira-Rakhti? If only I could gain more power every single time she nearly gives me a heart attack. I scoot aside and pat the mattress of my bed anyway. "Fine. Just for a while. And don't go out through the window later."

She climbs up and snuggles against me.

I wrap my arms around her as if it's the most natural thing in the world to do.

"Do you want to talk about Rashmatun's announcement?" I ask. She shakes her head. "Then what about a tale to lull you to sleep? Any particular favourites?"

"I don't know. My mother never told me any," she says. "I always read the stories myself."

I look at her, surprised. "Really? Not even one?"

She hugs me tighter.

"I see. Then I will tell you a story that my mother used to tell me many times when I was a child." I prop her on my lap so that I can face her properly. "This is a story so old that its origins have been forgotten. Its characters, older still. For this story is set during the Age of Fire, when the gods walked amongst us and humankind prospered in their presence. This is the story of a being, its true name and face forgotten to history. And this is the story of the nameless and faceless being taking other names and taking other faces..."

I narrate "The Tale of Tashmi," of how an immortal being born without a face or a name desired to be worshipped and to be recognised. I weave landscapes, of villages hidden deep in mountains and of cities flourishing under the gods' care. Tashmi comes alive in my head, their pain and loneliness resonating deeply with mine, right until they are cruelly punished by the gods.

When I finish the tale, it is as though a veil that was draped over the atmosphere has been lifted. I can breathe, and I see Medha's expression, starry-eyed with wonder.

"What happened to them after that?" she asks.

"There is no official continuation, but..." I wink at her. "If you continue to be a good girl, I'll think of their story."

She giggles. Then her smile drops. Adarsh's face surfaces in her mind. "Is this what it is like to have a real mother?" she whispers.

"Don't say that, Medha," I chide her. "Your mother is still your mother, no matter what you think."

Not that I can say much about myself, but it is an automatic response. An expected response.

Medha buries her head in my stomach. "What was your mother like, Binsa?"

My fingers stiffen. "Kind, loving, nurturing," I say. "Everything you'd expect of a mother."

"What happened to her? Why don't I see her?"

Of all the questions in the world she could ask. "She...disappeared." I pull myself away from her. "She used to stay in Ghanatukh with me. Then she up and left one day, all trace of her gone."

This is the official truth that has circulated throughout the temple.

Except that no one bothered to find out how she disappeared. No one bothered to search for her. If they had scoured the chasm beside the Bakhal, they might have found the shattered body of a woman with all her belongings scattered around her. But they were relieved when she was gone.

You were born for greatness, my daughter, Kavita's voice echoes in my head.

A chill grips my entire body.

"Binsa, it's okay," Medha says, breaking through the bubble of terror encasing me. "You don't have to talk about your mother if you don't want to. I'm sorry I asked."

I force myself to take a deep breath. I am here, real and breathing and alive, with Medha cradled in my arms. Kavita is not.

"You should be glad your mother is still around, Medha," I say. *You could make amends with her one day*, I think.

Medha nods and stays silent as she remains encased in my arms. I am a blood shaman, I remind myself. I should not feel sympathy for people I will use to achieve my goals.

Yet when I think about saying goodbye to Medha, my heart feels like it's being rent in two.

30

Accusation

I opt to skip my lessons for today. I do not have the time to entertain Ykta, nor do I have the capacity to deal with Medha's moping about her coronation. The girl stayed with me until just before dawn cracked over the sky last night, seemingly content to remain in silence. Yet before we parted, her mood dampened, and there was a mournful pang that struck deep to my core.

There are far more pressing matters to attend to than estranged brothers and clingy girls.

At my behest, Jirtash calls Nali to my room. The maidservant appears before my door in a flash, as though she were waiting all day to be summoned.

I gesture for her to take a seat. She insists on standing; I do not pressure her. Instead, I pluck a tome that is over twice the length of my hand out of the bookshelf. Its cover is inscribed with *A Brief History of Aritsya*, but once I open it, it is an empty box that houses Privindu's book. Ykta had gifted it to me, gleefully divulging that this was how Dahlu students smuggled kobir leaves and raksi and anything remotely illegal. My tongue sours at the memory, and I shove it away and take Privindu's book out.

"I hope the priests aren't mad at me for stealing you away so frequently," I say, teasing.

"They won't miss my presence," Nali replies, her words clipped with impatience. "More importantly, what do we do about this book? How—how do we reveal that Nudin is a blood shaman?"

"What time of day is it?"

The half-Dennarese stares at me as though eggs are growing out of my ears. She looks outside the window, trying to gauge the sun's position. "About four in the afternoon?" Her brows knit together in confusion. "I caught a glimpse of the clock in the Yharuda's main hall when you summoned me."

"Wonderful contraptions, aren't they? We can only hope to catch up to the technological marvels of Shur," I say, sitting at the table.

"Rakhti Binsa," Nali says, "I do not believe I was summoned to talk about clocks."

"Of course, of course." I prop my chin on my palm. "How has your translation work been? I've heard that Shurran is a remarkably difficult language, with the various conjugations and strange word orders. If you successfully translate a complex literary work such as *Collection of Folktales*, I'm sure the priests will be happy to assign you more work."

"*Binsa.*" Her expression stiffens. "Nudin killed my sister. I do not want to talk about the Shurran language or clocks."

This is your strategy? Ilam asks, tone dry. *Agitating her?*

It seems to be working just fine. Aloud, I release a huff. "Lower your voice," I chide her. "Don't let the entirety of Ghanatukh know you're accusing one of their beloved priests of a crime."

Nali's face pales, but she still quivers with rage.

"That attitude will get you killed, Nali," I continue, putting on a grave expression. "Do you know what we can do about Nudin? Nothing."

Her eyes widen in fury. "*Nothing?*"

I shake my head. "Nothing."

"You're the Rakhti of Bakhtin, vessel of one of the ten Forebears of Aritsya. And you're telling me you can do nothing?" she hisses.

"He killed innocent girls, Binsa. You may have been the lucky survivor, but those nine girls had family. People who were waiting for them to come home if they were not chosen by Rashmatun. But they were killed. And by one of your priests, no less! Tell me, what *can* you do, then?"

I narrow my eyes at her. "Perhaps I have been too cordial with you, Nali. Need I remind you that you are a mere servant and I am your Rakhti?"

She clenches her jaw and drops her head. Interesting. Does she care about Anju that much? Or is she only trying to break free of her stepmother's clutches?

Watch, Ilam. I don't have to use your magic to control someone.

The demon cackles.

"Listen to me. I may be Rakhti in name, but the priests have control over the entire temple—and Bakhtin, in turn." I intertwine my fingers and place them on the table. "Nudin's family, in particular, has been serving the temple for the past five centuries. What makes you think the people will believe that a member of such an eminent family has committed such a terrible sin?"

"Then—what can we do? Hide the truth forever?" Her lower lip trembles; her eyes glisten with silver. "What about Rashmatun? Is she not enraged by this injustice?"

By my estimation, almost ten minutes have passed, Ilam says.

I get onto my feet and walk to her side, then place a hand on her shoulder. She does not flinch from my touch. "Rashmatun's power is not one we can exploit on a whim," I say. "Besides, I do not think the matter is so simple. Nudin was only fifteen years old during the previous Rakhti Selection—do you really think he would have done anything without his father's permission?"

Her expression drops. "It's Harun who's the murderer?"

"That sounds more likely. Besides, Nudin was not even boruvinda at the time, while Harun was the Thiravinda-in-training. If anything, Harun had more opportunities to kill them."

"Why would he do something like that?" Nali's face has gone so white she looks like she is about to faint. "Anju..."

"She must have been important to you," I say sympathetically.

"She was the only one in the house who treated me like a human." Nali turns her face to the side. "Even the servants there . . . called me a Dennarese dog and treated me like one. She was the only one who played with me and taught me how to read."

She takes in a shuddering breath. "She was so kind—the sort of girl who would cry when someone else's cat died and when a bird hurt its wings. My stepmother may have coerced me into entering Ghanatukh Temple, but I was partly driven by my own desire to find the truth. I know that now. Her kindness has fuelled me for all these years. If not for her, I might have used my hadon to kill many people by now."

A chill snakes down my spine. I did not know how important Anju was to her, the same way Chandri was to me. "I'm sorry," I say. Then my sympathy dies down, and I add, "I found something interesting in Privindu's book that might help us."

Her expression brightens. "What is it?"

So impatient. So easy to manipulate.

Even if I cannot read her mind, I am able to draw out her thoughts and twist them the way I want, all the same.

"Here." I hand the tome over to her; Nali holds it as though it might burst into flames. "I have a translation note for page one hundred and seven."

She flips to the corresponding page, her face paling as she scans the paper I clipped over the original writing; I am lucky that she does not know how to read Ritsadun. Then her hands stop moving, and murmurs fall from her lips: "Crushed roots of dalle jhar, two spoons of honey ingested by birds, and one drop of blood from a goddess's vessel . . ."

Her eyes widen in horror and elation. "A truth serum? This is . . . Is this real? Can we even do this?"

Internally, I release a small sigh of relief. "It's not impossible," I say. "Look. Medha's coronation will come next Jhokti, and all of Bakhtin will be attending. If we get Harun to speak the truth of the Bloodbath, would that not be a far better option than barging into his room and demanding an answer?"

Nali's eyes lift to meet mine, an unsettling void that adds to the eerie quietness of her mind. "But we're not blood shamans. How—"

Somewhere in the Bakhal's courtyard, I hear dozens of footsteps stomping across the ground.

"Nowhere does it say that you have to be a blood shaman to create a truth serum," I cut in before she can question the matter any further. "This is our only hope, Nali. You know it."

"But—"

I take a step closer to her, hands hovering over the book. "Do you want justice for Anju or not?"

The footsteps are running up the stairs, the dull tremor of their weight like distant storm clouds gradually rolling in.

"I . . . Of course I do," she whispers. "Still—"

"Nali Yankaran!" someone roars from outside the door. "Come face your crimes!"

It's Harun. Nali and I exchange a panicked glance. I place a reassuring hand over hers and gently tug Privindu's book away from her. "It's okay," I say. "You have me."

She gives a frightened, determined nod. I walk to the door and open it, admitting the temple's entire procession of orange-robed boruvindas. Harun and Nudin stand at the head of the group, and several Holy Guards flank their sides. All of a sudden, it is suffocating to take even a single step.

"What happened, Harun?" I ask. The chief priest's face is purple with rage, making his frog-like eyes appear as if they were bulging farther out of their sockets.

He jabs a fat, stubby finger towards Nali. "She stole something from me," he snarls, "which I found in *her* bed. A statuette of Rashmatun, made of Yeruvian gold and inlaid with the finest Nasthar rubies and yellow sapphires. A family heirloom that has been around for nearly three centuries, and *she* dared to sully Rashmatun's brilliance with her dirty hands."

Nali stares at him in disbelief. "This is ridiculous! I am on library duty this week!" she protests. "Ask any of the servants who share quarters with me. They can testify that I have been doing translation work. My name is not on the roster assigned to the priests' quarters."

"I saw you last night," Nudin says in a reedy voice. "I couldn't sleep, so I was wandering around the temple. Then I saw a silhouette coming out of my father's place. I immediately recognised you because you look . . . different."

Nali flinches from the indirect insult. A pang of pity hits me; perhaps she wouldn't have to suffer if she looked more like her Aritsyan father, like how maybe I wouldn't have suffered so much if I had Kavita's beauty.

But as of now, the prejudice against her works to my advantage.

"My son is known to be a light sleeper," Harun affirms.

"There must be a mistake." Nali shakes her head vehemently, her shoulders hunching more and more by the second. "I wouldn't do anything like that. My sister is about to become Rakhti. Even if I were a thief, I would not dare to do anything that would tarnish her reputation!"

"Are you saying that Boruvinda Nudin is lying?" one the priests retorts, his sneering expression resembling a cross-eyed owl.

"I—" Her expression crumples with realisation. "Someone must have put it near my bed to sabotage me!" she cries, voice cracking. "I know it! Everyone hates me. Everyone wants to see me punished. I—"

"Hold your tongue, Nali," I finally step in. Then, directing my next words towards Harun: "Do you have proof that the statuette was found in her room?"

"All the priests here can bear witness," he answers. "As well as the Holy Guards and the servants within the vicinity."

Ilam tells me that the priests genuinely believe Nali took the statuette. Good. Nudin is upholding his end of the bargain.

"Are you sure you were not trying to search for this?" I say, raising Privindu's book for all to see.

Collective gasps ring out. I sense everyone's blood running cold. *Impossible*, they all think, horrified. *This book should not exist.*

Harun's attention narrows towards me as his priests fly into a panic. *Does she have a part in this? But why?*

He suspects me of planting the statue. But he doesn't know who else is conspiring against him. And perhaps he would never suspect Nudin, even in his wildest dreams.

The errs of great men often go unnoticed, after all.

"Where did you find this?" Nudin demands.

"From the Thiravinda's room while I was cleaning it last week." The lie falls out smoothly from Nali's lips. Good girl.

"You filthy urvas!" Harun roars. "How dare you make such a baseless accusation against me!"

"You're presenting it to us now?" Nudin says. "At such a convenient time?"

"I—I didn't know what to do when I found it, so I gave it to the Rakhti." Nali lowers her head. "How could I accuse the great Thiravinda of Bakhtin of being a blood shaman?"

The silence that follows is deafening; tension strings taut across the air, as if the tiniest movement would spark a wildfire.

"How do we know this book isn't yours?" Harun suggests quietly. His gaze slides towards me, as sharp as the fangs of a snake. "Or perhaps it was the Rakhti who found this book?"

A burst of laughter escapes my lips. "Whyever would I do that, Harun? Rashmatun would sooner strike me down than allow me to even *think* of using blood magic. Besides, I see no reason for Nali to need the book either. She is a practitioner of Dennarese magic."

A muscle works in Harun's jaw. "Yet you imply that I am a blood shaman, when I have served Rashmatun's temple for nearly forty years. Are you saying that Rashmatun is ignorant of my apparent sins?"

"Perhaps she wishes for you to repent." I smile sweetly at him. "Even the holiest of men commit sins, both unknowingly and consciously."

If his mental state had a physical manifestation, it would be a steaming teapot, emblazoned in red and threatening to shatter from the heat at any given moment.

I'd like to see that happen, Ilam purrs, clearly enjoying the theatrics.

I too am revelling in the play I have staged.

"Hand that book to me, Rakhti Binsa," Nudin intervenes in a low tone. "And we'll forget whatever happened. Including the urvas's thievery."

Nali tugs at my sleeve, eyes wide with desperation. I lean towards her and whisper in her ear, "We'll give it up for now, Nali. You have to protect your position—and your integrity as the future Rakhti's sister."

Her shoulders slump at the mention of Medha. Reluctantly, she loosens her grip on me.

I pass the book to Nudin.

"Thank you," he says. Then he wheels around and declares, "None of you have seen or heard anything here. Let us leave."

Everybody whispers among themselves even as they heed Nudin's orders. Soon, my room is empty, with only Nali, Nudin, Harun, and I left rooted in our original spots.

"I will not forget this, urvas," Harun growls. "You will pay the price of shaming me in front of my own people."

Nali does not deign to give a response.

Harun scoffs, confident he has done nothing wrong. He turns around and stalks off. Nudin inclines his head towards us before trailing after his father.

Nali bursts into sobs.

I startle, then rub a hand between her shoulder blades. I'm not sure if the motion brings comfort, but I have seen plenty of maid-servants being offered condolences in this manner after one of Jir-tash's infamous scoldings. It takes a while for her to calm down. "I will make him pay," she grits out, scrubbing her eyes. "He killed Anju. He killed those girls. He does not deserve to live—not when he stole so many lives."

A nail hammered into place. The piece that will convince Nali to go through with my plan.

"Indeed," I echo in agreement. "He does not deserve to live."

Be careful what you wish for, Ilam laughs.

I study Privindu's book late into the night, with only a lit candle to keep me company. Nudin secretly passed the book back to me earlier in the evening. My eyelids keep drooping, and a dull pulsing pounds in my ears. Fatigue wracks my bones, but I force myself to keep going, to keep studying and make up for all the years I hadn't had the opportunity to learn more.

Occasionally, Ilam drops a snide comment or two—*I'm anything but prideful*, he snorts when I come across a passage characterising demon traits, which apparently includes narcissism—but I am alone in my thoughts otherwise.

Just as I am about to pitch forward in exhaustion, I find a chapter that truly catches my interest.

"The Properties and Uses of Blood."

I remember what I told Ykta the night he tried to stop me from taking more soulstream—how Kavita had poisoned the other girls at the Bloodbath, and how she had fed me her blood in the weeks leading up to the Bloodbath.

But I never quite understood how she did it—and why I survived. Now the answers lie right before me.

I see Privindu slitting his wrist and storing his blood in a tiny vial. I see him dropping the blood into a cup of wine before serving it to a man wrapped in heavy, elaborate robes. Then the man drops dead, his unfinished cup of wine spilled onto the carpet. His body has decayed, and his mouth is contorted in unvoiced agony.

The same method Kavita used to poison the girls.

Our blood has been infused with the demon's, and hence contains a portion of the demon's otherworldly energies, Privindu explains. *These energies are poison to regular human beings. The severity of the poisoning depends on how they ingest our blood. Pure blood will kill the victim almost instantaneously; blood and water mixed with a ratio of one to ten will take effect within a week. However, any solution that is more diluted than the one-to-ten ratio will not kill the victim. Rather, taken regularly, it will help the individual develop immunity to the poison.*

The scene at the Bloodbath resurfaces in my mind. The nine girls, downing the purifying wine before Chandri entered the temple. The nine girls, faces glowing with smiles and bright, eager eyes. The nine girls, blackness gradually searing their skin and tearing screams out of their throats, their radiant faces contorted in grotesque expressions of agony.

Then there was nothing left of them, save for charred piles of flesh.

I study my hand, recalling how my skin blackened every time I tapped into too much of Ilam's power.

I cannot bear to imagine the pain they suffered during their final moments—the thoughts that must have run through their heads.

My fingers curl into a determined fist. I can do nothing for them. They are dead. Anju is dead. What I can do is to move forward, to continue forging my own path on blood that has already been shed.

You have become just like me, Kavita chants in singsong. *You have become just like me.*

Peace settles over me, despite the incessant cackling in my head.

I have found the final piece in my puzzle—the poison that will seal Medha's and Nali's fates once and for all.

31

Loose Ends

The days trickle past all too quickly. Pitch-black skies meld into blushing dawns, and sunrises bleed into sunsets. Every night, I pore over Privindu's book, learning all I can: how demons are summoned, how they reveal themselves when their vessels are harmed, and the inherent lust for power within all demons.

All the while, Privindu's memories flash before my eyes.

They are vivid and real, as though I were there watching everything unfurl. I see how he pens his memories down in the first place, his brows furrowed in concentration as he inks his illustrations. I learn that all blood shamans have the ability to make their memories visible to other blood shamans when writing, and that these memories will be stronger if the blood shamans are related. Would I have been able to learn more about blood shamanism if I'd kept Kavita's belongings? But she didn't know how to write, so I couldn't have seen her memories anyway.

A knot in my stomach loosens.

I continue browsing through the book. I see how Privindu bound himself to Ilam. They talk to each other under the moonlight; the scene is quiet, serene, dissonant from what is actually taking place. When the memory fades, I learn how blood shamans are able to bind a demon to their bloodline, and how the demon grows stronger the longer they remain with the family. But their strength comes at a great price, as the demon will gradually lose their sense of ambition and purpose. In the end, they may even forget who they are.

Ilam stirs in my head.

Are you sure your wiped memories don't have anything to do with this? I ask him.

Someone manipulated me, he growls. *That's all there is.*

Why did you agree to such a contract in the first place?

Do I look like I have all the answers?

I take this as a cue to move on to another chapter: "Unsealing a Bound Demon"; I've read this several times before already, but I keep coming back to it, as if there were an invisible presence guiding my fingers. Privindu does not have an embedded memory for this section, only showing me what he was doing while writing. Ilam—in weasel form—slinks around his legs.

"Unsealing a demon is dangerous, even for me," Ilam says to Privindu. "Are you sure you want to write this down?"

"I need to make sure that whoever succeeds me knows everything about blood shamanism. *Everything.*"

My hand drifts to the yellow sapphire around my neck. The night air is completely still, but the candle-flame at my desk flickers vigorously.

"Tempting, isn't it?" Kavita murmurs.

Wind brushes past my shoulder. I look up. Kavita is perched on the edge of my table, smiling down upon me, her eyes glowing a devilish red. "Ilam told you about the terms of our contract, right? That he would give me power if I helped him find Rashmatun."

She vanishes into a trail of smoke.

I scan the room. Her breath tickles the back of my neck—and there she is, looming behind me, her grin growing wider with each second. "Now you have the chance to do what I couldn't," she says. "You can become a true goddess."

She dissipates into the air. This time, she does not return.

So will you attempt to unseal Rashmatun? Kavita's and Ilam's voices meld into one.

Seal. Unseal. Goddess and demon. Such fine lines between opposing concepts, a single inversion of meanings that transitions one into the other. Even if Rashmatun were a demon, she has been worshipped and revered as a goddess all this while. Wouldn't that make her a real goddess to her devotees, never mind the truth of her nature?

Who is Rashmatun? Who are the demons, exactly? How is Ilam unaware of his past, yet is bold enough to seek Rashmatun out?

All the answers lie with the demoness herself.

I release a slow breath, dragging it out for as long as I can. My veins thrum with excitement. Ilam's power already fills me with euphoria when I tap into it—and Rashmatun's power promises even more. It will be the magic of an ancient demon that I am carrying, magic that could easily destroy me.

Or exalt me.

"I will," I reply to Ilam and Kavita—whoever it is who actually spoke.

You are confident you will succeed in taming her? Ilam says. *She'll be volatile, unpredictable.*

With your help? I'm sure we'll find a way.

Ilam harrumphs loudly. Yet I detect some semblance of satisfaction from him. *You know I will not deny an opportunity to grow stronger.*

My lips curl at the corners. *Perhaps that is why we are partners.*

Purple smoke suddenly wreathes around my arm. It pulls away from me, and there sits Ilam, his sinewy body blending in seamlessly with the shadows shrouding my room. Only his eyes, a bright and luminous silver, pierce through the dark.

To my surprise, he nuzzles his head against me, much like a normal house cat.

Except that Ilam is enormous, and he topples me from my seat.

As I huff at him indignantly, he emits a yowl that resembles laughter.

My remaining time as Rakhti is surprisingly lazy and idyllic; I indulge myself in whatever I want, whenever I want. I still take lessons with Ykta and Medha—even if my brother ignores me most of the time—and stroll outside the Bakhal grounds. The blatant exploitation of my newfound freedom earns quite a few disapproving frowns from Jirtash, but she holds her tongue. *The girl will be gone soon*, she reminds herself every time.

I see Nali and Nudin separately to finalise their roles during the coronation. Neither one has any idea that the other is involved in this grand scheme, which is exactly how I want it.

I am doing this to survive, I keep telling myself.

As for Medha, the girl is so quiet. Nothing I do or say stirs her interest. She merely takes in everything with a benign smile and a resigned nod, and goes back to contemplating her future. Fear and anxiety grip her, mostly at the prospect of finally obtaining the answer to her question: *I want to know what it means to be Rakhti.*

The day before her coronation—or the day of my retirement—we lunch in the Bakhal's courtyard; the temperate weather is perfect for dining outside. The cooks have prepared a feast for my last day here, a vast array of lamb and mutton and buffalo, grilled and curried and marinated with an explosion of spices. Plates are lined with mushy dhindo and sour gundruk, and there is an entire tray of yomaris for dessert. It seems they are intent on stuffing me as much as possible before I leave. I happily indulge myself, no longer worried about my bleeding.

The maidservants have moved a table down to the courtyard to accommodate the sheer volume of dishes. As I savour the feast, Medha barely touches her food.

This will be the last time I eat with Binsa, she thinks morosely.

"What's wrong, Medha?" I ask.

She jerks, then quickly shakes her head. She stuffs handfuls of rice into her mouth, nearly choking on the last shove. I get up and rush over to her side as she coughs, splattering bits of rice back onto her plate.

"What did I tell you about chewing slowly?" I chide, tone light.

The coughing fit continues for a while. When it subsides, she washes her food down with gulps of water. Then she looks at me. "Will I get to see you again?"

I offer her a sympathetic smile. "No. This will be the last time you ever talk to me like this, Medha."

Her expression immediately crumples. "But—I will miss you," she says. "I've been so lonely here, and you have been the only real friend to me. My sister will probably be stuck at the Yharuda, and I can't talk to the servants whenever I please."

"There's Ykta," I say.

She sniffs loudly. "He's not *you.*"

I do not know what to say, so I keep quiet.

"I . . . I only talked so much around you because I felt comfortable around you," she continues. "And I don't know. I knew I would have to be Rakhti one day, and that you would leave. But now that it's tomorrow . . ."

Her nose reddens at the tip, and tears stream down her cheeks. "I'm scared, Binsa," she whispers, struggling to steady her tone. "I don't know what I'll do without you. I don't know if I'll be able to fill your shoes. Worst of all, you won't be here to guide me."

I purse my lips, heaving a sigh. Then, allowing myself one last moment of weakness, I wrap my left arm around her at an awkward angle—my right hand is still sticky from bits of rice and curry. A vague recollection tugs my mind: me clinging to Chandri, bawling my eyes out, and her soft, gentle hands pressing the yellow sapphire into my palm.

"Rashmatun will guide you," I murmur, echoing the very words she used that day. "Fret not if the weight of being Rakhti seems too heavy to bear. Remember this—Rashmatun chose you for a reason."

"Chandri's words," she chokes out, recalling the Sacred Scrolls. The name triggers a new stream of thoughts. "Did you and my sister manage to learn more about the Bloodbath?"

Desperation edges her voice. A face surfaces in her mind—her mother's.

I shake my head. "Remembering the ghosts of people who can never return will do you no good, Medha," I say, my voice low and heavy. "You cannot bring them back to life, no matter what you do. Do not be like your mother, who is so trapped in her past that she cannot move on, refusing to live a new life with her husband and her family."

The little apsara slowly squeezes her way out of my grip and gapes at me. "How do you know?"

"How could I not know after that night?" I say, voice soft. "You looked so sad when I mentioned your mother."

She blinks; she wants to ask more, but decides that it does not matter anymore. "You think I should give up," she concludes.

"It is not wrong to be curious, Medha," I say. "Sometimes, though, it is safer to remain ignorant."

"How do you know that?"

I close my eyes. *Please, stop thinking about the Bloodbath*, I want to beg her. *Forget it. Forget your mother's teachings and set yourself free. It is not worth the cost of your life.*

Yet I know that those words will be futile, even if I say them out loud.

"It will be best for us to forget, Medha. Not just you or me, but the entirety of Bakhtin."

My hand hovers over hers; I hesitate before lowering it.

My perspective shifts. I am still in the Bakhal's courtyard, sitting under the mellow sky and presented with a vast array of food, but my limbs are even smaller now, and my toes barely graze the ground. I look up to see Binsa's face staring back at me; turmoil tears at my guts as I consider what she has just said. How am I supposed to forget everything so easily when my entire life has been built for the purpose of exacting justice for Anju? How am I supposed to forget when my mother won't let me?

"Can I do it?" I whisper. "Forget?"

"It's not a matter of if you can do it," Binsa says. "You *must*."

My mind instantly clears, even if my heart remains heavy. All of a sudden, I cannot recall why I was so anxious, so obsessed with finding the truth of the Bloodbath. I blink and stare upwards; the dark silhouette of an eagle soars across the sky, perhaps searching for prey, perhaps simply wanting to stretch its wings. It is free. Unbothered by tragic pasts.

What does it mean to become Rakhti? I wonder. Curiosity plumes at the question, a slow burn that scratches at my chest.

I decide that I will find that out for myself—without the shadow of Anju or my mother looming over my head.

I blink, and my perspective snaps back into Binsa's body; my hand is placed over small, smooth fingers. I look at Medha, the little girl's eyes ablaze with energy. My chest swells with pain and warmth. My head spins.

She trusts you, Kavita murmurs.

More precisely, she trusts Binsa, the strong yet gentle Rakhti of Bakhtin.

If she knew the actual Binsa, she wouldn't be so trusting anymore.

What am I thinking? *I* am Binsa. It must be the after-effects of Ilam's blood magic. It feels surreal, to have carved a direct pathway to her mind and *become* Medha while retaining my own consciousness.

Medha leans her head against my arm. "Binsa?"

"Hmm?"

"I will never forget you."

The smile on my face stiffens as I stroke her head with my clean hand. The memory of my first contract with Ilam plays in my head, the one where he took my womb in exchange for his power. I wonder if it's because he knew this would happen—that I would feel such a strange connection to this little girl. And so he took away any possibility of my entertaining maternal instincts. I wonder if it's because he no longer wants to be bound to my bloodline.

I wonder if this is what Kavita felt when she combed and braided my hair in our dilapidated room, back before *everything* happened.

The final remnants of guilt twinge within me; I clamp down on the feeling without mercy, until nothing but cold determination remains.

It will be best for all of us to forget.

I pull her into another embrace and say nothing.

The eighth bell of the night rings, and I am escorted into the room adjacent to mine—Rashmatun's room. Traditional braziers light the room instead of modern gas lamps; the fires form an eerie halo that encases the area. Harun is the only priest here, and he sits in the middle of the space. A bowl of water is placed before him. He is to perform a ritual to cleanse me and ensure that I depart with utmost purity and virtuosity of heart.

Jirtash quietly shuffles out of the room. The chief priest and I are left alone.

I take my place on the floor across from him. A seven-pronged star dots the centre of his forehead in vermilion paint instead of the usual seven-lobed leaf—a crude imitation of the one usually painted on my forehead when I am Rashmatun. His eyes follow my every motion, caution sparking in them.

Meanwhile, right behind Harun, the yellow eyes of Anas watch me, the light from the fires setting a dim glow within them.

"I would start the ritual," he says in a withering tone, "but you and I both know it is not necessary."

I smile at him. "Come now. I've done my duty perfectly for all these years."

"Where is Rashmatun? What have you done with her?" he asks.

"I did not answer Asahar when he posed the same questions to me," I reply. "What makes you think I will answer you?"

He clenches his teeth in frustration. "You promised Rakhta Asahar you would reveal her whereabouts in two years."

"Ah, but that was assuming I'd still be Rakhti then." I bare my teeth. "Since Rashmatun has already announced that she will take a new vessel, I don't see how that agreement holds true."

"You!" His fingers twitch, and heat coats my body; the yellow sapphire at my throat hums in response to his magic.

Then the heat dies down. Good. He is aware that he is no match for me.

"Rakhta Asahar will make sure you pay," he says through his teeth. "Did you think your antics would go unnoticed?"

I tilt my head. Harun has not spoken a single word of protest since my announcement, despite his evident alarm. Of course he'd reported everything to Asahar. "I'm not interested in how he intends to take Rashmatun from me afterward. Rather, why are *you* so intent on finding her, Harun?" I ask, genuinely curious. "Why do you serve a demoness?"

He is taken aback by the question. "At first I was merely following tradition. A legacy passed down to my father and his father, and the many fathers before them," he replies, slightly sardonic. "Besides, what can one priest's word do against a demon, when all believe them to be a god? It was easier to keep my head down and follow the rules.

"Eventually, I came to believe in Rashmatun herself. She is a demon, yes, but one cannot deny that she has led the city with the wisdom and strength of a goddess. She has done good for us and protected us from disasters, again and again. Regardless of what she does to maintain her power, she has served us well."

His words contain nothing but the barefaced truth.

"You're so desperate for her return that you would resort to killing people yourself," I mutter. "Why did you drop the goats on unsuspecting commoners?"

He flinches at the mention of the accidents. "Our magic is weak," he argues. "We were not able to control the location of the incantations."

The same excuse Nudin gave. Like father, like son, despite how the latter would hate the idea. "You went ahead with it anyway," I say. "Does that make you any better than me?"

He glares at me. "Is that why you raised pandemonium the other day, just to remind us of the goats?"

I emit a chuckle. "That? I wanted to have some fun before I left. The looks on all your faces were worth it. Not even my own mother had been so concerned about me."

His lips curl into a snarl. "You—"

"How will you proceed with the new Rakhti," I interrupt, "now that Rashmatun will not be with her?"

He releases a snort, as if he cannot be bothered to remain furious at me anymore. "Nudin and I will personally oversee her upbringing. And I am sure Rakhta Asahar will find Rashmatun—no matter if you're willing or unwilling. This city will not survive long without its true goddess."

Anas's yellow eyes bore into me.

"I see," I reply softly.

I wait a few hours after the "ritual" has finished, skulking out of my room and speeding towards the Yharuda. The servants' quarters lie right behind the library, in a low, shoddy length of bricks that is the unsightly younger sibling of the priests' quarters. I stop at the entrance, reaching into the folds of my cloak and extracting a vial. It sloshes with a dark, viscous liquid—the "truth-teller concoction."

Quiet as a whisper, I place the vial right beside the door-frame, ensuring that it lightly taps against the wood. Then I am gliding off, another shadow melding into the night.

From a distance, I hear the scuffling of cautious footsteps.

32

A New Goddess

It is the day of the coronation.

The temple is engulfed in a swirl of excitement, and nerves buzz in the atmosphere. In fact, everyone seems busier today than on the day of the Rakhti Selection. A tangible readiness strings taut across the air, as if everybody could spring into action at a moment's notice.

For the last time in Binsa's life, I am taken into Rashmatun's room. I am dressed in the red-and-gold jama, my hair pinned into an elaborate topknot. Four necklaces are draped around my neck, and the royal headdress is fixed onto my head. All I am missing is the Star of Rashmatun on my forehead. But that will come later, when the goddess's spirit is to be officially transferred into Medha.

For the last time in Binsa's life, I step onto the palanquin, Medha beside me. She clings to my hand, her face white beneath the makeup. I do not say anything to comfort her, but I hold on to her hand as well.

For the last time in Binsa's life, I descend from Ghanatukh Temple and into the city centre, to greet the citizens who have come to bid me goodbye.

They are a solid mass of heat, pressing against one another in attempts to be near me, to throw their offerings, or to touch me, in hopes that I will grant them my final blessings. They seem to have forgotten how I brought the calamities of the Prophecy of Geerkha to them in the first place. The Holy Guards who escort us wall them off, and the priests and handmaidens of Ghanatukh form a snaking file that cuts through the crowd.

All too soon, we arrive at Shiratukh Temple. The place where it all began.

I wear a polite, if slightly downcast, smile on my face.

The bearers gently place the palanquin down. I step out, stumbling slightly.

Nudin snickers at the display.

Medha exits the palanquin after me. I turn to face the crowd, a sea of faces that blur before me. I vaguely make out coarse brows, wrinkles, unmarred skin, thick lips, thin noses. Other than that, everything seems to be draped in a haze.

I open my mouth. I'm supposed to give a speech.

And then I see them.

Ykta, watching me from a distance, as he always does. Nali, hunching herself against the horde of people, but standing out with her pale skin and crescent eyes, nonetheless. Kavita, a smile plastered on her face. Keran, sometimes there, sometimes not. Chandri, appearing regal and kind in spite of her haggard expression. Their faces ripple at the edges, lending them an incorporeal quality. Both the living and the dead are here, although they are not supposed to be, reminding me of who I was and who I want to be.

You made a choice, Binsa, they seem to say. *We hope you are happy with it.*

My mouth goes dry.

"Rakhti Binsa," Harun calls out, jerking me back into the present. "On behalf of the entirety of Bakhtin, we would like to thank you for your services for our city, and for your devotion and dedication to our goddess. Now, if there is anything you wish to say while you are still our Rakhti, make it known."

This is not the time to be hallucinating, I scold myself. I take a deep breath.

"As your Rakhti, I have nothing much to say. But as someone who will soon stand amongst you, I wish to make this known. The goddess has watched over us during this period of suffering," I say, finally getting the words out. "She has delivered us from times of darkness and brought us back into the light. Praise be to Rashmatun, who continues to protect us with her strength and wisdom.

"It was my honour to serve her, and I will continue to serve her to the full extent of my abilities for the rest of my life." I pause for a while, drawing myself tall and sweeping my gaze across my audience. "Wisdom be upon all of you!"

"Wisdom be upon you!" the crowd roars in return.

I turn towards Harun, wearing a magnanimous smile. "Now, let us toast to the coming of our next Rakhti, the dawn of a new age! May she lead us with Rashmatun's strength, and may she guide us with the wisdom of Rakhtis long past. May our goddess continue to bless us through her!"

The crowd erupts into raucous cheers.

The maidservants step forward with the ceremonial wine, each of them carrying a single cup on their tray. Jirtash serves me mine, her expression etched with the resignation of one who has seen many a season pass by, one whose life weathers through the fleeting of many others.

I will miss her, honestly, she thinks. *Mischievous sometimes, but it was a joy to serve her.*

I lift the cup from the tray and raise it slightly towards her.

I wheel around. Nali is serving Harun his wine, to everyone's shock—especially the priests, considering they think she stole a precious heirloom from their chief priest. The half-Dennarese maidservant looks as though she wants to burrow herself into the ground. Still, she holds the tray out towards him; he takes the cup.

My attention quickly flits towards Nudin. He was in charge of the ceremonial details today, including the assignment of specific maidservants to specific priests. It had not been easy to convince Harun that Nali should be serving him. *As a gesture of the temple's acknowledgment of the Yankaran family's honour*, he argued vehemently.

Harun lifts his cup from the tray, the light *clink* of his nails against bronze cutting my thoughts. He raises the cup towards me.

I blink, taking a moment before returning the gesture. The boru-vindas echo the motion as they shuffle into a perfect circle around me.

"In honour of Rashmatun," I say.

"In honour of Rakhti Binsa," Harun says.

We lift the cups to our lips. My hands tremble ever so slightly, and bile rises to my tongue. Before I can hesitate any further, I tip the cup and guzzle its contents in one go, the trail of alcohol setting my throat aflame. In my peripheral vision, Harun downs the wine as well. He grimaces, but makes no mention of the terrible taste. We replace the cups on their trays.

Now, to wait.

"Let the ceremony officially begin!" I announce.

My people explode in another round of cheering.

I stand before Shiratukh's entrance, facing little Medha. This is the only time when the public is allowed to witness the summon-ing of Rashmatun. Harun takes his paints and stands between us, turning towards me first.

"I wish you luck in your life," he murmurs, not bothering to hide the malice in his tone.

I grin at him, as if we are friends. "And may Rashmatun bless yours."

A slight furrow creases his brows, but it quickly clears away. *It will be for the best*, he tells himself. *The girl will only continue to be a nuisance if you allow her in the temple. She is unpredictable, uncontrollable. Rashmatun would have never chosen a vessel like her if she had the choice.*

Too bad Rashmatun didn't have a choice, Kavita laughs.

He dips his brush into the paint. Nudin rings the bell that hangs from the frame of the entrance. In perfect synchrony, the priests begin to chant the summoning incantation. Harun paints my fore-head with the Star of Rashmatun—the very last time he will do so. The priests' voices condense in the atmosphere; where the mantra is usually light and soothing, a certain heaviness clouds it today.

Open, open, open, and see, Ilam chants along with them, almost cackling.

Harun takes his time painting the star. First, the white prongs that form the base, then the yellow layer atop it.

He closes the last prong.

The chants stop as soon as he finishes the painting.

Harun abruptly doubles over, the paints splattering onto the floor in a mess of white and yellow. Soon red colours the floor as well—as blood froths at his mouth and ash spreads across his fingertips.

A horrified scream pierces the brief peace—Jirtash.

Chaos follows soon after.

Some are stunned by the sight, their minds wiped blank. Others screech and scrabble away from the temple, declaring it cursed. The priests rush over to their leader, surrounding him but not daring to touch him, fearing that the infectious darkness lining his skin may be transferred to them as well.

And Nali—Nali stands there, mouth agape, the tray with the empty cup of wine still in her hands.

This is how her sister had died.

And she's witnessing it for herself. How the poison burns through the body. How the victim's eyes are filled with distilled agony, yet are glassed over, unseeing. How they open their mouth to scream, but not a sound comes out. How their body begins to collapse upon itself, consumed by the raging decay.

Meanwhile, Nudin stands over his father's body, stricken with fear. His gaze flickers between me and Harun; his mind is in a daze. He has not registered what is happening. All he knows is that his father is dying.

And that he had a hand in it.

Finally, when it is clear that there is no way to save Harun, he lifts his eyes and locks onto me.

I offer no response, maintaining my expression of blank surprise.

I wonder if Ykta is watching this from a distance. If he is, I wonder what he thinks of this—if he recognises the blackened skin from the Bloodbath. Perhaps he thinks that I have grown into a monster, just like Kavita.

It doesn't matter.

Binsa, isn't it high time you step in now? Ilam reminds me. The priests are a horrified huddle around Harun's body; all that remains of him are his clothes and a vague resemblance of a face that had once been human.

I lower my gaze. Then I lift my chin, snapping into my true self.

"Nali Yankaran, many a time have you committed grave sins, yet I forgave you each time," I say in the voice of Rashmatun. "Many a time have you transgressed the words of the Forebears, but you showed repentance, and I mercy."

She freezes in her spot. Then, disbelievingly, she turns towards me, as though she has just emerged from a trance. Her fingers, still gripped around the tray, have gone bone-white. If I could read her mind, I imagine she would think, *This was not part of the plan.*

"Yet would you go so far to unleash your rage, you who have been oppressed all your life? Would you go so far to take the life of a father, you who lost a sister?" I continue. Another wave of shock ripples throughout the crowd. "Would you give up on a life that is promised to you, for the sake of a life that has been long forgotten?"

Understanding dawns in her eyes. She is a mere scapegoat in the grand scheme of things. I never intended to help her in the first place.

Binsa has betrayed her.

"You, Nali Yankaran, had a choice—to walk the path of the Forebears and dedicate your life to them, but you chose otherwise." I take deliberate steps towards her. She shrinks away; I lengthen my gait in return. "You have committed the gravest of sins, the most heinous of crimes. You have taken the life of a man—and not just any man, but a man of utmost devotion to me, a loyal follower of mine. For that, you will pay."

"Rashmatun, stop!" Medha throws herself onto me, snapping out of her stupor. "Please! My sister didn't do anything! She wouldn't kill anyone! *Please!*"

Snot and tears mix down her face. Once, my heart would have knotted at the sight of the pure sorrow she emanates. Now there is nothing save for one thought.

She cannot be Rakhti.

I shove her away with an easy flick of my wrist. "Dare you question my judgment, girl?"

"Where's the proof that she did it?" Medha pleads.

Nudin steps forward, swallowing a lump in his throat. "You dare question your goddess? The very deity you are supposed to embody?"

"Peace, Nudin. The girl is right. Evidence must always be presented in the case of a crime." I jerk my head towards the Holy Guards. "Search her."

They fly into action, holding Nali's limbs and pawing through her clothing. Her head is bowed in the defeated manner of one who knows there is no use fighting.

The Guards extract a vial from her pocket. Tiny residues of the truth-teller concoction—my blood—still remain inside.

"Is that evidence enough?" I say to Medha.

"That doesn't prove anything!" she shrieks. "You have no idea what's inside the vial!"

"Don't I?" I raise a brow. "But your sister is the most conspicuous suspect here. She was the only maidservant assigned to handle Harun's wine, and she had reason enough to be furious at him— hate him, even, for the previous accusation of thievery. And why would she be carrying an empty vial around?"

I turn back to Nali, threading my fingers before me. "I am the goddess of wisdom. I see all, and I know all. And I know for a fact that you, Nali Yankaran, have taken the life of the former Thiravinda of Ghanatukh Temple. For committing the gravest of sins, you shall be sentenced to a life of isolation in Llaon."

No one says a word of protest.

I take a deep breath.

"As for you, Medha Yankaran, you whose blood has been tainted by one of a sinner, you are no longer fit to call yourself my vessel."

You have become just like me, Kavita whispers.

"You will be dismissed from your position as Shira-Rakhti, and you may never return to this position. You are to leave Ghanatukh Temple today, and while you are welcome to step through its doors as a devotee of mine, you are never to be granted an audience with me."

Don't tell me you're planning to be Rakhti forever, Ykta once said to me, back when I had no idea how and why I wanted to maintain my position.

A memory from a lifetime ago.

"Today, I declare Binsa to be the one and only Rakhti for as long as she lives. For she has served me well, and never have I found a vessel to be so pure of heart and bright of mind. She is a sign of a new era to come, my people. An era of change and enlightenment, of wealth and prosperity. She will guide Bakhtin for the many years before us, and she will do so with utmost wisdom and dedication."

I will never forget you, Medha had said to me.

I will never be forgotten now.

It takes a few moments before my words finally register.

Nudin is the first to pay his respects. He presses his palms together and falls into a deep bow. "To our goddess. May you illuminate our path now and forevermore!"

"To our goddess," the crowd follows. "May you illuminate our path now and forevermore!"

"To our goddess," Medha whispers, a single tear streaking down her cheek.

33

Sever

The temple denizens and the Guards are surprisingly efficient in removing Medha's and Nali's belongings and escorting the former out of the temple. The latter is taken straight to Llaon, accompanied by the older priests and Guards who have experience with the treacherous mountain path. Meanwhile, Medha is returned to her family in disgrace; I do not see her off.

I rest in my room, exhausted from having to project "Rashmatun" for so long. She occupied me for the rest of the procession, only leaving when we arrived back in Ghanatukh. I stumbled out of the palanquin, collapsing, pretending to be in a complete daze about everything that had happened. Nudin explained the entire event to me before the priests, his careful expression barely masking the turmoil beneath it.

Was this what I really wanted? he thought. *To live in a world where I do not have to answer to my father?*

Well, I did fulfil my end of the bargain.

I gave the appropriate reactions, of course: mourning, panic, and grief, all rolled into one. But I also took the news with the calmness of one fit to bear a goddess forever, displaying just the right balance of empathy and rationality.

The funeral rites for Harun are to take place today, after his body—or what remains of it—is properly washed and wrapped in sankti, the garments of the dead. I am allowed a brief moment of respite, to recover from the shock of the tragedy that just took place.

I sit on the edge of my bed, staring into the distance. Fulfilment floods me—knowledge that everything is in its rightful place. It is a pity that the Yankaran sisters have to go when I have taken a liking to them, but what's done is done. There is no use reminiscing about the past.

And not even the Rakhtas will be able to challenge me, for so long as I have Rashmatun, they will dance my tune. *Too bad, Harun*, I think. *Even your precious Rakhta Asahar is subject to my will.*

Soon, everything will be mine.

A slow grin creeps up my face; I cover it with my hand to stifle my laughter.

I did it, I tell Ilam. *We did it!*

He extracts himself from me, unfurling into his feline form. He bares his fangs. Strangely enough, I am not the least bit intimidated. "Indeed," he says. "You have far exceeded my expectations, Binsa."

Binsa. The name does not sound like my own anymore. It belongs to another girl, someone who fought against blood magic, someone able to bond with others, who thought twice before striking against anyone. Binsa wanted to remain Rakhti because of fear—she was terrified of the world outside, and she did not know what to do with herself.

Now I am Rakhti because I want to be Rakhti. Because I know this is my rightful position—that I was born into this role.

I am no longer Binsa. I realise this fact with an odd sense of resignation.

Ilam abruptly melds back into my body. I understand his disappearance only a few moments later, when I hear Ykta storming towards my room. Outside, he shoves past Jirtash and the handmaidens and slams the door open.

"What did you do, Binsa?" he snarls.

"The gall!" Jirtash shrieks, waddling in from outside. "How dare you—"

"It's all right, Jirtash," I say. "I'll talk to him."

The old matron thins her lips into a disapproving line. She shoots Ykta a glare before exiting my room.

My brother closes the distance between us in two quick strides, crouching and levelling his face with mine. "What are you doing, Binsa? Why did you kill Harun?"

The agony in his voice is unfiltered, raw. His eyes are rimmed with red, and he is holding back his tears. In his eyes, I look like the little sister he has always known—a little too small for her age, gaze sharp, movements composed. He tries to reconcile this image with the one he witnessed just this morning.

My heart clenches in pain. He sees me as a monster, an irredeemable murderer. As if to block myself from the heartache, I try to pretend that I am still Binsa for him—the innocent girl dragged into this, who had no idea that Rashmatun would charge Nali with Harun's murder.

The aching in my chest subsides.

"What do you mean, Ykta?" I frown at him. "I didn't kill Harun. Nali did. Rashmatun said so."

"And *you* are Rashmatun," he hisses.

I tilt my head in confusion. The goddess is a wholly separate being. "But I'm not. And it was Nali who did it, if Rashmatun judged it so. Her word is final."

His expression crumples in utter defeat. He gets up and tears through my bookshelf; Keran's face flashes in his head. *Look for the empty book,* he tells Ykta. My brother grabs *A Brief History of Aritsya*; he opens the tome to reveal another book inside the box. Ykta rapidly scans through the pages, his features morphing into pure horror.

Then he starts shredding the book, page by page.

I leap to my feet in shock. "Ykta! What are you doing?!"

"How could you?" he mutters, almost to himself. "I should have known this would happen. I should have tried to stop you. Keran was right. You're no longer the Binsa we know. You've given yourself completely to blood shamanism. Just like our mother."

Tears are freely streaming down his face now. I do not dare to go near him; there is an impermeable shield about him that drives me away. He's hiding his emotions behind a wall so thick that no amount of blood magic can break through it.

"Ykta, please!" I cry.

"Enough! I don't want to hear you!" And with that, he shreds the final page. "I won't be lied to anymore."

He bundles the scraps into his arms and marches towards the window.

He throws them out. They scatter like snow, lazily drifting away with the wind.

I stare at the remains of my book, stupefied.

"Goodbye, Binsa," Ykta says quietly. He casts one last look at me, heavy and forlorn. "And just so you know, I will find a way to stop you. Not for your sake, but for Bakhtin's."

He disappears like the ephemeral shadow of a candle-flame that had never been there.

Breathing heavily, I settle back onto my bed. The pain I managed to suppress returns as I discard the mask of Binsa. It floods my limbs and closes off my throat until I double over, wheezing. My skull feels as though it is cracking at the seams, and my hands tremble as I recall what has just taken place. What's wrong with me? I had genuinely believed that I had no recollection of the event, that Rashmatun had occupied my body, that Nali was the culprit behind Harun's death. I believed in the lies I told everyone and myself.

You are getting used to compartmentalisation, Ilam purrs.

Privindu's words from *Theories and Principles of Aritsyan Magic for Beginners* come to me: *When does a falsehood become truth? Very simply, when you believe it to be true.*

I bury my face in my hands, chuckling softly.

What are you doing, Binsa? I ask myself.

No. I'm not Binsa. And I'm not Rashmatun either.

I look out the window, at the pages from Privindu's book that are no longer there, destroyed by the hands of someone once so dear to me.

I will find a way to stop you.
As if I'd be intimidated by that.

Harun's funeral is grandiose for a man who was supposed to subscribe to a life of restraint and moderation—even until death. His
body has been placed atop a pyre, wrapped in a plain white sankti,
its only embellishment being the seven-pronged brooch on the
forehead. His personal memento, a symbol that represents his rank.
A new one will be made for Nudin soon, and he will be cremated
along with that brooch when his time comes.

The priests surround the pyre, clothed in white robes. Devotees weep as they present their offerings and press their foreheads
against the ground. Nudin is seated before the body of his father,
two incense pots on either side of him. Smoke coils around him,
like dragons draped around his shoulders.

I watch all of this from behind the pyre, to pay my respects to
the priest who had wholeheartedly devoted himself to looking
after me.

The hours tick past, slow and ponderous. An endless stream of
people filters into Ghanatukh. Some insist on staying, others leave
as soon as they have offered their prayers. The afternoon eventually
dwindles into night. I take occasional sips from the glass of water
placed beside me. Other than that, I am as still as stone.

Just as my eyelids are getting heavy, the eleventh bell rings.

The priests rise from their seats; I do the same. They bow their
heads and clasp their beads between their hands. Nudin takes a
deep breath.

He begins to sing.

> *"Bless your sons, your daughters,*
> *O Creator.*
> *Bless your creations, your destruction,*
> *O Destroyer.*
> *Our lives were never ours,*

> *Our lives are a fleeting night,*
> *O Namer."*

The Yktishar, the final rite for the dead. It is a prayer to Zirwathi, the god of all gods, the overseer of death and life itself. The final judge of all souls.

I wonder if he is just another demon like Rashmatun.

The rest of the priests join Nudin after the first verse, their voices a sonorous wave that ebbs and flows, washing throughout the courtyard. Everyone in the courtyard listens intently, not a single audible breath escaping their lips.

After finishing the twenty-eight verses, Nudin picks up a torch beside him, lighting it up over a brazier. He shambles towards Harun's body with a slight tremble in his arm.

"Farewell, child of Zirwathi," he whispers. "May you find rest."

He sets the pyre aflame.

The fire slithers along the wood, devouring it in an orange-and-yellow embrace. Nudin steps back; the heat from the pyre films a light tingling sensation over my skin. The flames roar and crackle, and for a few moments, only the sound of snapping wood fills the atmosphere.

Nudin turns towards the crowd and claps his hands together, bowing towards them—one of the very few times in his life that he will show respect to people of a lower status. "I thank you all for keeping vigilance over my father's soul. Go back. Rest. Do not fret, for he has returned to Zirwathi's side now."

Slowly but surely, the people trickle out of Ghanatukh, murmuring their pity and mourning between themselves. I prepare to leave too. There is no need for me to remain here any longer. The priests will oversee the cremation.

"Rakhti Binsa," Nudin calls out over the roar of the fire.

I raise my brows but walk to his side anyway.

"You must be pleased now that everything has worked out in your favour," he says.

I stare at him with some surprise. I expected him to accuse me, to scream and curse me in rage, just as Ykta had. Instead, he is filled with resignation, the confusion and horror from this morning already dissipated into empty dread.

"Everything lined up perfectly." His gaze cuts towards me. "I wouldn't want to cross a goddess like you."

"To be fair, no one should cross a goddess in the first place."

He turns his attention back to the pyre.

"I hated my father," he says softly, his eyes set aglow by the fire. "But you knew that already."

I lace my fingers behind my back, features schooled into a neutral expression.

"He was never much interested in me. A Thiravinda serving one of the most prolific gods in Aritsya will always be a busy man, after all," he continues. "Besides, I was his second son. My older brother was supposed to take his place; I was an unnecessary addition to the family.

"Then my brother died, and all of a sudden I came to his attention. He educated me, just as he had my brother, teaching me the ways of priesthood and offering me fatherly advice. He showed more affection to me than he ever had in the first fifteen years of my life.

"But even as he tried to reach out to me, I just couldn't reciprocate." He takes in a shaky breath. "His affair with the Dennarese woman resulted in a child. That was the real reason why my mother killed herself. She saw that child as a threat—a possible replacement for her dead son, no matter how impossible that seemed."

The corners of his lips curl into a sardonic smirk. "Officially, she died of an unknown disease. And that Dennarese woman is still out there somewhere, along with her son. My father carried on with life as if the entire affair had never happened."

He goes silent after that, still staring at the flames.

"So are you glad he is dead, or are you not?" I ask.

"I am neither gladdened nor saddened. I just feel...nothing." He sighs and looks upwards, at the embers that drift towards the sky. "Tell me, does vengeance always feel this empty?"

"Why are you asking me?"

"You're a walking, burning pile of hatred. Don't think I never noticed. It was prominent when your mother was still around

Ghanatukh, but you seemed to have tamped down on that once she was gone, so I thought that side of you had dissipated as well." He lifts a supercilious brow. "Besides, you're the goddess of wisdom and foresight. You should be able to give me an answer."

Does he know that I killed Kavita? "Was it that obvious? With my mother?"

"No one in Ghanatukh liked her either. They were more than willing to ignore her disappearance." He shrugs. "Your secret is safe. For now."

He has a vague guess of what happened, I read from his thoughts.

"By the way, I haven't seen your tutor around recently," he comments. "Ykta, I believe?"

I bristle at the mention of my brother. "What does his absence have to do with you?"

"I hope he hasn't met the same fate as your mother," he says. I grit my teeth. "And lest you forget, he is living off Ghanatukh's funds. My father may have been an exorbitant spender, but I have no intention of following in his footsteps."

"If you're so concerned about him, look for him yourself. You have the authority." I pause, watching the embers sparking from the pyre drift into the sky, like new constellations dotting across the universe. Silence follows. Finally, I ask, "Where does Medha live?"

He is surprisingly unperturbed by my sudden switch in topic. "Should I be wary of why you want to know?"

"I'm just curious."

He narrows his eyes at me, but his mind yields no traces of rebellion. "Rathar. The kisharis' district," he answers. "Their family's mansion is one of the largest there. There's a statue of Anas sitting at the gates."

I dip my head in thanks and wheel around, leaving Nudin to attend to his father's body.

34

Weave

At dawn, I join the procession to the Holy Mound as Binsa, along with the other temple denizens. We all go there on foot; even the Rakhti isn't exempt from this ruling. Only the dead are allowed to be carried on a palanquin for their final send-off. The entire journey takes about four hours, with the Mound being located in the southernmost tip of Bakhtin, the white tip of the stupa cutting above the menagerie of brick and clay buildings.

Nudin carries his father's ashes, leading the procession through the huge archway carved with the motif of Ulavaar, the white-scaled naga mount of Zirwathi. Inside, the Mound is an emptied dome, with nothing but a depression dug out in the ground, forming a giant bowl of ash. At the edge of the depression, Nudin sends the contents of the urn tumbling into the sea of grey with a whispered prayer.

We emerge out of the Mound a few minutes later, the hems of our white suruwals stained with soot.

Then Nudin, already slipping into the role of chief priest, summons Rashmatun in the temple. He paints the star on my forehead with a practiced hand and chants the prayers.

It is unnerving, to see him step into his father's shoes so effortlessly.

After the handmaidens have dressed me and left me alone in Rashmatun's room, I quickly scour all the statuettes of Anas, studying their eyes. There are at least ten Anases in here. Which means I have to look at them one by one.

Rashmatun's strength lies within us as well; if you do not know where to find it, look to the snake's yellow, discerning eyes.

It has to be Anas. There's no other snake god in the Aritsyan pantheon—not as far as I know, at least. And a Rakhti's access to the world is limited; Chandri would only have the chance to plant the fragments in Llaon or right here, within Ghanatukh grounds. And if I were her, I would have chosen a room that no one else but her could access.

Rashmatun's room.

Fragments will resonate strongly with the other fragments, producing tangible energy that manifests as a glow within the stones, I recall from Privindu's book. *This glow is not discernible to the naked eye. For blood shamans and their enhanced senses, however, it is easy to spot gemstones that contain a fragment of a demon.*

None of the statues particularly stand out, perhaps due to the sunlight that is pouring into the room, illuminating every corner and banishing every shadow. All of them seem to glow equally. I grit my teeth in frustration. I know it's not of immediate importance that I find the remaining fragments, but it would be nice if I could find them soon to further solidify my position—so that none of the other Rakhtas can oppose me when the two years are over.

You have two years. Why the rush? Ilam asks.

Why, indeed? Why do I need to find more leverage when I've already blackmailed the other Rakhtas to do my bidding?

But Rashmatun's power is so close. It is right in front of me. *Don't you want to find her?* I say to Ilam.

Of course I do, he says.

I wheel around to check another row of Anases on the opposite end.

And Harun is there on the floor, sitting cross-legged just as he did two nights ago. The orange sash thrown over his shoulder blazes like liquid fire, resembling the flames that had consumed his body into ash.

I gasp and stumble backwards, nearly knocking a chair over.

When I look up, Harun is gone.

I take deep breaths, trying to steady myself. Harun is dead. I saw his body being burned; I saw Nudin scattering his ashes. The funeral is over. His son has already taken his place.

Harun... The last time I talked to him was in this very room as we sat across from each other. And the eyes of Anas that bore straight into me—

Shock jolts throughout my body.

I circle the room, trying to recall the exact angle from which I had seen the statuette. Harun had sat facing the tapestry of Zirwathi on one side of the wall, I believe, so I was facing the opposite direction. I settle myself in that area and look straight ahead.

A golden statuette of Anas sits on a cedarwood shelf, his serpentine heads stretching over a figurine of Orun—the deer god of welcoming strangers. Anas's scales glitter under the sunlight, as though his bodies were a river of gold.

I scramble towards the statuette. If I recall correctly, nearly all of its eyes had been glowing that night.

I remove the yellow sapphire from around my neck and hold it close to one of Anas's eyes. It grows warm in my hand, and it is no longer sunlight spilling through the two yellow sapphires—if I concentrate closely, I see a glow coming from within the stones, like a fire kindling in its hearts.

I hold my yellow sapphire to another one of Anas's eyes. The stone glows as well.

I stare at the statuette in disbelief. Did Chandri really place all the fragments together just like that? Was she not concerned about someone finding them? She had been so meticulous with her plan. Why was she careless about hiding the fragments?

Then again, all are forbidden from entering Rashmatun's room, unless permission has been given.

My heart thudding wildly against my chest, I test each of the heads. True enough, all of them have one eye that is a fragment. The only exception is the head at the centre. My fingers tighten around my yellow sapphire, biting into its rough edges. This is the last stone—the stone that was supposed to go in the final head.

Until she decided to pass it to me.

I grin to myself. It seems I will be able to obtain a goddess today, after all.

Twelve Holy Guards kneel before me in the Paruvatar, their ankles and wrists bound in chains and their uniforms dirty and unkempt. None are to look at me, though I do not detect a trace of fear in them. An admirable trait.

"Your Holiness, these Holy Guards have been brought forth to you today, for they have failed in their task to ensure the safety of Bakhtin," Nudin announces, standing to the right of my throne. It still feels odd to see him in place of Harun. "They allowed Nali Yankaran to poison the former Thiravinda. They were negligent in their duties, and today we listen to your judgment upon them, Rashmatun."

I raise a hand. Nudin bows his head and steps back.

I scan the Paruvatar. While it is usually the Order of the Holy Guards that keeps their lines disciplined, this issue is so big that the Rakhti herself must deal with it. This was supposed to be a quiet trial, to be swept under the rug once it was over as though it never happened. Just like how Chandri had passed her judgment upon Gurrehmat and his other Guards.

But I told Nudin to open this to the public, to let them all see what it is like to have Binsa continue being Rashmatun's vessel. Now they are crammed outside the hall, squeezing against one another to catch a glimpse of the inside. More Holy Guards line the walls—ones who were not in charge of watching Shiratukh Temple.

It's like the entire city has come to watch me.

I suppress a smile. "Who will be your representative?" I direct the question at the Guards kneeling on the floor.

A woman finally lifts her head. "I will speak on behalf of my comrades, my goddess."

"Very well." I nod at her. "What is your name?"

"Aakshasuya Ramivelan, my goddess."

"Tell us how you prepared for the coronation ceremony, then,

Aakshasuya, and what happened during the time leading up to the ceremony itself."

"We did the usual routine checks. Scouted the premises. Cleaned up the interior of the temple. Ensured that no one entered and exited Shiratukh Temple three days before the coronation." She meets my gaze. "My goddess, if you permit me to say so, I believe that this incident was not the fault of the Holy Guards. If there is anyone to blame, it should be the temple priests. We were not in charge of checking the wine."

I hear gasps among the commoners.

"You must be quite confident in your case, if you have the courage to accuse the temple priests of being negligent." I raise a brow and study the other Holy Guards. They remain still as stone. "The fact is that this is not the first time the Holy Guards of Bakhtin have made deadly mistakes."

Aakshasuya bows her head. "We have indeed made mistakes, my goddess. I sincerely apologise for that."

"Your apology will bring neither Thiravinda Harun nor the nine girls back," I say, tone sharp.

"We understand that, Rashmatun. But we also want to ensure that everyone involved takes responsibility."

If you drag me down, she thinks, *I will drag your entire temple down with me.*

I narrow my eyes at her. Clever, to speak such words in the presence of other people.

She could be a useful asset someday, Ilam murmurs.

"I have had enough of your pretty little words, trying to obscure everyone's eyes to the truth. But I admire your boldness." I lean against my throne, feeling the solid wood against my back. "Kill the other Holy Guards, but spare their leader."

Everyone's jaws slacken.

"My—my goddess, surely it is an extreme punishment for Guards who have been doing their duty faithfully for all their lives," Nudin interjects. In a lower voice, he adds, "Not even Chandri punished them so harshly."

"I'm aware of that," I say. "But they have clearly not learned from the mistakes of their predecessors, so I believe a harsher judgment is due." I gesture at the Holy Guards hanging by the walls. "Hurry up. We don't have all day."

"*Bin*—Rashmatun, you want to execute them here? Now?" Nudin hisses.

"You did not mishear me."

Aakshasuya trembles with rage. The other Holy Guards also tremble with fear, their stoic masks crumbling to pieces. Finally. Laughter bubbles in my throat; I barely keep it down.

Their comrades by the sides place hands on the handles of their kukris, but do not draw their blades. *Why is she doing this?* they wonder, confounded. *Is this truly necessary?*

Yes, it is, I think. *So that all of you will fear me. So that the silly Holy Guards in my city will bow to me, and not Asahar.*

All this for power.

"You all test my patience," I say, rising to my feet and staring down at them. The entire Paruvatar goes still, as though all life has been choked out of it. "If you are too weak to execute my orders, I will do it myself."

I raise a hand.

Their minds go silent as my arm burns. *Don't let the decay show*, I tell Ilam.

It'll be more painful than usual, he says.

His magic gathers and sears my fingertips. It is nothing but brute force—there is no finesse to his power, no fine control like when he is peering into minds. It is like trying to push boulders out of my body, and I have to ensure that they roll in the direction I want. I focus on the Holy Guards other than Aakshasuya.

Ilam's magic escapes me. It slams into them. I curl my hand into a fist.

They collapse to the floor without another word; their hearts are crumpled from inside.

Someone screams.

I retake my seat, ignoring the commotion that has exploded. "Clean up their bodies," I tell the remaining Holy Guards. "And you"—I lock eyes with Aakshasuya, who gives me a defiant glare— "will be banished from Bakhtin, and all your land here will be returned to the Council of Land Duties."

"Just her land in Bakhtin, my Rakhti?" Nudin confirms. His face has gone pale, but his voice is firm and steady.

"That is right." A slow grin creeps up my face. "Outside my city, you are free to do whatever you wish."

Aakshasuya does not say anything. Her chest burns with hatred. Similar to mine. Similar to Nudin's.

I dust my jama even though it is not dirty. "Do not disturb Rakhti Binsa for the rest of the day. You are all dismissed."

Before they can say anything, I step off the dais of the Scarlet Throne.

Nudin quietly escorts me back to my room, and the handmaidens strip me of my clothing and remove my makeup. They move laboriously, as though the shock from these past few days hasn't quite exited their systems.

It takes a painstakingly long time before they're done and leave me to my devices. I wolf my lunch down and grab my kukri. Then with a satchel slung across my back, I climb out of my window, Ilam's magic reinforcing my limbs. My eyes cannot help but flick downwards, at the chasm beneath me. If I make a single misstep, even Ilam won't be able to save me.

I take a deep breath and steel myself. If Medha could do this, so can I.

I swing outwards and squeeze my fingers and toes between tiny crevices in the wall, scaling my way towards Rashmatun's room.

The statuette of Anas sits inside, his yellow sapphire eyes gleaming at me.

Now, how do I remove those eyes?

Ilam supplies the answer, forming shadowy needles that protrude out of my fingertips. With one hand gripping the base of the statuette, I pry the fragments out of their settings until I have the nine fragments in my possession. Bronze depressions in the snake god's heads are left in their absence.

I wrap the gemstones in a piece of cloth and stash it into my satchel. Then I swing out of the window again and scale the wall until I reach the other end of the Bakhal. With Ilam's magic coursing through my veins, I slip out of Ghanatukh Temple and head down to the city; no one in Bakhtin recognises their goddess walking among them. Without makeup, I am merely another girl going about her daily duties.

No one stops me as I walk into Rathar, the kisharis' district.

It is not a very big area, yet it takes me a while before I find the mansion that Nudin described—a large, sprawling building with strange roofs that curl upwards at the corners. A bronze statue of Anas sits above the entrance, the fangs of his ten heads gleaming ivory.

Quite a few people in their estate, Ilam says. *Nothing we can't handle, of course.*

His magic pulses through me, a tiger lying in wait, ready to pounce. I recall reading Privindu's book, about mind demons and the range of their abilities—about how short-term mind manipulation is possible with people who do not have a strong bond with the blood shaman. I smile and walk in.

The two mercenaries keeping watch at the entrance attempt to stop me. Ilam's magic bursts forth. They stop mid-action, their hands just about to grab my wrists. Their eyes have gone blank.

"You do not see anything here," I tell them. "It is a normal day, your normal routine. Nothing noteworthy happened."

Their shoulders relax. Their hands drop. They go back to where they were stationed.

This is only temporary, Ilam reminds me. *Make it quick.*

I march through the mansion grounds. Servants and mercenaries see me, but Ilam's magic keeps them at bay. I pass by a middle-aged man with a hunch and a stomach pouch in the study—presumably Ranjit Yankaran, former professor at the University of Dahlu. A grey-haired woman with protruding cheek bones and a wide, baleful gaze stands beside him—Adarsh, Medha's mother. I cast my spell over them as well.

I turn around to leave the study. Medha is at the entrance, staring at me.

"What are you doing here?" she whispers, stunned. "What happened to my parents? And I thought Rakhtis are not supposed to step out of temple grounds."

I walk towards her. She flinches. I place a hand on her shoulder before she can run away, and crouch so that my face is level with hers. "It's Binsa, not Rashmatun," I say as I slip into the mantle of Binsa—of the Rakhti who loved little Medha as though she were her own sister. "It's fine. You don't have to be afraid of me."

Her eyes are dull and lifeless, but a hint of her usual spark returns to them when she hears my voice. "Really?"

"Really. And I am here for a reason. There's a very special favour I must ask of you, Medha," I whisper. "You can get Nali out of Llaon. In exchange, you must help me do something."

Her eyes grow wide with anticipation and confusion. "What— what must I do?"

"Help me summon Rashmatun to this world. She will have the power to see the whole truth and set Nali free."

A crease forms between the little apsara's brows. "But it was Rashmatun who said Nali was guilty. And you can summon her yourself, no?"

I close my eyes, clearing my head of my own thoughts and shifting my focus towards Medha, allowing her musings to flood my mind. I take in all her questions, her unspoken joys and worries, the pain and sorrow coiling around her heart like a long, ferocious python. I see her mind, and I know her intimately, as though she were a part of me.

Amid the grey that clouds her internal world, a distinct warmth glows in her core, the gentle heat of an autumn sun. As though her mind were desperate to cling to a sliver of hope.

My eyelids flutter open, and I reach out to touch her.

I open my mouth, my tongue thick with the burn of blood magic.

"You have to believe me, Medha," I say, gradually guiding the flow of her thoughts, bending them so they travel the same route as mine. "Rashmatun must be summoned to save your sister."

The frown above Medha's brows dissipates. It takes a few more moments before she nods her head. "Okay."

Ilam laughs, slow and maniacal.

A grateful smile curves my lips, disguising my surprise—it had been so easy to manipulate her will. Disgust snakes down my spine—a remnant of Binsa's conscience—but the feeling soon fades. "Thank you."

I wrap my arms around her, and with a slight huff, I lift her up into my arms and walk into the garden. "Let us go. Do not worry about your parents. They'll be fine soon."

Ilam pours all his magic into my legs; a burning sensation lashes throughout my veins. I grit my teeth and endure it.

I leap into the air.

Medha's shriek is stolen by the wind, and she desperately clings to me. But her fear is soon replaced with awe—she is bearing witness to magic.

When breaking the seal on a demon, Privindu had written, *there are three important things to note.*

Tapping into my soulstream, Ilam weaves a cloak of shadows around us, and we avoid the attention of those we pass. It would have been easier if Ilam manipulated people's minds to forget us, but there are far too many for him to pay attention to every single one. If my body is burning with effort and magic, I do not notice it—Ilam moves like lightning, and it only takes a few quick bounds before we arrive at Aratiya. Llaon is no longer as derelict as when I last saw it, as some of the debris has been cleared from its structure, and several Holy Guards patrol the area. We do not make for the prison.

Instead, we head to the other side of the mountain, where a small plateau juts out at an altitude slightly lower than Llaon's. I set down Medha, who experimentally toes the snow beneath her feet. Wind cuts past us, and she wraps her arms around herself, shivering. It must be cold. I can't feel it, though; my limbs prickle with numbness.

"Wh-what are we doing here, Binsa?" she says through chattering teeth.

> One: The abrupt convergence of the fragments' energies will be extremely volatile. Hence, it is recommended that one unseals a demon in an open space.

I unsling the satchel from my back and set it on the ground, extracting the bundle of cloth from inside and unwrapping it to reveal the gemstones. They sparkle a brilliant yellow under the pure, undulating sunlight.

Medha gapes at them in fascination. "What are these?"

> Two: The demon that emerges will be extremely volatile as well. They will not listen to reason. In fact, they might not listen at all. The only way in which they can be subdued is by pure force.

"They are the stones we will use to summon Rashmatun," I answer, cradling the stones with trembling fingers. The heat of Ilam's magic seeps into my bones, but I ignore the pain. "Chandri left them behind for me."

Medha tilts her head. "Why would she do that?"

"Perhaps she foresaw the day we would need Rashmatun's full strength, and the day is now." I place the fragments down onto the snow. "Now, will you help me?"

> Three: The demon, while volatile, will also be extremely weak. They are most vulnerable at this point of time—especially to hadon.

Medha takes a deep breath, savouring the piercing air. She squares her shoulders and lifts her chin—something Binsa would do when she wanted to appear strong.

"Of course," she says.

The screech of an eagle tears through the air. An expansive pair of wings zip past us.

Before I can react, the eagle abruptly turns in a motion impossible for a normal bird. It rams itself straight into Medha.

And sends her plummeting from the mountain.

35

Last Lie

N^{o.} I dive after her without thinking. She extends a hand towards me, her mouth open in a silent scream.

I have to get her! I shriek at Ilam.

What are you thinking? You're supposed to kill her anyway! he snarls back.

Just let me save her! Tears water in my eyes; they must be from the wind cutting my face. *Please!*

He reluctantly releases more of his magic.

The heat within my body is amplified tenfold. I can scarcely feel myself anymore. But it doesn't matter. Not when Medha is plunging to her death. My weight seems to increase, as though there is a tether pulling me towards the earth, and I dive faster. The distance between us closes.

Closer, closer, closer...

Just as I am about to crash into her, I slow my fall.

I grab her wrist and pull her towards me, the momentum nearly flinging us apart instead. She clings to me like a lifeline.

My eyes are pinned to the ground as it rapidly draws closer. My stomach flies towards my mouth, and my vision greys a few times.

I cannot die. Not yet—not when there are so many things I want to accomplish. I grit my teeth and look for the threads that surround me—the weavings of the wind. I tell them to encase me, to cushion my fall.

Miraculously, the wind responds to my call. It swirls beneath our feet, and we slow to a pace that allows us to breathe.

We stumble onto the gravelly surface of the ground. Medha's knees immediately crumple beneath her, and she curls over, coughing violently. I maintain balance on my feet, although my head is still dizzy from the sharp descent.

"Binsa, you're burning!" Medha cries as soon as she has recovered enough.

I frown at her and look at my arms. They look as though they have been scorched. I regard them with mild surprise.

I'll have to ease the magic off, Ilam says. *Your body can't take much more.*

No. Just a little longer, I protest. *I feel fine. I'm not in pain at all.*

That's because your body has been obliterated to the point where your nerves aren't working anymore, Ilam responds, tone dry. He gradually withdraws his magic; a touch of leftover cold from the mountain settles over my shoulders.

"*No!*" I scream aloud, forcing Ilam to maintain his power.

"Binsa?" Medha stares at me, perplexed.

I curve my lips into what I hope is a reassuring smile. "Everything is fine, Medha. You're safe."

I feel around for my satchel. My fingers find nothing but air; dread forms in the bottom of my stomach.

The stones. They're still up there. On the plateau.

"Looking for something?" a familiar voice rings out from behind me.

I wheel around. The abrupt motion sends a few more grey spots dancing before my vision. I grit my teeth and focus. The last person I expected to see is here, his wide, expressive eyes watery and bright, his beard messy and untrimmed. The bundle of cloth is in his hands.

Ykta.

And he's not alone.

Keran stands beside him, nonchalant as ever, extending an arm as his eagle swoops in to land on it—the same eagle that knocked Medha off Mount Aratiya. Stone-faced Nudin is on the other side, radiating pure, black fury. Nali lags a little farther behind, still clad in the grey uniform of prisoners, her hands bound and her hair whipping freely in the wind.

Behind them are Holy Guards and all of Ghanatukh's priests.

"What is the meaning of this?" I snarl, partly upset that Ykta has taken my fragments, and partly upset that I hadn't been able to sense them earlier. My mind is still muffled by the sheer power thrumming through my veins.

Ykta dangles the pack from his fingers. "I told you I would stop you, Binsa."

My fingers curl into fists. "Give that back. It's mine."

"I am not that gullible, dear sister." He tightens his grip around the bundle. "I know what you can do, and I know what you're trying to do. I don't want to see you like this, Binsa. Please. Just stop while you can."

I burst into laughter, my sides coiling with stitches. He's still trying to play the role of the saintly sibling, I see. "What, exactly, did you think I was planning to do?"

"Nudin told me everything," he says. "About Chandri, the gods of Aritsya, Privindu's book—everything. And we suspected that you were going to try to unseal Rashmatun. Did you really think Keran wouldn't find out about Privindu's book?"

I finally hear all their thoughts.

I hear the revelations jolting through the Holy Guards and the Ghanatukh priests: the knowledge that the goddess they have been worshipping all their lives is a sham.

I hear their disbelief. The tumultuous crack of the foundation of their entire lives splits my bones as if the pain were my own. Everything they had been taught is a lie. Chaos rages throughout them, a clear yet hazy snowstorm that fills every crack and crevice with ice.

When did Ykta tell them? I wonder.

I remember the way Ykta strode to my shelf and tore Privindu's book apart. I remember how Keran told him of Asahar's plans to reveal me as a blood shaman.

I knew a long time ago that they were both working against me. Why didn't I do anything to stop them?

Like why didn't I let Medha fall?

Perhaps all this while I thought I could kill Medha without hesitation, to sever myself from my past once and for all. But perhaps a tiny, beating part of my heart says otherwise.

I chuckle. I am still a fool.

But no more. I need to kill that part of my heart.

"You broke your oath to me, Binsa," Nudin suddenly interjects. "We agreed to keep Rashmatun sealed."

"I didn't break my promise. The whole point is that Rashmatun must be under control—and I would have controlled her." I splay my arms. "Isn't that what you wanted? Wouldn't Chandri have been proud of us?"

"Stop twisting my words," he hisses. "You were never half the Rakhti Chandri was."

I bare my teeth at him. If he hopes that the mention of Chandri's name will awaken some semblance of regret in me, he will be disappointed.

"Please, Binsa," Ykta whispers. "Don't make us do this."

"She's right, Little Mantis," Keran says. That traitorous bastard. "All will be forgiven if you just—"

"Quiet, urvas. You, of all people, have the least right to give an opinion about anything here," I say. The slur is a visible slap across Keran's features. I turn my attention to Ykta. "And I thought we were past the point of showing mercy and forgiveness. You can stop pretending to be a martyr now. I'm sure everyone around you will soon realise that you are a hypocrite, only displaying kindness to boost your own ego. I may be selfish and ambitious, but at least I am honest about it."

His expression cracks, as if my words were a whip.

The sound of a foot slipping against the ground crunches behind me. Medha yelps as she falls on her rump, her gaze filled with disbelief. She recalls our time spent together in the temple, how we laughed together, how we pored over books and stories, the meals we shared.

Harun's dying face abruptly surfaces in her mind, his decaying skin and contorted expression grotesque.

"No, no," she whispers fervently. "This can't be real."

"Remember what I said?" I crane my head around to look at her. "It would be best for all of us to forget about the Bloodbath."

She slowly pieces everything together. Harun, dying by poison—in the exact same manner as Anju had. How I had been the only survivor among the ten girls at the Selection.

Medha's body stills, too stricken to even breathe.

"You should have just tried to forget everything—even me," I murmur.

The little girl's eyes gleam with silver. Fool, to think that crying will soften my conviction. I release a short huff. "Enough. I tire of this."

Purple smoke wreathes around my body, pulling away until Ilam's feline form manifests beside me. He is almost towering over me now.

"Medha! Get away from there!" Nali screams, lunging forward. Her palms begin to glow—the same blue I saw when she healed me.

I snap my fingers. "Ilam."

With a single bound, he pins Medha down, his fangs danger-ously close to her throat.

Nali freezes.

"It's unfair, you know, with so many people trying to bully me into a corner. So please do understand that I need some leverage." I lace my fingers behind my back and cock my head. "Give me the fragments."

The lump in Ykta's throat bobs.

"You had no qualms about pushing her off a cliff just now," I say. "Are you so desperate to hold on to the fragments that you would sacrifice her again?"

Medha hiccups.

"We would have saved her," Ykta snaps. "Her sister was prepared."

"But what if Nali failed to catch her? What if I didn't choose to dive after her?" I grin at him. "You claim to do things for someone else's sake, but you just completely disregard their well-being—all for your own goals. You did it to Medha, and you did it to me."

"Don't listen to her," Keran says as Ykta's face is drained of colour.

"Demoness," Nudin mutters.

"We don't have all day," I say. "The fragments, Ykta."

"You'll let Medha go if I hand you the fragments?" he says.

"Of course. I always keep my word."

No, she doesn't, he and Nudin think at the same time.

But they do not have a choice. If they truly choose to sacrifice Medha, they won't be much better than I am. And they know that even if they escape with the gems and leave her to die, I will find them—no matter how long it takes.

Ykta tosses the cloth bundle towards me.

I wave a hand, and Ilam gets off Medha. She remains motionless, her tiny frame gripped with terror.

Slowly, I pick the cloth bundle up and unwrap it. Nine fragments. I tug the last fragment off my neck and drop it into the pile.

I release a breath of satisfaction.

I reach beneath the waistband of my suruwal and unsheathe my kukri, stalking towards Medha, the gemstones gathered in one hand. The little girl stares at me, unable to move, unable to pull her eyes away. Then she is right at my feet, my shadow looming over her features.

"Binsa, you're falling apart," she whispers.

I see myself through her eyes. The decay has spread to one side of my face, like venomous veins that tear my skin apart. I am hideous. I am beyond recognition and reconciliation.

A blood shaman.

That's right. I am not Binsa. I cannot make the same mistake again. I cannot let myself care for anyone here. And I will kill anyone who stands in my way.

Ilam, hold them off, I say.

He lowers himself into a crouch.

I raise my kukri and slash it downwards.

At the same time, a brilliant flash of light sparks in my peripheral vision.

Hadon.

"Nali, stop!" Ykta screams.

Nali tears past Ilam in a streak of light and appears in the path of my blade.

36

Final Truth

My world slows.

A raw, primal scream tears from Medha's throat. Ilam snarls a warning, a split second too late. My kukri strikes downwards, following a path it cannot deviate from.

Nali steps in between me and her sister, taking the blow that was meant for Medha.

Red blooms across my vision, like rhododendrons that peek out of their buds following the tail end of a deathly winter. It splatters everywhere—onto my kurta, onto Medha, onto my blackening arm.

Onto the yellow sapphires I hold in my palm.

I release my grip on the kukri as I wrench it out. It clatters onto the ground, and so does Nali, writhing in pain.

Looks like Dennarese blood will have to do, I tell Ilam wryly.

The Holy Guards behind us surge forward, yelling anguished war cries. Vengeance clouds their minds—for Aakshasuya and for their comrades I killed. Ilam leaps between us, the fog steaming from his body forming an impermeable wall. Keran raises a glowing hand—but he is clearly not as strong as Nali. He pierces through a few layers of the shield; Ilam flares raw magic in return, sending a shock wave rippling that makes me feel as though my body were constructed out of paper.

The shield holds. Though probably not for long.

She'll be even more volatile, he says. *Demons hate Dennarese blood. It is poison to us.*

It'll still summon Rashmatun. I trust what Privindu says. I quickly place the stones in a circle around Nali's body, shoving Medha aside with my leg when she gets in my way. *She will accept no blood other than the first spilled onto her, no?*

Ilam emits a reluctant growl. *I hope you're prepared, Binsa.*

My knuckles turn white as they grip the last fragment—my fragment. The stone that Chandri gave me, the stone that has kept me alive for the past ten years. *I've been prepared since that first night in Dharun.*

As if I were bidding farewell to a lover, I kiss the stone.

I place it on the ground, completing the circle around Nali.

For a moment, all is still. A void that vacuums away everything that exists within and without.

White, brilliant light bursts from the stones.

I throw my arms over my eyes, gritting my teeth as a whirlwind erupts before me. I stand my ground, holding on with Ilam's magic. Medha is flung backwards from the explosion of energy, and she lands some distance away, groaning in pain. Ilam, surprisingly, recoils as well; I sense that he is barely keeping us from melting.

When the light dims, Nali's bloodstained body rises to its feet, as if invisible threads were tethered to her shoulders. It twitches violently, and her eyes have gone blank. She attempts to speak; only guttural groans emit from her mouth.

And Rashmatun is standing above her.

She bears a striking resemblance to her carvings and murals. Fierce, thick brows, inquisitive eyes, full lips, and an uncompromising expression. Her skin continues to glow with the same white light from earlier, as if she were a burning star. If I hadn't known the truth of her nature, if not for the telltale silver glow in her eyes and the smoke wreathing out of her body, I might have mistaken her for a true deity.

So much for "The Tale of Tashmi," where she had been one of

the furious gods who punished the wretched, nameless being for impersonating the Forebears.

She's here, Ilam murmurs.

"Who summons me?" Her voice is deafening yet gentle, all at once.

We've come this far, I tell Ilam. *You'd better not back out on me now.*

Of course not.

Rashmatun fixates her attention on Ilam. "*You*," she hisses, the single word slicing through the air. "How dare you show yourself to me again!"

"You," Ilam echoes. He blinks, as if he has just woken up from a long, dreamless sleep. "I remember now. You were the one who took my memories, *Mother*."

Mother?

My eyes flicker between Ilam and Rashmatun; one takes a humanoid form, while the other is a giant cat. One glows with light, while the other is wrapped in shadows. No two demons could possibly be more unalike, yet...

Rashmatun is the "goddess" of wisdom and foresight—of the mind.

"I was born from her desires—her greatest wishes, her deepest fears. I was her mind made real," Ilam said. "That is why I felt a connection to her—and why I want to tear her down so badly."

Rashmatun snorts. "Just because you've accumulated power over a few centuries doesn't mean you're strong enough to face me once more."

"Privindu and I were contracted because we wanted to take over the Forebears," Ilam explains to me. "We knew that I wouldn't have enough power with only his strength, which was why he bound me to his bloodline, in hopes that his ambitions would carry on in me and his descendants. But we tried to steal the Forebears' magic anyway during his lifetime."

"And you failed," I whispered.

"That's the real reason why blood shamanism was forbidden." Ilam's piercing silver eyes—Rashmatun's eyes, I notice—are focused on the demoness. "You feared my power. You feared Privindu's potential. You know that demons cannot kill demons, and so you chose to take my memories away instead of facing me head-on."

"A defeat is a defeat, no matter the method. Just because humans don't play by the rules doesn't mean they are strong enough to overcome us. Just because Privindu was powerful doesn't mean he could match us." Rashmatun sneers at Ilam. "There is a reason why I birthed you, why I am ranked above you. A maggot cannot become a dragon. Know your place."

"But you were sealed away," I cut in. "So perhaps you are not as invulnerable as you think."

She stares at me as if just realising my existence. "Who are you, blood shaman? Name yourself!"

Ilam, here's your chance, I think.

Keep her distracted, he says.

"I am the Rakhti of Bakhtin. Your servant." I press my palms together and offer a courteous smile. "I'm here to restore you to your rightful place, my goddess."

She mirrors my smile, a sardonic twist that splits her face in half. "You, who are contracted to my treacherous son? Why should I believe you?" She tilts her head in a mocking angle, not unlike mine. "What a desperate child, to have bartered away nearly your entire body for my poor, unloved son's power." Her arms sweep over Nali's head. "And to have used another child to secure your place. A Dennarese at that."

"That is exactly why I am presenting myself before you, O Holy One," I say. "You are the only one able to understand my plight."

She regards me, her otherworldly silver eyes piercing me as if she were peeling away the layers of my skin, as if she were seeing past the death and decay—and finding nothing but rot beneath.

"Do you think me a fool?" she murmurs.

She sweeps a hand towards me.

A wave of pain slams into my head.

I hiss and curl myself into a ball, hands pressed against my temples. Then I sense her—her silver eyes inside me, a pair of glowing orbs that illuminate the darkness in my mind as she peers deep into my soul. She is squirming inside, raking through every inch of *me*, of my sense of self. She presses herself against every crevice within me, until I am filled with nothing but her.

Breathe, I tell myself. *Breathe.*

When it feels like my body will actually fall apart, she withdraws.

"You are not suited to be a blood shaman, much less a goddess," she comments. "Put your pretty little ambitions to rest."

Rage kindles within me.

I hold it back, allowing it to stoke further.

I raise my head and look at her, and at the writhing, jerking body that is her current vessel. "You're right," I tell her. "I'm not suited to be a goddess. But I am much more than that. I am not bound to the rules that bind you. I am far beyond the rules of humans."

Ilam bides his time. I barely managed to maintain myself just now, ensuring that all the compartments of my mind were intact, tucked away from Rashmatun's gaze. Fortunately, she was so intent on exploring me that she did not notice Ilam chipping away at her being.

With that, he now has a steady link to continuously siphon her power.

"I'm a harbinger of a new era," I laugh, throwing my arms to the sky. "The fall of the Forebears, the rise of the nameless ones—I will see to it all! I will make sure Privindu's ambition lives on!"

"The insolence!" she shrieks, hurling a blast of wind towards my face.

Ilam stomps a paw against the ground; the dirt before me explodes to form a fortress.

Ilam, I say gently. *Are you—*

I will kill her, he replies with the quiet assurance of a tiger that has locked onto prey. *I do not care if demons can't kill one another. I do not care if she was the one who conceived me. She is the one who took my power. And I will kill her.*

Relief floods me for some reason.

"So why don't you attack now?" Ilam taunts. "It isn't like the great and almighty Rashmatun to hesitate!"

Rashmatun screeches in anger and sweeps a hand towards him, producing an invisible blast of raw energy. He shrugs it off, barely fazed by the impact. For all her haughtiness, Rashmatun is weak after over a decade of being sealed away. And she is further weakened by the subtle stream of magic that Ilam is absorbing.

Her energy is nothing compared to Ilam's.

But I also know that Ilam is barely maintaining his power. The numerous lives I consumed over the past few weeks are burning away at an alarming pace. Gurrehmat, Yhadin, the people of Dharun—their souls are being fed into Ilam as he continues to flare his magic.

Yet there is so much power to be obtained from a former goddess—even a weakened one. The taste of it thrills me, entices me. I want more. I want all of it.

And I am willing to give everything to obtain it.

Do it, I tell Ilam.

He pounces forward, all his energy gathered within that single bound.

I collapse onto my knees, no longer having the strength to even prop myself up. But the demons' magic is so staggering that no one would dare to come close.

Or so I thought.

I notice the small figure standing a healthy distance away from the demons.

Only then do I notice the blood, splattered across the ground in periodic intervals.

Only then do I notice that they form a perfect circle.

Another technique involves hadon, Privindu wrote in his book about sealing demons.

I didn't bother with reading the rest, since I don't have hadon. But if Keran and Ykta had read it...

Fool, Kavita mumbles.

Bastards! I think. *Ilam, get rid of Keran!*

But the demon is too focused on his clash with Rashmatun. It is not a physical battle, even though they are sniping and swiping at each other. Their colliding magic plays a turbulent, chaotic tune in my mind. Ilam's field of consciousness has narrowed to Rashmatun, and only Rashmatun.

I look around frantically. What could the sealing ritual involving hadon possibly entail? What would happen?

My eyes find Medha—her tiny, quivering figure right behind Rashmatun, but her presence so insignificant that the demoness hasn't even noticed her. Yet her attention is not pinned onto her sister.

It's fixed on Keran.

Keran, who points at Nali and draws a finger across his throat.

Medha takes in a sobbing gasp. I can no longer hear her thoughts, but I hear her despair, a tapestry of storming clouds woven around her. I hear her making a decision that tears her heart in two—a decision that no child her age should have to make. But she has no choice.

Just like how I had to kill the cat Kavita presented to me.

Carefully, Medha traipses across the space to where my kukri lies. She picks it up with both hands, her grip surprisingly steady for a girl her age and size.

Tears stream from her eyes.

She huffs a determined breath.

And rushes straight towards Nali, blade aimed at her heart.

I press my palm against the ground, attempting to push myself up. My body collapses again with the effort. I hear a sickening snap in my elbow, and I belatedly realise that it has twisted into an unnatural angle.

The tip of the kukri meets its mark.

Rashmatun releases an earth-shattering cry.

Nali's body glows white around the wound. Rashmatun's body crumbles, fading like dust dissipated in the wind.

A small laugh escapes my lips, though it sounds more like a croak instead. Darkness blots my vision.

No...No. I am not defeated. I have survived for so long. I just need to get up. Get up...

Nali flashes a smile—her own.

My vision completely fades.

"You have disappointed me," Kavita's voice echoes through the void.

My eyelids fly open. I am greeted by the dark, empty chamber that exists within my mind, a heavy, bloodred fog settling all over me.

Kavita steps into view, the fog parting before her. She crouches down so that her face is level with mine. Her face seems to be carved out of porcelain, her features so exquisite and perfectly arranged that I twitch with the urge to smash it in. She smiles at me.

Her perfect face morphs—a hideous decay spreads from beneath the collar of her jama, winding up her neck and blistering across her cheek. It crawls towards her right eye, which suddenly bleeds, and red intertwines with black, forming a grotesque yet fascinating pattern that makes her seem like she is not of this world.

It is my face, I observe.

"All your efforts, all the knowledge and power you've gained... and it all culminates in nothing," she continues. Her breath is a barb that coils around my heart, and every word is a thorn that digs deeper into my flesh. "What are you, really? What did you want to be?"

"I don't know," I whisper. "I just did whatever I could. This is the only way I know."

She gives me a long, hard look—a hateful expression of pity and sympathy. Then to my surprise, she takes me into her arms and caresses my head. "You are truly like me. We came from nothing, and we will return to nothing. We want to be remembered, but we will be forgotten."

Tears streak down my cheeks; I furiously wipe them away, only to have more gushing forth. "Why? Why did it turn out this way? Is it wrong to want things? To have desires? Why am I being punished for being myself?"

"Hush, child. It is no use questioning the ways of the world." She pulls away from me and squeezes my shoulders. "I am a disappointment as well. To both you and myself."

My mouth parts ever so slightly.

"But the time for us to make amends has long passed, my child." She tucks a lock of hair behind my ear; the smile she gives is genuine, and it lights up her entire face, despite her monstrous appearance. "There is blood on our hands. And nothing we do will ever wash it off. Remember the lives you've taken. Remember the sacrifices you've made thus far."

"Nali," I murmur, the name like a curse burning my tongue.

Nali is gone.

And with that, I've lost Medha as well. Bright, beguiling Medha, always quick with words and quicker with thoughts. Always ready with a question, always trying to make everyone happier. Always covering her own sadness, always hiding her desire for a real family.

The knowledge hollows out a part of me that I had been attempting to bury, a part that had the potential to bloom into something more—that was capable of loving, of feeling.

Of caring for a child.

Now that part of me will never come to light.

I shake my head. It doesn't matter anyway. It doesn't matter if I had been somewhat relieved when it was Nali who was sacrificed, not her. I was ready to sacrifice her for the sake of my ambitions.

I am like my mother now.

"You started from nothing. And you will return to nothing. Such is the way of the world," Kavita says. "Now go. Face the final truth—your truth."

I take a deep breath.

And open my eyes.

Epilogue

I am alone.

It is almost cathartic, to finally be free of everything I have carried for the past decade. There's no Ilam. No Kavita. No Rashmatun. No Binsa.

What is left for me, then? I wonder.

The days pass by drearily. There's nothing much to do in a holding cell except to stare at the four walls and contemplate your life.

Sometimes, I still dream of them, as though a small, subconscious part of my mind refuses to forget everything. I see Ykta's smiling face, his furrowed brows as he tinkers with his automatons. I see Nali, her polite exterior belying the emotional wounds puckering all over her. I see Keran, his expressions and actions always shadowed in mystery, even as a roguish grin lights up his face.

Then I see Medha. Her curious, inquisitive eyes drill into me, always asking me *why, why, why.*

Why indeed. Even when granted all the time in the world to come up with an answer, I have no answer to that question.

I wake up drenched in cold sweat after those dreams. Then I survey my surroundings, and remember where I am and what happened.

I am truly alone.

Back at the foot of Mount Aratiya, I had opened my eyes to a field of desolation, of nothingness. All that remained were the ten fragments of the yellow sapphire, and the broken body splayed beside them. Keran healed me, and Ilam deserted me as soon as he realised I was not strong enough to enable him to take Rashmatun— then she had been sealed off.

I should not have been surprised and hurt by Ilam's decision. It was the logical move—it was something I would have done.

And yet.

"You should have let me die," I told Keran as I lay on the ground, staring at an azure sky.

"I couldn't," he answered, voice cracking. "I don't want anyone else to die. Too many people from my life are already gone. I just . . . can't bear to lose another."

I'd nearly burst into laughter.

Even when I'm a monster? I wanted to ask, but didn't.

And with Ilam's departure, I am as good as useless. Still, the Guards in Llaon keep an impervious eye on me, with nary a gap between their shifts. They are always armed to the teeth too, with spears nearly as tall as them and full plates of bloodred armour. As if one little girl could abruptly kill them all. It is not far from the truth; I killed their comrades, after all.

But that was a lifetime ago.

It is always pitch dark here in the deepest depths of Llaon. No one is allowed to carry even a torch inside. The Guards are so well trained that they can easily adapt to moving in darkness. Perhaps they thought to drive me insane by depriving me of light. I heard that happens to some people. What they don't know is that I don't have a mind to lose anymore.

Why do they keep trying to break someone who has already been broken beyond repair?

One day, something changes. I hear the jangle of keys and the creaking of a cell door. It takes me a few moments to realise that the Guards are swiftly setting upon me, unclasping the chains that anchor me to the ground and tying a blindfold over my eyes. They handle me roughly; they are afraid that I will attempt something if they do not act fast.

What can one little girl do alone? I want to ask them.

They haul me to my feet. My muscles give up when I try to take the first step forward. The Guards hold me upright and, after judging that I am indeed too weak to do anything, drag me forward. The jagged ends of their gauntlets dig into my arms, and I feel a few bruises blooming along my skin.

A cold wind slaps me. I suppress a shiver, the frost penetrating deep into my bones. I am ill-dressed for the weather, but no one cares. Why should they, when they're about to send me to my death?

A smile plays on my lips.

The cold numbs my body so badly that I barely notice it anymore. The Guards keep walking. I can hear a retinue up ahead now. They are silent, but it is a silence so harsh that it takes the shape of a dozen people—perhaps Ykta and Keran are among them—anticipation held in their breaths and prayers filling their hearts. It is a silence audible to me, as if a remnant of blood magic still remains.

I have hosted Ilam for so long. Perhaps *something* of his magic has been left behind for me.

"Tashmi has arrived," the Guard to my right speaks, the cadence of her tone low and sombre. Not Aakshasuya, but her aura is similar.

Tashmi. The one with no name. They call me after a trickster god now. I nearly cackle aloud. But my throat is dry, and my lips are cracked, and no sound comes out.

"The preparations are complete," a familiar voice says. Nudin. The bastard. Still chief priest of Ghanatukh, I see, for all his talk of being betrayed by me. I wonder what story he conjured to have me branded a criminal when I am their only Rakhti.

I wonder if there's anyone sitting on the Scarlet Throne.

An image surfaces in my mind. Medha, utterly scarred on the inside, but maintaining a smiling façade for her followers. Something simmers in me—a rage that I thought had deserted me long ago.

But I can't do anything.

The Guards shove me forward. I stumble and fall face-first into the snow.

The voices around me begin to sing.

It's a dispelling chant, a rite for demons inscribed in the Nam-uru. Perhaps if Rashmatun were with them, there would have been magic laced into the song. But their words are empty, completely devoid of power. I want to tell them to stop, to not bother. If Ilam were here, he would have devoured them all in a heartbeat.

As if some part of me refuses to forget the demon, I instinctively open my mind to see what's going on around me.

I have no magic, but I imagine people, swathed in orange robes or white kurtas. I see their expressions, drawn and heavy, firm with determination. I see the city of Bakhtin below me, nestled safely in our basin, the lands flourishing as though they had never been touched by flood or drought. I hear the people thriving, laughing, forgetting I had ever existed.

Bitterness wells in my heart; I quickly tamp down on it. What good will it do me, to express regret and anger at everything that has happened? What's done is done.

It is for the best, I tell myself. To fall into a chasm of darkness and forget that anything had ever come to pass.

I do not fear death. I have already caught a glimpse of what the other side has to offer. I bartered with gods and demons; I gambled with life and death. How can I be afraid of death, when I have already experienced it?

So I welcome everything. The cacophony of voices surround-ing me, the hushed whispers that blanket the air once the ritual is done, the rough arms that haul me to my feet and drag me forward.

A blustering wind whips my frozen cheeks. I do not have to see to know that I am standing by the edge of Llaon's entrance, high above the Yaborun range—the mountains that overlook the tem-ple and the city that had once been mine.

It's a fitting place to die.

"Any last words, Tashmi?" Nudin asks, his tone devoid of emotion.

I laugh aloud, my breath carried away by the echoes of the mountain.

"It's probably a nice day today, isn't it? It's winter, yet I can feel the sun." I cast my face upwards, smiling. "Thank you."

Silence follows. Then a single set of footsteps crunches towards me. A heavy hand clamps down on my shoulder, a surprising bit of warmth amid the cutting cold.

"Begone, Tashmi," Nudin says. "May the gods forgive your sins."

The Guards release my arms.

Nudin shoves me forward.

This time, I do not tumble into snow. Instead, I plummet down, down, down, in a never-ending flight towards the earth. The wind slices into my marrow, and I feel like one of Ykta's failed bird automatons, designed to fly but only ever able to fall.

Up here, I am free.

Are you sure you want to give up? a voice whispers in my ear.

My fall suddenly slows, as if I were a toddler gently being laid down on its cot.

Tell me, do you truly accept this fate? the voice whispers again. It sounds so familiar. I should know this voice; it sounds like the tune of a long-forgotten lullaby. A voice close to my heart.

Then I recognise it. *Ilam?*

It is I, he replies. *Tell me. Will you accept your fate like this, after all we've done, after all we've accomplished?*

You were gone, I say, disbelieving. *You abandoned me.*

I had no choice, Binsa. You could not take my power any longer. One second more and you would have crumbled into dust.

Hearing my original name opens a floodgate of memories. The ambitions I had, the dreams I harboured. The goals I wanted to achieve, and how I achieved and lost them all. I am Binsa. I am Rashmatun. I am Tashmi. I am everyone; I am no one.

I am a former goddess sentenced to death.

Tell me, Binsa. Do you accept this? Ilam presses on. *Do you accept your fate?*

I do not have a choice, Ilam.

I'm offering one to you right now. I will give you power, Binsa. I can save you.

Why would you do that? I have no more influence. I am Binsa no more. I am nameless and worthless.

Because you are special, Binsa, Ilam says, his tone calm and steady. There is a determination I have never heard before in him. *You are stronger than all the humans I know, and you can give me what I want.*

You were the one who took my womb, I say. *You no longer want to be bound to my bloodline.*

He pauses before speaking: *That's right. But before that happens, I still need you. Rashmatun is gone, and someone must take her place. If I wish to become as powerful as her... I need a host.*

If the wind didn't tear away my voice whenever I opened my mouth, I would chuckle.

You are enraged, Binsa, even if you deny it. Why don't you take everything back?

How? I have nothing left.

No. You have me, he insists. *I was there since the beginning. I have watched over you since you became Rakhti, and I have guided you to rise to the highest of Aritsya. It will be us again. We, who understand each other best.*

Hesitancy flickers in me.

No one else understands us, Binsa, Ilam murmurs. *Not Ykta. Not Nudin or Keran. Certainly not Nali or Medha. Who has walked this path before? Who has ambition so fierce that they are willing to sacrifice everything for power?*

Then his voice is so close that it seems to brush against my ear: *I understand you, Binsa.*

I cannot deny the truth he speaks.

What do you want, Binsa? he asks, even though he knows the answer.

Revenge, I reply, the single word like a quiet reverberation of the temple bell.

And revenge you shall get. I finally sense his presence slinking around me, the familiar menace and fear his aura evokes blanketing me. *Tell me, Binsa. Do you accept me?*

I consider everything. The lives I have taken, the power that was taken from me. The loneliness I had wrapped around myself, the grief and sorrow I could share with no one. The sacrifices I'd made so the world could continue to believe in its precious Rashmatun.

Yet they all dared to judge me. Never mind that I held up my bargains, never mind the rain and the blessings I brought upon the city. They all turned against me the moment it was revealed that I was not the goddess they wanted.

Never mind the sacrifices I made. Never mind the life I could have led if I had not been shackled to the Scarlet Throne.

They all betrayed me.

The rage that sparked back at Llaon plumes to life, a furious flame that threatens to devour everything in its path—a storm that vows to sweep everything that crosses it into oblivion.

Do you accept me, Binsa?

I hold on to that rage, the old ember of wrath in me that had always been in Binsa. I spread my arms wide, as though I were a hawk taking wing. My lips curve upwards.

I accept.

The story continues in . . .

Book TWO of the False Goddess Trilogy

Acknowledgments

The Scarlet Throne is a book that gave me a purpose during a time when I felt lost in life. Likewise, this book would have remained lost forever without so many people supporting it from behind the scenes and giving it a wonderful home.

Thank you to my badass agent, Alice Sutherland-Hawes, who immediately believed in me and my writing; I cannot imagine a better, fiercer advocate for *The Scarlet Throne*. To Brit Hvide, editor extraordinaire—thank you for being an ardent supporter of Binsa's wrongs and calling out all the instances where I tried to suspend too much disbelief. To Roseanne A. Brown, thank you for guiding me and this book through some very weird times. And thank you to the DV Mentor program that brought us together—you will be sorely missed.

I am also extremely grateful for the fantastic team at Orbit. Especial thanks to Tiana Coven, Tim Holman, Jenni Hill, Angelica Chong, Alex Lencicki, Angela Man, Natassja Haught, and Kayleigh Webb. I am incredibly lucky to have all of you supporting me. To Rachel Goldstein and Crystal Shelley, thank you for your eagle eyes and for catching all the embarrassing mistakes that slipped past me. To Sandhya Jain-Patel, thank you for your kind and insightful comments on the cultural representations in this book. To Lauren Panepinto and Alexia Mazis, thank you for the gorgeous cover; it is *the* definition of "jaw-dropping."

The Scarlet Throne was such a chonky monster when I first sent it to Amber Chen and Jenny Pang, but the two of you somehow blew past the pages and overwhelmed me with your love for it. Thank you, my fellow青春美丽少女们. To the Chilichurls—is it "chili" or is it "chilli"?—thank you for always being ready to scream about my book and for being so chaotic and feral over Ilam. Cindy Chen, Trisa Leung, and Tsaika Sai—you will be my forever bros. To Ysabelle Suarez, Wen-yi Lee, and Megan Mahoney, thank you for being so kind and enthusiastic about this book when it was rough around the edges. The cows live on in our memory. Cath Gatmaitan, thank you for making my writing community brighter; here's to more beef ball noodles in the future.

To my earliest Wattpad readers of *The Scarlet Throne*, when it was known under a different title, thank you for supporting me through the horrendous first draft of the book. And to those sticking around since circa 2015, I am overwhelmed and overjoyed by your love. To Stefanie Saw, my very first writing friend, I cannot believe we are still here. Thank you for your friendship and for all your badass covers for my very first books. See you next year (jk)!

To Alina, thank you for keeping me sane and for your constant presence by my side. I'd literally be dysfunctional without you. Thank you to Travis, for being the annoying older brother I never had; and to Kayla, for being the best confidant and future Bangsar auntie—I hope we grab plenty more coffee at 103. To the Happy Apartment residents—Keng Yin, Wei Shan, Ching Siew, Jing Ning, Li Yuan—thank you for being the best housemates and for giving me such a safe and comforting space to stay.

To my family—Pa and Ma, thank you for raising me and for believing in my dreams, despite all your anxieties of having your eldest child making the most unconventional career choices. Beatriz, thank you for being the best unhinged and loving little sister, and thank you for all your weird WhatsApp stickers. Runty, you're definitely not reading this, but thank you for bringing lots of light and joy to our house, even if you always refuse my cuddles and bite my toes.

And to my Father, thank you for accepting me as I am, contrite and broken. Thank you for all you have given me, and I give my all to you.

extras

orbit

meet the author

Alina Lee

AMY LEOW is a Malaysian SFF writer currently residing in Kuala Lumpur. She graduated with a degree in linguistics and is currently pursuing a PhD in the same subject. When not reading or writing, she can be found consuming copious amounts of anime, boba, and random facts on the internet.

Find out more about Amy Leow and other Orbit authors by registering for the free monthly newsletter at orbitbooks.net.

if you enjoyed
THE SCARLET THRONE

look out for

THESE DEATHLESS SHORES

by

P. H. Low

Jordan was once a Lost Boy, convinced she would never grow up. Now she's twenty-two and exiled to the real world, still suffering withdrawal from the addictive magic Dust of her childhood. With nothing left to lose, Jordan returns to the Island and its stories—of pirates and war and the cruelty of youth—intent on facing Peter one last time, on her own terms.

If that makes her the villain... so be it.

Chapter 1

Nine years after leaving the Island, Jordan still hated the city heat.

She shoved her duffel bag back behind her hip, breathed through the soup of air that stuck her shirt to her skin. Sweating spectators jostled and leaned toward the ring below, where two fighters in similar gear jabbed and blocked and danced.

An otherwise equal match, except one of them was going through karsa withdrawal. Even from up here, Jordan could see him shaking.

"Are you really the Silver Fist?"

She looked down. A boy of about ten stared up at her, grubby fingers clenched around a fried dough stick. No parents or siblings that she could see—and he was thin and wary-looking in a way that reminded her of Peter, of the Island, of crawling through forest underbrush with Baron, senses pricked for the rustle of a pirate or a Pale or a hungry feral boar.

An aspiring fighter, then. Or perhaps one already.

She wondered if he'd ever dreamed of the Island. If he'd ever read the Sir Franklin novel or watched the many movie adaptations and thought it, for a moment, real.

"No," she said, serious. "It's just a costume."

The kid cast a long look at her hands. She spread them: the prosth on her right a glove of metal, the click of uncurling fingers masked by the crowd. "Pretty convincing, huh?"

"Sure," said the boy, but he did not shuffle away to his seat. As Jordan turned back to the match, he hovered on her periphery, gnawing his lower lip; stayed until her focus broke like a wave against stone.

"You should get out," she said finally. Smiled with all her teeth. "While you still can. Don't let them use you."

He backed away then, the stick of fried dough in his hand untouched.

The match below was not going well. Third rounds in general tended to be where the most bones broke, fighters both exhausted and amped on their drug of choice, but the karsa addict had fallen to his knees; when his opponent kicked him in the shoulder, he crashed backward and lay twitching on the sand.

As the referee raised his arms, a roar went up through the stadium, half triumph, half protest. This late at night, after the rookie matches and the polite international ones, the spectators hungered for fast punches and faster bets, snapped wrists and broken backs.

This late at night, they wanted a show.

And the addict had failed to provide.

As the medical team—not all of them certified—carried him out, Jordan caught a couple men in suits moving through the stands, wireless headsets hooked around their ears: syndicate muscle, most likely, deployed to ensure a quick disposal of the man's body. The karsa had rendered him useless as a fighter, but they couldn't have him shouting valuable intel in dark alleys, no matter how convincingly it came off as an addict's ravings.

"Pity," the man standing beside Jordan muttered to his friend. A dragon tattoo snaked down his shoulder, wrapped his wrist in flames. "I've been watching Gao Leng since I was in primary school."

"Happens to all of them. They're uneducated, desperate—" The friend's gaze flicked to Jordan. "Hey, isn't that—"

Jordan ducked toward the aisle, their eyes pressing into her shoulder blades.

Two purple cubes of karsa burned in her own pocket. She had deliberately kept her doses as low as she could stand, these past nine years, and not just because Obalang was a stingy arse who would withhold her next canister the moment she missed a rent payment. Karsa tore up your nerves and digestive system; spend too much time in its grip, and withdrawal would leave you vomiting and convulsing until you regretted the day you were born.

But she could not regret the choice she'd made, nine years ago. Not when the alternative, withdrawal from the Island's Dust, would have killed her.

Not when it might still.

As she shoved into the locker room below the ring, a hand clamped down on her shoulder.

From anyone else, it might have been a gesture of encouragement. From Obalang, it was anything but. Jordan rested her right palm casually on top of his tobacco-stained fingers; felt them quivering there, hot and trapped. In a single twitch she could crush his bones so finely he would need a prosth to match hers, and for a moment she reveled in that, even if he held sway over the rest of her pathetic little life.

"You owe me," he said.

Jordan's eyes narrowed. Her landlord-dealer's black eyes were jittering, thin lips parted in suppression of ecstasy. The eejit was sharp on his own drug.

"I said I'd run your errand in the morning."

"What, and count that as payment for a four-ounce can? It's a small deal. Weak stuff. I'll barely get enough to cover the cost of transport." His grip tightened; she shifted back.

"Then why didn't you ask Alya to do it?"

Obalang scowled. His breath smelled of scorpion curry and the rotted sweetness that came with karsa chewing. A hint of the same, she knew, tinged her breath as well. "You're replaceable, girl. I can find a dozen kids on the street quicker and hungrier than you. Don't forget that."

Jordan nodded at the stadium above. Ads for energy drinks and foreign cars blazed across the walls in four different languages, but beneath, the chant had gone up, faint but unmistakable: *Silver Fist. Silver Fist.* "Tell it to them."

Obalang's mouth twisted. It was his word that opened the Underground doors to her every Fifthday night, his karsa that kept her from melting into a drool-mouthed wreck.

Even so, it was not every day that one of his tenants made him big among the ringside betting circles.

"Make sure you win all three tonight," he said as she shrugged off his grip and made for the locker room. "Or I'll give that job to Alya after all."

As the door swung closed, she flipped him a two-fingered salute.

The locker room was, if possible, even hotter. She shoved her bag in her graffiti-encrusted compartment as fast as she could get it off her; fished out a near-empty tube of ointment, which she smeared over her arms and face to keep her skin from breaking. Then she downed the two karsa cubes dry, and the world sharpened, sweet and slow: the bone-rattling thump of eedro music, the shift of a thousand sweat-slicked bodies, the gleam of her opponent's smile as he prepared himself in an identical room on the other side of the ring. Shitty karsa, this—withdrawal would leave her sluggish and achy in thirty minutes, dry-heaving a couple hours after that—but she'd run out of the stronger stuff she'd nicked off errands, and she would ride this high for as long as she could.

And if her right arm prickled a warning beneath the prosth, if the very weight of her bones and blood simmered with the echo of pain—

Through the walls, a chime sounded. Jordan rolled her shoulders, shoved in her mouth guard, and pushed open the door.

The sound almost blasted her back into the room. She'd hovered at the outer edges of this crowd all night, but here at its center, the spectators' fury washed over her like a tide. Her heart was an adrenaline pump, her body electric. As she raised her arms—at once a V for victory and a giant *up yours* to Obalang, who stood, arms crossed, in the front row—the screams swept her up, drowned her, coated her veins in titanium and glowing ore. Two words, pounded into chests and rusted benches.

Silver Fist. Silver Fist.

She fought to pay for the karsa, yes, and for a rat-infested closet Obalang called a room. Fought to keep her other addiction, her Dust addiction, at bay. But as she rolled onto the balls of her feet, felt the slow hard stretch of muscle and joint, she also felt *alive*.

She was a burning star, hungry and inexorable, and she would not be broken.

A pale silhouette sliced the opposite doorway.

Jordan did not blink. She had stayed up nights to study this fighter in the Underground's video archives: his predator's gait, the kicks he snapped like mouthfuls of scorpion pepper. As the ref raised his arms, she mouthed along to the name that blasted from the flat, tinny speakers.

"Gentlemen, I present to you—the White Tiger!"

Jordan's opponent loped across the sand, his white-blond hair shining beneath the lights, and the crowd *howled*.

The White Tiger was the darling of the Underground, tall and lanky and arrogant—*and Rittan*, people whispered loudly behind their hands, as if in explanation. Jordan had fought him twice since she'd first shown up at the back gates of the arena. The first time, he'd knocked her out in seconds. The second, he'd snapped two of her ribs and whispered, as the medics carted her away, that he went easy on little girls.

But Jordan had come back. She'd wrapped her broken bones, iced her bruises. Learned to throw a punch with the full weight of gravity dragging her down, to stay light on her feet even when no Dust from the Island kept them in the air.

All in all, she'd gotten decent at fighting on sand.

And tonight, she would win back her pride—and her next week's worth of karsa.

As they bowed to each other, the Tiger's eyes locked on hers. His irises were giveaway Rittan, the cold pitiless blue of movie stars and senators' sons, and at the sight of them, an old heat seared across Jordan's chest.

"Pity you think you've already lost," he said, the words crisped by his accent. "It might have been a good match."

"Pity you're an arrogant kweilo," Jordan countered. "It'll be fun to beat you."

They stepped apart, and the scoreboard clock flicked into a countdown, digits burning red against the faded wall paint.

Ten seconds.

At the edge of the arena, Obalang flicked a cigarette. *Three for three.*

He did this sometimes, when someone big had bet on her and he was behind on rent or drugs or whatever increase in tribute money the Hanak were demanding from him that week. These days it was usually two for three, minimum, or that she hold out for a certain length of time—which gave her lower audience ratings, but fewer broken bones.

In the past few months, however, she'd been losing him fewer bets. Had even thrown a few matches on purpose.

Six.

The Rittan's white tank top was a paper ghost. The memory of his video matches sketched across the backs of her eyelids: the dancer-like lift of his back foot before a kick, a phantom gap between raised hands. She just had to catch him in real time.

If only it were that easy.

Three.

Fists raised, a meter and a half apart, they crouched as one.

Two.

She needed this, she told herself. A hundred times more than he did.

One.

Another chime rattled the air.

They circled each other. Jordan's ears pounded blood and bass; she didn't dare blink. The Tiger did not bounce as some of the newcomers did, established no rhythm that would betray his first strike. His fists were points of light, the metal studs on his knuckles jeweled like snake eyes. The crowd above them stirred and murmured as sweat clung to their backs.

This late in the night, they wanted blows. They wanted blood. They wanted—

Strapped down to the hospital bed, screaming as Dust withdrawal burned through her veins—

Focus, dammit.

In Jordan's periphery, Obalang scratched his nose.

She lunged. The crowd roared as she and the Tiger became a flurry of limbs, and she fell into muscle memory, blocking again and again as his kicks and alloy-capped fists barreled toward her. A roundhouse wrenched her left arm in its socket and she slammed it with her other forearm, teeth rattling as he shoved her to the ground. Then his heel smacked her shoulder—a starburst of pain, too close to her head—and she was rolling away, back on her feet, her eyes acrid with sweat. Her chest heaved. No shame in breathing hard, here. As they circled each other again, her vision embrittled into sand, light, shadow.

This time, he attacked first.

He fought with the grace of someone trained in classical martial arts—quick and elegant, kicks snapped perfect from the knee. Countering even the punches from her right hand with blows that would have fractured her ribs again if she'd sidestepped a millisecond more slowly. When she showed up five years ago, she had fought with the unrefined flailing she'd picked up on the Island: a child who'd always had the option to fly away, snuggle back into bed at the end of the day. But she'd figured out gravity. Figured out her arm. Now she lashed out with all she had, struck kidney, elbow, crotch—

Another chime, the clock over their heads blazing zeros, and amid the surge of shouting and uncreative slurs involving her anatomy, the ref shoved between them, arms outstretched. Jordan spun away and wiped her face—though that was a stupid move, since sand gritted her knuckles. The White Tiger limped, still tender, toward his locker room. A one-minute break, and no question that she'd ended on top.

Two more to go. A splash of water from the drinking fountain, a stimulant patch slapped on the back of her neck, and she strode back out to the center of the arena.

Even crouching with his legs slightly too far apart, the Tiger looked murderous.

"Just remember," she called as time ticked down, "I took it easy on you."

He bulldozed into her with a thud and she crashed breathless to the sand, kicking and struggling as his knees pinned her midsection. A silent fury in those glacier eyes, a studded fist swinging down toward her head, and small suns exploded behind her eyes *shit shit shit*—

She threw out an elbow, bucked her hips. Dove for him as he tipped off-balance. Her vision was fuzzing in and out—one moment narrowed to the bead of sweat at his temple, the next dazzled by the shine of the surrounding fence. Then she was punching torso, neck, head, her pulse a crack-snap of bone, red echo of tearing teeth—

"Time," someone bellowed, "*time*," and multiple refs' arms vised around her, carrying her off the ground; the Tiger's chest heaved as he glared and staggered to his feet. They had bowed to each other only minutes ago, yes, but there was no thought of sportsmanship inside the match itself—only this animal hate, the blue lightning of her body, the tang of ozone on her tongue. As Jordan was set back on the sand, she raised her arms again, and the crowd bore her up, heady as the name she had chosen for herself.

Round three.

The White Tiger was desperate now: humiliated by a girl, even if she was slightly more augmented than he was. It would make him reckless, but also dangerous. If he managed to get the upper hand, she had no doubt he'd break *all* her ribs tonight.

The clock blinked down its intervals.

One last time.

They circled again, briefly—both of them hot and loose now, the ring blurring with the sweat in Jordan's eyes—and then he rushed her once more: head shot after head shot, lightning jabs and arcing kicks. Pushing her out of center, aiming for the knockout. She blocked, both arms shuddering with impact, huffed as his fist caught her full in the chest. Pivoted away, panting, toward the wire fence, the pounding sea of faces.

And paused.

Something was wrong.

Her ears felt stuffed with cotton. The taste of iron clogged her tongue. She was standing at the bottom of a giant fishbowl, the crowd a sick sea of gaping mouths and dead eyes, and a slow convulsion twisted her gut—separate from the pulse of her shoulder, the bruises blooming on her arms. A high tight tremor in her knees, her spine.

She thought of Gao Leng, twitching in the sand, and a cold void slid open inside her like a door.

Jordan edged farther away, both hands raised and clenched to stop the shaking. Obalang might have fucked her over—might have discovered she'd been skimming from clients, degraded the karsa he gave her on purpose, and then bet against her so he would profit anyway. But if he hadn't—if this was the usual dose and it was her body that was habituating, demanding more—

When she was thirteen, she had sought him out at the convenience store near her parents' house: a shifty, greasy-looking bastard with only the shopkeeper's gossipy suspicions to recommend him. She had bought herself a few years, thinking to stave off the Dust withdrawal shredding her system hour by hour, and paid for it in people she'd left behind.

But she had always known it would return. Pain, after all, was the only thing that stayed.

Three paces away, the Tiger cocked his head. Understanding loosened the set of his shoulders—and wary triumph.

Jordan met those hard blue eyes. Jerked her head: *Well, come on, then.*

And when he plunged forward, his leg a flawless scythe toward her temple, she let her fists drop just enough that her head snapped to the side, and she tumbled into the dark.

"What the fuck?" Obalang snarled as Jordan emerged from a back entrance of the Underground, still bruised and raw despite the anti-inflammatory patches she'd slapped over her shoulder and temple. One of the other fighters had tossed her an extra cube of karsa for the withdrawal, but she now owed them a cut of A-grade from tomorrow's deal, and lurking beneath her skin was the promise that this would happen again—and again and again, until her body gave up altogether. Obalang shoved her against the wall, and the world jarred. "You threw that match."

"I didn't," she said, shouldering around him, but he stepped in front of her, the tip of his cigarette flaring orange.

"I don't need to show you the godsdamned replay. You dropped your fucking hands."

Jordan sighed. She had taken her time in the locker room precisely to avoid this. The reek of old sweat and rotting food filled the passageway, turning her stomach; across the street, people stumbled laughing out of bars, chattering in Burimay and Hanwa and Yundori, and she briefly envied them—the way they could lose themselves in the city without bracing for a knife or a fist or the cold kiss of gun to temple.

"These things happen," she said evenly. "I'd fight better if I had a cut of the A-grade—"

"No," Obalang snapped, as she'd known he would. "And you're still running that errand tonight. Two a.m., or I'll sell that silver fist of yours to the Hanak bosses. It'll almost pay off the debt you just racked up, along with your next three weeks' worth of karsa."

Jordan shifted her gear bag on her hip. She'd always expected to part ways with Obalang eventually—though whether by hotwiring a motorcycle and hightailing it out of the city, or being shot and dumped in an alley like this one, was yet to be seen. Now, as borrowed drug sang in her veins, she imagined their relationship as a timer, counting down.

Three weeks' worth. Even if she skimmed off deals, called in every favor owed her, she would break by next Fifthday. And the fighter she went up against then might not be as merciful as the White Tiger.

She would rather die a quick death than a slow one. Would rather go up in flames while she was ahead than shrivel in a slow decay of consequences.

At the edge of her hearing, a little boy's giggle, as if from inside a black-mouthed cave.

And now?
And now?
And now?

"Everything pays a price to survive," Obalang said. Darkness eddied over his face, thumbprints of shadow dappled by the light of a nearby restaurant. He ground his cigarette out on the wall. "I've paid, all this time. And I'll keep paying."

"As will I," Jordan said, and walked past him into the brightness of the city. She would pick up his godsdamned karsa—but not on his behalf, or the syndicate's. By this time tomorrow, she'd be long gone. "I'll be there. Two o'clock sharp."

if you enjoyed
THE SCARLET THRONE

look out for

FATHOMFOLK
Drowned World: Book One

by

Eliza Chan

Welcome to Tiankawi—shining pearl of human civilization and a safe haven for those fleeing civil unrest. Or at least, that's how it first appears.

But in the semiflooded city, humans are, quite literally, on top: peering down from shining towers and aerial walkways on the fathomfolk—sirens, seawitches, kelpies, and kappas—who live in the polluted waters below. And the fathomfolk are tired of it. When a water dragon and a half-siren join forces, the path to equality is filled with violence, secrets, and political intrigue. And they both must decide if the cost of change is worth paying, or if Tiankawi should be left to drown.

Chapter One

A late arrival elbowed past Mira, knocking her out of position. His jaw was tight, and he wrinkled his nose as he met her eye. "Keep in formation, saltie."

Mira fist-palm saluted sarcastically. She had heard it all before; got into fights with pettier human bureaucrats than him. The delegates continued at a snail's pace, ambling as if perusing market stalls on a Tiankawi festival day rather than inspecting a rooftop military parade in the baking midday sun. The wax coat of Mira's border guard uniform was akin to a simmering claypot. If she strained, she could hear the ocean below, but thirty floors up where they stood, the breeze didn't provide much reprieve. Sweat dripped from her forehead and she cricked her neck.

The captain of the kumiho – the city guard, led the politicians down the line. "And this is Mira, newly appointed as captain of the border guard." The older man was de facto Minister of Defence, but he stroked his silver moustache like an indulgent grandfather offering candied lotus seeds. Mira had seen the other side of him. She saluted the delegates, the Minister of Ceremonies and two junior officials.

"Ah, we've heard a lot about you," said the Minister of Ceremonies, a tall middle-aged woman. "Helping out the Minister of Fathomfolk. The siren."

Helping out was not how Mira would have phrased it. It was more of a partnership really. She pushed a smile into the corners of her mouth. "Half-siren actually. I'm glad to be here today."

"You should be," the man on the left said. "First fathomfolk in the military and now the first to reach captaincy. Integration at its finest." The words were well-meaning enough but she could hear the abacus beads clicking in his head. Not satisfied with putting her name out as a fathomfolk success story, now they wanted to paste billboards all over the city. Mira had refused. It was difficult enough to do her job without her face staring back from every sky-bridge, walkway and tram platform. "With all due respect, sir, I hope to inspire fathomfolk to join *all* branches." Her emphasis was deliberate. While she was a trailblazer, there were only four other folk in any aspect of government. All on the military side, all in her chinthe border guard rather than the more influential kumiho city guard. Titans forbid that folk get into the offices of agriculture or transport; the glamour and influence they could have . . .

The remaining official who had not spoken simply pinned Mira's captain badge on the front of her coat: the golden liondog name-sake of the chinthe. His hand shook, eyes decidedly not meeting hers. He was afraid. Afraid of the siren mutt without a leash. He did well not to flinch. Mira nodded and smiled, went through the motions of small talk the same way she got dressed in the morning: automatically, perfunctorily, with her mind sorting through end-less lists and jobs that needed to be done. If she kept pretending it didn't bother her, one day it might be true.

"Did you see the look on his face? Pale as a sail," a voice whis-pered behind her as the delegates moved on. One of her lieutenants.

"Bollocks, he'd probably forgotten where he was. Doddering fools refuse to retire until they have to be carried out." Lieutenant Tam's baritone carried above the other voices.

Mira allowed herself a half-smile. At least some people had her back.

Despite everything, it had been a good day. Two of her good friends had been promoted and a rusalka had just completed advanced training. The border guards were never invited to the kumiho celebrations in City Hall. The steamed dumplings and free-flowing wine would be missed, but the entitled city guard would not be. They flaunted their ceremonial swords like children's toys. The chinthe only got symbolic daggers, another slight to add to the heap. Mira ran her thumb down the worn hilt of hers.

This group had been with her for nearly as long as her chin-the dagger; patrolling the waters in the southern districts of the sprawling Tiankawi city state. The border guards' jurisdiction was supposedly only around resettlement and trade. But over the decades, the city guard had refused to have anything to do with the folk-concentrated south. The whole region would have fallen into the hands of gangs had it not been for the chinthe.

From the rooftop training ground, sea level was quite a drop. In her younger days, Mira had clambered across buildings, vaulted and scrabbled through various shortcuts. But the long way had its own charm. The city stretched out, monolithic pillars a canopy above the shanty towns below. At low tide the planks of the walkways oozed with muddy water, threatening to warp faster than they could be fixed. At high tide they were completely submerged, beholden to the mercies of the waters that surrounded Tiankawi. Not that this presented a problem for the folk.

Mira's usual after-work haunt was nothing more than a street stall near the port in Seong district. An elderly couple of stallholders seared skewers of spiced tiger prawns and whole fish over coals, bottles of moonshine floating in the water by their feet.

"To the new captain, Mira o' the chinthe, we are not worthy," Lieutenant Tam said with a mock bow.

"Oh piss off." Mira prodded him with the toe of her boot.

"Don't forget about us when you're a lofty council member," he added. Mira rolled her eyes, not wasting her breath on a retort.

"He has a point," said Mikayil, her other lieutenant, his thick eyebrows wiggling at her from an amiable brown face. He wiped his hands neatly on a square of cloth from his pocket.

"They want you for leadership," Lucia agreed. She was one of the newest ensigns, her uniform still pressed every morning and her face free from the worn river lines the others had. She held her sheathed dagger like they'd given her a nugget of gold. Mira remembered that elation. Wished she had a little of it left.

"They want a tick box in the Council; a head-bobbing, arse-kissing recruitment pamphlet. Well, what do you think?" Mira said, posing with her hand on her hip, a caricature of an enrolment notice. They laughed, clinking bottles and turning to talk of other things. Mira took a long swig of the local brew. She wished it was that easy to brush it off inside as well. The faces of the delegates today confirmed what she already knew. All they saw was a half-siren. No matter the uniform she wore, the exams she passed, the ideas she brought to the discussion; they always saw her as fathomfolk first. She'd never lived in an underwater haven – the semi-submerged city was her only home – and yet she'd always be an outsider.

She helped herself to another bottle, raising it until the stall-holder auntie nodded in acknowledgement. Heard the merry-making fall silent suddenly.

A group of folk made their way down the walkway. Walking four abreast, they took up all the space. Mira recognised some of them: the whiskers of the ikan keli catfish twins, the swagger of the broad-shouldered kelpie leader in front. Drawbacks: a group of dissident folk who had been openly sceptical of her appointment. They walked with confident purpose, stopping too close to the border guards' celebration for comfort. Mira felt the wariness of her colleagues, drinks being placed down on tables, hands inching towards baston sticks.

"Congratulations are in order, *Captain*," Lynnette, the Draw-back leader said. Sarcasm tugged on the edges of her words. As if she wasn't tall enough, her tousled mohawk added inches to her height, like the crest of a wave.

Mira stood slowly, closing the distance in their heights a little, trying to defuse the situation with a light-heartedness she did not truly feel. "My thanks, you're welcome to join." Eyes glanced over the makeshift seats; nothing more than upturned wooden crates. The table a couple of damp pallets, mildewed around the edges.

The younger catfish twin was staring at Ensign Lucia, baiting her to look away first. He bared his teeth with a sudden hiss, barbed fins fanning down otherwise human-looking forearms. The effect was startling. Disquieting. Lucia toppled off the wooden crate she was sitting on. Only the quick reactions of those beside her prevented her from falling entirely into the water. The folk cackled.

"We've somewhere to be," Lynnette said.

"Another time perhaps." Mira kept her voice steady. Neutral.

The kelpie flexed her generous biceps, the sand god amulet around her neck swinging. "Unlike some, we're busy making a difference for folk in the city."

Mira heard Tam curse quietly behind her, the tension thick. Despite the alcohol, she suddenly felt very sober. Of course, just because she'd been made captain didn't mean all folk approved her appointment. "Should you have any suggestions for change, I'd be glad to hear them."

"Try changing yourself," a whisper from the back of the new group snarked. Loud enough for all to hear. Not enough of an insult to warrant anything really. What was Mira – the first folk captain in the history of the city – going to do? Arrest the most vocal protest group on her first night? The Drawbacks knew it as well, Lynnette seemingly swaggering up to make this exact point.

"Good night, *Captain*. I'm sure our paths will cross again soon."

The Drawbacks did not wait for the response. They jumped, cannonball-diving and flipping from the walkway into the water on either side with whoops and jeers. Making splashes so big that the border guards were drenched completely.

Saltwater ran down Mira's face and coat as her colleagues swore and stood up around her. She sat back down, taking a sip of her now salty beer. She'd hoped to enjoy her promotion for at least one day, but there would be no such respite.

Mira had almost succeeded in putting the Drawbacks out of her mind by the time she caught the tram. It was mostly empty apart from a drunk sleeping in the corner and a fathomfolk couple talking in whispers by the doors. The carriage lurched forward on the raised rails as it headed towards the central Jingsha district. Here stood the proud buildings at the heart of the city, the steel-boned monuments to humanity's prowess. Built during the Great Bathyal War, when it became clear that fighting between humanity and fathomfolk would not change the rising water levels; before the decades of floods. Built to endure. The rest of the city was made up of scattered semi-submerged neighbourhoods sprawled around Jingsha. Mira herself came from one of those districts, a shanty town really. She'd never thought that one day she'd live in the centre.

When she opened the door to her apartment, it was snowing. A layer of white covered everything as if a flurry had passed through the room. It was like the stories her ama had told, tales set in winter palaces on top of mountains she'd never known. Flakes like tiny flowers drifted towards her and despite herself, she stuck out her tongue. The cold sliver melted and sharpened her senses. She could've stayed there all night, head tilted as if towards the sun, and let it fall on her face. The sound of familiar footsteps made her turn. Her partner Kai stood waiting for her to notice.

"You have no idea how much I love you right now," he said with a smile that spread from his mouth into his warm brown eyes. He soaked the scene in, clearly pleased with himself.

"What did you do, you mad fool?" she said, unable to stop herself from laughing.

He came towards her, hugging her tight and warm. "Congratulations!"

"What, what is all this?" she said again. Insisting this time. She extracted herself briefly, even though she just wanted to bury her nose in his shirt. He smelt of home. Of soup broth and lemongrass soap. Though he was impeccably dressed, his fingers were nonetheless stained with black ink. She took one of his hands, rubbing at the smudges as he talked.

"I have to be impartial, I know. And you didn't want it to be a big deal. But how can I not celebrate this? You made captain!" he said. Mira cupped the side of his jaw, the bristles on his chin tickling her palm. He could still make her heart sing after two years. "So," he continued, turning to plant a gentle kiss on her hand, "we can celebrate your promotion here – at home – with all the fuss I want to lavish on you."

"Yes, but what is *this*?" She gestured around. Now that she had a moment to look, she realised he had covered the furniture with blankets, rendering the sofa and the dining table into soft white mounds. The snow falling around her was real though. It was all Kai. He demonstrated, flicking water into the air and using his waterweaving powers to freeze the droplets as they fell in perfectly defined snowflakes. It hardly looked like he was putting any effort into it, a level of skill that would make any other fathomfolk sweat with exertion. Delicate precision that only someone of his upbringing could achieve.

"You wanted to see snow; you've never been north. Honestly, I want to take you there. I *will* take you there! But for now, this will do."

Despite the cold, Mira felt her skin tingle where it touched his. Her head spun with his words. Kai was never one to do things by halves. Even after all this time together, he could still surprise her. She wondered if all folk born in the sea havens were like this, but she doubted it. He was pure sincerity and joy.

He presented her with a scroll in both hands, bowing ceremoniously. The lotus-leaf paper was protected by a glass tube. It had become a tradition of theirs to give each other mock documents: salacious newssheets, penalty notices for missed dinners, or strongly worded complaint letters about the quality of lingering glances. His eyes laughed merrily as she struggled with the wax, finally cutting it loose with her ceremonial blade. He'd made a certificate in flowing legalese, a document verifying that she was captain not just of the chinthe, but of all fathomfolk. And beneath it, images brought to life by a couple of deft brushstrokes. Mira leading a parade of dancing, laughing, singing folk along a riverway. His light touch had captured familiar faces, the idiosyncrasies of people they both knew.

"It's, it's . . . " she began.

"I know," he quipped.

She pushed him lightly onto the sofa, the snow puffing up on impact and making them both laugh as she sat across his lap. A tremor ran through her, the whole room swaying. Kai's face was the one clear thing. "Look at me, I'm shaking," she said in a whisper.

"As much as I'd like to take credit, that's an actual earthquake." He put his hands on her hips and anchored her.

The overhead light was swinging but nothing else was out of place. Growing up on the water, Mira barely noticed the minor tremors, but in the imposing towers of Jingsha she felt them more acutely. They waited for it to pass. She piled the fluffy snow on Kai's topknot, dabbing it into his dark facial hair and on his nose. Giddiness bubbled up through her as he shook himself free, the snowflakes flicking onto her face and down the front of her top. And when he complained of cold, she kissed him better; butterfly kisses down his neck and shoulders. Her hands untied his robes to reach down across his smooth skin, her lips caressing the pearlescent smattering of scales on his collarbone, across his torso and down one arm. She loved that he wore his true colours even when in human form. A water dragon, the only one in the whole city state. The notion still took her by surprise now and then. The closest thing to fathomfolk nobility, and here he was, looking up at her with hungry eyes.

He ran his hands across the fabric of her chinthe green uniform, tracing the braiding, rubbing the brass buttons in a way that made Mira involuntarily exhale. "*I'm* supposed to be treating *you*, remember?" he murmured. The coat fell away and his hands ran down her back. Their lips met and she leaned in, pushing her hips, her chest, her mouth into him, pressing close so he could feel the ache that filled her entirely.

"So . . . how do you want to celebrate?" he asked.

Her response required no words.

Follow us:

/orbitbooksUS

/orbitbooks

/orbitbooks

Join our mailing list
to receive alerts on our
latest releases and deals.

orbitbooks.net

Enter our monthly
giveaway for the chance
to win some epic prizes.

orbitloot.com